George Mercer Dawson

Report on an exploration in the Yukon district, N.W.T., and adjacent northern portion of British Columbia

George Mercer Dawson

Report on an exploration in the Yukon district, N.W.T., and adjacent northern portion of British Columbia

ISBN/EAN: 9783742841704

Manufactured in Europe, USA, Canada, Australia, Japa

Manufactured and distributed by brebook publishing software (www.brebook.com)

George Mercer Dawson

Report on an exploration in the Yukon district, N.W.T., and adjacent northern portion of British Columbia

GEOLOGICAL AND NATURAL HISTORY SURVEY OF CANADA.
ALFRED R. C. SELWYN, C.M.G., LL.D., F.R.S., Director.

REPORT

ON AN EXPLORATION IN THE

YUKON DISTRICT, N.W.T.,

AND

ADJACENT NORTHERN PORTION OF

BRITISH COLUMBIA.

1887.

BY

GEORGE M. DAWSON, D.S., F.G.S.

PUBLISHED BY AUTHORITY OF PARLIAMENT.

MONTREAL:
DAWSON BROTHERS.
1888.

To Alfred R. C. Selwyn, C.M.G., LL.D., F.R.S,
Director of the Geological and Natural History Survey of Canada.

Sir—I beg to present herewith a report on a portion of the Yukon District, N.W.T., and adjacent northern part of the Province of British Columbia. The exploration upon which this report is based was carried out as part of the work of the Yukon Expedition, of which I had the honour to be placed in charge. The further explorations and surveys carried out by Messrs. R. G. McConnell and W. Ogilvie will form the subject of separate reports.

It may be explained that the greater part of the present report was completed in June last, but that having been engaged in field work during the summer, it was impossible to send the manuscript to the printer at that time.

I have the honour to be, sir,

Your obedient servant,

GEORGE M. DAWSON.

Ottawa, Dec. 1, 1888.

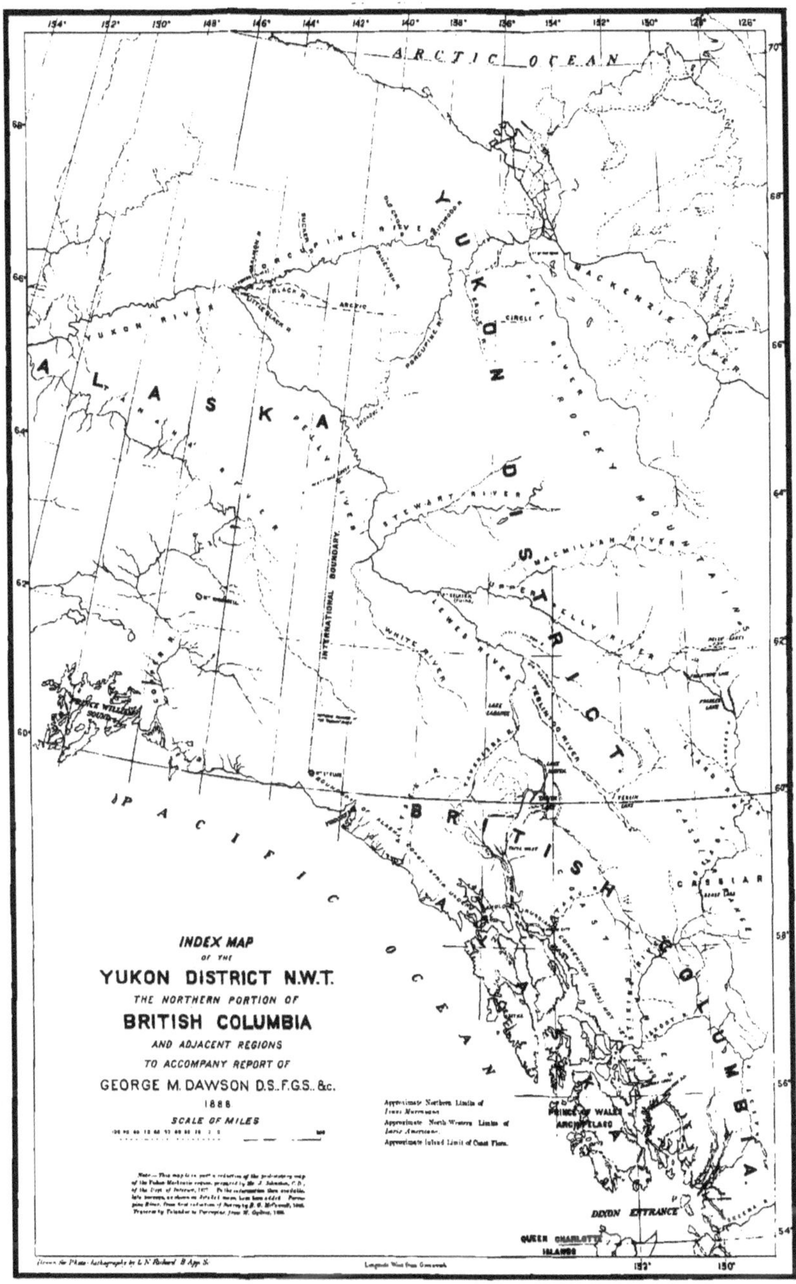

ARCTIC OCEAN
ALASKA
YUKON DISTRICT
BRITISH COLUMBIA
PACIFIC OCEAN
PRINCE WILLIAM SOUND
INTERNATIONAL BOUNDARY
YUKON RIVER
PORCUPINE RIVER
MACKENZIE RIVER
ROCKY MOUNTAINS
STEWART RIVER
MACMILLAN RIVER
PELLY RIVER
LEWES RIVER
WHITE RIVER
TESLINTOO RIVER
CASSIAR
PRINCE OF WALES ARCHIPELAGO
QUEEN CHARLOTTE ISLANDS
DIXON ENTRANCE
INDEX MAP
OF THE
YUKON DISTRICT N.W.T.
THE NORTHERN PORTION OF
BRITISH COLUMBIA
AND ADJACENT REGIONS
TO ACCOMPANY REPORT OF
GEORGE M. DAWSON D.S., F.G.S., &c.
1888
SCALE OF MILES
Approximate Northern Limits of
Ixxus Marmereus
Approximate North Western Limits of
Laris Americanus
Approximate Inland Limit of Coast Flora.
Longitude West from Greenwich

·REPORT

ON AN EXPLORATION IN THE

YUKON DISTRICT, N.W.T.,

AND

ADJACENT NORTHERN PORTION OF

BRITISH COLUMBIA.

BY

GEORGE M. DAWSON, D.S., F.G.S.,

Introductory.

The Yukon expedition, to which the present report relates, was undertaken for the purpose of gaining information on the vast and hitherto almost unknown tract of country which forms the extreme north-westerly portion of the North-west Territory. This tract is bounded to the south by the northern line of the Province of British Columbia (Lat. 60°), to the west by the eastern line of the United-States territory of Alaska, to the east by the Rocky Mountain Ranges and 136th meridian, and to the north by the Arctic Ocean. The region thus generally defined is referred to as the Yukon district, this name being rendered appropriate from the fact that the greater part of its area lies within the drainage-basin of the river of that name.

The Yukon district, as above defined, has a total area of approximately 192,000 square miles, of which, according to the most recent information, 150,768 square miles is included in the watershed of the Yukon. The superficial extent of the district may perhaps best be realized when it is stated that it is nearly equal to that of France, greater than the United Kingdom by 71,100 square miles, ten times the area of the province of Nova Scotia, or nearly three times that of the New England States. It is unnecessary to add that the present report must be considered merely as a first contribution to our knowledge of this wide country.

Purpose of the Expedition.

The immediate necessity for the exploratory and surveying work undertaken by the expedition, arose from the fact that somewhat important developments of placer gold-mining had of late been attracting a yearly increasing number of miners and prospectors into a portion of the district in question; and the work decided on, included the preliminary determination of the point at which the Yukon or Pelly River crosses the 141st meridian, which here constitutes the boundary between the North-west Territory and Alaska.

Organization.

The writer was placed in general charge of the expedition, with Mr. R. G. McConnell, B.A., and Mr. J. McEvoy, B.Ap.Sc., also of the Geological Survey, as assistants, while Mr. W. Ogilvie, D.L.S., was intrusted with the conduct of instrumental measurement and the astronomical work in connection with the determination of the position of the 141st meridian.

Work by Mr. Ogilvie.

In consequence of information gained from persons having some knowledge of the region to be traversed, it was decided that Mr. Ogilvie should carry out an instrumentally measured traverse of the route from the head of Lynn Canal to the Lewes and along the line of the river to the 141st meridian, where he was to make arrangements for wintering, and in the spring and summer of 1888 continue his surveys north-eastward to the Mackenzie River and up that river to connect with previously surveyed lines on Athabasca Lake.

Work by the writer.

Having ascertained that there was a fair probability of his being able to carry a line of survey and exploration from the Cassiar district in northern British Columbia, by way of the Upper Liard and across the height of land to the Yukon basin, the writer decided on attempting that route, which, though known to be difficult, appeared to offer, in conjunction with Mr. Ogilvie's work, the best opportunity of adding to our knowledge of the country as a whole.

Work by Mr. McConnell.

Mr. McConnell was entrusted, in the first instance, with the instrumental measurement of the Stikine River, from the point to which surveys had previously been carried, as far as the head of navigation, and subsequently, with the exploration of the lower portion of the Liard River; the original intention being that he should return after reaching the Mackenzie, in the autumn of 1887, by the ordinary trade route up that river.   Before we finally separated from Mr. McConnell,

Change of plan.

at the confluence of the Dease and Liard, however, so many unexpected delays had occurred, that it was considered advisable to instruct Mr. McConnell to endeavour to make arrangements for passing the winter of 1887-88 on the Mackenzie, and subsequently to descend the Mackenzie, cross the northern extremity of the Rocky Mountains to the Porcupine River, and by following that river and ascending the Lewes, to return to the Pacific Coast at Lynn Canal.   This arrangement further

provided for the examination of a great additional region of which the
geological structure was altogether unknown. Mr. McConnell has Reports.
since successfully completed the arduous journey thus outlined. A
preliminary report of his work, as far as the mouth of the Liard, is
given in conjunction with that of the writer, in Part III, Annual Report of the Department of the Interior, 1887. A progress report of
Mr. Ogilvie's work forms a portion of Part II of the same volume.

The present report relates exclusively to the exploration by the The present
writer in 1887, with the following exceptions:—(1.) Mr. McConnell's report.
traverse and geological observations on a portion of the Stikine are
included in the description of that river and are incorporated on the
accompanying map. (2.) The Lewes River, as laid down on the map,
(with the exception of the mountain features in its vicinity and some
additions to the outlines of the lakes), is from the survey of Mr. W.
Ogilvie. The results of Mr. McConnell's work, carried out after his
separation from us at the mouth of the Dease, will form the subject of
a separate report of the Geological Survey, and Mr. Ogilvie will also
prepare an independent report of his survey on his return.

In order to present within a reasonable compass the results of the por- Arrangement
tion of the work of the expedition here reported on, the daily record of matter.
of progress, which the unknown character of the country traversed
might otherwise appear to warrant, has been discarded, and but slight
allusion is made to the modes of travel adopted and the numerous
vicissitudes encountered during our journey. This, while resulting in
the loss of interest which a connected narrative might possess, has
distinct advantages in other respects. On account of the extent of the
region treated of, the descriptive portion of the report has been divided
into separate chapters, each treating of a distinct portion of our route
and constituting practically a separate short report. In the pages
immediately following this introduction, some general notes on the
region as a whole, are given.

Summary of Proceedings.

The following summary of our proceedings in connection with the Journey to the
expedition is substantially the same as that given in my preliminary Stikine.
report before alluded to.—

We left Ottawa on the 22nd of April, 1887, travelling by the
Canadian Pacific Railway to Victoria, but, in consequence of irregularity in the sailing dates of the Alaskan mail steamers, were unable
to reach Wrangell, at the mouth of the Stikine River, where our work
may have said to have begun, till the 18th of May. Here Mr. McConnell
stayed behind, for the purpose of getting Indians and canoes to enable
him to make a micrometer survey of the Stikine from the end of the

line measured by Mr. J. Hunter in 1877, to Telegraph Creek, while I proceeded up the river by the first steamer of the season to Telegraph Creek, the head of navigation. From this place, goods are carried by pack animals to Dease Lake, the centre of the Cassiar mining district; and here again a delay of several days occurred, as the animals had not been brought in from their range or shod for the season's work at the date of our arrival. Finally, on June 5th, we reached the head of Dease Lake, and found the greater part of the lake still covered with ice. It was not till the 9th that we were able to reach the point on the shore near Laketon at which two men, previously sent on in advance with an Indian packer, were sawing lumber for boats. Seven days were here busily employed in this work and in constructing three boats for the purposes of the expedition. On the evening of the 16th, a strong wind having broken up the remaining barrier of ice, we reached Laketon with our boats, Mr. McConnell, with a crew of five Coast Indians intended for my work on the Upper Liard, having meanwhile joined us. On the 18th, having completed our supplies and outfit at Laketon, we left that place, and on the 23rd reached the " Lower Post " at the confluence of the Dease and Liard Rivers. Here Mr. McConnell, with one boat and two men, separated from us for the purpose of surveying and geologically examining the Lower Liard.

Journey to Dease Lake.

Building boats.

Departure from Dease Lake.

On leaving the confluence of the Dease and Liard, my own party included, besides myself, Mr. McEvoy, Messrs. L. Lewis and D. Johnson, engaged at Victoria, two Tshimsian and three Stikine (Thlinkit) Indians, all good boatmen. Two local Indians hired as guides, and to help in portaging, deserted a day or two after engaging, and from the " Lower Post " to near the confluence of the Pelly and Lewes, for an interval of more than six weeks, we met neither whites nor Indians.

Personnel of parties.

The ascent of the Liard and Frances rivers to Frances Lake proved unexpectedly difficult and tedious, the rivers being swift throughout and three bad cañons having to be passed through. Frances Lake was reached on the 8th of July, and after spending a few days in examining and mapping the lake, making the observations necessary to fix its position, and in the endeavour to find some Indian trail by which we might travel across to the Pelly, we began the work of portaging on the 17th.

Journey to Frances Lake.

As we had been unable to discover any route now in use by the Indians, and no trace whatever remained of the trail employed by the Hudson Bay Company in former years; and further, as no local Indians could be found to act as guides or to assist in carrying our stuff, it was evident that the crossing of this portage (which had been estimated by Mr. Campbell at about 70 miles in length) would be a difficult matter,

Journey overland to Pelly River.

and that we might indeed find it impossible to carry over a sufficient
supply of provisions for work on the Pelly. We therefore, constructed
a strong log *cache* on the shore of Frances Lake, and left there, to be
taken to Dease Lake by the Indians when they returned, everything
we could possibly dispense with. Had we been unable to effect the
portage, there was in our *cache* a sufficient supply of provisions to enable the whole party to return to the "Lower Post." After a very toil-
some journey, we were, however, so fortunate as to reach the bank of the
Upper Pelly on the 29th of July, with still nearly a month's provisions
for four persons, our instruments and a small camping outfit, a
canvas cover from which a canoe might be constructed, and the tools
and nails for building a wooden boat, should that prove to be necessary. Our Indians, who had for a long time been very uneasy because
of their distance from the coast and the unknown character of the
country into which they had been taken, were here paid off, and to
their great delight allowed to turn back.

As a dangerous rapid was reported to exist on the upper part of the Descent of the
Pelly, it was decided to construct a canvas canoe in preference to Upper Pelly.
building a boat, which it might prove impossible to portage past the
rapid. Having completed the canoe, we descended the Pelly, making
a portage of half a mile past Hoole Rapid or Cañon, and arrived at the
confluence of the Lewes branch with the Upper Pelly on the 11th
of August. We had now reached the line of route which is used by the Proceedings at
miners, and expected to find, at the mouth of the Lewes, a prearranged Lewes.
memorandum from Mr. Ogilvie, from whom we had separated in May.
As we could not find any such notice, and as Mr. Ogilvie had not been
seen on the lower river by a party of miners whom we met here on
their way up the Lewes, we were forced to conclude that he had not
yet reached this point. The same party informed us that there had
been few miners during the summer on the Stewart River, where most
of the work had been carried on in 1886, but that in consequence of the
discovery of "coarse" gold on Forty-mile Creek, over 200 miles
further down the river, most of the men had gone there. We were
also told that Harper's trading post, where I had hoped to be able
to get an additional supply of provisions should we fail to connect
with Mr. Ogilvie, had been moved from the mouth of the Stewart
to Forty-mile Creek. From the place where we now were we still
had a journey of nearly 400 miles to the coast, with the swift waters
of the Lewes to contend against for the greater part of the distance.
If therefore it should have become necessary to go down stream
200 miles to Forty-mile Creek for provisions, so much would have
been added to our up-stream journey that it would become doubtful
whether we should be able to afford time for geological work on

the Lewes, and yet reach the coast before the smaller lakes near the mountains were frozen over. I therefore decided to set about the building of another boat, suitable for the ascent of the Lewes, and on the second day after we had begun work, Mr. Ogilvie very opportunely appeared. After having completed our boat and obtained Mr. Ogilvie's preliminary report and map-sheets, together with the necessary provisions, we began the ascent of the Lewes, from the head-waters of which we crossed the mountains by the Chilkoot Pass and reached the coast at the head of Lynn Canal on the 20th September.

In addition to the physical obstacles to be encountered on the long route above outlined, some anxiety was caused by reported Indian troubles on the Yukon. We heard a most circumstantial account of these from a couple of miners who followed us in to Dease Lake, the report being that the hostile Indians had retreated up the Pelly. As it was impossible either to confirm or refute these reports without practically abandoning the scheme of work, it was determined to proceed according to the original arrangement. On reaching the mouth of the Lewes we ascertained that the story was entirely false, but it had none the less kept us in a state of watchfulness during a great part of the summer.

Building our fifth boat.

Reach Lynn Canal.

Reported Indian troubles

Main Geographical Results.

The main geographical results of the Yukon expedition, in so far as those are covered by the present report, are best shown by the accompanying maps, which may be compared with previous maps of the same region. Mr. Ogilvie's instrumentally measured line from the head of Lynn Canal to the intersection of the Yukon or Pelly by the 141st meridian, will form a sufficiently accurate base for further surveys. In addition to this we now have an instrumental survey of the Stikine from its mouth to the head of navigation (Telegraph Creek), which is connected with Dease Lake by a carefully paced traverse. This is continued by a detailed running- or track-survey following the lines of the Dease, Upper Liard and Pelly rivers, and connecting with Mr. Ogilvie's line at the mouth of the Lewes, the total distance from the mouth of the Stikine to this point, by the route travelled being about 944 miles. Adding to this the distance from the mouth of the Lewes back to the coast at the head of Lynn Canal (377 miles), the entire distance travelled by us during the exploration amounts to 1322 miles. This, taken in connection with the coast-line between the Stikine and Lynn Canal, circumscribes an area of about 63,200 square miles, the interior of which is still, but for the accounts of a few prospectors and reports of Indians, a *terra incognita*. The same description,

Geographical data obtained.

Length of route traversed.

with little qualification, applies to the whole surrounding region outside the surveyed circuit, but much general information concerning the country has been obtained, which will facilitate further explorations.

Along the routes thus travelled numerous points have been carefully fixed in latitude by sextant observations, and a sufficient number of chronometer longitudes have been obtained by which to lay the whole down within small limits of error. Special attention was paid to the sketching and fixing of mountain topography in sight from the line of travel, and the approximate altitudes of a number of the more prominent peaks was ascertained. *Positions fixed.*

No reference is made here to the further work carried out by Messrs. Ogilvie and McConnell in 1888, which will, as above stated, be separately reported on.

OROGRAPHY AND GENERAL FEATURES.

The region traversed by the routes just mentioned, including the extreme northern part of British Columbia and the southern part of the Yukon district (as previously defined), is drained by three great river systems, its waters reaching the Pacific by the Stikine, the Mackenzie, (and eventually the Arctic Ocean,) by the Liard, and Behring Sea, by the Yukon. The south-eastern part of the region is divided between the two first named rivers, whose tributary streams interlock, the Stikine making its way completely through the Coast Ranges in a south-westerly direction, while the Liard, on a north easterly bearing, cuts across the Rocky Mountains to the Mackenzie valley. The watershed separating these rivers near Dease Lake has a height of 2730 feet, and both streams may be generally characterized as very rapid. *Drainage system.*

To the north-westward, branches of the Stikine and Liard again interlock with the head-waters of several tributaries of the Yukon, which here unwater the entire great area enclosed on one side by the Coast Ranges, on the other by the Rocky Mountains. As the general direction of this line of watershed is transverse to that of the main orographic ridges of the country, it will probably be found, when traced in detail, to be very sinuous. The actual watershed, between the Liard and Pelly, on our line of route, was found to have an elevation of 3150 feet, but it is, no doubt, much lower in the central portion of the region between the Rocky Mountains and Coast Ranges. *Watershed.*

To the north of the Stikine, at least one other river, the Taku, cuts like it completely across the Coast Ranges, but its basin is comparatively restricted and little is yet known of it.

It will be noticed, that while the several branches of the Yukon con- *Courses of Rivers.*

form in a general way to the main orographic axes, the Stikine and Liard appear to be to a large degree independent of these, and to flow counter to the direction of three mountain ranges.

Relief of the region.

The region as a whole, being a portion of the Cordillera belt of the west coast, is naturally mountainous in general character, but it comprises as well important areas of merely hilly or gently rolling country, besides many wide, flat-bottomed river-valleys. It is, moreover, more mountainous and higher in its south-eastern part—that drained by the Stikine and Liard,—and subsides gradually, and apparently uniformly, to the north-westward; the mountains at the same time becoming more isolated and being separated by broader tracts of low land. The general base-level, or height of the main valleys, within the Coast Ranges, thus declines from about 2500 feet, to nearly 1500 feet at the confluence of the Lewes and Pelly rivers, and the average base-level of the entire region may be stated as being a little over 2000 feet.

Trend of ranges.

Disregarding minor irregularities, it is found that the trend of the main mountain ridges and ranges shows throughout the entire region here described a general parallelism to the outline of the coast. In the south-eastern and more rugged tract, the bearing of such ranges as are well defined is north-west by south-east, while beyond a line which may be drawn between the head of Lynn Canal and Frances Lake the trend gradually changes to west-north-west.

The Coast Ranges.

The Coast Ranges, with an aggregate average width of about eighty miles, the whole of which is closely set with high, rounded or rugged mountains, constitutes the most important orographic uplift in the entire region, and here reproduces geographically and geologically the features characteristic of it in the more southern portion of British Columbia. Beyond the vicinity of Lynn Canal, this mountain axis runs behind the St. Elias Alps, ceasing to be the continental border, and may be said to be entirely unknown, as any indications of mountains which have appeared on this part of the map are purely conjectural. Notwithstanding the great width of the Coast Ranges, it is not known that any of their constituent mountains attain very notable altitudes, but it is probable that a great number of the peaks exceed a height of 8000 feet. These ranges are composed of very numerous mountain ridges, which are not always uniform in direction, and, so far as has been observed, there is no single culminating or dominant range which can be traced for any considerable distance.

Rocky Mountain Ranges.

The mountain axis next in importance to that of the Coast Ranges, is that which forms the water-parting between the Upper Liard and Yukon, on one side, and the feeders of the main Mackenzie River on the other. This represents the north-western continuation of the Rocky Mountains proper. Its eastern ridges were touched on during

the present exploration in the vicinity of Frances Lake and the head
waters of the Pelly River, and are there designated on the map as the Too-
tsho Range. This forms, so far as has been ascertained, the culminating
range of a number of more or less exactly parallel ridges, and summits
in it attain heights of from 7000 to 9000 feet. It has, however, been
traced to a comparatively limited distance only, and it appears probable
that a very complicated mountain system remains to be worked out in
this portion of the region.

A third notable mountain axis, which I have designated on the map Cassiar Range.
as the Cassiar Range, is cut through by the Dease River in its
upper course, and further to the north-westward appears to form the
line of water-parting between the tributaries of the Upper Liard and
those of the branches of the Yukon. Peaks near the Dease, in this
range, exceed 7000 feet, but it is probable that none much exceed
8000 feet, and that the range in a general way becomes lower to the
north-westward.

In the north-western and less elevated moiety of the region, the
mountain ranges and ridges are in general lower and become discon-
tinuous and irregular, or while retaining a general parallelism, assume
an overlapping or echelon-like arrangement.

In each of these mountain chains above described granitic rocks Granitic rocks.
appear in greater or less force, as more fully noted on succeeding pages.
In the intervening and subordinate mountain systems of the south-east,
granitic axes are not found and do not exist as prominent features.

Scarcely anything is known of the character of the country drained Orography of
by the Macmillan, Stewart and White rivers, but it is probable that neigbouring regions.
the basins of the two first-named streams closely resemble that of the
Upper Pelly, which is described in following pages. Miners who have
ascended the Stewart for a hundred miles or more, report the existence
of a continuous range of mountains of considerable height, which runs
parallel to the river on the north, from a point about fifty miles from its
mouth onward. The absence of tributaries of any size along the south-west
side of the Lewes below the Tahk-heena, with the general appearance
of the country in that direction, so far it has been overlooked, seems to
show that the basin of the upper portion of the White River must be
comparatively low, and situated as it is within the St. Elias Alps, this
country must possess most remarkable features, both geographically
and from a climatic point of view, and well deserves exploration. It
would further appear to be nearly certain that the sources of the Tanana River are to be looked for in this district, well to the east of the
141st meridian.

The topographical features of the entire region here described have Effects of the glacial period.
been considerably modified by the events of the glacial period, and the

changes produced at that time have more particularly affected the drainage-basins and the courses of the various streams. The valleys and lower tracts of country are now more or less completely filled or covered by extensive deposits of boulder-clay, gravel, sand and silt laid down during that period. To these deposits are due the flat floors of the larger valleys, and also to a great extent the appearance which the more irregular mountain regions present of being partly submerged in level or rolling plains. Many changes in direction of flow in river-valleys have doubtless also been produced during this period, though most of these yet remain to be worked out. The general result has been to produce systems of "inconsequent" drainage wherever the natural slopes of the country are easy and the limiting ranges irregular. Most of the rivers at the present day have done little more than cut out new channels in the glacial *débris*, touching only here and there upon the subjacent rocky floor.

Sources of the Yukon and Nomenclature.

Confused nomenclature.

Such particulars as have been ascertained relative to the various rivers examined in the course of the exploration, are given in a subsequent part of this report. As, however, some confusion has arisen in respect to the nomenclature of the Yukon and its tributaries, and erroneous statements have been made as to the "source" of the river, it may be appropriate here briefly to note the facts in the case in so far as I have been able to ascertain them. Further details of the early exploration of the river are given on page 136 B.

First exploration of Yukon.

The estuary of the Yukon appears to have been first explored by the Russian, Glasunoff, in 1835 to 1838, and the river was then named by the Russians the Kwikhpak, which name, according to Mr. W. H. Dall, is in reality that of one of the channels by which it issues to the sea. The lower part of the river, however, continued to be known under this name for a number of years, and it is so called on the (Russian) map of Lieut. Zagoskin, made from reconnoisance surveys which, in 1842-43, he carried up as far as Nowikakat. The mouth of the river is shown on Arrowsmith's map of 1850, but is there nameless.

Origin of the name.

The name Yukon was first applied in 1846 by Mr. J. Bell, of the Hudson Bay Company, who reached the main river by descending the Porcupine, and called it by what he understood to be its Indian appellation. The head-waters of one of the main tributaries of the Yukon had previously been attained by Mr. R. Campbell (also an officer of the Hudson Bay Company) in 1840, and in 1850 he descended the river as far as the mouth of the Porcupine, naming the whole river thus traversed the Pelly, and naming also the Lewes, White and Stewart rivers, as well as numerous smaller tributaries. Campbell's nomenclature and his Connection of Yukon and Kwikhpak. sketch of the river appear on Arrowsmith's map published in April, 1854, and Campbell practically established by his journey the identity of his Pelly River with the Kwikhpak of the Russians. The connection between the two is given by a sketch (shown in broken lines) on the map just cited, on which also the mouth of the Tanana River (under the name Mountain-men River) is shown, and other details represented with reasonable accuracy. The sketch of the river below the mouth of the Porcupine appears to have been due to the Hudson Bay Company's traders, who, before Campbell had communicated his geographical information in London (in 1853), had already met the Russian traders at the mouth of the Tanana. Much later, in 1863, I. S. Lukeen, of the Russian Trading Company, ascended the river to the Hudson Bay post, Fort Yukon, at the mouth of the Porcupine.*

The name Yukon does not appear at all on Arrowsmith's map of Usage on subsequent maps. 1854, that of the Pelly standing for the whole length of the river explored by Campbell, but since that date the term Yukon has gradually become applied to the main river. The next map in order of publication in which original data are employed is, I believe, that accompanying Mr. Whymper's paper of 1868, in the Journal of the Royal Geographical Society,† which is also reproduced in his book, Travels in Alaska and on the Yukon (1869). His general map gives the name Pelly for the whole river above the mouth of the Porcupine, " Kwich-Pak or Yukon," for the lower part. In his large-scale map, on the same sheet, the river above the Porcupine is named the Yukon or Pelly. Whymper refers to the river as the " Yukon (or Pelly) as it has long been called on our maps."‡   In the United States Coast Survey map dated 1869§ the main river between the Porcupine and Lewes is definitely named the Yukon; but in the map accompanying Raymond's official report (1871) this name is again confined to the river below the Porcupine, and the statement is made in the report (p. 21) that from Lake Labarge to Fort Yukon the river is called the Lewes.

---

* By a singular oversight, Mr. W. H. Dall states in the first part of his work, Alaska and its Resources 1870 (p. 4), that "the identity of the Yukon [Pelly] River with the so-called Kwikhpak of the Russians" remained to be established when the explorations of the Telegraph Survey commenced on the river in 1865, while giving the credit of this achievement to Lukeen on a subsequent page (p. 277). Raymond repeats this error in his Report of a Reconnoissance of the Yukon River (1871). Mr. Dall's work above cited constitutes a veritable mine of information on the subjects of which it treats, and is frequently referred to in the sequel. Where, therefore, as in the above case, criticisms are offered, it is in no spirit of detraction.

† Vol. xxxviii.

‡ Op. cit., p. 223.

§ In United States Coast Survey Report for 1867 the same nomenclature is adopted, as it is also in the map accompanying Mr. Dall's Alaska (1870), in the Ethnological map of Alaska by the same author (1875), and in most later maps. These, however, do not embody any original data for this region.

Much later, Lieut. Schwatka, in the maps accompanying the official report of his explorations of 1883 and in other maps elsewhere published, in defiance of the fact that the name of the Lewes had a published priority of thirty years, erased it completely, extending the name Yukon so as to include under that designation the Lewes River. This extension of the name Yukon appears to be justified by Lieut. Schwatka on the ground that the Lewes is the larger branch at its confluence with the Upper Pelly. As elsewhere stated, this is no doubt true, but from what is now known of the Upper Pelly, that river is almost certainly the longer, its sources are furthest removed from the mouth of the Yukon and its course is more directly in continuation of its main direction than is the case with the Lewes. Granting, however, that the Lewes excelled in all these particulars, it would still, I believe, be unjustifiable to alter an old established name for the sole purpose of giving to a river a single name from its mouth to its source. In any case it is incorrect to state that the Yukon (Lewes) rises in Lake Lindeman, or streams flowing into it, as is done by Schwatka, for by far the greater part of the water of the river enters by the Taku arm of Tagish Lake.

With respect to the substitution of the name Yukon for that of Pelly on the portion of the river between the Porcupine and Lewes, it is simply a question of well established priority *versus* *use*. It is possibly a matter of small importance which shall be employed in future, but no valid excuse can be offered for the attempt to substitute any new name for that either of the Lewes or Pelly above the site of old Fort Selkirk.

From the point of view of the physical geographer, and apart from the question of nomenclature, the position of the furthest source of the great Yukon River is, however, an interesting subject of enquiry; though it may yet be some years before we are in possession of sufficient information to settle this question definitely. It may be confidently assumed that this point is to be found by following up either the Pelly or the Lewes from their confluence at the site of old Fort Selkirk. As already stated, the Lewes there carries the greater volume of water, but draining as it does a considerable length of the humid Coast Ranges, which bear throughout the year great reserves of snow and numerous glaciers, it does not compare on terms of equality with the Upper Pelly, which unwaters a region relatively dry. Whether reckoned by size or distance from its mouth, the source of the Lewes must be placed at the head waters of the Hotilinqu River,* explored by Byrnes, of the Telegraph Survey, in approximate latitude 59° 10′,

---

* The Tes-lin-too occupies the main orographic valley above its confluence with the Lewes, but is smaller than the Lewes, and besides doubles back on its course, as is shown on the map.

longitude 132° 40′. In regard to the Pelly, it is not yet absolutely certain that the Pelly proper rises further from the common point at Fort Selkirk than its great branches, the Macmillan and the Ross rivers, but it is highly probable that it will be found to do so.

With the above facts premised, we may compare the respective dis-*Comparison of tributaries.* tances of assumed or probable sources of the Yukon as below, the distances being in each case measured in a straight line from the common point at Fort Selkirk :—

Fort Selkirk to summit of Chilkoot Pass, source according to
        Schwatka (position fixed)....................... 224 miles.
"   " to head of Hotalinqu River of Telegraph Survey
        (position approximate)....................... 294   "
"   " to "Pelly Banks" (position fixed)............ 213   "
"   " to head of Pelly Lakes (above "Pelly Banks,"
        according to Campbell's sketch)........... 276   "

The upper lake on the Pelly must be fed by a considerable stream or streams, the addition of the length of which, if known, would add considerably to the last of the above distances.

I must confess to having been somewhat disappointed in the size of *Size of the river.* the Pelly or Yukon where we saw it below the confluence of the Lewes. The river is there, when undivided by islands, about 1700 feet only in width, with a maximum depth scarcely exceeding ten feet when at a stage which may be considered as its approximate mean. It appeared to me to be about equal in size and velocity to the Peace River at Dun-vegan and Mr. Ogilvie, who is also familiar with the Peace, concurred in this estimate. Below this place the river, of course, receives a num-*Comparison with Mackenzie River.* ber of important tributaries, but at any fairly comparable point on the two rivers I believe that the Mackenzie must far exceed the Yukon in volume. Numerical data on this point are unfortunately still almost entirely wanting, but the comparison of the drainage-areas of the two rivers, according to the latest available information, strongly bears out the statement just made, that of the Yukon being 330,912 square miles as against 677,400 square miles in the case of the Mackenzie.* In other words, the drainage area of the Mackenzie is more than double that of the Yukon, while nothing is known to show that the mean annual precipitation over the two areas, as a whole, differs very greatly. Exaggerated statements which have been made, to the effect that the Yukon discharges a volume of water approaching that of the Mississippi, appear to carry their own refutation in the fact that the basin of the latter river has an area of no less than 1,226,000 square miles.

---

* Of the area drained by the Yukon, about 150,768 square miles are in Canadian, 180,144 square miles in United-States Territory.

Discharge of rivers.

Some attempt was made by us to gage the flow of several of the rivers in the Yukon basin, as more fully stated further on. The discharge of the several rivers above the site of the old Fort Selkirk may be roughly summarized as follows. The figures given in heavy type are derived from measurements more or less approximate, the others are based merely on comparisons made by eye and without any attempt to cross-section the streams. The scheme may, however, serve to give a general idea of relative dimensions. All the figures represent cubic feet per second and refer to the latter part of the summer, when the rivers may be assumed to be at their mean height. In common with all the streams of the interior region these are highest in the early summer and lowest toward the end of the winter.

Pelly River, at "Pelly Banks"	**4,898**
Ross River, at mouth	4,898
Macmillan River, at mouth	9,796*
Tes-lin-too, at mouth	**11,436**
Lewis River, above confluence with last	**18,664**
Big Salmon	**2,726**
Total thus accounted for	52,418
Pelly or Yukon at site of Fort Selkirk	**66,955**
Difference from above total, not accounted for	14,537

Upper Pelly and Lowes compared.

By adding two-thirds of the water thus not accounted for to the Pelly and one-third to the Lowes, to represent the flow of numerous smaller tributaries not enumerated, the discharge of these two rivers above Fort Selkirk will stand thus :—

Lewis	37,672
Pelly	29,283
Total as above	66,955 †

* The discharge of the Ross is taken as equal to that of the Pelly at "Pelly Banks," that of the Macmillan as equal to the combined waters of the Pelly and Ross.

† For the purpose of comparison, the following extract from a table of various rivers, contained in the General Report of the Minister of Public Works for the fifteen years from 1867 to 1882, is quoted :—

NAMES.	Area of drainage in square miles.	Length in miles.	Discharge in cubic feet per second.		
			Low Water.	Mean.	High Water.
Mississippi	1,226,000	4,400	447,200	....	1,270,000
St. Lawrence	565,000	2,600	....	900,000	....
Ganges	432,000	1,680	36,300	207,000	494,200
Nile	520,200	2,240	23,100	220,000	....
Thames	5,000	215	1,330	....	7,900
Rhone	38,000	560	7,000	21,000	204,000
Rhine	88,000	700	13,400	33,700	164,000
Ottawa (Grenville)	80,000	700	35,000	85,000	150,000

Navigable Waters and Routes of Travel.

The numerous large and important rivers by which the Yukon district and the adjacent northern portion of British Columbia is intersected, constitute the principal routes of travel, and during the summer months render inter-communication comparatively easy. The Stikine is navigable by stern-wheel steamers for a distance of 138 miles, as more fully stated in a subsequent part of this report, where also details respecting the connecting trail to Dease Lake are given (pp. 46 B, 64 B). This constitutes the travelled route to the Cassiar mining district. A trail was, at one time, opened from Fraser Lake overland to Dease Lake by which cattle were driven through, but of late no travel has occurred on it (p. 89 B). The Dease River can scarcely be considered as navigable for steamers, though constituting a fairly good boat route (p. 91 B). The Upper Liard and Frances rivers, above the mouth of the Dease, are also passable for large boats, with occasional portages, but not so for steamers (p. 102 B). The difficulties of the Lower Liard, however, are such as to render it an undesirable route, even for boats, and scarcely suitable as an avenue of trade between Cassiar and the Mackenzie. Numerous tributary streams in this district may also be ascended by boat or canoe for considerable distances, though with many interruptions from rapids and bad water.

Communication may easily be established by railway from the mouth of the Stikine to the centre of the Cassiar district and beyond, when this shall be called for, and it is probable also that this district might, without difficulty, be connected by rail with the more southern portions of British Columbia by one or more routes of which the main outlines can already be indicated. Following the river-valleys, by a route practicable for a railway, from Rothsay Point at the mouth of the Stikine to the mouth of the Dease, the distance is found to be 330 miles. Thence to Fort Simpson on the Mackenzie, is a further distance of 390 miles, making the total distance by this route, from the Pacific to the navigable waters of the Mackenzie about 720 miles only.

Little is yet known of the Taku River, but the Indians ascend it in canoes to a point at a distance of about eighty miles from the head of Taku Inlet, and Indian trails lead south-eastward from this vicinity to the Tahl-tan, eastward to Tes-lin Lake and north-eastward to the lakes near the head of the Lewes. From what has been ascertained of these, it is probable that it would not be difficult to construct a trail suitable for pack-animals, if not a waggon road, from the vicinity of the head of navigation on the Stikine to these lakes connecting with the navigable waters of the Lewes.

Tributaries of Yukon.

The rivers draining the Upper Yukon basin, have in general lower grades, and afford better navigable water than those above referred to, and are in consequence likely to prove of greater importance in connection with the exploration and development of the country. The distance to which they may be respectively ascended by boat or canoe, has as yet been determined in only a few cases.

Navigable lengths of rivers.

It may, however, be stated that the Yukon is continuously navigable for small steamers from its mouth, on Behring Sea and following the Lewes branch, to Miles Cañon. Thence, after an interruption of about three miles, to the head of Bennett Lake and to an additional considerable—though not precisely determined distance—by the waters extending south-eastward from Tagish Lake (p. 165 B). The Tes-lin-too is probably navigable for stern-wheel steamers for a hundred and fifty miles or more from its mouth, (p. 154 B) while the Tahk-heena and Big Salmon rivers may probably both be ascended by steamers of the same class for some distance. From the site of old Fort Selkirk, again, the Pelly might be navigated by small steamers of good power to within about fifty miles of the site of old Fort Pelly Banks, (p. 133 B) and the Macmillan branch is also navigable for a considerable, though not ascertained distance (p. 129 B). The same may be said of the Stewart River, but White River is, so far as known, very swift and shoal.

Aggregate length of navigable waters.

The total length of the waters which may be utilized for navigation by light stern-wheel steamers on the main river and its branches to the east of the 141st meridian or Alaskan boundary, measured in straight lengths of fifty miles, is therefore at least 1000 miles, and following the sinuosities of the various streams would be very much greater. This does not include the Porcupine River, and with the exception of the single break above referred to on the Lewes, forms a connected system, all parts of which lie to the east of the above meridian. If the upper portion of these rivers, above the first obstacles to such navigation, were included, the total here given would doubtless be greatly added to.

Means of access to Yukon District.

At the present moment but three routes of access to the Yukon district are employed. (1). That of the portage by the Chilkoot Pass from the head of Lynn Canal to the navigable waters of the Lewes. (2). That from Peel River, near its confluence with the Mackenzie by portage to La Pierre's House on a branch of the Porcupine. (3). That from Behring Sea by the main river. The first is that almost exclusively used by the miners, the second is employed only by the Hudson Bay Company, and the last is that of the Alaskan traders.

There are now three small stern-wheel steamers on the lower river, which ascend each year as far as the trading post at Forty-mile Creek, bringing the greater part of the goods used in trade with the Indians and for the supply of miners. It is not possible, however, for miners to reach the scene of their operations by this route in time to make a season's work, and the chances of reaching or leaving the Yukon mouth are few and precarious. Particulars relating to the Chilkoot Pass and Lewes River will be found on pages 173 B, 174 B. The character of the pass is such that it would scarcely be possible to construct a useful trail across it for pack-animals, but the White Pass appears to offer a better opportunity for making a trail or road which, if constructed, would render the entire region much more easy of access. Another route, also leading from the head of Lynn Canal to navigable water connecting with the Lewes, is that by the Chilkat Pass. This was formerly much employed by the Indians, but entails a much longer land carriage, one which is said to occupy the Indians for twelve days when carrying packs, as against two days of packing by the Chilkoot Pass.

The Indians inhabiting the region to the south and east of the site of old Fort Selkirk are poor boatmen and follow the various rivers in the course of their periodic journeys to a very limited extent. Most of their travelled routes appear, indeed, to run nearly at right-angles to the direction of drainage, the rivers being crossed in summer on rafts, the remains of which may frequently be observed. In travelling thus they carry their entire small camping outfit on their backs.

Indian routes.

Climate, Agriculture and Flora.

While the available information as to the climate of the northern portion of British Columbia and the Yukon district is necessarily as yet very imperfect, its general features are sufficiently obvious, repeating as they do those met with in the similarly circumstanced region to the south, with such modification as is produced by their higher latitude. The coast and coastward slopes of the Coast Ranges constitute a belt of excessive humidity and great precipitation, with somewhat equable temperatures, while the interior region to the eastward of these ranges is relatively dry, with a temperature of extremes.* In the interior, however, the climate is largely influenced by the altitude of each particular district, and in consequence of the general lowering of the country beyond the 60th parallel (constituting the north line of British Columbia), it is certain that the climatic conditions are there much more favorable than in the Cassiar district.

General character of climate.

The mean annual temperature of the coast region is considerably higher than that of the interior; yet, in consequence of the great

Regions of heavy and light rainfall.

---

* A mean of the total annual precipitation for Fort Tongass, Wrangell and Sitka gives a general mean for the coast of 86·81 inches.

depth of the snow-fall and persistently clouded character of the skies, the Coast Ranges are found to support numerous and massive glaciers, while these are almost or altogether absent in the Cassiar Mountains, in the mountains about Frances Lake and in the other ranges seen by us in the interior. The heavy accumulation of snow upon the Coast Mountains and in their valleys, retards the progress of spring, as is very clearly evidenced on the Stikine, and explained more fully elsewhere. (p. 58 B). The depth of snow in winter continues to be inconsiderable or moderate, at least as far down the Pelly (Yukon) as the mouth of Stewart River and Forty-mile Creek, while at Nulato, on the lower river and in a similar latitude, but 500 miles further west, the depth of snow from April to November is said to average eight feet and often to reach twelve feet.*

Progress of spring. Mr. Dall also writes: "The valley of the Lower Yukon is somewhat foggy in the latter part of summer; but as we ascend the river the climate improves, and the short season at Fort Yukon is dry, but pleasant, only varied by an occasional shower." Relatively to the country of the Upper Yukon basin, the advent of spring is much retarded in the country to the west, and it is stated that on the river below Nulatto alder buds were found just opening and tender leaves beginning to appear on the 4th of June. These and other facts seem to show conclusively, that in the absence of a continuous mountain barrier in that region, the humid winds of the Pacific are enabled to push eastward a long way up the Yukon valley, carrying with them the belt of heavy snow-fall, which ceases to be conterminous with the Coast Mountains, as it is to the south-eastward.

Dry belts. As in the more southern parts of British Columbia, the dryest country is found to occur in a belt bordering the eastern or lee side of the Coast Ranges, and this phenomenon recurs, though in a less marked degree, in connection with each of the well-defined mountain ranges of the interior. Thus a region of greater humidity is found near Dease Lake, on the western side of the Cassiar Mountains, with a dry belt on the east side of the range; while humid conditions, with recurrent showers in summer, characterize the district in the vicinity of Frances and Finlayson lakes. Further illustrations of this fact, with other climatic observations, will be found in the body of this report and in Appendix VI.

Summer and winter winds. A noteworthy circumstance in connection with the Stikine valley, the passes leading from the head of Lynn Canal, and doubtless in all the low gaps in the Coast Ranges, is the change in direction as between the summer and winter winds. During the summer strong winds blowing up these valleys inland, are of very frequent occurrence and they commonly freshen in the afternoon and die away toward night. In

---

* Alaska and its Resources. W. H. Dall, 1870, p. 437.

the winter months the conditions are precisely reversed, the strongest winds blowing seaward. The summer winds are doubtless homologous with the sea breezes observed in many other regions, while the direction of the winter winds probably depends on the existence of a persistent anti-cyclonic area in the interior during that season.

The temperature of Wrangell, just off the mouth of the Stikine, may probably be taken as fairly representative of that of the coast in these latitudes. For the interior region, here particularly treated of, we are unfortunately without a series of thermometer readings extending even over a single year, but some idea of its climate may be formed from that of Fort Yukon, which is, however, situated far to the north, almost exactly on the Arctic circle. The mean seasonal temperatures for these two stations may be compared as below.*—

	Wrangell.	Fort Yukon.
Spring	40.4	14.6
Summer	57.1	56.7
Autumn	43.0	17.4
Winter	28.3	—23.8
Year	42.2	16.8

In the central provinces of European Russia the thermometer descends to —22° and —31°, and occasionally even to —54°, in the winter months, but rises at times to 104° and even to 109° in summer. The rain-fall is small, varying from sixteen to twenty-eight inches, the maximum precipitation taking place during the summer months, and not, as in western Europe, in the winter, while the months of advanced spring are warmer than the corresponding months of autumn.† So far as our information goes, the above statement might almost be adopted as characterizing the climate of the southern half of the Yukon district.

At Telegraph Creek and in its vicinity on the Stikine, to the east of the Coast Ranges (lat. 58°), wheat, barley and potatoes are successfully grown with the aid of irrigation. Their cultivation has so far been attempted on a limited scale only, on account of the want of any market, and wheat has been grown only experimentally, as it cannot, like barley, be employed for feeding pack-animals. None of these crops can be successfully grown or ripened on the coastward side of the mountains. At Fort Yukon (situated, as above noted, on the Arctic circle) Mr. Dall states he was informed that barley had once or twice been tried in small patches and had succeeded in maturing the grain, though the straw was very short.‡ A few cattle were also

---

* From the United-States Coast Pilot, Alaska, Part I, 1883, p. 269.
† Encyclopedia Britannica, vol. xxi. p. 67.
‡ Op. cit., p. 441.

kept here at one time, when the post was in the possession of the Hudson Bay Company. Petroff, in his Census Report on Alaska, endeavors to discredit Dall's statement as to the growth of barley at this northern point, but I am fortunately in possession of independent evidence as to its accuracy, the late Mr. James Anderson, of the Hudson Bay Company, having noted in an official report on the district that both potatoes and barley have been grown at the fort.

Conclusions as to possible agriculture

Taking into consideration all the facts which I have been able to obtain, as well as those to be derived from an examination of the natural flora of the country, and the observed advance of vegetation, which, in the absence of actual experiments, are capable of affording valuable data, I feel no hesitation in stating my belief that such hardy crops as barley, rye, turnips and flax can be successfully cultivated in the Yukon district as far north as the former position of Fort Selkirk, near the 63rd parallel, or in other words about 1000 miles north of Victoria. Taken in conjunction with the physical features of the region, this means, that chiefly within the drainage area of the Yukon, and for the most part to the north of the 60th parallel, there exists an area of about 60,000 square miles, of which a large proportion may, and doubtless in the future will—be utilized for the cultivation of such crops, and in which cattle and horses might be maintained in sufficient number for local purposes, without undue labor, as excellent summer grazing is generally to be found along the river-valleys and natural hay-meadows are frequent. I do not maintain that the country is suitable for immediate occupation by a large, self-supporting agricultural community, but hold that agriculture may before many years be successfully prosecuted, in conjunction with the natural development of the other resources of this great country, of which by far the most valuable portion lies to the east of the line of the Alaskan boundary.

Trees.

A note on the distribution of the various species of trees and on that of some of the herbaceous plants forms a separate section of this report (Appendix I), while in Appendix III, Prof. Macoun gives a list of the plants collected.

Timber.

Remarks on the quantity and quality of timber along the various routes are given under the local headings. It may suffice here to state, in this connection, that the country is generally wooded,* and that in all portions of it, in valleys and on low lands, there is an abundance of white spruce, of fair to good quality, well suited for purposes of construction. The other species of trees present are of inferior economic importance.

---

* No areas of *tundra* or frozen morass, such as are stated to be characteristic of the country of the Lower Yukon, were found in the region here reported on.

Fauna.

The fauna of the region traversed by us, does not differ notably from that of other parts of the northern country which are already moderately well known. There are, no doubt, many interesting points yet to be determined in respect to distribution, but our opportunities for obtaining information of this kind were very limited. The smaller black-tailed deer (*Cariacus Columbianus*) occurs on the islands of the southern portion of Alaska and the adjacent mainland coast, but is nowhere found on the inland side of the Coast Ranges. The mountain goat is moderately abundant in the Coast Ranges, and is also found in the mountainous inland regions, probably throughout. The big-horn or mountain sheep occurs, together with the last-mentioned animal, on the mountains about the head of the Lewes and other parts of the inland spurs of the Coast Ranges, but does not inhabit the seaward portions of these ranges. It is also found generally in the mountains of the interior, including the Rocky Mountains. *[Larger animals noted.]*

The moose is more or less abundant throughout the entire inland region, and together with the caribou, which is similarly ubiquitous, constitutes a great part of the food of the Indians. We found the moose particularly plentiful along the Upper Liard River, and it is stated that the country drained by the White River is noted among the Indians as a moose and beaver region. The caribou is everywhere common, but is scarcely seen in the valleys or lower country during the summer. when it ranges over the high, alpine moors and open slopes of the mountains.

The black and grizzly bears roam over the entire region and are often seen along the banks of the rivers in the latter part of the summer when dead or dying salmon are to be obtained with ease. Wolves are not particularly abundant, but the cross-, black- and silver-fox are more than usually common.

The smaller fur-bearing animals, being similar to those found generally in the northern parts of the continent, do not require separate enumeration. The entire Upper Yukon basin, however, yields furs of exceptionally high grade. Some notes as to the quantity of furs annually obtained from the region will be found in a subsequent paragraph (p. 28 B). *[Smaller fur-bearing animals.]*

Among a few skins brought back by us, is that of a mouse which Dr. C. H. Merriam has found to be a new species, and has described under the name of *Evotomys Dawsoni*.*

The salmon ascend the Lewes River as far as the lower end of Lake Marsh, where they were seen in considerable numbers early in Sep- *[Salmon.]*

---

* American Naturalist, July, 1888.

tember. They also, according to the Indians, run almost to the head-waters of the streams tributary to the Lewes on the east side. Salmon also run up the Pelly for a considerable distance above the mouth of the Lewes, but their precise limit on this river was not ascertained. The lakes and rivers generally throughout the country are well supplied with fish, and a small party on any of the larger lakes would run little risk of starvation during th o winter, if provided with a couple of good gill-nets and able to devote themselves to laying in a stock of fish in the late autumn.

Other fishes.

As might be anticipated from the interlocking of streams tri-butary to the Mackenzie and Yukon in this region, the fishes in both drainage-areas appear to be identical, so far as I was able to observe, with the exception of the salmon, which is, of course, confined to the Yukon tributaries. The principal fishes noticed are white-fish (*Coregonus Nelsoni*), lake trout (*Salvelinus Namaycush*), grayling (*Thymallus signifer*), pike (*Esox lucius*), and sucker (*Catostomus catostomus*). The names above given are on the authority of Dr. T. H. Bean, of the U. S. Commission of Fish and Fisheries, who has very obligingly examined for me the photographs of fishes which were taken. No photograph, unfortunately, was obtained of the salmon seen on the Lewis, etc., but Dr. Bean informs me, from my description of its size, that he has little doubt it was the king salmon, *Oncorhynchus chuicha*.

Insects.

Appendix IV includes a list by Mr. James Fletcher, F.R.S.C., of the species of insects collected

Mining and Minerals.

Placer gold-mining.

Mining has so far been confined within the Cassiar district and in the Upper Yukon basin to the working of gold placers, and in the latter, almost entirely to river-bar mining, the inception of which indeed dates only from 1880. Particulars with reference to the rich creeks of Cassiar will be found on page 83 B, and facts relating to the rivers tributary to the Yukon on page 181 B. Almost all the large streams which have been prospected in the Yukon basin have been found to yield placer gold in greater or less quantity and the aggregate length of the rivers thus already proved to afford gold is very great, but little has been done toward the examination of their innumerable smaller feeders. Similar river-bar mining on the Stikine and Liard rivers proceeded the discovery of the smaller creeks in which the richer deposits of "heavy" gold were obtained, and a few miles in length each of Dease, Thibert and McDame creeks produced the greater portion of the $2,000,000 worth of gold credited to Cassiar in 1874 and 1875. Discoveries similar to these may be expected to occur at any time in the Yukon district, the generally auriferous area of which already proved is very much greater than that of Cassiar. Scarcely anything has been done as yet even in the Cassiar district toward the search for or proving of metalliferous veins, and practically nothing in the Yukon district, but there can be no reasonable doubt that such deposits exist.* The present activity in mining enterprise in the southern part of British Columbia will, before long, spread to this northern region also, and then, if not before, its valuable character as a portion of the metalliferous belt of the continent will be realized. *[Metalliferous veins.]*

The Yukon district with the northern part of British Columbia, measured from the vicinity of Dease Lake to the intersection of the Pelly (Yukon) with the 141st meridian comprises a length of over 500 miles of the Cordillera belt of the west, which, wherever it has been examined, has been found rich in minerals and particularly in the deposits of the precious metals. The width of this particular part of the Cordillera belt is also great, as it appears, so far as our explorations have gone, to extend from the coast to the eastern ranges of the Rocky Mountains in the vicinity of the Mackenzie River. This portion of the Cordillera region, together with that of the more southern part of British Columbia, gives an aggregate length of between 1200 and 1300 miles, almost exactly equal to the length of the same metalliferous belt contained by the United States, and in all probability susceptible of an eventual mining development equally great. *[Importance of Metalliferous belt.]*

In the northern districts here reported on, it is true that the winter climate is a severe one, rendering the working season for ordinary placer-mines short and likely also to present some special difficulties in the way of "quartz mining." There is, however, on the other hand an abundance of wood and water, matters of great importance in connection with mining, and means of communication once provided, mining operations should be carried on here at less cost than in dry and woodless regions such as are great portions of Arizona. *[Bearings of climate on mining.]*

Statistics of the former and present gold production of Cassiar are given in connection with that district, on page 82 B. It is difficult if not impossible to arrive at even an approximate statement of the total amount of gold which has been so far afforded by the Yukon district, but from such enquiry as I was able to make in 1887, I estimated the value of gold obtained in that year at a minimum of $60,000; the number of men engaged in mining at 250. *[Statistics of gold.]*

A specimen of asbestus (chrysotile) being part of a small vein of that material about half an inch in thickness, has been brought from *[Asbestus.]*

---

* A specimen of galena obtained from McDame Creek, Cassiar, was found to contain 75 ounces of silver to the ton (see p. 86 n) and of seven specimens of vein stuff collected by us on the Upper Pelly and Lewes, five proved to contain distinct traces of gold on assay.

the Stewart River, and the occurrence of serpentine in large mass else-where, tends to show that workable asbestus deposits may yet be found in the region.

Platinum.   Platinum is found in small quantities along all or nearly all the tributaries of the Yukon, in association with the gold. It has also been observed in the Cassiar district.

Fur Trade.

Exports of furs.   Gold and furs are at present the only articles of value derived from the great region here referred to as the Yukon district. It is impossible to secure accurate information as to the value of furs annually obtained, but sufficient is known to show that it must be very considerable. Petroff, in his report, states that the total annual value of the furs shipped by the Yukon probably does not exceed $75,000, * and it is known that a great, if not the greater, portion of this total is derived from the region lying east of the 141st meridian. Dall states, that at the date of his visit (1867), the value of furs annually obtained at Fort Yukon, then maintained by the Hudson Bay Company, was not less than $50,000. Captain Raymond notes that the total number of skins collected in 1869, at this place, was stated at 10,000, but adds that he believes this estimate to be excessive.† Practically the whole of these may be regarded as having been brought by Indians from the region east of the Alaskan line. An approximate estimate of the furs derived from Canadian territory and taken down the Yukon, obtained from Mr. François Mercier, who spent many years trading on the river, places the annual value at about $27,000. The annual catch is made up, according to the same authority, about as follows :—

Beaver	1200 to 1500	skins.
Cross fox	100	"
Black fox	100	"
Red fox	300	"
Bear	300	"
Marten	4000	"
Otter	200	"
Mink	2000	"
Lynx	600	"
Wolverine	150	"
Wolf	100	"
	9350	"

---

* Report on the Population Industries and Resources of Alaska, p. 5, U. S. 10th Census, vol. viii.

† *Op. cit.* p. 115.

In addition, however, to the furs taken from the Yukon district by Routes of export of furs. this route, the Hudson Bay Company obtains a large quantity of skins from their posts on the Porcupine, which reach the market by the Mackenzie River route. A certain number of skins derived from the country north of British Columbia is, further, annually traded at the little post at the mouth of Dease River, and taken out by the Stikine. A considerable quantity of furs also each year finds its way by the Chilkoot and Chilkat passes to the head of Lynn Canal, and some are brought down by the Taku River to the coast, though the greater part of these last is probably derived from the north-western corner of the province of British Columbia. Information obtained on the spot indicates that the value of the furs reaching Lynn Canal from the interior is from $12,000 to $15,000 annually.

Economic Importance of the Region.

Without including the northern part of British Columbia, respecting Value of the Yukon district. which more has already been made known, but restricting ourselves to the great area of 192,000 square miles situated to the north of the 60th parallel and west of the Rocky Mountains, which I have referred to as the Yukon district, it may be said that the information now obtained is sufficient to warrant a confident belief in its great value. Very much yet remains to be learned respecting it, but it is known to be rich in furs, well supplied with timber, and it is traversed by a great length of navigable rivers. It is already yielding a considerable yearly product in gold, and presents every indication of a country rich as well in other metals, and including deposits of coal. In its southern portion, situated between the 60th and 65th degrees of latitude, is comprised an area of probably not less than 30,000 square miles, suitable for eventual agricultural occupation, and presenting none of the characters of a sub-Arctic region, which have, in advance of its exploration, been attributed to it by some writers. In each of these particulars and in climate it is greatly superior to the corresponding inland portion of the territory of Alaska. It may, in fact, be affirmed with little room for doubt, that the region here spoken of as the Yukon district surpasses in material resources the whole remaining northern interior portion of the continent between the same parallels of latitude.

The winter climate of the whole of this great region is known to be Isothermal lines. a severe one, and its northern extremity lies within the Arctic circle, but it must be remembered that the climatic conditions on the western and eastern sides of the continent are by no means comparable, and that the isothermal lines, representing the mean annual temperature, trend not westward but north-westward from the Manitoba region. The lines, in particular, which would represent the mean summer temperature would assume, in the far north-west, a proximate parallelism with the Pacific coast, instead of tending to follow lines of latitude. It is needless here to recapitulate the well known causes which produce this remarkable difference in climate, but the lines as already approximately drawn upon the maps, represent in a generalized form the aggregate of influences which, working together, produce at the site of old Fort Selkirk on the 63rd parallel of latitude in the Upper Yukon basin, an attractive landscape, decked with well-grown forests and with intervening slopes of smiling meadow, while in the same latitude in Hudson Strait we find, even at midsummer, merely a barren waste of rocks and ice.

Comparison with province of Vologda. To instance a region which reproduces the general conditions of the Yukon district and adjacent northern portions of British Columbia, we must turn to the inland provinces of Russia, to which allusion has already been made in connection with climatic features. (p. 23 b.) The province of Vologda, in European Russia, appears to offer the nearest parallel. It is circumstanced relatively to the western shores of Europe, as is this district to the western shores of the North American continent. Its area is 155,498 square miles, situated between the 58th and 65th degrees of latitude. The climate in both cases is a continental one, in which severe winters alternate with warm summers, and the actual degrees of cold and heat, so far as our information goes, are not dissimilar. There is no very heavy rainfall in either region, such as we find near the western coasts bordering on the Atlantic and on the Pacific respectively. The agricultural products from the province of Vologda are oats, rye, barley, hemp, flax and pulse. The mineral products comprise salt, copper, iron and marble, but the precious metals do not appear to be important, as in the Yukon district. Horses and cattle are reared, and the skins of various wild animals, as well as pitch and turpentine, are among the exports. The population of the province is stated at 1,161,000.

Ultimate development assured. While the Yukon district and the northern portion of British Columbia are at present far beyond the limits of ordinary settlement, we may be prepared at any time to hear of the discovery of important mineral deposits, which will afford the necessary impetus, and may result, in the course of a few years, in the introduction of a considerable population into even its most distant fastnesses. To-day it may well be characterized by the term which has been employed in connection with the Mackenzie basin, a portion of "Canada's Great Reserve." It appears meanwhile eminently desirable that we should encourage and facilitate, in so far as may be possible, the efforts of the miners

and others who constitute our true pioneers in the region, and to
whom, in conjunction with the fur companies and traders, the peaceful
conquest of the whole of our Great West has been due. In the future,
there is every reason to look forward to the time when this country
will support a large and hardy population, attached to the soil and
making the utmost of its resources.

General Geology.

In a reconnaissance carried out along a single line, in which
the greater part of one's time is necessarily occupied in overcoming
the difficulties of the route and in securing the necessary geographical data, it is difficult to obtain any very complete knowledge of a
region geologically complicated. In the present case this difficulty is
increased by the circumstance that the geology of the corresponding
portion of the Cordillera belt in the southern part of British Columbia,
is as yet very imperfectly understood, though considerable attention
has been devoted to it; while with respect to the older rocks of the
analogous region in the western part of the United States very little
published information of a systematic kind is available.

Speaking broadly, however, and with reference to the general features of the region, the rock-series represented are evidently similar to
those found in the southern portion of British Columbia between the
Rocky Mountains and the coast, and an important general result of
the work here reported on, is the further demonstration of the great
constancy in lithological characters of the several formations, when
followed in the direction of the main north-west and south-east axes
of uplift—a constancy which contrasts markedly with the diversity
found when comparisons are made as between localities situated at
right angles to this direction.

The Coast Ranges, where traversed by the valley of the Stikine, and
again where crossed still further north by the Chilkoot Pass, are found
to consist, for the most part, of granite and granitoid rocks, almost
invariably of gray colour and frequently rich in hornblende. With
these are occasionally included stratified or stratiform masses of mica-
and hornblende-schists, and both these and the granites are frequently
traversed by pegmatite veins, diabase dykes and intrusive masses of
coarse diorite. The schistose portions of these ranges may possibly
represent the still recognisable remnants of rocks of Archæan age, or
may be merely portions of much newer series which have suffered
extreme alteration.

No demonstration of the date of the origin of the granitic rocks of
the Coast Ranges was obtained in this region, but there is every reason

to believe that it is comparatively recent, and due to a time lying between the Triassic and the Cretaceous, as has been found to be the case with their continuation to the south, near the northern part of Vancouver Island. *

Rocks of the coast archipelogo.   The argillites of Wrangell, together with those met with near Juneau, and at Sitka, on the Alaskan coast, and also in various places along the east side of Lynn Canal, together with the altered volcanic rocks found in association with these on Lynn Canal and elsewhere (examined by me particularly in the vicinity of Seduction Point), closely resemble rocks of the same class composing the Vancouver group of the Queen Charlotte and Vancouver Islands. Though no fossils were obtained at these northern localities, the rocks may, like those just referred to, be provisionally classed as Triassic, with the reservation, (as made in the case of the similar series of the Queen Charlotte and Vancouver Islands), that Palæozoic strata may also be represented.

General features of coast belt.   The width of the belt of granitoid rocks composing the Coast Ranges is, on the Stikine, about sixty-five miles, measured from their sea-border inland at right angles to the main direction of the mountains. It is somewhat less in the latitude of the Chilkoot Pass, but may be assumed to occupy a border of the mainland about fifty miles in width along the whole of this part of the coast. Broadly viewed, however, the coast archipelago in reality represents a partly submerged margin of the Coast Ranges, and granitic rocks are largely represented in it also. The examination of these two northern cross-sections of the Coast Ranges, serves, with observations previously made, to demonstrate the practical identity in geological character of this great orographic axis, from the vicinity of the Fraser River to the 60th parallel of north latitude—a length, in all, of about 900 miles.

Formations of the interior region.   East and north-east of the Coast Ranges, the interior region traversed is, for the most part, floored by Palæozoic rocks of very varied appearance, and probably referable to several of the main sub-divisions of the geological scale. In so far as the information obtained in the region here in question enables conclusions on the subject to be formed, the lowest part of the rocks, (1) consists of greenish and grey schists, generally felspathic or hornblendic, but often quartzose and including distinctly micaceous and talcose schists, with some bands of limestone; the lithological character of this sub-division being exceedingly varied. Apparently overlying these are, (2) grey and blackish, often lustrous and sometimes more or less micaceous calc-schists and quartzites, including beds of limestone of moderate thickness, which are often more or less dolomitic. These are associated with, or pass up into, (3) black

---

* See Annual Report Geol. Surv. Can., 1886.

argillites or argillite-schists, also containing thin beds of limestone, which, at one locality on the Dease, have afforded a small number of graptolites of Cambro-Silurian age (see p. 99 B). Next above these is a series (4) consisting chiefly of massive limestones, generally of grey or blue-grey colour where unaltered, but often locally changed into white or variegated crystalline marbles. These are closely associated with quartzites which usually show the peculiar fine grained cherty character of those of the typical Cache Creek series on the Fraser and Thompson rivers. The thickness of this sub-division cannot (any more than that of those previously mentioned) be stated with precision, but that of the limestones alone must be several thousand feet in some places. On the Dease, on the Frances, and again on Tagish Lake fossils of Carboniferous age, including more particularly a species of *Fusulina*, have been detected in some beds of this limestone series, probably belonging to its upper portion. Forms of the genus *Fusulina* are characteristic in certain zones of the Carboniferous limestone in California. They have been found by the writer in a number of places in British Columbia, which, with the discoveries here reported on, occur at intervals along a belt of country to the north-east of the Coast Ranges for a distance of over 800 miles. The limestone last-mentioned appears to be conformably followed or even in part interbedded with (5) a great mass of more or less evidently stratified rocks of volcanic origin, comprising amygdaloids, agglomerates, and other more massive materials which apparently represent old lava-flows. All these are highly altered, so much so that in some cases their original physical character is scarcely demonstrable, while they have suffered changes also in constitution, having been converted for the most part into diabases.

Analogy with the southern portions of British Columbia which I have examined, leads me to believe that the greater part of these volcanic materials are also to be classed as of Carboniferous age, but it is quite probable that here, as to the south, they comprise as well rocks of similar appearance which are of Triassic age, but which we are at present unable to separate from them. This is further rendered probable by the occurrence in certain black argillites at Glenora, on the Stikine, of Triassic fossils (p. 56 B) and by the discovery by Mr. McConnell of fossils of this age on the Lower Liard River, some distance to the east of the region covered by this report.[*]

No unconformity has been proved to occur throughout the whole of the above Palæozoic series, but the examinations made were scarcely of a sufficiently detailed nature for the detection of any stratigraphical break unless of a very obvious character. Respecting the first-mentioned of the above sub-divisions, I feel some doubt as to whether

---

[*] See Summary Report of the Operations of the Geological Survey for 1887, p. 11.

it really constitutes a lower member of the series or whether it may represent some of the other members—particularly the rocks of volcanic origin—in a highly altered state, as seems, from late observations, to be the case with rocks of similar appearance in southern British Columbia. The proximity of the rocks classed under the first sub-division to certain granitic axes is equally explicable on either hypothesis. It must also be added that there appears to be a recurrence of rock materials originally volcanic in greater or less force in several parts of the series, and that important beds of serpentine occur at one or more horizons.

Geological notes on map. For the purpose of assisting future more complete enquiry, and in view of the tentative character of the classification here offered, the more important details observed are noted on the face of the map accompanying this report, for which it would be premature to attempt a geological colouring.

Interior granitic axes. The preponderantly Palæozoic floor of the region east of the granites of the Coast Ranges, is broken through on two main lines by granitic axes. The first of these is cut across by the Dease River, a short distance below Dease Lake, and was again met with—over 300 miles north-westward—on the Pelly near the mouth of the Macmillan. Though referred to as a single granitic axis, this uplift probably consists rather of a series of alternating and more or less irregularly shaped granitic masses, which, however, preserve a general alignment. There are on the Upper Pelly in fact three separate granitic ridges in place of the single one met with on the Dease. In close association with these granites are some gneissic rocks and holocrystalline mica- and hornblende-schists, which have not been referred to in previous paragraphs as they are regarded as probably Archæan, rather than as representing highly altered Palæozoic rocks. A small tongue of granite occurs on the Lewes a few miles above the mouth of the Little Salmon, which may be con_nected with the south-western side of this granitic axis, but with this ex.ception its continuity between the Dease and Pelly is indicated merely by the statement of Mr. J. McCormick that granites and mica-schists occur on the south-west side of Quiet Lake and near the Big Salmon River, below that lake. Its further extension in a north-westerly bearing is, however, proved by the occurrence of a great preponderance of rocks of the same character in the collection made by Mr. Ogilvie* on the lower Pelly or Yukon, between the mouth of the Lewes and Forty-mile Creek.

Connexion of gold with the rock series. On comparing the position of this irregular granitic axis and its surrounding altered rocks (in part referable to several of the Palæozoic sub-divisions previously described) with that of the richer deposits of

---

* Sent out by him in charge of the latest party of miners in the autumn of 1887.

placer gold so far discovered and worked, it will be found that they
are closely associated. The chief placers and river-bars are, in fact,
scattered along this line or belt, and extend, like it, all the way from
Dease Lake and McDame Creek to Forty-mile Creek. Evidence was
moreover found on the Pelly, to show that the development of quartz
veins in the Palæozoic rocks had occurred contemporaneously with the
upheaval of the granites, and probably by some action superinduced
by the granite masses themselves while still in a formative condition.
While cutting the stratified rocks, the quartz-veins seldom or never cut
the granite masses in this district. These observations should afford
an important clue to the further search for auriferous ground, as well
as for the lodes from which the placer gold has itself been derived.

Of the second granitic axis of the interior region very little is yet Granites of
known, but it is probable that it is still less regular in character than Range.
the last. It occurs in the mountainous region to the east of Frances
Lake and River, and probably also in the vicinity of the Pelly Lakes
(see p. 121 B). Its lithological characters and those of the rocks in its
neighborhood are similar to those of the last described, and here again
in its vicinity, on Frances Lake and on the Liard (pp. 105 B, 113 B)
paying gold placers have been found. The district is, however, so
difficult of access that it can scarcely as yet be said to have been at all
prospected.

I am inclined to believe that the two granitic axes of the interior Age of granites.
region above described are of much greater age than that of the Coast
Ranges. The reasons for assigning a comparatively late date to the
latter have already been alluded to. It is found, too, that while the
stratified rocks usually conform to an ascending order in receding from
these granitic axes, there is evidence along the north-eastern flanks
of the Coast Ranges of an irregular line of junction, and though on the
Stikine the Palæozoic rocks appear to rest upon the granites of the
Coast Ranges, the supposed lower members of the series are not seen,
while on the lakes near the head of the Lewes some of the upper portions of the Palæozoic are directly in contact with and have apparently
been broken through by the granites. The granitoid rocks of the
interior region are, moreover, different in general appearance from
those of the Coast Ranges, and resemble more closely the probably
Archæan granites of the Gold Ranges in southern British Columbia.

Lithologically the granites and granitoid rocks of the Coast Ranges Lithological
are generally fresh and unaltered in appearance, grey in colour and character.
not often distinctly foliated, while those of the ranges of the interior
show evidence of considerable alteration subsequent to their formation,
are more highly quartzose and often reddish in tint. Some particulars
respecting a few of the granites of the region which has been microscopically examined by Mr. F. D. Adams will be found in Appendix V,

Cretaceous and Laramie rocks. Besides the Triassic rocks previously referred to, the Mesozoic period is represented also by strata of Cretaceous and Laramie age. These rocks are distinctively more recent in appearance than, and rest quite unconformably on all the older formations, though they have since been to some extent involved in their flexures. On the lower part of the Lewes, below the mouth of the Little Salmon, these rocks are cut across by the river for a distance of at least thirty-five miles. Some fossil molluscs and plants have been obtained from this area, from which it would appear to include beds referable to the Middle or Lower Cretaceous and to the Laramie period (p. 146 B), and it is not improbable that the series is a consecutive one between these limits, as the total thickness represented must be very great. The strike of these beds varies much in direction, and the angles of dip are so irregular that no even proximate estimate of thickness could be formed, and it is impossible to arrive at any definite conclusion with respect to the trend of the basin in which they lie. The rocks comprise, in their lower portion, coarse conglomerates, grauwacke-sandstones, yellowish and grey quartzose sandstones and dark calcareous slates. The upper portion, in which Laramie plants are found, consists chiefly of rather soft sandstones, shales and clays, generally of pale colours. Evidence of contemporaneous volcanic action is observable in both parts of the series, and the higher beds include lignite-coal of good quality (p. 148 B).

Some miles further up the Lewes, midway between the Little and Big Salmon rivers, peculiar green, grauwacke-sandstones and green, highly calcareous conglomerates occur, which are also provisionally referred, though with some doubt, to the Cretaceous. They are at least newer than the Palæozoic rocks, being composed of fragments of these and of the granites.

Cretaceous of Lake Labarge. Conglomerates and sandstones similar to the last are again found near the lower end of Lake Labarge, on the east side, and are associated with black calcareous slates, which recur in several places along the same side of the lake, further up, and from which a few fossils have been obtained. These seem to show that the beds are on or near the horizon of Series C. of the Queen Charlotte Islands, which is of Middle Cretaceous age, approximately equivalent to the Gault (p. 158 B).

Cretaceous of Upper Pelly. On the Upper Pelly River, forty-three miles below Hoole Cañon, a single low outcrop of hard, dark shales, containing fossil plants of Cretaceous or Laramie, age was found, but in the absence of further exposures along the river in that vicinity, nothing can be said of the extent of this area, except that it must be quite limited in width. Again, on the Stikine River, between Glenora and Telegraph Creek, there are local occurrences of conglomerates and soft sandstones which may be regarded as probably Cretaceous, though no palæontological evidence is forthcoming.

The position of these last-noted areas, as well as that of those along the Lewes River, occurring as they do in a zone of country immediately within the line of the Coast Ranges, is analogous to that held by Cretaceous rocks on the Skeena and in other localities still further southward in British Columbia. Further investigation will probably show that rocks of this age occur in many additional places, and occupy somewhat extersive areas in this belt of country. In the vicinity of the Lewes, particularly, it is noted that the plane of the original base of the Cretaceous, now thrown into a number of folds, is about that of the present surface of the country, and these rocks may therefore be expected to recur frequently in the form of troughs or basins, more or less strictly limited and only to be discovered in detail by thorough examination. The loose material brought down by the Big Salmon River, appears to indicate the existence of a considerable development of these rocks not far up the valley of that stream.

Relations of the Cretaceous.

No wide-spread Tertiary areas like those of the southern interior portion of British Columbia appear to occur in the region here described. The most important occurrence of beds of this age met with, is that which occupies the wide valley of the Upper Liard, but its extent to the north-west and south-east was not ascertained. The rocks are soft shales, sandstones and clays, generally of pale color, and holding beds of lignite in some places. Flows of basalt either cap these rocks or are included in their upper portion, and from the considerable angles of dip observed, the formation would appear to have suffered some flexure subsequent to its deposition (p. 101 B).

Tertiary rocks.

In the Stikine valley, east of the Coast Ranges, important local basalt-flows are met with, overlying old river- and valley-gravels (p. 57 B), and the lignite reported to exist some miles up the Tahl-tan is, doubtless, also of Tertiary age and inferior in position to the basalts. Basalt effusions of a sporadic character may be frequent in other places in the region, as such were actually noted in three other widely separated localities, viz., above Hoole Cañon on the Pelly, at Miles Cañon on the Lewes, and again at the confluence of this river with the Pelly.

Basalts.

The basalts are at least pre-glacial in age, and though no characteristic fossils were observed in the associated bedded deposits, both may be provisionally classed from their analogy with similar deposits in the more southern portion of British Columbia, as Miocene.

Age of basalts.

Occurrence of Jade on the Lewes.

Occurrence of jade pebbles.

Having become interested in the question of the origin of nephrite or jade, on account of its former extensive employment by the natives of the west coast for the manufacture of implements, * I kept a close watch for this mineral along our route, and ultimately succeeded in finding several rolled pieces of it in gravel-bars along the Lewes (p. 147 D). Of the pebbles collected by us, at least five have the specific gravity and other physical characters of jade, though they have not yet been subjected to chemical or microscopical analysis. Several of these are evidently, however, pure and typical jade, of which the finest and most characteristic was found by Mr. W. Ogilvie, near Miles Cañon. This specimen is a pale-green translucent to sub-transparent variety weighing a pound and three-quarters, after a piece, probably equal to about one-fourth of the original mass, had been broken off and unfortunately lost. Some of the specimens collected, but not referred to in the above remarks, appear to show the passage, by admixture of other materials, of the pure jades into various altered rocks of volcanic origin, as described in the publication above referred to. So far as I have been able to ascertain, the discovery of jade here noted is, with one exception, the first actually direct one made in the region of the Pacific slope. The exception above alluded to is that of jade found at the Kwichpak mouth of the Yukon during Captain Jacobson's stay in that vicinity and which was obtained by him and taken to Berlin.†

Glaciation and Surface Deposits.

Such details as appear to be of interest respecting glaciation, and the superficial deposits, are given in the subsequent descriptive portion of this report. The general bearings of these are here merely summarized in the briefest possible manner.‡

Previous observations in British Columbia

Previous observations in British Columbia§ have shown that at one stage in the Glacial period—that of the maximum glaciation—a great confluent ice-mass has occupied the region which may be named the Interior Plateau, between the Coast Ranges and the Gold and Rocky Mountain ranges. From the 55th to the 49th parallel this great glacier has left traces of its general southward or south-eastward movement, which are distinct from those of subsequent local glaciers. The southern extensions or terminations of this confluent glacier, in

---

* See Canadian Record of Science, vol. ii. No. 6, April, 1887.

† See paper by Prof. A. B. Meyer, Jahresbericht des Vereins für Erdkunde zu Dresden, 1884.

‡ The substance of this summary has been published in advance in the Geological Magazine. Decade III, vol. v. p. 347 (Aug. 1888).

§ Quart. Journ. Geol. Soc. vol. xxxi. p. 80. *Ibid.* vol. xxxiv. p. 272. Canadian Naturalist, vol. viii.

Washington and Idaho Territories, have quite recently been examined
by Mr. Bailley Willis and Prof. T. C. Chamberlin of the U. S. Geological Survey,[*] and their observations tend to confirm the views above
outlined, which had previously been stated by the writer. There is,
further, evidence to show that this inland-ice flowed also, by tranverse
valleys and gaps, across the Coast Ranges, and that the fiords of the
coast were thus deeply filled with glacier-ice, which, supplemented by
that originating on the Coast Ranges themselves, buried the entire
great valley which separates Vancouver Island from the mainland, and
discharged seaward round both ends of the island. Further north, the
glacier extending from the mainland coast touched the northern shores
of the Queen Charlotte Islands. The observed facts on which these
general statements are based have been fully detailed in the publica-
tions already referred to, and it is not here necessary to review former
work in the region, further than to enumurate the main features
developed by it, and to connect these with the observations made during the summer of 1887, in the more northern region described in the
present report.

The littoral of the south-eastern part or "coast strip" of Alaska, pre- Glaciation of the coast.
sents features identical with those of the previously examined coast of
British Columbia, at least as far north as lat. 59°, beyond which I have
not seen it. The coast archipelago has evidently been involved in the
border of a confluent glacier which spread from the mainland and was
subject to minor variations in direction of flow dependent on surface
irregularities, in the manner described in my report on the northern
part of Vancouver Island. † No conclusive evidence was here found,
however, in the valley of the Stikine River or in the pass leading inland from the head of Lynn Canal, to show that the inland-ice moved
seaward across the Coast Ranges, though analogy with the coast to the
south favours the belief that it may have done so. The front of the
glacier must have passed the outer border of the archipelago, as at Stika,
well-marked glaciation is found pointing toward the open Pacific ‡
(average direction about S. 81° W. astr.).

It is, however, in the interior region, explored and examined by Glaciation of the interior region.
us in 1887, between the Coast Ranges and the Rocky Mountains
proper, and extending northward to lat. 63°, that the most interesting facts have come to light respecting the direction of movement of the Cordilleran glacier. Here, in the valleys of the Upper
Pelly and Lewes, traces were found of the movement of heavy

---

glacier-ice in a northerly direction.   Rock-surfaces thus glaciated
were observed down the Pelly to the point at which it crosses the
136th meridian and on the Lewes as far north as lat. 61° 40', the
main direction in the first-named valley being north-west, in the second
north-north-west.   The points referred to are not, however, spoken of
as limiting ones, for rock exposures suitable for the preservation of
glaciation are rather infrequent on the lower portions of both rivers,
and more extended examination may result in carrying evidence of the
same kind further toward the less elevated plains of the Lower Yukon,
as elsewhere detailed.   Neither the Pelly valley nor that of the Lewes
is hemmed in by high mountainous country except toward the sources,
and while local variations in direction are met with, the glaciation is
not susceptible of explanation by merely local agents, but implies
the passage of a confluent or more or less connected glacier over the
region.

On Lake Labarge, in the Lewes valley, both the sides and summits
of rocky hills 300 feet above the water were found to be heavily
glaciated, the direction on the summit being that of the main (north-
north-west) orographic valleys, while that at lower levels in the same
vicinity followed more nearly the immediate valley of the river, which
here turns locally to the east of north.

Glaciation was also noted in several places in the more mountainous
country to the south of the Yukon basin, in the Dease and Liard valleys,
but the direction of movement of the ice could not be determined satisfactorily, and the influence of local action is there less certainly elim-
inated.

Deposits of the
glacial period. While the greater part of the area traversed is more or less completely mantled with glacial deposits, it will be observed, in referring
to subsequent pages, that true boulder-clay was found in certain parts
only of the southern and more mountainous portion of the region,
while it spreads over almost the entire length of the Upper Pelly
and Lewes valleys, though not found exposed quite to their confluence.   The boulder-clay generally passes upward into, and is
covered by, important silty beds, analogous to the silts of the Nechacco
basin, further south in British Columbia, and to those of the Peace
River country to the east of the Rocky Mountains.   It may be stated
also that the country is generally terraced to a height of 4000 feet or
more, while on an isolated mountain-top near the height of land between the Liard and the Pelly rivers (Pacific-Arctic watershed) rolled
gravel of varied origin was found at a height of 4300 feet, a height exceeding that of the actual watershed by over 1000 feet.

Mastodon
remains. No remains of mastodon or mammoth were observed in the country
traversed by us, but according to Campbell such remains occur not far

from the site of Fort Selkirk, and they are known to be moderately abundant at points further down the river. Sir J. Richardson speaks of a tibia of *Elephas primigenius* sent to England by Roderic (Robert) Campbell from this region.*

Reverting to the statements made as to the direction of the general glaciation, the examination of this northern region may now be considered to have established that the main gathering-ground or *névé* of what I have called the great Cordilleran glacier or confluent glacier mass of the west coast, was included between the 55th and 59th parallels of latitude, a region which, so far as explored, has proved to be of an exceptionally mountainous character. It would further appear that this great glacier extended, between the Coast Ranges and the Rocky Mountains, south-eastward nearly to lat. 48°, and north-westward to lat. 63°, or beyond, while sending also smaller streams to the Pacific Coast. General facts
established.

In connection with the northerly direction of ice-flow here ascertained, it is interesting to recall the observations which I have collected in a recently published report of the Geological Survey, relating to the northern portion of the continent east of the Mackenzie River.† It is there stated that for the Arctic coast of the Continent, and the Islands of the Archipelago off it, there is a considerable volume of evidence to show that the main direction of movement of erratics was *northward.* The most striking facts are those derived from Prof. S. Haughton's Appendix to M'Clintock's Voyage, where the occurrence is described of boulders and pebbles from North Somerset, at localities 100 and 135 miles north-eastward and north-westward from their supposed points of origin. Prof. Haughton also states that the east side of King-William's Land is strewn with boulders of gneiss like that of Montreal Island, to the southward, and points out the general northward ice-movement thus indicated, referring the carriage of the boulders to floating-ice of the glacial period. Other instances
of northward
glaciation.

The copper said to be picked up in large masses by the Eskimo, near Princess-Royal Island, in Prince-of-Wales Strait, as well as on Prince-of-Wales Island,‡ has likewise, in all probability been derived from the copper-bearing rocks of the Coppermine River region to the south, as this metal can scarcely be supposed to occur in place in the region of horizontal limestone where it is found.

Dr. A. Armstrong, Surgeon and Naturalist to the *Investigator*, notes the occurrence of granite and other crystalline rocks not only on the south shore of Baring Land, but also on the hills at some distance

---

* Am. Journ. Sci. and Arts, vol. xix., 1855, p. 132.

† Notes to accompany a Geological Map of the Northern Portion of the Dominion of Canada East of the Rocky Mountains, p. 57 R., Annual Report Geol. Surv. Can., 1886.

‡ De Rance, in Nature, vol. xi. p. 492.

from the shore. These, from what is known of the region, must be supposed to have come from the continental land to the southward.

Dr. Bessels, again, remarks on the abundance of boulders on the shore of Smith's Sound in lat. 81° 30', which are manifestly derived from known localities on the Greenland coast much further southward, and adds : " Drawing a conclusion from such observations, it becomes evident that the main line of the drift, indicating the direction of its motion, runs from south to north."*

It may further be mentioned that Dr. R. Bell, has found evidence of a northward or north-eastward movement of glacier ice in the northern part of Hudson Bay, with distinct indications of eastward glaciation in Hudson Strait. † For the northern part of the great Mackenzie valley we are as yet without any definite published information, but Sir J. Richardson notes that Laurentian boulders are scattered westward over the nearly horizontal limestones of the district.

Two great glacier-masses. Taken in conjunction with the facts for the more northern portion of the continent, already pretty well known, the observations here outlined would appear to indicate a general movement of ice outward, in all directions, from the great Laurentian axis or plateau which extends from Labrador round the southern extremity of Hudson Bay to the Arctic Sea; while a second, smaller, though still very important region of dispersion—the Cordilleran glacier-mass—occupied the Rocky Mountain region on the west, with the northern and southern limits above approximately given, and a length, in a north-west and south-east direction, of at least 1200 miles.

It is inexpedient at the present moment to enter into any detailed discussion of the glaciation of the extreme north-west, as Mr. McConnell's observations, made in the prosecution of his portion of the work of the expedition, are likely to add much to our store of facts bearing on the subject.

Economic importance of facts elicited It may be added, that while the study of the phenomena of the glacial period is one not without its bearings on economic problems even in the eastern part of the continent, it has, in British Columbia and the Yukon district, a direct value in its connection with the distribution of the placer gold deposits and on the existence and position of the buried channels of rivers and streams, in which some of the richest of those deposits are often found to occur. Thus the greater part of the " fine " gold found along the river-bars and banks of the larger streams in the Yukon district is doubtless proximately derived from the gravels

---

* Nature, vol. ix.

† Annual Report Geol. Surv. Canada, 1885, p. 14 D.D. and Report of Progress, 1882-84, p. 30 D.D.

and other superficial deposits in which those streams have re-excavated
their beds since the period of glaciation. By the general dispersion
and intermixture of these materials, composed of the *débris* of the older
rock formations, it is even possible that the existence of a few comparatively limited areas of great richness might account for the wide-
spread auriferous character of the alluviums of the Upper Yukon basin.
In the former direction of ice-movement, and consequently that of its
transport of material, we obtain an important clue as to the source of
the finer gold which may now be found in any particular area. This
subject is too wide in its ramifications to be followed out here, but it is
one to which considerable attention has been devoted, and to which I
hope to return at an early date in greater detail.

Volcanic Ash Deposit.

A circumstance of some interest in connection with the later superficial deposits of that part of the Upper Yukon basin drained by the
Lewes and Pelly rivers, is the occurrence of a wide-spread layer of
volcanic ash or pumiceous sand. The existence of a peculiar white
line or band in the upper parts of scarped banks along the river, was
first remarked not many miles below the point at which we reached
and embarked on the Pelly. As its character was not at first understood, I omitted to note the precise point at which it was first
seen but am of opinion that it probably extends to the east of the place
where we reached the river. After recognizing its character and importance, however, it was looked for and noticed almost continuously
along the whole course of the Pelly, as far down as the mouth of the
Macmillan, beyond which, to the site of Fort Selkirk at the mouth of
the Lewes, it was not distinctly recognized, but according to Mr. Mc-
Connell (1888) it extends down the river for about ten miles below
Fort Selkirk. It is likewise seen along nearly the whole course of the
Lewes, being last noted at the narrows between Lake Nares and
Bennett Lake, known as Caribou Crossing. *

This ash deposit appears to be entirely due to a single period of
eruption. It is homogeneous in character wherever seen, forming a
single layer not divided by intercalations of other material, and has
been spread everywhere over the entire area characterized by it. It is
much more recent in date than the white silt deposits, which are the
last of those properly referable to the glacial series, having been deposited after the river-valleys were excavated in the glacial materials,
and at a time when the rivers had cut down nearly or quite to their

Extent of the deposit.

Origin of the deposit.

---

* I found subsequently that Schwatka had observed this peculiar layer along the Lewes and
correctly characterized it as a volcanic ash.   Along Alaska's Great River, p. 106.

present levels, a fact rendered evident by the circumstance that it overlies the deposits of river- and valley-gravels and sands in all cases, except in those of some low river-flats, where these deposits sometimes
cover it to a depth of several feet. In most places it is overlain merely
by the surface soil with a depth of six inches to two feet, and in a few
instances it was noted as constituting the actual surface of terraces of
moderate height, the present forest being rooted in it.

Mode of deposition and thickness. The ash appears to have fallen tranquilly, much in the manner of
snow deposited from a calm atmosphere. The examination of scarped
banks along the two rivers showed it to occur near the surface of
terraces about 200 feet in height, as well as on lower terraces and river-
flats down to within about ten feet of the actual river-level in August
and September. It was also detected in some places on the sloping fronts
of terraces. The thickness of the layer was no doubt originally pretty
uniform, and it still retains this uniformity where it rests upon wide
flat terraces. Its average normal thickness for the Pelly, as a whole,
was estimated at about five inches, but this is somewhat exceeded
along the part of the river immediately above the Macmillan. On the
Lewes, below Rink Rapid, its normal thickness is about a foot, but
above this point it becomes much less and where last seen, at Caribou
Crossing, is not over half an inch thick, and only to be recognized when
carefully looked for.

Local accumu-
lation. In addition to these differences in normal thickness, however, and
much more striking than them, is an irregularity due to local circumstances. Thus in hollows, and particularly when these occur at the
foot of steep slopes, the material has evidently been washed together
by rains occurring shortly after its deposit, and sometimes attains a
thickness of as much as three feet. In correspondence with this it has
been completely removed from some sloping or exposed surfaces. The
same local circumstances explain the varying depth in different localities of the soil or ordinary sand which overlies the ash deposit.

Where the ash deposit rests undisturbed upon the original surface,
this appears very generally to be a yellowish or reddish quartzose
sand. There are, in some cases, remains of burnt trees at the base of
the layer, and traces of similar forest fires are found as well in the sand
or soil overlying it.

Source of the
ash deposit. So far as the observations I was able to make go, the volcanic ash is
thicker on the lower part of the Lewes than elsewhere, and the thickest
part of the deposit on the Pelly lies nearly due east of the portion of
the Lewes just referred to. The greater mass of the deposit in that
direction, seems to show that it was derived from the westward, and a
line drawn across the portions of the Pelly and Lewes above defined, lies
between the 62nd and 63rd parallels of latitude, with a nearly east-and-

west bearing, so that if produced to the westward it would pass, at a distance of about 200 miles, through the mountain region near the Copper River, of Alaska, which includes Mount Wrangell. Mount Wrangell is the nearest known volcano,* and this or one of the

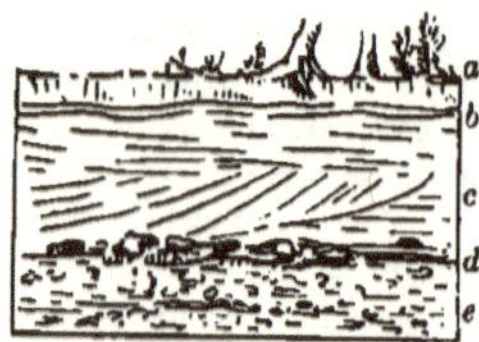

Fig. 1.　RELATIONS OF ASH-BED ON THE LEWES RIVER.

a. Soil.　*b.* Ash-bed.　*c.* Stratified sands and gravels.　*d.* Buried drift-wood.
e. Stratified gravels.

neighbouring mountains in the same group, may not improbably have been the source of the material which has been so widely spread over the Upper Yukon basin. It should be stated, however, that the Indians report the existence of a burning mountain near the head-waters of the White River, and that it is uncertain whether this report refers to Mount Wrangell or to some still unknown mountain which may be even nearer to the district here described.

Respecting the date of the eruption to which the ash-bed is due, very little can be said with certainty. As already noted, the rivers have not certainly cut their beds perceptibly deeper since the deposit occurred on their flood-flats, so that the period to which it belongs cannot be an exceedingly remote one. It was further observed in one place, on the Lewes, to rest upon stratified sands a few feet thick, which in turn overlie a mass of drift logs still quite sound and undecayed. This fact, with the general appearance and mode of occurrence of the deposit, leads me to believe, that while the eruption must have happened at least several hundreds of years ago, it can scarcely be supposed to have taken place more than a thousand years before the present time. Dall, in his work on Alaska, gives a list of volcanic eruptions (derived from Grenwingk) which have occurred in the Aleutian Islands and along the western part of the Alaskan Coast from the year 1690. † While it is quite improbable that any of these was connected with the formation here described, it is interesting to note that great quantities

Date of the eruption.

----

* See Lieut. H. T. Allen's Reconnaissance in Alaska, Washington, Government, 1887.
† Alaska and its Resources, 1870, p. 466.

of ash were observed to fall on several occasions, notably in 1825, when the whole peninsula of Alaska was covered with black ashes.

Volume of ash ejected. That the eruption of which the occurrence is marked by the ash-bed of the Lewes and Pelly, was on a great scale, is sufficiently evident from the extent of the deposit; which must necessarily be very much greater than the area to which the present observations refer. By drawing a line such as to include the outer limits of the observed extent of the ash, a roughly triangular area of about 25,000 square miles is outlined, and if we assume the average depth of the layer over this area alone to be three inches, the mass represented would be equivalent to a prism one mile square, with a height of 6240 feet or (making allowance for interspaces in the comminuted material) equal to nearly a cubic mile of rock.

Lithological character. It has not been considered necessary to make a complete examination of the character of this ash. In appearance it is a fine, white, sandy material, with a harsh feeling when rubbed between the fingers. Microscopically it is found to consist chiefly of volcanic glass, part being merely frothy and pumiceous, but of which the greater portion has been drawn out into elongated shreds, frequently resembling the substance known as "Pele's hair," in which the enclosed vesicles become more or less completely tubular. In addition to this glass, fragments and small perfect examples of sanadine felspar crystals occur together with portions of minute crystals of hornblende and probably of other minerals.

THE STIKINE RIVER.

General Features.

River cuts across the Coast Ranges. Since the year 1873, when the placer gold mines of Cassiar were first developed, the Stikine River has become a somewhat important avenue of communication from the coast to the interior of the northern part of British Columbia. Like the Fraser, the Skeena, the Nass and several other smaller streams, it rises to the east of the broad belt of mountains which constitutes the Coast Ranges, and cuts completely through this belt with a nearly uniform gradient. In size and general character the Stikine closely resembles the Skeena, which reaches the coast 200 miles further south. It is navigable for stern-wheel steamers **Route to the interior.** of light draft and good power, to Glenora, 126 miles from Rothsay Point, at its mouth, and under favourable circumstances to Telegraph Creek, twelve miles farther. Above Telegraph Creek is the "Great Cañon" which extend for many miles and is quite impassable either for steamers or boats, though traversed by miners in winter on the ice. The head-waters of the Stikine are unknown, but lie for the most part to the south of the 58th parallel of north latitude, in a country said to be very mountainous, interlocking there with northern branches of the Nass and western feeders of the Black or Turnagain River, a tributary of the Liard. From Telegraph Creek, the head of navigation, a pack-trail sixty-two miles and a-half in length, constructed by the British Columbian Government, follows the valley of the Stikine, generally at no great distance from the river, and eventually crosses from the Tanzilla or Third North Fork to the head of Dease Lake, which may be regarded as the centre of the Cassiar mining district. This route has long been known to the Indians, the Stikine having been to them from time immemorial an important avenue of trade, by which, as by the Skeena, the coast tribes penetrated a considerable distance inland.

My personal acquaintance with the Stikine, as far as Telegraph Creek, _Information obtained._ was such only as could be made from the deck of the little steamer in which we ascended the river to that point, and merely enabled me to note the main features of the valley. This was supplemented, however, by the observations of Mr. McConnell, who remained behind for the purpose of making a micrometer survey of the river from the furthest point reached by Mr. Hunter's survey of 1877 to Telegraph Creek. Mr. McConnell's notes and map with specimens collected by him have been consulted in the following sketch of the river, and are drawn upon particularly in respect to its geological features.

As the result of Mr. McConnell's survey, taken in conjunction with _Map of the river._ that of Mr. Hunter, we are now for the first time in possession of a correct map of the river to the head of navigation. The best general map of the river and route to Dease Lake previously in existence, was a sketch made by Mr. G. B. Wright and published in the report of the Minister of Mines of British Columbia in 1875. This map also includes Dease Lake and part of the Dease River, and I may take this opportunity of stating that much credit is due to Mr. Wright for its general accuracy, taking into consideration the circumstances under which it was made.

The general trend of the Stikine valley for twenty miles from the _Trend of the main valley._ sea, is east-and-west, corresponding in direction to Bradfield Canal, which penetrates the coast thirty miles to the south, and also to part of the northern portion of Behm Canal and Burroughs' Bay, still further south. At this distance from the coast the river bends through a quadrant of arc, and assumes a nearly due north direction, which it maintains for about sixty-six miles, beyond which the valley is continued in a nearly direct north-eastward course to the vicinity of Dease Lake, but in its upper portion is occupied, not by the main river, but by the Tanzilla or Third North Fork, the main river entering this continuous valley from the southward.

The Coast Mountains.

The particular range of the Coast Mountains, which locally assumes a culminating or axial character on the Stikine, is that which is traversed by the river-valley near the great bend above alluded to. As seen from the sea, at some distance off shore, it is notably higher and rougher to the north of the river-valley than to the south of it, and is surmounted by sharp, jagged, rocky pinnacles in some places. The highest summits in this range here probably average about 8000 feet. It carries much snow throughout the year, and in it are the sources of the principal glaciers which debouch along the north-and-south part of the river above the great bend. The inland border of the Coast Mountains may be said, on the Stikine, to be near Glenora, giving a transverse width, from the coast, for this rugged belt of country of nearly eighty miles.

Current of the river.

The current of the navigable portion of the Stikine is swift throughout, but there are no rapids properly so called, though the Little Cañon (fifty-three miles above the great bend) forms a serious impediment to navigation when the river is at its highest stage in June or July, in consequence of the great velocity of the current in this narrow and rocky though deep gorge. Near the mouth of the river the current scarcely surpasses two miles an hour, but it increases as the river is ascended, till it attains a rate of six to seven miles in many places between the great bend and Telegraph Creek, the swifter water being chiefly met with above the Little Cañon. The average rate of flow of the navigable portion of the river must be about five miles an hour. The width of the Stikine immediately opposite Telegraph Creek was found on May 29th to be 480 feet only, but it is here deep; and had a velocity of 6·08 miles per hour, as determined from several observations. A few days later it was rising fast, and the velocity was considerably greater.

Navigation.

Stern-wheel steamers for the navigation of the river should have good engine power, and should draw not more than four feet of water when loaded.

The height of the river above sea-level at Telegraph Creek, as deduced from simultaneous barometric observations at the mouth and at this place, is 540 feet, giving an average fall of over four feet to the mile by the course of the stream. The actual fall on the upper part of this length of the river must, however, considerably exceed this figure, while that of the lower portion is inconsiderable. Under ordinary circumstances the ascent of the river to Telegraph Creek, with a suitable steamer, occupies about three days, and it is generally necessary to carry a line ashore at a few places. The extensive flats near the mouth of the river render it necessary to enter it about high-tide. Mr. Hunter ascertained that the channel across these flats has from one to two feet only of water at low tide. A considerable proportion of the traffic is carried on by Indians with canoes, and the Stikine Indians are very expert in all the necessary operations of tracking and poling in swift water.

Notes on the dates of opening and closing of the river will be found on page 60 B.

The entrance to the Stikine from the sea is not distinguishable in its main orographic features from that of many of the salt-water inlets by which this part of the West Coast is dissected. The lower portion of this river-valley may, in fact, be regarded, like that of the corresponding part of the Skeena, as an inlet which has become filled with detritus in consequence of the great size and sediment-carrying capacity of the river which has emptied into it. Unlike the Skeena, however, the *débris* brought down has in this case been projected seaward so as to completely block the wide channel between the mainland coast and Mitkoff Island with shallow tide-flats and bars, above which several smaller, high, rocky islands project. The mountains immediately bordering the valley of the Stikine at its seaward entrance are from 2000 to 3000 feet in height, and rise abruptly from the wide alluvial flats, through which the river there winds, often without even touching the lower spurs of the hills. *(Lower part of river at one time an inlet.)*

The flats are generally covered with fine groves of cottonwood, mingled with spruce and other trees, and are often cut through by sloughs and channels, which become so numerous in some places as to render it difficult to decide which is entitled to rank as the main stream. The valley-bottom maintains an average width of from two to three miles as far up as the Little Cañon, which place may be regarded as nearly marking the head of the old salt-water inlet which has been silted up by the river. The cañon is about three-fifths of a mile long, and in places not more than fifty yards wide. It is bordered by massive granite cliffs, 200 to 300 feet in height, above which, on the west side, rugged mountain slopes rise. On the east, are low rocky hills representing part of a former spur of the mountain, through which the cañon has been cut. A tract of low land separates these hills from the eastern side of the main valley, and it is difficult to explain under what circumstances the river has taken its present course. *(Character of valley to Little Cañon.)*

For some distance above the Little Cañon the Stikine valley appears to cut very obliquely through a series of somewhat irregularly parallel ranges. Eight miles further up is the "Kloochman Cañon," which to some extent repeats the features of the last, but it is nearly 300 feet in width and offers no impediment to navigation. At four miles above the "Kloochman Cañon" is the so-called "Grand Rapid," which, in consequence of recent changes in the river, is now by no means formid- *(Valley above Little Cañon.)*

4

able, though the water is still particularly swift and the river wide and shallow. Here the valley begins very markedly to open out, the mountains retiring further from the river and decreasing in altitude, while irregular, basaltic hills, of no great height appear between the river and the bases of the mountains. This, taken in conjunction with the dry climate which characterizes the country to the east of the mountains, and the fact that most of the slopes have been bared of timber by fire, gives an entirely different aspect to the landscape.

Iskoot River.

The Stikine is joined by some important tributaries in the part of its course above described, though none of these have yet been examined in detail. The Iskoot or Skoot, which flows in from the eastward about thirty-five miles from the mouth, or just within the locally culminating range of the Coast Mountains, is known to be navigable for some distance by canoes, and one branch is said to head not far from the extremity of Portland Canal, to the southward. By following this river to its head and there making a portage, the Indians are reported to be able to reach the Nass River without difficulty. The Iskoot has been prospected by a few miners, but apparently without any notable result, though the Indians report the occurrence of coal. The northern branch of the Iskoot, to the east of the Coast Mountains, was traversed in 1867 by P. J. Leech, of the Western Union Telegraph Exploration Survey, who crossed from it to the head of the First South Fork of the Stikine. The valley is there reported to be from 2500 to 3700 feet above sea-level, generally timbered, but with some open, grassy slopes.

Scud River.

About seven miles below the Little Cañon, the valley of the Scud River opens to the east, but the exact position of the mouth of the stream has not been fixed on the map. Some gold has been found by prospectors on this stream, but no workable placer deposits. It is said to head in a low country behind the Coast Mountains, and if this be correct, must nearly inosculate with branches of the Iskoot and First South Fork of the Stikine.

Clearwater River.

Six miles above "Kloochman Cañon," the Clearwater River enters the Stikine on the west side, by several mouths. This is a stream of considerable size, and is navigable for canoes for some distance. It is said to head near the sources of one branch of the Taku River, and is noted by the Indians on account of the great number of salmon which ascend it.

First South Fork.

The First South Fork joins the Stikine about a mile and a-half below Telegraph Creek. It is a large turbid stream, and for a number of miles from the main river, flows in a rough narrow gorge, between high hills and mountains. Further up, according to the Telegraph Exploration sketch, it is bordered by level, partly timbered terraces or

" benches."   The summit between its head-waters and those of the
Iskoot, on the route followed by Mr. Leech, is given on his authority
at 5000 feet.   Salmon do not ascend this stream.

Telegraph Creek is an inconsiderable stream, which falls rapidly to
the river through a narrow rocky cleft in the bordering hills of the
right or north-west bank of the Stikine.   Its name is due to the
fact that here the Western Union Telegraph line was intended to
cross the Stikine.   The little town of Telegraph Creek occupies the
narrow delta of the stream and the lower terraces bordering it on both
sides, its site being identical with that of "Fort Mumford" of the
older maps.   Glenora, twelve miles below Telegraph Creek and on the
same side of the Stikine, consists of a single row of houses built along
the edge of the river at the foot of a steep bank.   Both places were at
one time busy little towns, but are at present very much reduced in
importance, though I believe it will probably not be long before further
mining developments in the Cassiar district will lead to the renewal
of their activity.

Telegraph Creek and Glenora.

Glaciers.

The glaciers constitute one of the most remarkable features of this
part of the Stikine valley.   There are a number of these on both sides
of the river, in its lower part; but four only of special importance, all of
which are situated to the west of the river, and all but the first on the
eastern slopes of the most massive central ranges of the mountainous
region.   The only detailed previous notice of these glaciers is that
given in a report by W. P. Blake.*   Mr. Blake's account of the
glaciers is transcribed in the Fifth Annual Report of the United
States Geological Survey, where it is placed under the somewhat misleading title of Glaciers of "Alaska."   Two of the glaciers
are illustrated in the last-mentioned volume by reproductions of photographs taken under the direction of Dr. J. W. Powell, Superintendent
of Indian Affairs in British Columbia.   That named the "Orlebar
Glacier" represents part of the front of the Great Glacier of the
miners and of Mr. Blake's map.   The "Bernard Glacier" I am unable
to identify with any certainty, but the illustrations evidently represents part of either the Flood or Dirt Glacier.

Previous notes on the glaciers.

Mr. John Muir, who spent some time on the Stikine in 1879, gives
an interesting popular description of its glaciers in a letter dated from
Sitka in December of that year, and published in the San Francisco
Bulletin.   Mr. Muir informs me that no more systematic account of his
observations in this region has yet been made public.   The glaciers

---

*Geographical notes upon Russian America and the Stikeen River. W. P. Blake, Washington,
Government. 1868.

are also noticed at some length in an account of a trip on the Stikine by Mr. W. H. Bell in Scribner's Monthly, 1879, Vol. XVII. The accompanying illustrations, though striking and artistic, have been idealized so far as to be scarcely recognizable.

Little Glacier. The glacier known as the First or Little Glacier by the miners (named the Popoff Glacier by Blake) fills a high valley on the north side of the river, about ten miles from its mouth. As seen from a distance it offers no features of particular interest, resembling many other minor glaciers of the Coast Mountains.

Great Glacier. The next and most important glacier, is that universally known on the river as the Great Glacier, and so named also by Mr. Blake, who gives an excellent description of its main features. The high snow-fields from which this glacier must take its rise are not seen from the river, the glacier entering the wide valley of the Stikine nearly at right-angles, through a break in the mountains two to three miles distant from the river bank. Before entering the Stikine valley, the glacier has a width estimated at from one-half to three-quarters of a mile, but upon freeing itself from the bordering mountains immediately expands in a fan-like manner, its actual front upon the river being from three to three and a-half miles in width. The slope of the surface of the glacier where it issues from the mountains was estimated — as seen at right angles — at above five degrees. Beyond this point it flattens out, and portions of the surface become extremely rugged, breaking off near the front in series of descending steps, as described by Mr. Blake. When seen by us, on the 20th of May, much of the surface was still covered by the new snow of the preceding winter, but notwithstanding this, a great quantity of rocky *débris* was visible, giving a grey tint to portions of the ice. The front of the glacier appears to be quite close to the edge of the river, but is actually about a third of a mile distant at the nearest points. This interval is occupied by moraines and marshy pools, the outer tier of moraines, or that nearest to the river, forming wooded hills about one hundred and fifty feet high. The newer moraines were partly covered and overridden by the front of the decaying ice. Large streams issue from beneath the ice, the position of outflow frequently changing from year to year.

Next to its size, the most remarkable feature about this glacier is the regularity of the fan-like form in which it terminates. It resembles in this respect the Davidson Glacier on Lynn Canal.

Recession of the glacier. The miners state, that during the few years which they have known the Stikine the Great Glacier has steadily and notably receded, though the total amount of such recession can evidently not have been more than the distance from the wooded bordering-moraine to the present ice-front. The Indians relate as a tradition, that at a former period the glacier stretched completely across the valley, the Stikine passing beneath the ice through a tunnel-like opening. It is, however, impossible to determine whether this is a remembered fact or a fancied inference. Curiously enough, a copious hot spring is situated immediately opposite the glacier on the east side of the Stikine valley.

Ten miles above the Great Glacier, and also on the west side of the valley, is the Dirt Glacier, so named by the miners because of the great quantity of rocky *débris* with which its surface is covered.* This is much smaller than the last, having a width estimated at a quarter of a mile, but possibly greater than this. Like the Great Glacier, it comes quite down on the river-flats. *(margin: Dirt Glacier.)*

The last important glacier, sixteen miles still further up the river, is the Flood Glacier. This also comes down to the level of the river-flats, but does not closely approach the river. From the valley of this glacier a great rush of water occurs almost every year towards the end of the summer. This, no doubt, arises from the blocking by the glacier of the mouth of some lateral valley in which a lake is formed and from time to time breaks through the glacier dam. The quantity of water thus liberated is so great as to raise the river from a low stage to half-flood level for a short time. There is a large quantity of *débris* also on this glacier, though less than on the last. *(margin: Flood Glacier.)*

Geological Notes on the Stikine.

The only information as to the geology of the Stikine, up to the present time, has been that embodied in notes in Mr. Blake's report, already referred to,† and these include the lower portion of the river alone, as his furthest point was a few miles above the Little Cañon. The results of Mr. Blake's examination are by himself summed up in the following terms:—"The mountains of the Stikine valley, from the Little Cañon down to near the coast, are formed of syenite and granite, with some metamorphic beds at intervals. The walls of the Little Cañon are granite. At the mouth of the river, and below the Indian villages, the rocks are quite different, being formed of the great sandstone and shale formation already described. The direction of uplift of these strata is about N. 80° W. magnetic. This formation is some thousands of feet thick, and resembles the rocks of San Francisco, but is more changed by metamorphic action. They are probably of the secondary period. It appears to pass into mica- *(margin: Mr. Blake's observations.)*

---

* Also so named on sketch map in Report on Customs District, Public Service and Resources of Alaska Territory, by W. G. Morris, 1879.

† Mr. Blake's notes on the geology of the river are also given in Petermanns Mitteilungen, vol. x, 1861.

slate just above the site of an old stockade or fort of the Hudson Bay Company, where I found a locality of garnets like those of Monroe, in Connecticut."*

Rocks of Wrangell Island.

The rocks seen along the west shore of Wrangell Island, in the vicinity of the town and harbor, are chiefly black, flaggy argillites, remarkably uniform and regular in their bedding and with a westward dip. They are considerably indurated and contain small staurolite crystals in some layers, while on the surface of others crystals of mica have been developed. Similar rocks are found on other parts of the coast, both to the north and south, and from a lithological point of view, they much resemble the Triassic argillites of the Queen Charlotte Islands, though no fossils were found at this place. The ridge behind the town of Wrangell is chiefly composed of rather fine-grained grey granite, which is probably intrusive and may have been the cause of the incipient crystallization observed in the argillites. The north point of the island is formed of similar granite, probably a continuation of the same mass.

Rocks at month of river.

On crossing to the mainland, to the eastward, mica-schists and granites are met with, and beyond Rothsay Point (which may be regarded as the entrance to the Stikine River) granitic rocks only were seen for some miles. Near Rothsay Point, at a short distance from the shore,

Garnets.

is the locality from which are obtained fine claret-colored garnet crystals, sometimes an inch or more in diameter. The matrix of these, as seen in hand specimens, is a dark, highly crystalline mica-schist, but the locality was not visited. The general strike of the rocks west of Rothsay Point is about S. 35° E., with prevailing westward dips.

Rothsay Point to Great Glacier.

From Rothsay Point to the Great Glacier, the mountains bordering the river are chiefly composed of granites and granitoid rocks. These alternate with gneissic and schistose rocks of similar composition, including mica-schists; but massive granites probably form much the greater part of the whole. The granites are usually grey in colour, and contain both hornblende and mica, with white felspars, which are often porphyritic, giving the rock a spotted appearance.† Some varieties become granitoid diorite, while others are highly quartzose, and contain little or no hornblende. The series as a whole closely resembles that cut across by the Fraser River in its lower course, and generally characteristic of the Coast Ranges of British Columbia.‡

Rocks brought down by the glacier.

The Great Glacier, rising many miles back in the higher ranges of the mountains, in the material which it has brought down and deposited in its moraine, affords a mode of ascertaining the gen-

---

* This does not appear to be the locality near Rothsay Point, subsequently mentioned.
† See note on the lithological character of the granites, Appendix V.
‡ Compare Annual Report Geol. Surv. Can., 1886, p. 11 B.

eral composition of the central ranges. This material was found by Mr. McConnell to consist almost entirely of grey granite of medium grain, composed of felspar, quartz and hornblende in nearly equal proportions, but holding also a little mica and occasional crystals of sphene. Diorites and mica-schists occur in smaller quantity, together with coarse pegmatite, which is evidently derived from veins intersecting the granite.

Similar granitoid rocks, with occasional schistose areas, constitute the whole of the rock-exposures seen along the river to the so-called Grand Rapid, about four miles above "Kloochman Cañon". The mountains bordering the valley also appear to be entirely, or almost entirely, composed of the same materials, though at one place, (nearly opposite the site of the Hudson Bay Company's old post) the upper portion of a mountain seems to show a massive bedding, recalling that of the Cretaceous quartzites of Tatlayoco Lake, which occur there in a similar position relatively to the Coast Ranges.* No further evidence was, however, met with tending to show that rocks of this age occur here. *[margin: Kloochman Cañon to Grand Rapid.]*

A short distance below the "Grand Rapid," distinctly stratified rocks of dark colour are seen capping some of the mountains and resting upon the granites. These beds have a dip of N. 70° E. < 30°, which brings them down to the level of the river near the rapid. They are there found to consist of hard argillites and grauwacke-quartzites, interbedded with shaly, grey and brownish impure limestones, the whole being considerably disturbed and cut near the granites by coarse grey porphyritic dykes of that rock. The argillites were not observed to hold staurolite, mica, or other crystalline minerals like those of Wrangell, and otherwise differ somewhat in appearance from these, though their relation to the granitic rocks appears to be similar. They are followed in ascending order by a massive grey-blue subcrystalline limestone of considerable though undetermined thickness, which can be traced in the mountains for some distance on both sides of the valley. These limestones are believed to represent those afterwards noted on the Dease and there referred to the Carboniferous period. *[margin: Stratified rocks at Grand Rapid]*

About two miles and a-half above "Grand Rapid," near the mouth of the Clearwater, the limestone is followed—apparently still in ascending order—by a series of altered volcanic rocks which are, for the most part of grey and greenish colours. These are apparently chiefly diabases, but include also porphyrite-like rocks. The rocks are generally rather fine grained, and would require microscopic examination before they can be named in detail.† Though clearly forming a *[margin: Altered volcanic rocks.]*

---

* Report of Progress, Geol. Surv. Can., 1875-76, p. 253.

† One of these which has been microscopically examined by Mr. F. D. Adams is described in Appendix V. as a diabase-porphyrite (Stikine No. 16.)

stratified series, evidence of bedding can seldom be detected in the exposures, in consequence of their homogeneous composition and shattered state. They seem to be identical with those forming a part of the Cãche Creek group, in the southern interior of British Columbia, and though no fossils were found in the limestones previously mentioned, they, and possibly also the argillites beneath them as well, may be referred with considerable probability to the same Upper Palæozoic age.

Argillites and limestones.   Altered volcanic rocks only, like those above noted, were seen along the river for about twelve miles above the Clearwater, but there is reason to believe that outliers of Tertiary basalt also occur in this part of the valley. At the distance just mentioned above the Clearwater, and about six miles and a-half below Glenora, exposures are found of slaty argillites and dark shaly rocks, containing some impure limestone, all very much broken and disturbed, and associated with altered volcanic materials. Some beds of these shaly limestones prove on microscopical examination to consist chiefly of organic fragments which are not, however, sufficiently distinctive for the reference of the beds.

Triassic fossils.   Dark shaly rocks occur near Glenora which were not specially examined. It is probably from these that some specimens containing Triassic fossils, which were given to me some years ago by Mr. J. W. McKay, were derived. The form represented is a species of *Holobia*, probably a finely sculptured variety of *H. Lommeli.*

Tertiary volcanic rocks.   From this point to Telegraph Creek, basaltic and other comparatively modern volcanic rocks become prominent features, the basalts appearing as remnants of horizontal flows, the broken edges of which form scarped cliffs. These rocks are due to a period antecedent to that of the glacial deposits, and are of Tertiary age. Analogy with neighboring parts of British Columbia indicates that they may be assigned with probability to the Miocene. The basalts have evidently flowed along and partially filled the old river-valley, and unconformably overlie the old altered volcanic rocks previously alluded to, as well as all the other rock series.

About two miles below Glenora, the basaltic rocks were noticed in one place to have filled the old river-bed, conforming in their lower layers to the slopes of its sides, and to have been subsequently cut across obliquely by the present river. Other examples of this character are mentioned on following pages and are of special interest in connection with the occurrence of placer deposits of gold.

Palæozoic and Cretaceous rocks.   Between Glenora and Telegraph Creek, the rocks seen below the basalts include at least two distinct series. The first and oldest of these is represented by a number of occurrences of altered volcanic rocks, like those previously referred to, as well as by considerable exposures (beginning about a mile above Glenora) of grey and blackish, rather cherty quartzites, often nearly on edge. The second consists of slightly indurated conglomerates, sandstones and shales, the conglomerates being often very coarse and containing pebbles both of the older volcanic series and of the granites and granitoid rocks. These lie at comparatively moderate angles of inclination. No fossils were observed in them, but in their lithological character as well as in their position relatively to the Coast Ranges, they resemble rocks of Cretaceous age met with in other parts of British Columbia, both to the south and north of the Stikine, and may be provisionally referred to that period.

In the immediate vicinity of Telegraph Creek, the prevalent rock is a grey-green, speckled, altered volcanic material, which proves to be a fine-grained diabase-tuff. *   The high hill immediately opposite Telegraph Creek, on the other side of the river, is composed of similar old volcanic rocks, comprising compact diabase and a massive diabase-agglomerate. *[margin: Rocks near Telegraph Creek.]*

About two miles below Telegraph Creek, on the right bank of the river, a portion of the basaltic filling of the old valley forms a range of columnar cliffs about 200 feet above the present water-level. A second similar remnant occurs just above Telegraph Creek, on the same side, and a portion of it extends up Telegraph Creek itself for a mile or more. Basaltic dykes, which may have served as sources of supply of molten material at the time of eruption, are found cutting the older rocks. Though in some cases simulating the appearance of terraces, the basaltic shelves along the sides of the valley are quite distinct from, and of earlier date than these. *[margin: Basalt flows.]*

Notes on the various rocks met with will be found on the face of the map accompanying this report. The country to the east of the granitic rocks of the Coast Ranges would require much time and attention before its somewhat complicated geological structure could be properly defined. *[margin: Notes on map.]*

In the gorge of Telegraph Creek, a large boulder of grey sub-crystalline limestone was found, closely resembling in character and degree of alteration that seen near the "Grand Rapid," but in this case containing large branching corals and numerous *Fusulinæ*, indicating its Carboniferous age. It is of course impossible to state with certainty whence this boulder was derived, but it may very probably have come from the mountains to the north within the drainage-area of Telegraph Creek. *[margin: Fossiliferous limestone.]*

The portion of the Alaskan coast which I have seen, viz., that to the south of the 59th parallel, shows the same general absence of

---

* See Appendix V. (Stikine No. 25.)

Terraces.

terrace deposits which has already been noted and commented on in the case of the British Columbian coast. In the vicinity of the mouth of the Stikine, terraces fifteen to twenty feet in height are found, resembling the wooded flats met with further up the river, but as they are here upon tide-water, indicating, doubtless, an elevation of the coast-line to that amount. Further up the river, the first appearance of high-level terraces is at about two miles below the Great Glacier. Those here seen are quite narrow, and were estimated to be 500 and 700 feet, respectively, above the river. The river, for the first time, shows bordering-terraces of from thirty to fifty feet in height, about six miles below the Little Cañon, and similar terraces are frequently seen above this point. On the mountain above Glenora a distinct but small terrace was seen from a distance at an estimated height of 1500 feet above the river. At Telegraph Creek the two principal terraces are 90 and 200 feet respectively above the river-level.

Gold.

The mode of occurrence of gold on the Stikine, and the placer mining which has occurred along the river, are described on a subsequent page, in connection with facts on gold mining in the Cassiar region generally. (See p. 79 B.)

Climate.

Two distinct climatic regions.

The traverse of the Coast Ranges by the Stikine River, from its mouth to Telegraph Creek, affords an excellent illustration of the difference between the coast and inland climates, repeating to a great extent the phenomena met with in making a similar traverse of the same ranges in the southern part of British Columbia. It is here, however, all the more remarkable, as so great a difference between these climates would scarcely be anticipated in this northern latitude. Some records of observations in Appendix VI may be referred to for details, but it may be stated here, as showing the broad general contrast, that while the annual precipitation at Wrangell, at the mouth of the Stikine, is over sixty inches,* that in the vicinity of Telegraph Creek on the inland side of the mountains, is so small that it is necessary to irrigate cultivated land.

Nor does this comparison of rain-fall sufficiently mark the great diversity which actually obtains between the two climates, the prevalence of clouded skies in the coast region being accompanied by a saturated state of the atmosphere, while precisely opposite conditions are found on the eastern side of the mountain belt, at not more than

---

* U S. Coast Pilot, Alaska, Part I, 1883, p. 271. The precipitation at Wrangell is moreover much less than that at more exposed parts of the Coast, for at Tongass and elsewhere it exceeds 100 inches annually.

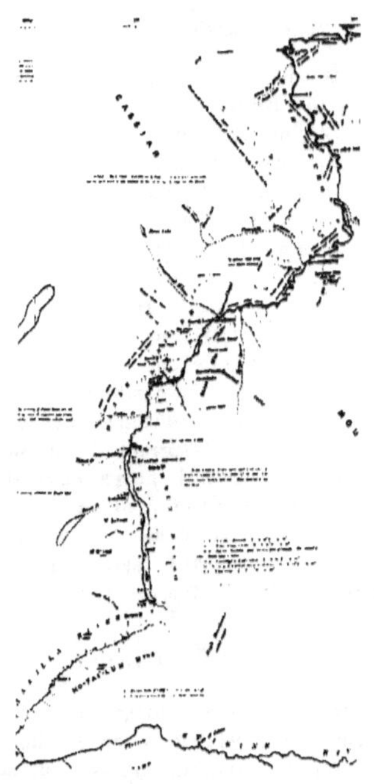

Terraces.　terrace deposits which has already been noted and commented on in the case of the British Columbian coast. In the vicinity of the mouth of the Stikine, terraces fifteen to twenty feet in height are found, resembling the wooded flats met with further up the river, but as they are here upon tide-water, indicating, doubtless, an elevation of the coast-line to that amount. Further up the river, the first appearance of high-level terraces is at about two miles below the Great Glacier. Those here seen are quite narrow, and were estimated to be 500 and 700 feet, respectively, above the river. The river, for the first time, shows bordering-terraces of from thirty to fifty feet in height, about six miles below the Little Cañon, and similar terraces are frequently seen above this point. On the mountain above Glenora a distinct but small terrace was seen from a distance at an estimated height of 1500 feet above the river. At Telegraph Creek the two principal terraces are 90 and 200 feet respectively above the river-level.

Gold.　The mode of occurrence of gold on the Stikine, and the placer mining which has occurred along the river, are described on a subsequent page, in connection with facts on gold mining in the Cassiar region generally.　(See p. 79 n.)

Climate.

Two distinct climatic regions.　The traverse of the Coast Ranges by the Stikine River, from its mouth to Telegraph Creek, affords an excellent illustration of the difference between the coast and inland climates, repeating to a great extent the phenomena met with in making a similar traverse of the same ranges in the southern part of British Columbia. It is here, however, all the more remarkable, as so great a difference between these climates would scarcely be anticipated in this northern latitude. Some records of observations in Appendix VI may be referred to for details, but it may be stated here, as showing the broad general contrast, that while the annual precipitation at Wrangell, at the mouth of the Stikine, is over sixty inches,* that in the vicinity of Telegraph Creek on the inland side of the mountains, is so small that it is necessary to irrigate cultivated land.

Nor does this comparison of rain-fall sufficiently mark the great diversity which actually obtains between the two climates, the prevalence of clouded skies in the coast region being accompanied by a saturated state of the atmosphere, while precisely opposite conditions are found on the eastern side of the mountain belt, at not more than

---

* U S. Coast Pilot, Alaska, Part I, 1883, p. 271. The precipitation at Wrangell is moreover much less than that at more exposed parts of the Coast, for at Tongass and elsewhere it exceeds 100 inches annually.

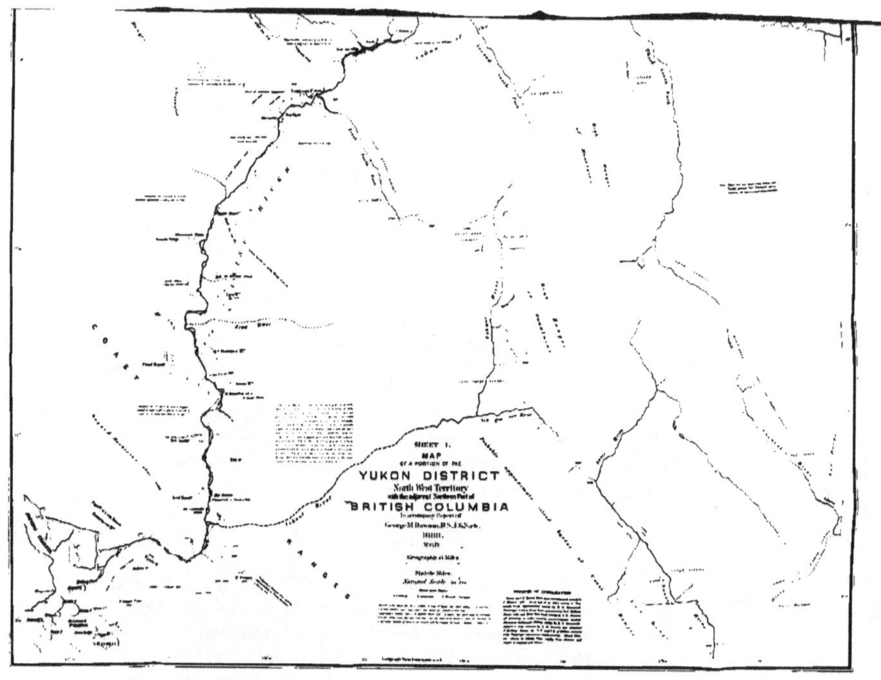

SHEET 1.
MAP
OF A PORTION OF THE
YUKON DISTRICT
North West Territory
with the adjacent Northern Part of
BRITISH COLUMBIA
To accompany Report of
George M Dawson, D.S., F.G.S. etc.
Scale
Geographic Miles
Statute Miles
Natural Scale
COAST
RANGES
HIGH

594

No. 2. PART B, 1887.

SHEET I.

YUKON DISTRICT & BRITISH COLUMB

eighty miles inland from the general line of the coast. The coast climate is, of course, much more temperate than that of the interior, which, even no further off than Telegraph Creek, becomes one of extremes. It is probable that the total annual precipation is even greater in the vicinity of the culminating and central ranges of the Coast Mountains than at Wrangell, and as a large proportion of this occurs as snow, it sufficiently accounts for the existence of the important glaciers and the heavily snow-covered appearance of the mountains till late in the summer. Miners state that the snow accumulates on the river-flats of the lower part of the Stikine, within the mountains, to a depth of from eight to ten feet, while at Telegraph Creek and on the Tahl-tan River it seldom exceeds eighteen inches, and at the latter places horses and mules have been wintering out for a number of years. The great depth of snow retards the advance of spring all along the portion of the river where it occurs, and thus by a cumulative effect conserves the already large quantity of snow for the supply of the glaciers, which are consequently due rather to the extremely heavy snow-fall than to the actual latitude of the region.

Bearing of snowfall on existence of glaciers.

When we left the coast, on the 19th of May, the hills near the sea were generally denuded of snow to a height of several hundred feet, but on entering the river patches of snow began to appear on the low flats, and a few miles further on these flats and the gravel-bars of the river were almost entirely covered with the old snow, quite down to the water's edge. The quantity of snow was observed to diminish somewhat where the river first turns to the north, but was again greater in the vicinity of the glaciers, and it was not till the Little Cañon was reached that the flats were found free from snow. From this point on, the improvement in the climate became quite marked, and the limit of snow retreated far up the mountain sides.

Observations on depth of snow.

In correspondence with the above facts, the vegetation is much further advanced in spring on the inland side of the Coast Ranges than elsewhere. Thus, at the date above mentioned, the cotton-woods and other deciduous trees at the mouth of the Stikine and along its lower part showed merely a general faint greenish tint as the buds opened. Four days later, in the vicinity of Telegraph Creek, the appearance was almost that of early summer. *Shepherdia Canadensis, Amalanchier alnifolia, Corydalus aurea* var. *occidentalis, Actæa spicata* var. *arguta, Prunus Virginiana, Arnica cordifolia, Viburnum pauciflorum, Saxifraga tricuspidata, Androsace septentrionalis,* amongst other plants, were in flower, and butterflies and humming-birds were abundant.

Climate and vegetation.

The change in species of plants met with in ascending the river is also clearly indicative of that from a very moist to a dry climate, as a reference to the lists in an appendix to this report will show. The devil's club (*Fatsia horrida*) extends only a few miles above "Kloochman Cañon," while *Elœgnus argentea* and other forms characteristic of a dry region were first seen at Telegraph Creek. The state of progress of the season at this place appeared to be nearly, if not quite, equal to that found at a similar date in the vicinity of Ottawa or Montreal.

Local climatic
differences. The local differences of climate are, however, quite important. Thus Glenora, though about twelve miles only from Telegraph Creek, is said to experience much greater cold in winter, and the snow-fall is also greater, being estimated at three feet and a-half. Less snow falls on the Tahl-tan than elsewhere, the amount increasing both to the east and west of that place. Strong winds blowing up stream or inland are prevalent in the Stikine valley in summer, but occur in the reverse direction, as a rule, in winter. Further observations on the winter climate of the Stikine are given in Appendix VI.

Notes at
Telegraph
Creek. During the few days spent at Telegraph Creek, in the latter part of May, the wind generally blew up the river and was often strong. The high distant ranges of the Coast Mountains to the west, were usually enveloped in clouds and heavy showers were there evidently of constant occurrance. The sky at Telegraph Creek was also as a rule largely obscured, but after passing over the Coast Mountains the clouds were more broken and produced merely a few drops of rain now and then, the conditions being similar to those met with in the dry country to the east of the same range in the Fraser valley, much further south.

Cultivation. Cultivation in the vicinity of Telegraph Creek and Glenora is practically confined to the raising of small quantities of vegetables and of barley and fodder for animals. There is, however, in this vicinity, in the aggregate, a considerable area of land which might be tilled if there were sufficient local demand to warrant it. Excellent potatoes are produced, and though the leaves are occasionally touched by frost, the crop is seldom affected. It has further been ascertained by actual trial on a sufficient scale that not only barley, but wheat and oats will ripen, and that all ordinary garden vegetables can be produced. The record is a remarkable one for the 58th degree of north latitude.

Opening and
closing of the
river. According to Mr. J. C. Callbreath, of Telegraph Creek, the Stikine generally opens for navigation between April 20th and May 1st.* Ice or 'sludge' usually begins to run in the river about the 1st of November, but has been noted in some years a fortnight earlier. The river generally freezes over before the end of November. Mr. Callbreath

---

* The season of 1887 was unprecedentedly late, the first canoe from the upper river reaching the coast only on May 18th.

states that the first sludge ice coming down from the smaller tributary mountain streams ceases to appear in the Stikine for a time after these are frozen over. As in the case of other rivers rising in the interior, the highest water occurs in the early summer, generally in June. Horses and mules find grazing on the Tahl-tan from April 20th, or May 1st to about December 1st, after which date they require some hay.

Discovery and Exploration of the Stikine.

Though the position of the Stikine* is indicated on Vancouver's charts by the open channels of the river, and the shoals about its estuary are mapped, the existence of a large river was not recognized by that navigator, who visited this part of the coast in 1793. According to Mr. W. H. Dall,† the river was first found by the fur traders. "The sloop *Dragon*, Captain Cleveland, visited the Stikine delta in April, 1799,‡ and in the journal of the sloop *Eliza*,§ Captain Rowan, for the same year, we find the locality alluded to as 'Stikin'." It was, no doubt, visited as well by many of the trading vessels which about this time frequented the coast. In 1834 the Hudson Bay Company fitted out a vessel named the *Dryad* for the purpose of establishing a post and colony at the mouth of the Stikine, but the Russians being apprised of this circumstance sent two small armed vessels to the spot, and constructed a defensive work which they named Fort Dionysius, on the site of the present town of Wrangell. Finding themselves thus forestalled, the Company retired. This dispute was compromised in 1837, when an arrangement was made by which the Company leased for a term of years all that part of the Russian territory which now constitutes the "coast strip" of Alaska, and the "fort" was handed over to the Company, the British flag being hoisted under a salute of seven guns in June, 1840. In the same year, the post, which had been renamed Fort Stikine by Sir James Douglas, was attacked by the Indians, and in the following year a still more serious attack was threatened, and averted only by the timely arrival of Sir George Simpson, as recorded in his "Narrative of a Journey Round the World" (II, p. 181). In 1847, the coast Indians (Thlinkit) are stated to have attacked and taken possession of the fort. In the spring of 1840, the

Early notices of the river.

Establishments of the Hudson Bay Co.

---

* The modes of rendering the native name of this river has been very varied, Mr. Dall enumerates *Stakeen, Stahkin, Stickeen, Stachin* and *Stikine*. (Pacific Coast Pilot, Alaska, Part I, 1883, p. 109; foot note.) The last mentioned has been generally employed by good authorities and is adopted here. Mr. J. W. McKay informs me that the name Stikine is a corruption of the native (Thlinkit) word *ta-kane*, meaning "the river," and equivalent to "the great river."

† U. S. Coast Pilot, Alaska, Part I, 1883, p. 110. From this work, and from Bancroft's History of the Pacific Coast, vol. xxxiii, several of the facts mentioned below are also derived.

‡ Cleveland's Voyages, Cambridge. Mass. 1842.

§ MS. in possession of Mr. Dall, but unpublished.

Hudson Bay Company established also a second fort on this part of the coast which was named Fort Durham. This fort was situated at a place named by the late Sir James Douglas, "Locality Inlet," about thirty miles southward from the mouth of Taku River and near the entrance of the Inlet of the same name, in sight of Douglas Island. It was abandoned in the spring of 1843, and is sometimes referred to as Taku Fort.

Discovery of upper part of river.

Previous to this time, in 1834, Mr. J. McLeod, had in the interest of the Hudson Bay Company, reached the banks of the upper part of the Stikine, near Dease Lake, coming overland from the Mackenzie River. Subsequently, Mr. R. Campbell spent the winter of 1838-39 on Dease Lake, but established no fort on the Stikine.

Discovery of gold.

No further events of importance appear to have occurred in connection with the river till, in 1861, two miners named Choquette ("Buck") and Carpenter, discovered placer gold on its bars. In the following spring, some excitement being created by the announcement of this discovery, several prospecting parties were fitted out in Victoria, and a number of men passed the summer in mining on the river. In 1863, the Russian authorities, hearing of the discovery of gold, despatched the corvette *Rynda* to ascertain whether the mining was being carried on in Russian territory. A boat party from this vessel, under Lieutenant Pereleshin, ascended the river to a point a few miles above the Little Cañon, occupying May 23rd to June 1st on the expedition. Mr. W. P. Blake accompanied this party, and in addition to the sketch-map published by the Russians, his report on the Stikine, previously alluded to, is based on it.*

Hudson Bay Company's post.

A Hudson Bay post was established on the east side of the river in 1862 or 1863 and maintained till about 1874, when it was moved to the vicinity of Glenora, were it remained till 1878, when it was abandoned.

Telegraph exploration.

In 1866, explorations for the line of the Western Union or Collins' Telegraph Company were extended to the Stikine under Major Pope. These were continued in 1867 by Messrs. M. W. Byrnes, Vital Lafleur, W. McNeill and P. J. Leech, and embraced most of the principal tributaries of the river. The results of this work were not separately published, and the whole enterprise of which they were a part was, as is well known, abandoned. The sketch-maps then made were, however, partly embodied in the small map accompanying Mr. W. H. Dall's work on Alaska (1870), and with greater completeness in other subsequent maps of the region. The surveys made at this time, while doubtless sufficient for the object in view, and serving to

---

* Geographical Notes upon Russian American and the Stickeen River; Washington, 1868. Also, Am. Journ. Sci. and Arts, vol. xliv, 1867, p. 96.

represent the main features of the country traversed in a general way,
leave much to be desired in the matter of accuracy.

In 1873, Messrs. Thibert and McCullough, travelling westward from
the Mackenzie, discovered gold in the Cassiar region, and fell in with *Subsequent history of the Stikine.* the miners already engaged in placer work on the Stikine in the
autumn of that year. The subsequent history of the river depends on
that of the Cassiar mining district, and need not be further followed in
detail.

Some years after the acquisition of Alaska by the United States, the
Stikine came prominently into public notice for a time in connection
with difficulties respecting territorial jurisdiction which occurred in
regard to customs and other matters. A full account of these difficulties, together with a report by Mr. J. Hunter of his survey of the
lower part of the river, made for the purpose of approximately determining the position of the line of boundary between Alaska and the
province of British Columbia, is given in the Canadian Sessional
Papers, Vol. XI, No. 11, 1878.*

A description of the Stikine is given in the U. S. Pacific Coast Pilot,
previously quoted, as well as an itinerary of the river, but as no correct
survey of the Stikine existed at the time (1883), the distances and details
are only approximately correct.

Published Maps of the Stikine.

The following reference-list of published maps of the Stikine is based
on that given by Mr. Dall in Appendix I to the Coast Pilot of Alaska,
1879.—

Russian Hydrographic Office chart No. 1396, Pacific Ocean on the *Russian maps.*
North-west coast of America (published 1848). Also, Russian chart
No. 1493-4 (published 1853), Alexander Archipelago. [These two
charts, Mr. Dall informs me, show a part of the Stikine in such a way
as to prove that it must have been surveyed.]

Plan of the Stikine River from observations by officers of the corvette *Rynda* in 1863. Russian Hydrographical Department, 1867.

Sketch-map of the Stickeen River from the mouth to the Little *Blake's map.*
Cañon, W. P. Blake, *Op. supra cit.*, 1868.

Map of Cassiar District in Report of Minister of Mines of British *Wright's map.*
Columbia, 1876. [This has remained the most complete map of the
river up to the present time, and is a very praiseworthy sketch.]

Plan of Stachine (Stikine) River, by J. Hunter. [This, with other *Hunter's map.*
subsidiary maps, is contained in the Sessional Papers, Vol. XI, No. 11,
1878. It includes the lower part of the river only, but is from actual

---

* See also Report by W. G. Morris, elsewhere referred to, p. 43 *et seq.*

survey and on a scale of 8000 feet=1 inch. It shows the provisional boundary line adopted without prejudice until the true line shall have been determined.]

Morris' map.

Map showing boundary line in Morris' Report on Alaska. U. S. Senate, Ex. Doc. No. 59, 1879.

The river is shown on a small scale, according to the result of surveys here reported on, in a map accompanying a summary of the results of the expedition, in Science, Vol. IX, April 2, 1888.

CASSIAR TRAIL* (*Telegraph Creek to Dease Lake.*)

Route followed

The trail from Telegraph Creek to the head of Dease Lake was opened by the Government of British Columbia in 1874. It has since been kept in a fair state of repair, and is a good route for pack animals. It follows the north side of the Stikine and Tanzilla valleys, and is sixty-two miles and a-half in total length As already mentioned, the same important valley which is occupied by the Stikine below Telegraph Creek, continues in a north-eastward direction to Dease Lake, the main stream of the Stikine entering it from the southward about midway between these two points.

Telegraph
Creek to Tahl-
tan. —

On leaving Telegraph Creek, the trail makes a steep ascent to the level of a broad terrace, and runs along at a considerable height above the river, and often at some distance from it, till it descends again, at eleven miles, to the valley of the Tahl-tan or First North Fork, near its mouth. The main valley of the Stikine is here about four miles in width, and is bordered by high hills and by mountains of rounded forms, those to the north often nearly bare, while those on the opposite side are generally either wooded or strewn, where fires have passed, with burnt logs. The river occupies a cañon, with precipitous banks often 300 feet in height, which has been cut in the bottom of this great valley. It is very rough and rapid, but there are no true falls. Terraces are well developed at several levels on both sides of the river, which is frequently bordered by vertical basaltic cliffs. The basalts have manifestly filled the bottom of the ancient valley in a series of nearly level flows, which have since been cut through by the present river, while the bordering hills are all composed of much older and probably Palæozoic rocks. A general summary of the geology of the country from Telegraph Creek to Dease Lake is given on a later page.

The country traversed by the trail between Telegraph Creek and the Tahl-tan is wooded only in patches, the trees being chiefly black pine (*Pinus Murrayana*) and aspen (*Populus tremuloides*), with occa-

---

* See note in Appendix II (p. 198) on the origin of the name Cassiar.

sional specimens of white birch, and alder and willow in the hollows.
The soil is reddish and rather sandy, and appears very dry, being but
scantily clothed with thin, tufty grass and bear-berry (*Arctostaphylos uva-
ursi*).   The strawberry (*Frajaria Virginiana*) was abundant and in full
flower on May 31st, while *Polemonium pulchellum* was also very conspicuous, and *Linnæa borealis, Echinospermum Redowskii* and *Arnica cordifolia* were also locally abundant.   Thickets are composed principally
of *Shepherdia Canadensis*, high-bush cranberry (*Viburnum pauciflorum*),
roses, service-berry (*Amelanchier alnifolia*), red dog wood (*Cornus stolonifera*) and willows.

The Tahl-tan Indian village is seen near the trail, about a mile Indian village.
before the river of the same name is reached, but was at the time we
passed quite deserted.

The Tahl-tan River is crossed near its mouth by a good bridge. Tahl-tan River.
It is a large and rapid stream, which rises about thirty miles to the
north-westward.   Its valley is narrow and almost cañon-like where
it reaches the Stikine, and has cut through basalt flows and heavy
underlying gravel deposits to a depth of about one hundred and fifty
feet, though its right bank, just above the crossing, is composed of the
older rocks.   It is resorted to by the Indians for salmon fishing during
a part of the summer, and there are several temporary houses and a
number of graves.   The angle between this river and the Stikine, on
the right bank, shows three clearly defined, superposed, columnar
basalt-flows.   The opposite angle, up which the trail zig-zags, is in the
form of a long, narrow point, the surface of which is extremely rough,
being composed of large pieces of basalt lying in great confusion, with
deep interspaces and crevices.   This is generally known as the "lava
bed," but its broken character appears to have been produced by the
washing out of the underlying gravelly deposits, resulting in slides and
irregular settlement of a once uniform basalt sheet.   Notwithstanding
its relatively recent appearance, the basalt here, as elsewhere along the
Stikine, is of pre-glacial age, and was found, like the other basalt
flows, to pass beneath the higher terraces.   Gold mining was at
one time carried on successfully for some miles up the Tahl-tan valley.

According to M. W. Byrnes, one of the Telegraph Company's ex- Sources of
plorers. the sources of the Tahl-tan are at a distance of about thirty Tahl-tan
miles from its confluence with the Stikine.   It occupies a portion of an
important valley which, still further to the north-westward, carries
the upper branches of the Taku and the furthest sources of the Lewes
River.   The Indians travel along this valley, and it appears worthy of
attention as a route from the navigable waters of the Stikine to the
Yukon basin.

Tabl-tan to Tooya. The distance from the Tabl-tan to the Tooya, or Second North Fork, is about six miles. For about half this distance, to Ward's house, (now, like other places of call along this route abandoned) the trail runs near the Stikine River, the immediate valley of which still continues to be occupied by basaltic flows. Above these, however, the sides of the valley are generally formed of very regular and high terraces, composed of horizontally stratified sands, gravels and earthy deposits, which though generally very fine, are rather silts than true clays. The gravels frequently include large boulders. At Ward's, the trail turns away from the river and cuts across a high point to the Tooya, the highest terrace-level crossed being about 1000 feet above the river. On these high terraces the vegetation was perceptibly less advanced than in the lower parts of the valley. Swampy spots are frequent, and the country, as we recede from the vicinity of the Coast Mountains, has evidently a somewhat more humid climate and is more subject to summer frosts. Potatoes and other crops are successfully grown at Ward's, situated on one of the lower terraces, but irrigation is there necessary.

Tooya valley. The Tooya valley, where it is crossed by the trail, is a great gorge, about 600 feet in depth, cut out through the terrace deposits. The river, which is spanned by a small bridge, is a wild torrent—almost a series of cascades. Its scarped banks show a section of about 400 feet of the terrace deposits, which are of the character above noted, but include rough, bouldery and gravelly layers, and a number of large granite boulders occur in the bottom of the valley, resembling in their lithogical character the granites of the Coast Ranges.

Sources of Tooya. Scarcely any authentic information is available regarding the head-waters of the Tooya, though these have been reached by prospectors from Dease Lake. A lake of considerable size is reported to exist on its upper part, as indicated in the accompanying map, and the volume of water in the river is such as to lead to the belief that it must drain a large area to the south of the Yukon watershed.

Plateau beyond Tooya. About a mile beyond the Tooya, on the summit of a wide, undulating terrace, is Wilson's house. Here turnips and potatoes have been grown, but the potatoes do not fully mature. From Wilson's to Caribou Camp, about twelve miles, the trail crosses an extensive high terrace or plateau, with a nearly level or slightly undulating surface, which is generally wooded with aspen, black pine and white spruce of fair growth. A few very small streams, which flow toward the main valley, are crossed, but the river is generally some miles distant and scarcely visible from the trail. The Tooya valley is here said to run nearly parallel with the main valley of the Stikine and at no great distance from it, but is invisible from the trail. No mountains were

FIG. 2.   VIEW OF THE TANZILLA RIVER, LOOKING SOUTH-EASTWARD FROM 'CARIBOU CAMP.'
Illustrating the character of the level terrace-country, based on stratified later-glacial deposits.   (From sketch by J. McEvoy.)

here seen to the north-eastward, but high, rounded mountains, with broad, bare summits, continue to border the south-east side of the Stikine valley. About midway between Wilson's and Caribou Camp, the Stikine, or Too-dessa of the Tahl-tan Indians, coming from the southward, enters the main valley, cutting through the bordering mountains in a narrow cañon, which the Indians report impassable. Their route to the upper waters of the river crosses the mountains to the west of this cañon. They state that after again reaching the Stikine, above the cañon, they can ascend it in canoes without difficulty for a long distance.

No rock exposures were seen along this part of the trail, and only occasional groups of boulders. The soil appears to be excellent, but the altitude is probably too great for the successful cultivation of any but the most hardy crops. The vegetation and appearance of the country afford evidence that the climate is still a rather dry one.

The trail reaches the edge of the valley of the Tanzilla, or Third North Fork, about a mile south-westward from Caribou Camp. This valley is cut out to a depth of 450 feet below the level of the plateau, and is about a mile in width from rim to rim. The sides show evidence of extensive landslips, both old and recent. The river is a comparatively small though swift and muddy stream, with an estimated width of 180 feet and depth of about three feet. No rocks are exposed in the valley, the entire depth of which appears to be excavated in bedded clays and silts, which weather to grey, earthy slopes. No true boulder-clay was seen, but the occasional presence of large granitic boulders, with the singularly contorted character of some of the clay-beds, appear to indicate the existence of floating ice in the body of water in which the deposits were originally laid down. The clays and silts are evidently the same with those seen in the Tooya, but here, so far as observed, want the rough bouldery and gravelly beds which are there intercalated, and which are doubtless connected with the entry of the former representative of the Tooya into the lake in which the silty deposits have been formed. Flat or lenticular calcareous nodules are abundant at certain horizons in both places, and are also reported to occur at some distance up the Tahl-tan, where the same silty deposit is probably continued. The level country based on these deposits has a width of several miles on both sides of this part of the Tanzilla.

From Caribou Camp to the vicinity of Dease Lake, or for about twenty-six miles, the trail runs along the north-west side of the Tanzilla. The valley of the stream gradually loses its depth, owing to the fact that, while the grade of the stream is considerable, the terraces at its sides continue at about the same level. These consist, so far as can be seen, of similar silty and clayey materials, but the edges of the terraces are less marked, and they show a tendency to merge into slopes, which rest upon the bases of the mountains bordering the valley. The mountains which extend to the south-east of the river here become higher than before, and take the form of a well-marked range, which is known to the Indians as *Ho-taï'-luh.** Swampy spots become frequent and the vegetation more alpine in character, with evidence of a considerably greater rainfall. The white spruce is relatively more abundant, and *Betula glandulosa* and *Ledum latifolium* were here met with for the first time. A great part of the forest all along this portion of the valley has been destroyed by fire. Rock is seen in place only on approaching the bases of the mountains.

Opposite the head of Dease Lake, the Tanzilla turns off abruptly, and is seen to take its rise in a high range of mountains, holding much snow and running in a north-east and south-west bearing, at a distance of seven or eight miles. The main valley, which has heretofore been occupied by the river, turns northward, through a right-angle, and becomes continuous with that of Dease Lake. The distance from the head of the lake to the Tanzilla, at the nearest point, is about three miles, the level of the Tanzilla being somewhat lower than that of the lake. The height of land is about seventy feet above the lake, or 2730 feet above the sea, and constitutes the watershed between the Arctic and Pacific slopes. *Valley connecting Tanzilla with Dease Lake.*

The part of the valley which connects the Tanzilla with Dease Lake is floored by terrace deposits, and is without doubt very deeply filled with such material, as no solid rock is seen in it. It has evidently been part of a through river-course of very ancient date, but in which direction the stream which originated the valley flowed, it is now difficult to surmise. It has, however, been again occupied by a river in comparatively recent post-glacial times, subsequently to the formation of the terrace deposits, as it is traversed by a well-marked river-bed, filled with rolled stones and gravels. This old channel appears to rise slightly toward Dease Lake, and there can be little doubt that the stream by which it was formed flowed out of the lake. *Origin of the valley.*

Geological Notes on the Cassiar trail.

Respecting the older rocks which characterize the greater part of the country between Telegraph Creek and Dease Lake, few details were noted, and no approach to a general section was obtained, as they are not usually exposed except along the bases of the mountains, which are, as a rule, at some distance from the route of travel. They *Rocks chiefly Palæozoic.*

---

* The names of geographical features which have not been previously recognized, whether Indian names or names applied by myself, are throughout the descriptive portion of this report printed in italics, on the occasion of their first occurrence.

may be described as consisting of grey and greenish-grey quartzites and grauwackes, with a large proportion of altered volcanic materials, generally felspathic, but passing into diabases and becoming in some cases more or less schistose. Rocks originally of volcanic origin notably preponderate in the vicinity of Telegraph Creek, while near Dease Lake they are less abundant, and at about two miles from the lake, on the trail, massive grey fine-grained limestone occurs, in exposures which are nearly continuous for about a mile. None of the mountains in sight on either side of the valley are distinctly granitic, and rocks of this character were observed only in one locality, where they occupy a relatively small area.

Limestone.

At about two miles along the trail to the south-west of the Tahl-tan, a dark, blackish-green, highly crystalline hornblende-rock occurs in considerable mass, and is much broken and shattered by a grey porphyritic and hornblendic granite, which appears to be of later date, and which may have a width of about two miles on the trail. In the bed of the Tooya River rocks differing in appearance from any seen elsewhere on this trail were found. They are reddish and purplish in colour, fine-grained, and in some beds slightly porphyritic, and appear to be chiefly felspatic in composition.* One of these is identical with a rock met with in the lower part of the bedded series, a short distance above "Grand Rapid," on the Stikine. No fossils were found in the limestones above alluded to, and the rocks, as a whole, can at present only be classed as Palæozoic, though showing many points in common with those of the Cāche Creek group of southern British Columbia, which is believed to be, in great part at least, of Carboniferous age.

Hornblende-rock and granite.

Purple felsites.

The pre-glacial age of the basaltic rocks is shown, as already noted, by their relation to the terraces of the valley, and also by the occurrence upon them of large granitic boulders, the transport of which must be attributed to glacial action. This is seen particularly in some places between Telegraph Creek and the Tahl-tan. The basaltic rocks, at the period of their eruption, have filled the old river-valley, and may very probably have at one time done so continuously from below Glenora to the Tooya, or perhaps considerably further. There is no reason to suppose that the basalts were erupted from a single volcanic centre, and indeed the existence of basaltic dykes cutting the older rocks at Telegraph Creek would appear to lead to an opposite conclusion. Subsequent to the period of basaltic eruption, the river, still flowing in the same great valley, has cut down through the basalts in several places, exposing sections of the gravel deposits of the ancient river. The new channel thus formed is not, however, coincident

Basalts filling old river-valley

* See Appendix V. (Cassiar Trail No. 4.)

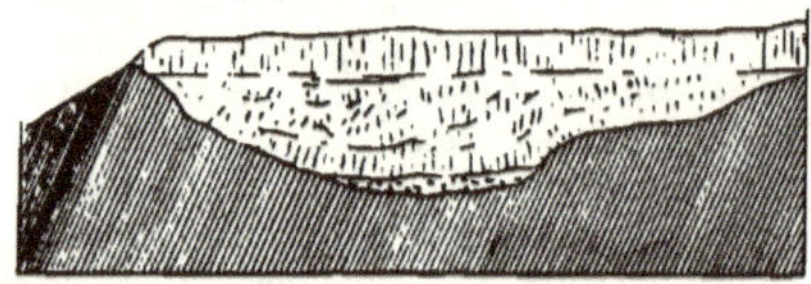

FIG. 3.—SECTION SHOWING OLD RIVER-CHANNEL CAPPED BY BASALTS.   EAST BANK
STIKINE RIVER BELOW TAHL-TAN.

FIG. 4.—SECTION SHOWING OLD RIVER-CHANNEL FILLED WITH BASALT.   MOUTH
OF TAHL-TAN.

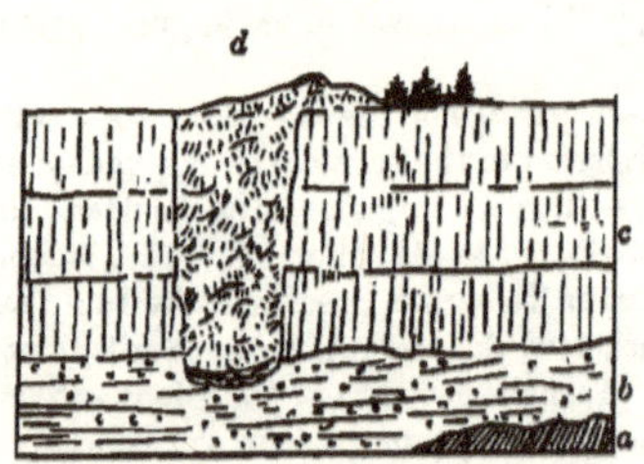

FIG. 5.—SECTION SHOWING RELATIONS OF BASALTS AND GRAVELS.   STIKINE RIVER,
EAST BANK, ABOVE TAHL-TAN.

a. *Old basal rocks.*
b. *Old gravels.*
c. *Superposed basalt flows.*
d. *Basaltic filling of a later gorge.*

with the old, but cuts across it at several points, and above Telegraph Creek, the excavation of the new bed has been carried to a depth estimated at from forty to seventy feet below the earlier one.

A few miles below Glenora, where the basalt filling of the old valley has been cut across, it seems, however, that the old river-bed is below the present water-level, indicating, in connection with the previous observation, that the grade of the original river was greater than that of the present.

Directly opposite the mouth of the Tahl-tan River, on the left bank of the Stikiné, a good section of the old river-bed is exposed, in the truncated end of a point which forms a spur of the plateau to the south, the basalts filling it like a great ingot and resting, at the bottom, on the old gravels, at the sides, directly on the rocky banks of the old channel.

The angle between the Tahl-tan and the Stikine, on the upper side, has already been referred to in connection with the peculiarly disturbed character of the basalt layer by which it is capped. Beneath the basalt at this place is a great thickness (apparently not much less than one hundred feet) of well-rounded gravel and boulders. It is probable that this deposit does not reach to the water-level, but its disintegrated material has formed a slope which conceals any basis of old rocks which may be beneath it. The eruption of basalt has, moreover, not been confined to a single period, but must have occurred at several different times separated by rather wide intervals. The occurrence in some places of three or more superposed flows, shows this to have been the case, but a still more striking proof of the same fact is found in a section observed from a distance, on the left bank of the Stikine above the Tahl-tan. At this place a thick and apparently extensive deposit of gravels has been covered by three superposed basaltic flows. Through these, a narrow vertical-sided cañon has been cut by some tributary stream, which has even excavated a portion of the gravels beneath the lowest basalt. A fourth basaltic flow has then occurred, which has completely filled the cañon and partly overflowed on the surface of the highest of the three earlier basaltic layers.

Though the basalts of Tertiary age actually seen by me are confined to the Stikine valley, it is highly probable that further explorations will prove their occurrence in other valleys, and possibly also the existence of similar rocks, in the form of plateaux of some size, in the region east of the Coast Ranges.

The basaltic formation of this part of the Stikine has been described in some detail, on account of the importance which it possesses in respect to the distribution of gold. The gold along the Stikine was said by the miners to be "spotted," or irregular, in its occurrence, but the greater part of the "heavy" gold was found just along that portion of the stream now characterized by the basalts, and it appears even possible to trace a connection between the richer bars which have been worked and those places in which the present river has cut through or followed the old basalt-protected channel. This being the case, it seems very desirable that the old channel should be fully prospected, which I cannot learn has ever been attempted. If gold should be found in it in paying quantity, it might easily be worked, and would give rise to a considerable renewal of activity in mining. It is not known to what extent similar conditions may occur up the Tahl-tan valley, where also remunerative bars were worked some years ago.

Superficial Deposits and Terraces.

No true boulder-clay was recognized either on the Lower Stikine or in the country between Telegraph Creek and Dease Lake; neither were any striated rock surfaces actually seen. The last-mentioned fact is to be attributed to the want of suitable localities for observation in the vicinity of the route followed and to the necessarily cursory character of the examination, as evidence of glaciation of a general character, shown in the rounding of rocky hillocks and the transport of large boulders, is abundant. The most characteristic later formation of the country between Telegraph Creek and Dease Lake, is the silty and clayey deposit which has already been referred to in several places. The whole of the great valley has evidently in later-glacial times been filled with this deposit, which must have been laid down in a comparatively tranquil lake-like body of water, into which coarser material was in some places washed by entering torrents, as in the case of the Tooya. It appears to me possible that this body of water was held in by means of glacier-ice accumulated on the Coast Ranges on one side and those of the Cassiar Mountains on the other, and the increased height of the terraces in the vicinity of Dease Lake, as compared with those near Telegraph Creek, may show that the terrace-deposits have been laid down near the front of a retreating glacier-mass, the water-level of the lake being reduced *pari passu*, with its recession. The highest terrace-level observed near the Tahl-tan, is at an approximate elevation of 1700 feet above the sea, while half way between the Tooya and Dease Lake the terraces run up to a height of about 2800 feet. At the head of the lake a well-marked terrace-edge was observed at 520 feet above the lake, or 3180 feet above the sea. The irregular surface of the same terrace sloped upward to a further height of about 100 feet, and granite boulders were found on the summit of a limestone hill 1000 feet above the lake, or 3660 feet above the sea. If the supposition of the considerable inland extension of the glaciers of the Coast Mountains at one epoch of the glacial period be correct (and it is strictly paralleled by similar circumstances in the more southern part of British Columbia), the greater part of the granitic erratics met with may probably have been derived from the Coast Ranges, though the Cassiar Mountains, and possibly other ranges in the region, are characterized by similar rocks.

Route for Waggon-road or Railway.

Dease Lake is the central point of the Cassiar district, and though, as shown by statistics subsequently quoted, the yield of gold has greatly fallen off since the palmy days of its first discovery, it is very probable that further placer mines of value may yet be found in this region, (of which a great part still remains to be carefully prospected) and there is every reason to believe that quartz mining and other industries will before long be developed on a considerable scale. Even at the present moment this district is more easily accessible than that of Cariboo, and when a waggon-road shall have been built from the head of navigation on the Stikine to Dease Lake, it should be easy to lay down goods at the latter point at very reasonable rates.

The construction of a waggon-road, with moderately favorable grades, between Telegraph Creek and Dease Lake, would not be very difficult or expensive. The first ascent from Telegraph Creek is steep, but might easily be overcome. Between eight and ten miles from Telegraph Creek, or for a distance of about two miles, the road would have to follow a rough hill-side above the cañon, where some blasting and grading would be required. The descent to the Tahl-tan would entail some heavy side-hill cutting in rock and earth and a bridge would be necessary. The ascent and crossing of the "lava bed" would entail about a mile of rough work on the opposite side of the Tahl-tan, and should the line of the present trail be followed, a long and steep ascent, with grading in gravel and clay, would be required at Ward's, and again in descending to and ascending from the Tooya valley, but no rock work would be necessary. It seems quite probable, however, that a better route might be found for a road, at a lower level, from Ward's to the mouth of the Tooya, in following along the side of the main valley. In either case a good bridge would be required at the Tooya. Beyond this, all the way to Dease Lake, no further serious obstacle is met with. Portions of the route are clayey and swampy, and to render these easily passable, from eight to ten miles of corduroy in all would be required, for which suitable material could be obtained near by in all cases.

Should the construction of a railway be contemplated, the difficulties to be surmounted would be greater in proportion, particularly

between Telegraph Creek and the Tahl-tan, where the line would have
to follow the side of the cañon, which is very rough and rocky. Beyond
this point, so far as the valley could be seen from the trail, it presents no
very serious impediments. Below Telegraph Creek, to Glenora, or a
little further, a railway would involve some moderately heavy side-hill
work; but further down the Stikine, to the sea, it might follow the
river-flats at a nearly uniform level. The greatest difficulty to be
apprehended on this part of the line would be that likely to arise in
winter from the very heavy snow-fall on that part of the river below
the Little Cañon.

It may be pointed out in this connexion that the survey of the
Stikine and of the valley leading by the Tanzilla to Dease Lake shows
that the route is an exceedingly direct one to Dease Lake, and that,
taken in conjunction with the valleys of the Dease and Liard Rivers, it
affords almost an air-line from the Pacific Coast to the great Mackenzie
River. (See p. 19 B.)

The present rates for goods, from Wrangell to Dease Lake are about
as follows :—Wrangell to Telegraph Creek by steamer, 2½ cents per lb. Freight rates.
Thence to Dease Lake by pack animals, 6 cents. Thence by lake to
Laketon, ¾ to 1 cent. Total, about 9½ cents per lb., or $195 per ton.
The result of such high prices is to discourage prospecting in the dis-
trict and seriously to retard its further development.

DEASE LAKE.

We reached the head of Dease Lake on June 5th, and eventually left Proceedings at
the lake on the morning of June 19th, spending thus thirteen days in Dease Lake.
all upon the lake. At the date of our arrival the lake, with the exception
of a small area at its head, was still covered with the decayed but
unbroken ice of the previous winter, and this did not finally break up
and disappear till the 16th. Meanwhile, almost all our time and attention were devoted to sawing out boards and building three boats. It
would have been impossible to have left sooner, even if we had had
boats ready at the outlet of the lake, which had long been open, in
consequence of the entire exhaustion of supplies in the district, from
which it was necessary that we should depart provisioned for the
greater part of the summer's work. As it was, our boats were finished
a few hours before the final disruption of the ice, which occurred in
the end with extraordinary rapidity, under the influence of a strong
wind. It will easily be understood that we had but little time or
opportunity for the examination of the surrounding country, which is
nevertheless of considerable interest on account of the rich gold-
producing character of some of the streams.

Opening and
closing of lake.

The disappearance of the ice must always be late in this lake, in consequence of its high altitude, the want of any large entering streams and its contracted outlet. It was, however, in 1887 later than ever before known since mining operations began. The following dates, obtained from Mr. Robert Reid, of Laketon, are those of the opening and closing of the lake for the past few years.—

Year.	Lake opened.	Lake closed.
1882	June 9	December 5 or 6
1883	May 30	December 5
	(Clear from end to end.)	
1884	June 2	December 2
1885	June 3	December 1
		(Frozen completely across.)
1886	June 5	December 16
		(Crossing on 17th.)
1887	June 16	

Further particulars respecting the climate of Dease Lake will be found in Appendix VI.

Dease Lake.

Dease Lake has an elevation of 2660 feet above the sea, and lies nearly due north-and-south on the 130th meridian. It has a total length of twenty-four and a-third miles, with an average width of rather less than one mile, being somewhat narrower at the northern than at the southern end. Dease Creek, on the delta of which is situated Laketon, the chief place of the Cassiar district, enters on the west side at sixteen miles and three quarters from the head of the lake, and is the largest tributary stream. It is also the most important, as being that on which the richest of the gold deposits were discovered, and

Mining camps.

on which gold is still worked to a limited extent. A certain amount of business is still carried on here, and it is the head quarters of the present Gold Commissioner, Mr. Crimp. At the south end, or head of the lake, there are a few buildings, now virtually abandoned, and at Porter's Landing, on the west side of the lake near its north end, goods are landed for Thibert's Creek. The old Hudson Bay Post was situated about two miles from the lower end of the lake, on the east side. A small steamer was put upon the lake when the mines were in a flourishing condition, and is still employed in making occasional trips up or down the lake with supplies.

Country sur-
rounding the
lake.

The country about the lake is everywhere wooded, though trees large enough for lumber are found only in sheltered valleys or on low land. It is not roughly mountainous, though several prominent summits occur. The most conspicuous of these lies four miles back from the lake, about half way between the head of the lake and Laketon. As I could not ascertain that this is recognized by any name, I propose

naming it *McLeod Mountain*, in honour of the discoverer of the lake. Mountains.
Its height is about 6300 feet.   Between McLeod Mountain and Dease
Creek is *Mount Sullivan*,* not so elevated as the last, but nearer the
lake-shore and very conspicuous from it. On the opposite, or east
side of the lake, a couple of miles back from the shore, is a group of
rounded and wooded mountains, somewhat exceeding 1000 feet in
height above the lake, or about 3800 above the sea. *Beady Mountain*,
another notable landmark, is also on the east side of the lake, about
three miles from its lower end and near the creek of the same name.
Its height was not determined, but is less than that of McLeod Mountain. With the exception of these and some other nameless
mountains, the country near the lake is merely hilly, or rises in long,
light slopes from the shores to undulating wooded uplands, a few
hundred feet only above it, which coalesce with the bases of the mountains. Only near the northern end of the lake do the mountains begin
to crowd down more closely to the water's edge. The lake is shallow
and marshy at both ends, but is elsewhere evidently very deep, though
no soundings have been made in it.

Rock-exposures are infrequent along the margin of the lake, which, Superficial
deposits.
when scarped, generally shows only stratified, sandy, clayey and
gravelly terrace-deposits, like those seen on the trail to the south-
eastward. None of these were recognized as true boulder-clay. The
lake is probably held in at its northern end by the accumulated delta
deposit of Thibert Creek.† It is much constricted, further up, by the
similar deposit of Dease Creek, and has narrowly escaped being divided
at this place into two lakes. It is rimmed round at its head by somewhat irregular terrace deposits, which have already been alluded to as
filling the ancient valley which communicates with that of the Stikine.

The vegetation gives evidence of a greater rainfall and conditions
more alpine and less favorable than those met with on the trail to the
south-eastward, and sharply contrasting with that of Telegraph Creek Vegetation and
cultivation.
and the Tahl-tan. The effect of the ice upon the lake in spring, in
retarding the vegetation in its immediate vicinity, was extremely
apparent. Agriculture can scarcely be regarded as practicable in this
region, and the results of gardening, however carefully conducted, are
small. Potatoes can be grown, but in some years they are much
injured by frost, and carrots, lettuce, cabbage, cauliflowers and turnips
may be made to afford a fair return.

Such rock-exposures as could be reached near the shores of the lake Rocks.
were inspected, and the material brought down from the hills by sev-

---

* So named for Mr. J. H. Sullivan, first Gold Commissioner of the district, lost in the wreck
of the *Pacific* in 1875.
† A stream about fifty feet wide.

oral streams was examined, the evidence afforded being in favor of the belief that the whole country is underlain by Palæozoic strata resembling those described to the south-eastward. In addition to the limestone already noted as occurring at the head of the lake, there are grey and greenish rocks, representing altered materials of volcanic origin,* associated with leek-green serpentine, in which some minute veins of chrysotile or asbestos were noted. Besides these, and probably predominant as a whole in the valley of the lake, are argillite-schists, which vary from a black plumbaginous to a grey, finely micaceous character, and are often lustrous and not unfrequently highly calcareous. The rocks, as a whole, closely resemble those of parts of the gold bearing series of Cariboo district.

Dease Creek.

Dease Creek, is said to be about twelve miles in length and to rise in a lake about five miles long. It has cut a deep, narrow V-shaped valley through a series of terraces, which have evidently been formed at its mouth when the lake stood at various levels higher than the present. The ancient pre-glacial valley has, at the same later-glacial period, been filled with clayey and gravelly deposits, among which large and often glaciated boulders are common. These deposits frequently resemble boulder-clay, and are possibly entitled to be so called. The present valley has been cut down through them, and often to a considerable depth into the rock beneath them. The mining has occurred chiefly in the bed of the stream, along the surface of the solid rock, in the sides of the valley, and in various places in the gravel deposits which still remain ; also at the head of the flat on which Laketon stands, where the stream issues from the narrow recent valley. Much quartz occurs in the wash of the stream, and the gold, being "coarse," is evidently of local origin and has been liberated by the disintegration of the rocks in the immediate vicinity of, if not entirely within, the actual drainage-area of the stream.

GOLD MINING IN CASSIAR DISTRICT.

Yield of gold.

The following table, based on the reports of the Minister of Mines of British Columbia, clearly illustrates the sudden rise and gradual decadence of the gold yield of Cassiar district.—

Estimated value of Gold produced by Cassiar District, from 1874 to 1887.

1873	Not known.
1874	$1,000,000
1875	830,000

---

* One of these, representing a numerous class having a more or less distinct schistose structure, is described in Appendix V. (Dease Lake, No. 8.)

1876	556,474
1877	499,830
1878	519,720
1879	405,200
1880	297,850
1881	198,900
1882	182,800
1883	119,000
1884	101,600
1885	50,600
1886	63,610
1887	60,485
Total	$4,886,069

No estimate has been formed for the yield of the mines in the first year of their operation (1873,) but as that for the following year appears probably to be overstated, it may, for the purpose of arriving at a general estimate of the whole, be assumed that the sum of one million includes both years. The value of the gold may be stated as from $16 to $17 per ounce, though that of Dease Creek is usually priced at about $15·50 only.

In the Report of Progress of the Geological Survey for 1886-87, I was enabled to give a general note on the various creeks worked for gold in Cassiar and on the Stikine.* The information there given was chiefly furnished by Mr. G. B. Wright. I am now able to add to this, particulars as to the actual condition of the workings in 1887. These were largely obtained through the kindness of Mr. J. S. Crimp, the present Gold Commissioner for Cassiar district, though facts were also gathered from several old miners who were among the first to enter the country. As explained on a previous page, my opportunities of personally investigating the Cassiar district were restricted by the necessity we were under of pushing on to our main field of exploration. Chiefly from the sources above-mentioned the following summary account of the different localities is derived.

Sources of information on mining.

Summary of Facts relating to Gold on the Stikine and various Creeks in the Cassiar District (1887).

Stikine River.—Gold discovered, 1861. Very fine gold can be found on almost all parts of the river, but very little profitable work was ever done below the mouth of the Clearwater. The rich ground may be said to have begun about nine miles below Glenora, and to have extended thence to the Grand Cañon, above Telegraph Creek. Here Sheck's or Shake's Bar, and Carpenter's, Fiddler's and Buck's

Localities of gold mining.

---

* *Op. cit.*, pp. 138-140.

Localities of
gold mining,
continued.

Bars were situated, the richest being between Glenora and Telegraph Creek, though gold was also worked in a few places in the Grand Cañon. With the exception of a few spots in the lower part of the cañon, below the Tahl-tan, and one nearly opposite Wilson's, all the gold was very fine. Coarse gold was also found on the lower part of the Tahl-tan, which proved quite profitable, and bars were worked for a distance of ten or fifteen miles up the river. Pellets supposed to be of silver but probably of arquerite or silver-amalgam were also found on the Tahl-tan. The bars on the Stikine at first averaged $3 to $10 a day to the hand, and as much as two to three ounces was sometimes obtained, but not more than $1 to $3 can now be got, and work has practically ceased. It is stated that none of the higher benches so far prospected will pay for hydraulic work, but it is doubtful whether these have been examined with sufficient care, as the area of such benches is very considerable.

Dease Creek.—The bed of this creek has been gone over several times, and is now nearly worked out. It formerly yielded $8 to $50 a day to the hand, and paid well from the head of the flat, at its mouth, for six miles up. Above this a few isolated good claims were found, particularly the Cariboo Company's claim, eight miles up, from which much heavy gold was obtained. This claim has been worked over four times. The best remaining claims are bench claims on the south side of the creek, some of these being upon an old high channel which yields well in places. Some hydraulic work on a small scale is being carried on. In 1886 there were sixteen whites and thirty-five Chinese at work, and the total amount produced was about $15,000. The gold is generally well water-worn and somewhat mixed in character, varying in value from $15.50 to $16 per ounce.

Thibert Creek.—The bed of this stream is also worked out. It paid for about six miles up from the mouth, yielding at about the same rate as the last. Bench claims are now being worked, two by the hydraulic method, the rest by tunnelling. An old high channel had also been found on the south side of this creek, upon which two claims are being worked, one paying very well. Yield in 1886, nearly the same with Dense Creek, about twenty-two whites and twenty-five Chinese being employed. Gold valued at $16 per ounce. On a tributary named Mosquito Creek very good prospects have lately been obtained,—as much as $40 to a six-foot set of timbers. Work is now going on here.

Defot Creek.—A tributary of Cañon Creek, on the same (west) side of Dease River with the last. It rises on a plateau high above the river, where great numbers of quartz reefs occur, and the gold found is quite rough and full of quartz. Large nuggets have been obtained, including one of fourteen ounces in weight. Some work is still in

progress, though the creek-bed is worked out.   Gold worth $17 per Localities of gold mining, continued.
ounce.

Cañon Creek.—No paying deposits found.

Cottonwood Creek.—This large stream heads in the same mountains with the last, but no paying deposits have been found upon it.

Beady Creek.—A little mining was done here in 1874 and 1875, but nothing of importance ever found.

Eagle River.—No mining ever developed.

McDame Creek.—Discovered 1874.   The highest average daily yield varied from $6 to $100 to the hand when mining was at its best.   Most of the gold was obtained in what appeared to be an old high-level channel, which crossed points of terraces or benches on both sides of the present stream.   A very small proportion of the yield was from the stream-bed.   Four or five Whites and forty Chinese are now at work here, the greater number of the Chinese being employed on wide flats, which occur about nine miles up the creek.   Bench claims run for about seven miles up the creek or to Holloway's Bar.   Gold worth from $17·75 to $18 per ounce.

Snow Creek, a tributary of the last.—The richest claim found in Cassiar was near the mouth of this creek, yielding for a week 300 ounces for six to eight men.   Only two men now at work.

Quartz Creek, a branch of Trout Creek, which is also a tributary of McDame Creek.   Good claims were worked here, yielding rough gold full of quartz.   Much quartz in the vicinity.   Two miners now at work.

Rosella Patterson and Dennis Creeks.—Yielded moderate amounts of gold, paying "wages," say, at $6 a day.   Now abandoned.

The remaining creeks mentioned in the report cited, *viz.*, *Gold Creek, Slate Creek, Somer's Creek* or *First North Fork of McDame, Third North Fork of McDame, Spring Creek* and *Fall Creek*, are now abandoned, though several of them yielded a considerable amount of gold at one time.

Sayyea Creek.   Near the head-waters of the Upper Liard, yielded excellent prospects, but has never been properly examined.   The gold obtained was found in the benches, and some of it was very coarse. The creek yielded at the rate of $10·90 a day to the hand for a short time, to three miners who discovered it.

Walker Creek.—Said to be distant about seventy miles in an easterly direction from the mouth of McDame Creek.   Some work has been done here, but no great quantity of gold obtained.

Black, Turnagain or "Muddy" River.—Reached by trail running easterly from a point opposite the mouth of McDame Creek, and said to be ninety miles distant.   Fine gold stated to have been obtained to the value of $20 per day to the hand, and it is generally believed that coarse gold may occur on its head-waters.   In 1874 prospectors found streams about seventy miles south-east of Dease Lake, which are supposed to be tributaries of this river, and yielded $6 a day in coarse gold, but at the time this was considered too poor to work.

Frozen ground.   Considerable difficulties were experienced in mining operations in some parts of the Cassiar district on account of frozen ground, often met with below the wooded and mossy surface.   It is on record that on Dease Creek, the ground continued to be frozen to the end of a tunnel driven in one hundred and fifty feet from the slope of the hill, and at a depth of forty feet from the surface.   After the woods and moss had, however, been burnt off, little further complaint was heard of frozen ground.

Metalliferous veins.   Very little has yet been done in the way of prospecting for metalliferous veins in this district, but from what I have been able to learn it would well repay a thorough examination, and the comparative ease with which it may be reached from the coast, together with the facility it affords for the construction of a good road to the very centre of the district, should not be forgotten.   A specimen of galena, holding a little copper and iron pyrites, from the "Acadia Claim," South Fork of McDame Creek, was given to me some years ago by Mr. J. W. McKay.   This has since been assayed by Mr. C. Hoffmann, and proves to contain 75 ounces of silver to the ton of 2000 lbs.   A piece of native copper, fifteen pounds in weight, was at one time found in Boulder Gulch, Thibert Creek.

Prospects of further placer mining.   Taking into consideration the great extent of generally auriferous country included in the Cassiar district, it must be conceded, that apart from the immediate vicinity of the well known productive camps, it has been very imperfectly prospected.   A great part of the district has in fact merely been run over in search of rich diggings, the simplest and cheapest methods of prospecting only, having been employed in the quest.   It is not improbable that additional rich creeks like those of the vicinity of Dease Lake, may yet be discovered elsewhere and it may be considered certain that these are great areas of poorer deposits which will pay to work with improved methods, and will eventually be utilized.   It is also to be anticipated that "quartz mining" will ere long be inaugurated and will afford a more permanent basis of prosperity than alluvial mining, however rich.

DISCOVERY AND EXPLORATION OF CASSIAR DISTRICT.

Discovery.   The Cassiar district of the northern interior of British Columbia may be said to have been twice discovered, first by officers and employees of the Hudson Bay Company, and again, after a considerable interval, by the gold miners.

The unsuccessful attempt made by the Hudson Bay Company in 1834, to reach the trade of the interior country west of the Rocky Mountains from the mouth of the Stikine, has already been noted. (p. 61 B). Efforts were at the same time being made to open up routes from the eastward. In the summer of 1834 Mr. J. McLeod, chief trader, was employed exploring the Liard River above Fort Halkett, and in endeavoring to discover some stream flowing to the westward. He found and named Dease Lake,* crossed to the head-waters of the Stikine, which he proposed to name the "Pelly River," and travelled westward in the valley apparently as far as the Tooya or Second North Fork. The Indian bridge (afterwards named Terror Bridge by Mr. R. Campbell), by which this river was crossed at the foot of "Thomas' Fall," was of such a character that neither McLeod nor any of his eight men dared to attempt it, and from this point he and his party retraced their steps.

The geographical information obtained by McLeod is incorporated in Arrowsmith's map of 1850, on which, however, the upper part of the Stikine, which McLeod had proposed to call the Pelly, is named "Frances River," and is placed much too far north and is not connected with the Stikine. The name Frances is still retained as an alternative one to "Stikeen" on the edition of 1854, though it has since fallen entirely into disuse. McLeod's route from the head of Dease Lake, as shown on these maps, crossed the Tanzilla within a few miles of the lake, and followed its left bank, recrossing before the main Stikine enters the valley, probably by an Indian suspension bridge, which is reported still to exist, within a mile or two of this point. On careful consideration of the facts there can scarcely be any doubt that the Tooya River was McLeod's furthest point, and the Indian bridge probably crossed it near the position of the present bridge, though it may have been at some point further up the stream which has not yet been mapped.

In 1836, McLeod's successor at Fort Halkett was instructed to establish a post across the mountains and to extend the trade down the Stikine, or "Pelly," as it was then called from McLeod's naming. For this purpose he left Fort Halkett early in June, with a party of men and two large canoes, but the expedition entirely miscarried. The appearance, or reported appearance, of a large force of hostile Indians at Portage Brulé, ten miles above Fort Halkett, so alarmed the party that they turned back in great haste, abandoning their goods, and lost no time in running down stream to Fort Simpson.

---

* Dease Lake and River were so named by McLeod after Peter Warren Dease, the Arctic explorer.

Exploration by Campbell. For most of the above particulars I am indebted to Mr. Robert Campbell, who was at the time of the return of the last-mentioned party in temporary charge of Fort Simpson. The news brought back by these expeditions was of a character to discourage further enterprises in the region, the extremely difficult and dangerous navigation of the Liard River, which constituted the avenue of approach from the Mackenzie, being an additional deterrent. In 1838, however, Mr. R. Campbell volunteered his services to establish a trading post at Dease Lake, and in the spring of that year succeeded in doing so. He was accompanied by a half-breed and two Indian lads only. After ascertaining that the "Pelly" of McLeod was identical with the Stikine, he returned to Dease Lake, where, to employ his own words, " we passed a winter of constant danger from the savage Russian [coast] Indians, and of much suffering from starvation. We were dependent for subsistance on what animals we could catch, and, failing that, on '*tripe de roche*.' We were at one time reduced to such dire straits that we were obliged to eat our parchment windows, and our last meal before abandoning Dease Lake, on 8th May, 1839, consisted of the lacing of our snowshoes."* After being thus abandoned, the post was not again re-occupied. It had become unnecessary, owing to the leasing of the "coast strip" of Russian America by Sir George Simpson for the Company, in consequence of which the trade of the interior was entirely controlled on both sides by the Company.

Further history From this time the country appears to have been practically forgotten for many years. The furs produced by it found their way, through the Coast Indians down the Stikine, by the Liard to the Hudson Bay posts on that stream, or across country southward to Fort Connelly (established by Douglas in 1826), on Bear Lake, at the head of the Skeena River. The exploration of the Telegraph Survey in 1866-67, has already been referred to. It did not extend inland as far as Dease Lake.

Gold discovery. Such was the state of the Cassiar district when Messrs. Thibert and McCulloch, by the discovery of gold in 1872, brought about an entire change in its conditions. Henry Thibert, a French-Canadian, left the Red River country in 1869 on a hunting and respecting expedition to the west. In 1871 he met McCulloch, a Scotchman, and together they passed the winter near the abandoned site of Fort Halkett, on the Liard River, suffering no ordinary hardships from scarcity of food. Near this place, probably on what was known afterwards as McCulloch's Bar, gold was first found. In 1872 they reached Dease Lake, having been informed that it was a good locality for fish, with the intention

---

* The Discovery and Exploration of the Yucon (Pelly) River. Winnipeg, 1885.

of securing a sufficient supply for the ensuing winter. Being told,
however, by the Indians, that white men were engaged in mining on
the Stikine not far off, they crossed by the trail from the head of the
lake and reached the mining camp of Buck's Bar. Early in 1873 they
set out on their return to the original discovery of gold, but meeting
with success on Thibert's Creek, at the lower end of the lake, they were
deterred from going further and remained working there during the
summer, being joined afterwards by thirteen other miners from the
Stikine. Dease Creek was discovered during the same season, and Capt.
W. Moore was among the first to begin work there. Thibert is still
mining in Cassiar, but McCulloch lost his life some years since on a
winter journey on the Stikine.

The subsequent history of Cassiar is that of a mining district.

In 1874 the population, exclusive of Indians, was estimated to Gold mining, 1874.
have reached 1500. The placers of McDame Creek were discovered.
Miners descended the Liard a long distance, and worked McCulloch's
Bar and other river-bars. Prospectors ascended the same river, and
reported having been within sight of Frances Lake. The little town
of Laketon was built at the mouth of Dease Creek, and beef cattle were
for the first time brought across country from the Upper Fraser. The
total yield of gold from the district (which, from a mining point of
view, includes the Stikine) is roughly estimated to have been equal to
$1,000,000.

In 1875 the population is estimated to have been 1081, and the yield 1875.
of gold equalled about $830,000. Three hundred head of cattle were
brought from the Fraser overland. This and the preceding season
were the best years of the district. Of a small party which spent
the winter of 1874-75 far up the Liard River, four died of scurvy.
Prospecting was actively carried on in outlying regions, Sayyea Creek
being discovered near the Liard head-waters, and the Frances River
also apparently examined.

Owing to the flattering accounts sent out, a great influx of miners 1876.
occurred in 1876, the population being at one time estimated at 2000.
Profitable work could not, however, be found for so many men, and
the yield of gold fell to $499,830. Walker Creek, said to be seventy
to eighty miles east of McDame Creek, was discovered, but this
stream never proved very remunerative. Defot Creek was also found,
and in 1878 proved rich for a limited area.

Since this time the production of the district and the number of Decline of gold mining.
miners employed have gradually declined, and no important new creeks
have been discovered, though reports to that effect have from time
to time been circulated. The Black or Turnagain (Muddy) River is
the most recent of these, some attention being drawn to it in 1886.

It appears, indeed, that after the first few years very little prospecting or exploring has been done at a distance from the main creeks, of which Dease, Thibert and McDame have throughout been the most important and permanently productive.

DEASE RIVER.

We left Dease Lake with quite a little flotilla, consisting of the three boats we had built, with an Osgood canvass boat, which it had been intended to keep in reserve, but which the amount of dead weight which we had to carry obliged us to press into the service. Besides myself, the party consisted of Messrs. McConnell and McEvoy, four white men, five Coast Indians and one Indian woman, the wife of the leading Indian boatman.

Cassiar Range. Though the region about Dease Lake is as a whole rather low, with isolated mountains·and ridges here and there prominent, that to the east and north-east is very different, being studded with rugged mountains, and in effect constituting an important mountain range with north-west and south-east trend, and a transverse width of nearly fifty miles. This range appears to represent a continuation of that which in various maps has been named the Peak Mountains or Blue Mountains, but as its connection to the south-eastward is as yet quite uncertain, and as neither of these names possesses either a distinctive character or any special fitness, I believe it will be most appropriate and convenient to call the range the *Cassiar Range*, and shall accordingly so designate it.

Lower end of Dease Lake. Looking down the Dease River from Porter's Landing, near the north end of the lake, the view is one of the most picturesque possible, embracing a portion of the lake itself, bordered by the marshy flats of the mouth of Thibert Creek and bounded by the rugged and extremely varied forms of the eastern ridges of these mountains, towards which the Dease River flows, and through which it cuts in a direction almost directly transverse to the run of the range.

Three main courses of the Dease. The Dease River has, up to the present time, been very inaccurately represented upon the maps. My survey of the river, as shown on the accompanying map, proves that its course is somewhat remarkable. Disregarding minor flexures, which are numerous and sometimes involved, it may be described as following three principal directions.— From Dease Lake its general course is N. 56° E. for forty-seven miles, to a point near the valley of Rapid River. Here, before it has freed itself from the Cassiar Range, it turns nearly at a right-angle to a bearing of N. 15° W., which it maintains for thirty-one miles. Thence it again turns for a second time through a right-angle to a course of

N. 55° E., which it follows to its junction with the Liard. Its entire length, thus measured in three straight reaches, is one hundred and ten miles, but measured in straight lengths of one mile it is one hundred and twenty-seven miles, or, following all the sinuosities of the stream, one hundred and eighty miles.

The height of Dease Lake, as previously stated, is 2660 feet, within small limits of error. That of the confluence of the Dease and Liard about 2100 feet. The last mentioned elevation is a fair approximation only, as no simultaneous barometer readings were available for purposes of comparison, and the weather during our stay at the forks was rather unsettled. The total fall of the river, according to these figures, is 560 feet, giving a slope of four feet to the mile for its entire length, which, judging from analogy with other western rivers, is about what might be expected from the appearance of the stream. The velocity of the current was estimated at about three miles an hour, as a general average, but there are several little rapids, as well as some rather long tranquil reaches. *Fall of the river, and current.*

The river, from Dease Lake to the Liard, may easily be descended in two days, but the ascent is a comparatively slow process, depending much on the height of the water, and when the bars and beaches are not bare for tracking is a tedious affair. It is possible that the river might be navigated by small stern-wheel steamers of good power, as there are no insuperable obstacles, but doubtful whether such an enterprise would be a remunerative one, even if the traffic were to assume proportions much greater than at present. Such goods as are now required at McDame Creek (fifty-five and a-half miles below Dease Lake by the course of the stream) and at the little trading post at the mouth of the river, are easily taken down stream in large flat-bottomed boats, which go back light, by poling and tracking, without great difficulty. The boating on the river has been done principally by crews of Coast Indians, who are engaged and brought into the interior for the purpose. *Navigability of the river.*

On leaving Dease Lake, the river is a small stream, estimated to average from 100 to 150 feet only in width, with a general middle depth of about three feet. It is extremely tortuous and rather swift, meandering in a wide, flat valley. At about eight miles from the lake, it may be said distinctly to enter the mountains, the valley at the same time gradually narrowing and becoming bordered by mountains from 4500 to 5000 feet in height, which, on the 19th of June, still bore much snow on their summits. At about thirteen miles from Dease Lake, it expands into a little lake about a mile and three-quarters in length, and between this and the mouth of Cottonwood Creek it flows through three more similar lake-like expansions, which are, respectively, a mile and a half, two miles and one mile in length. These are probably formed *Upper part of the river.*

in all cases by the partial blocking of the valley by *débris* brought in by tributary streams, of which Cottonwood Creek itself is the last and most important. These lakes constitute somewhat serious impediments to navigation, as they freeze over in the autumn long before the ice takes on the river, and remain frozen till late in the spring.

Small lakes. The mountains by which the valley is hemmed in on both sides from *First Lake* to the Cottonwood are very rough and high, and chiefly, if not entirely, composed of granitoid rocks. About three miles and a-half north-west of *Second Lake* is a remarkable broken summit, with a height estimated at 7500 feet, which, from the peculiarity of its form, has been named *Anvil Mountain*. Running parallel with this and *Third Lake* is a straight, well-defined range, the higher peaks of which attain an equal elevation, and which, for the sake of distinction and in consequence of the long slopes of broken rocks which descend from it, has been indicated on the map as the *Skree Range*. It is probable that actual measurement will show that several of the peaks in this vicinity exceed 8000 feet. The vegetation was observed to be further advanced as soon as the Dease River was fairly entered, showing how great must be the effect of the ice which lingers on Dease Lake, in its immediate vicinity. There is also evidence of a less abundant rain-fall along the river.

Tributaries. Dease River rapidly increases in size, and after the lake is left, soon doubles its volume, owing to the number of affluent streams, of which Cottonwood Creek is the first which may be called a river. This stream occupies an important valley, which may be observed to run for many miles in a north-westward direction, bordered by continuous high ranges. It is remarkable that no paying deposits of gold have ever been found either on this or on Eagle River, which enters the Dease from the south about four miles further down. Eagle River also flows between high mountains, and its valley appears to be parallel to, and analogous with, that occupied by Dease Lake. It is evidently the "Christie River" of McLeod,* but this name has entirely passed out of use, and it appears hopeless to endeavor to reinstate it. Cottonwood Creek is shown on Arrowsmith's maps, according to McLeod and Campbell, but is not named.

Terraces. Rock exposures are unfrequent in the banks of the portion of Dease River above described, though stratified gravel deposits are often cut into. There is also a considerable development of terraces at high levels on the sides of some of the mountains, particularly in the part of the valley which runs along the base of the Skree Range. Well-

---

* I have endeavored in all cases to identify the original names given by the first explorers in this country, and to ascertain as well the native names of places, but where these have passed entirely out of use by the miners and traders now in the country, it becomes necessary to drop them, though in so doing the strict law of priority is, no doubt, transgressed.

marked terraces were here seen on the west side of the valley, at an estimated height of 2000 feet above the river, or about 4600 feet above the sea.

Immediately below the mouth of Cottonwood Creek is the Cottonwood Rapid, in which the course of the river is impeded by a number of boulders. The rapid is not a formidable one, or at all dangerous to run, with ordinary care. The river below Cottonwood Creek runs nearly due east for about ten miles, with a rather strong current. It then turns more to the northward, and after making several large flexures, reaches Sylvester's Landing, at the mouth of McDame Creek, in about eight miles. In this reach the current is slack, and the river averages 300 feet in width. The flat land of the river-valley is rather wide in this part of its length, but the mountains to the north and south are high and bold, many of the summits ranging from 6000 to 7000 feet. The lower slopes of the mountains are usually light, and in general thickly wooded, but their higher parts are treeless, and from the quantity of snow borne by them in June, must retain some snow throughout the summer. Immediately opposite the mouth of McDame Creek is a remarkably prominent and abrupt rocky mountain, which it is proposed to name *Sylvester Peak*. It height was estimated at 7000 feet, but the circumstances did not admit of its measurement.

Sylvester's Landing is the point of supply for the miners on McDame Creek, also a post for Indian trade, and there are here a few log-houses and store buildings. Mr. R. Sylvester has been resident here for a number of years, and readily gave us all the information and advice in his power. McDame Creek was discovered to be auriferous in 1874. It has since been constantly worked, and, with its tributaries, has yielded much gold, but is now believed to be nearly exhausted. Its valley is wide and important, running north-westward for about seven miles, and then turning nearly due west. At the angle thus formed a low, wide pass leads through the mountains to the north-eastward, where it connects with the valley of the Dease. The appearance of this pass, as seen from a distance, is such as to suggest that the Dease River itself may at some former period have flowed through it.

The mountains bordering McDame Creek, viewed from Sylvester's Landing, are singularly different from any before met with. They are evidently composed for the most part of limestone, and characterized by the occurrence of long, bare slopes of shattered rock-fragments. They are scarcely at all wooded, and in this respect resemble the bare limestone crests of parts of the Rocky Mountains in more southern latitudes.

Potatoes and turnips of large size are grown every season without difficulty on McDame Creek.

Nine miles below Sylvester's, the Dease makes its great bend toward the north, the intervening portion of the river somewhat changing its character from that above described, rock exposures being comparatively frequent in its banks and bed, where they produce several little rapids. Four-mile Creek enters from the south at somewhat less than the specified distance below Sylvester's. It appears to be the "Stuart River" of McLeod, shown on Arrowsmith's map of 1850, but neither on this nor on that of 1854 is McDame Creek indicated. Sylvester's trail to Turnagain or Black River (Muddy River of miners) runs up this valley, and follows a tributary—Sheep Creek—to the south-eastward, passing near the base of *Sheep Mountain*, a high rugged peak estimated at 8000 feet, situated about five miles and a-half south of the Dease. The distance to the trading outpost on Turnagain River is estimated at ninety miles, but is probably less. Horses are employed in packing over the trail.

The valley of the Rapid River joins that of the Dease at its great bend, just alluded to, but the stream, running parallel with the Dease for some distance, enters it several miles lower down, and its actual confluence was not observed. Beyond the great bend the mountains near the river decrease rather notably in height and abruptness, and at the same time retreat from the vicinity of the river, the valley becoming very wide, and long, hummocky slopes, or groups of low hills, coming in between the river and the mountains.

The northerly course of the river here carries it very obliquely through the eastern portion of the Cassiar Range. The precipitation in this part of the valley is evidently inconsiderable. The quantity of snow resting upon the mountains was observed to be very small, and here Sylvester successfully winters his horses, without cutting hay or otherwise providing for them, the depth of snow in winter being so small that it does not seriously interfere with grazing. This favored district is, in fact, homologous with that in the vicinity of Telegraph Creek, being in the dry lee of the Cassiar Range, just as that is in a similar situation with respect to the Coast Mountains. Much of the valley, with the slopes of the hills, is open or partially wooded with groves of black pine (*P. Murrayana*) and aspen poplar. The grass has the tussocky bunch-grass character usually found in dry regions, and it is intermixed with the small sago (*Artemisia frigida*). The bear-berry (*Arctostaphlyos uva-ursi*) is not uncommon, and the strawberry and lupin (*Lupinus Nootkatensis*) were in flower. *Anemone patens* was here also observed for the first time, but long past flowering. Making allowance for the time occupied in reaching this place from Telegraph Creek, the progress of vegetation here was palpably less advanced, but the showing was still a remarkable one for the latitude, elevation and distance from the sea of the region.

Below the Rapid River the Dease changes its character considerably, becoming relatively wide, with numerous gravel-bars, and in some places many islands, with frequent "drift piles" or accumulations of timber. Terraces are well shown on the sides of the mountains and reach a height of about 2000 feet above the river.

A few miles before reaching the second great bend, a stream joins from the west, which has become known to the miners as French Creek, and is probably the "Detour River" of old maps. It rises on the north-east slope of the Cassiar Mountains, and is not large.

The last main reach of the Dease is that which extends from the second great bend to its mouth, a distance of thirty-one miles in a direction of N. 55° E. Though the course of the river is far from being direct, the general bearing leaves the base of the Cassiar Range nearly at a right-angle. The country becomes low and uninteresting, and assumes a rather dreary aspect, being covered generally with forest of inferior growth, often degenerating into swamp on northern aspects, and with only occasional grassy openings on slopes with sunny exposures. In descending this part of the river, the mountains soon become invisible from the river-valley, which is bordered by undulating lowlands, or low diffuse hills which rise to a plateau at some miles distant, from 400 to 500 feet above the stream. Banks of frozen soil were seen in one or two places beneath a peaty or mossy covering. The climate is evidently somewhat more humid than before and less favorable to vegetation. The current of the river is rather swift, and there are two or three inconsiderable rapids, but none of importance till within about four miles of the mouth, where there are several strong rapids, which at certain stages of the water are reported to be dangerous, and in which all our boats shipped more or less water. Terraces, as much as 300 feet in height, approach the river in some places in this part of its course, and when cut into generally show stratified gravels which sometimes rest directly on low exposures of rock.

The larch (*Larix Americana*) was first seen five miles below the second great bend, and below this place becomes quite abundant in cold, swampy spots, where it grows with the black spruce (*Picea nigra*.)

Blue River (the "Caribou River" of Campbell) joins the Dease twelve miles below the second great bend. It is a stream fifty feet wide at the mouth, with clear water, and derives its supply from the north-eastern slopes of the Cassiar Range, to the north of French Creek.

The "Lower Post," which is the furthest outwork of "civilization" or trade in this direction, is situated at the edge of a terrace forty

Dease below Rapid River.

French Creek.

Lower part of the Dease.

Larch.

Blue River.

"Lower Post."

feet in height on the left bank of the Liard, about half a mile above the mouth of the Dease. It is of a very unpretentious character, consisting of a few low log buildings, in the vicinity of which the woods have been entirely destroyed by fire.

The soil is poor near the post and the climate evidently unfavorable, but potatoes and turnips have been grown here in small patches.

Opening and closing of the river. The Liard River is here said to open, as a rule, from the 1st to the 5th of May, though in 1887 this did not occur till the 18th of that month. In the autumn of 1886 it was frozen over on November 21st.

Mr. Egnell, in sole charge, received us on our arrival here with all distinction possible, displaying his Union Jack and firing a salute from his fowling piece. Before leaving we were indebted to him for many other courtesies, all of which are here gratefully acknowledged.

Geology of the Dease River.

Rocks west of granite range. It would be impossible, without the expenditure of much time, to make anything like a complete geological section on the line of the Dease, in consequence of the infrequency of rock-exposures on the river itself and the distance and rough character of the bordering mountain-slopes. The main geological features are, however, sufficiently apparent. For about twelve miles below the lake the rocks composing the mountains seem to be referable to the same Palæozoic series, which has been described as occurring on Dease Lake, but the exposures examined appeared to be somewhat more highly altered, and in some cases to approach the character of crystalline schists. One bedded rock is probably a diabase, with somewhat lustrous division planes and kernels of epidote.

Granitic rocks of Cassiar Mountains. Beyond the point above defined, at the first little lake, a granitic area is entered on, which may be regarded as constituting the axis of the Cassiar range, and which extends on the river to the mouth of the Cottonwood, constituting the entire Skroe Range, and apparently also Anvil Mountain and the surrounding high mountain region, with a tranverse width of about thirteen miles. The granite here seen differs somewhat from that found on the Stikine in being more highly quartzose and occasionally garnetiferous. Mica is present in great abundance, and is in some specimens black, in others of characteristic pale, silvery colours. The existence of distinctly gneissic rocks was not ascertained, but the lithological character of the series resembles that of the lowest rocks of Shuswap Lake and other districts in the interior of British Columbia to the south, which have been provisionally referred to the Archæan.

East edge of granites. The valley of Cottonwood Creek appears to coincide with the northeastern edge of the granites for a number of miles. The mountains to

the north of it, and extending eastward along the north side of the
Dease, are evidently composed of stratified rocks, including important
beds of limestone, the average dip being about N. 45° E. < 30°.   The
northern spur of the mountain which terminates the Skree Range,
opposite the mouth of Cottonwood Creek, shows the overlap of the
stratified rocks upon the granites at a considerable height above the
river.   The mountains which run southward on both sides of Eagle
River valley seem to be also granitic for the most part, though a
greenish-grey felsite was collected on the river from the northern spur
of the mountain to the east of the valley.

Little was ascertained respecting the rocks composing the mountains between Eagle River and Sylvester's Landing, but granite does not
reappear in them.   The range to the east of McDame Creek is largely
composed of limestone, which, striking in a north-west and south-east
direction, constitutes also the mountains on the south side of the Dease.
The dip is generally westward, at varying angles, and the limestones
are associated with reddish shales, and near the mouth of Rapid River
were observed to be interbedded with dolomitic layers and calcareous
schists.   The total thickness of the strata brought to the surface along
this part of the river must be very considerable.   The lithological
resemblance is close to the upper part of the Palæozoic section on the
Bow Pass, including the Banff, Intermediate and Castle Mountain
limestones of Mr. McConnell (Annual Report, 1886, part D).   Limestones near the western or upper part of the river-section contain
numerous obscure fossils, including brachiopods, corals, and apparently
a sponge-like organism.   I also satisfied myself of the occurrence of
Fusulina on weathered surfaces, proving the Carboniferous age of the
rocks in question.   The pure limestones are usually grey and are
not highly crystalline.

The mountains bordering the valley in the north-and-south part of
its course, between the first and second great bends, appear to be composed throughout of similar rocks, though those on the west side are
much better exposed than those on the east.

Eleven miles south of the second great bend, on the right bank of
the river, is a low, rocky cliff, about fifteen feet above the water,
capped by about ten feet of bedded white silts.   The rocks are blackish, sandy shales, rather hard in some places, carbonaceous, and holding a little impure lignite.   They are extremely irregular in dip, and
are broken and jumbled up with a hard, grey quartzite, which is seen
in places as the underlying rock, but is even then singularly shattered.
The aspect of the shales is that of those of the Tertiary rocks, and it
is possible that this locality represents an old shore-line, but more probable that the rocks form part of an ancient slide, or are upon the line
of disturbance of a fault.

At the second great bend there are a few exposures of a peculiar character, consisting of regularly bedded, dark, calcareous, flaggy argillites, alternating with grey, flaggy and massive limestones. Lithologically, these much resemble the Triassic of the West Coast, but no fossils could be found, though carefully sought for, and the evidence is quite too imperfect for the reference of the beds. The limestone is rather cherty, and gives out a fetid odor on being struck. The beds, as a whole, appear to form a synclinal.

From the second great bend to the mouth of the Dease, the underlying rocks consist of grey and black schists, the former generally calc-schists, and the latter more or less highly carbonaceous. They are interbedded with thin limestones, which often weather brown. The calc-schists are frequently glossy, and in some places form very thin, paper-like layers. Some of these rocks closely resemble those met with at the " Grand Rapid " on the Stikine p. 55 B. The general strike is north-west by south-east, but the direction and angle of dip is very varied, and the beds are frequently much disturbed and twisted, and traversed by veins of quartz and calcite. There are probably frequent repetitions of the same horizon, but the general arrangement may be synclinal, the dark shales and schists occupying the higher position, and being most abundant about the middle of this length of the river-section. Graptolites were found in the dark shales, particularly at a locality in a north bend of the river, eleven miles westward in a direct line from the mouth, and in appearance the whole series is much like that of the Cambrian calc-schists and Cambro-Silurian graptolite-shales of the Kicking Horse (Wapta) valley, west of the summit, on the line of the Canadian Pacific Railway.

The general aspect and association of the rocks to the east of the granite axis of the Cassiar Range closely resembles that of the Rocky Mountains about the 51st parallel, but differs in the large proportion of metamorphic materials of volcanic origin, which, from the *débris* brought down by streams, must be even more abundant than the exposures along the river would indicate. This difference is paralleled by the similar change which is met with on the 51st degree of latitude, in passing from the Rocky Mountains proper to the interior plateau of British Columbia.

A small collection of graptolites, made at the point above indicated, has been submitted by Mr. J. F. Whiteaves to Prof. Charles Lapworth, of Mason College, Birmingham, who has kindly examined them, and furnishes the following note.—

"The graptolites collected by Dr. Dawson from the Dease River are identical with those examined by me from the rocks of the Kicking Horse Pass, some time last year. The species I notice in the Dease River collection are :—

> *Diplograptus euglyphus* (Lapworth).
> *Climacograptus,* comp. *antiquus* (Lapworth).
> *Cryptograptus tricornis* (Carruthers).
> *Glossograptus ciliatus* (Emmons).
> *Didymograptus,* comp. *sagittarius* (Hall).
> New form allied to *Cænograptus.*

"The graptolite-bearing rocks are clearly of about middle Ordovician age. They contain forms which I would refer to the second or Black River Trenton period, *i.e.,* they are newer than the Point Levis series and older than the Hudson and Utica groups. The association of forms is such as we find in Britain and Western Europe, in the passage-beds between the Llandeilo and Caradoc limestones. The rocks in Canada and New York with which these Dease River beds may best be compared are the Marsouin beds of the St. Lawrence valley and the Norman's Kill beds of New York. The Dease River beds may, perhaps, be a little older than these. {.marginal}

" Mr. C. White described some graptolites from beds in the mountain region of the west, several years ago, which may belong to the same horizon as the Dease River zones, though they have a somewhat more recent aspect.

"The specific identification of the Dease River fossils I regard as provisional. While the species correspond broadly with those found in their eastern equivalents, they have certain peculiarities, which may, after further study or on the discovery of better or more perfect specimens, lead to their separation as distinct species or varieties.

" It is exceedingly interesting to find graptolites in a region so far removed from the Atlantic basin, and also to note that the typical association of Llandeilo-Bala genera and species is still retained practically unmodified."

Overlying these old rocks, in several places at about eight miles from the mouth of the Dease, are shaly clays and coarse, soft sandstones, associated with which a thin bed of lignite was observed. These are evidently Tertiary, and referable to the series afterwards found more extensively developed on the Liard, above the mouth of the Dease. Some very obscure remains of leaves were noticed, but none were collected. The beds dip at various angles, sometimes as high as 15°, and thus appear to have been, to some extent, affected by flexure subsequent to their deposition. It is not improbable that a considerable part of the higher plateau by which the river is here bordered on both sides, is composed of these newer rocks resting upon the upturned edges of the schists.

Drift deposits and terraces.   Some notes respecting the superficial geology of the Dease have already been given in connection with the general description of the river. It now only remains to add the following general observations.

The scarped banks along the upper part of the river, to the first great bend, generally show stratified sands and gravels only, all or most of which may be classed as old river-gravels. Between the first and second great bends, well-bedded, yellowish-white silts appear and are frequently exposed. The bedding is sometimes inclined and large boulders are occasionally enveloped in the silts, which are in some places seen to rest upon and pass into true boulder-clay, while they are generally capped by a variable thickness of stratified gravels. The silts, occasionally, rest directly upon the underlying rocks, and in other places have been removed, so that the gravels lie upon the boulder-clay or upon the underlying rocks. Below the second great bend, the silts still occur, but are not so important, being largely replaced by stratified sands and gravels. The approximate level of the highest observed beds of the silt formation may be stated at 2400 feet above the sea. The highest observed terraces on the sides of the mountains have an estimated elevation of about 4600 feet. Glaciated rock-surfaces were observed in a single locality, a few miles below the mouth of McDame Creek. They appeared to indicate a flow of ice eastward or down the valley, but were not sufficiently distinct to afford completely satisfactory evidence on this point.

UPPER LIARD RIVER.

Proceedings at mouth of Dease.   We arrived at the little post at the mouth of the Dease on June 23rd, in rain, which continued during the whole of the next day, rendering it impossible to obtain observations, which were here necessary. On the morning of the 25th, however, I secured a fair series of observations, and having completed such arrangements as we had to make before entering the entirely untravelled country to the north, left the same afternoon. Mr. McConnell was here detached with two men and a boat for the examination of the Lower Liard. We had arranged that a couple of local Indians should accompany each party for the purpose of assisting at portages and acting as guides, but those who went with us deserted after a few days, and we afterwards learned that Mr. McConnell's Indians behaved in the same manner.

Country near the confluence.   The country about the confluence of the Dease and Liard is low and uniform, rising from the rivers in a series of more or less regular terraces, to a plateau 400 feet or more above the water-level, or approximately 2500 feet above the sea. The extent of this low country is considerable.

The name of the Liard River, or Rivière aux Liards, refers to the abundance of the cottonwood or poplar, and was no doubt originally given to its lower portion. This name has been corrupted to "Deloire," in which form it is generally in use by the miners of the Cassiar country. It is often spoken of as the West Branch by traders on the Mackenzie, and has also been named the Mountain River, and sometimes the Great Current River or Courant-fort. It is called Too-ti' by the Indians of the country along its upper part, while, according to Petitot, the Indians nearer the Mackenzie name it Eréttchichié and Thétta-désse.*

The Liard River, though one of the principal affluents of the great Mackenzie, has remained up to the present time practically unknown, or at least undescribed, though sketched from observations by officers of the Hudson Bay Company on Arrowsmith's maps, and copied from those on other maps. It has long been in use as an avenue of communication by the Company, but since the abandonment of the posts to the west of the Rocky Mountains, its upper part has been traversed only at rare intervals, by a few prospectors and miners from the Cassiar district. With Mr. McConnell's work on the lower part of the river, and the examination of its upper part here reported on, we now have a survey extending from Fort Simpson, at its mouth, to one of its furthest sources, in Finlayson Lake.

This river and the Frances appear to have been ascended by McLeod, about 1834, as far as Simpson Lake, but in 1840 Mr. R. Campbell explored the same route to Frances and Finlayson Lakes (as subsequently mentioned in greater detail), and obtained the most accurate geographical information available to the present time. Sir J. Richardson, however, in his Arctic Searching Expedition (1851) gives such particulars of the Liard as he was able to gather from hearsay (Vol. I, p. 167; II, p. 203), and mentions having received in 1848, while on the Mackenzie, Honolulu papers of late date by this route from the Pacific. On the older maps, the Black or Turnagain River is designated as the main continuation of the Liard, but it is much smaller than the "North-west Branch" of these maps, to which the name is now applied. In the present report that part of this branch above the confluence of the Dease is, for purposes of description, distinguished as the Upper Liard.

The Upper Liard, just above the mouth of the Dease and opposite the post previously referred to, is 840 feet in width, and on the 24th of June 1887 was found to have a maximum velocity of 4·54 miles per hour. The river was not cross-sectioned, but, with an estimated depth of six feet for one-third of its width, the quantity of water car-

---

* Bulletin de la Société de Géographie, vol. x, p. 152.

7

ried would amount to about 19,000 cubic feet per second.* This may be regarded as a rough approximation for the mean stage of the river, which, when in flood, probably carries at least double this volume of water. It is a turbid yellowish stream, and contrasts in this respect with the clearer water of the Dease, which river, at its confluence with the Liard, probably carries about half the volume of water above assigned to the latter.

Character of Liard and Frances Rivers. From the mouth of the Dease River to the confluence of the Frances River, the general bearing of the Liard is nearly due north-west, the distance, in a straight line, being thirty-three miles, or following the course of the river, forty-five miles. The Frances River, which was followed from the last-named point, disregarding its minor flexures, has a nearly direct north-and-south course. A straight line drawn from the mouth of the Dease to the lower end of Frances Lake is ninety-four miles in length, but the distance between these points, following the flexures of the river, is one hundred and thirty-five miles. Almost every foot of this distance had to be made by poling or tracking against the rapid stream, and as our boats were heavily laden and not as well suited in build as they might have been for the work, the ascent to Frances Lake occupied twelve days, or an average distance of about eleven miles a day only. As the river was entirely unknown to us and some time was unavoidably lost in reconnoitering rapids and selecting portages, besides the delays incident to surveying work and geological examination, I believe, that with a good boat and crew, the ascent to the lake might be made in about half the above time at the same stage of water. In very high water it would be extremely difficult to pass through some parts of the cañons, while at exceptionally low stages of water, when it would be possible to substitute tracking for poling in many places, the distance might be accomplished in even less time.

Lower Cañon. Six miles above the mouth of the Dease, by the course of the river, the entrance of the *Lower Cañon* is reached. The full height of the plateau through which the river here cuts, is about 500 feet, but banks of this height seldom abut directly on the river. The upper parts of these banks are composed of stratified sands and gravels, but the lower part of the gorge is cut through shaly and slaty rocks, which are perpendicular or form very steep slopes, averaging about a hundred feet in height. The cañon is three miles in length, and at high water it is said to be necessary to portage the whole of this distance. We were obliged to lighten the boats and make four small portages over rocky points, where the current was dangerously swift. The latitude,

---

* Estimated by approximate formula, Trautwine's Engineers' Pocket-book, 1882, p. 562. The depth above assigned to the river is probably too small.

observed at noon near the middle of the cañon, was 60° 01′ 06″. Find-ing that we were so near the northern boundary of British Columbia (Lat. 60°), we made a small cairn of stones on a prominent rocky point, in the centre of which a post was erected, on which the latitude was marked. The 60th parallel may be said to coincide almost exactly with the lower end of the cañon.

The rocks seen in the Lower Cañon resemble those described as cha-racterizing the lower part of the Dease River and Dease Lake, being shales or schists, which in some places show slaty structure. They are generally dark with plumbaginous matter. With these are associated grey, somewhat glossy schists, and calcareous schists which pass in some places into pretty pure, thin-bedded limestones. Quartzites are also present, and all the rocks are occasionally locally silicified. The whole series is much disturbed and contorted, and is broken by innu-merable small, irregular seams and veins of quartz and calcite, with some dolomite, though no well-marked or important lodes were seen. Galena is reported to have been found in some of the veins, and to have yielded a small return in silver on assay. *Rocks of Lower Cañon.*

Above the Lower Cañon the river continues swift, the current aver-aging about four miles an hour, and much exceeding this rate in many reaches. It is wide and shallow, and in places becomes a complete maze of islands and gravelly, half-submerged bars, causing much diffi-culty and loss of time from the frequent necessity of crossing from one to another of these to avoid under-cut banks, with water too deep for poling. Our actual travelling time from the Dease to the mouth of the Frances, deducting all stoppages, was thirty-eight hours and a-quarter. *River from Cañon to Frances.*

The river-valley averages about two miles in width, and is cut out to a depth of 300 feet or more in the plateau, which occasionally rises directly from the river-bank to its full height, though the stream is usually bordered by terraces of inferior height, alternating with low flats, which occupy the concave sides of the bends. The higher ground is generally wooded with spruce, while the black pine (*Pinus Murrayana*) is abundant on dry terraces, and groves of cottonwood of medium size often occur on the flats. Aspen poplar is not uncommon, and a few birch and larch trees were seen. Little of the timber is of useful size or quality. The dry bars and gravelly flats were, when we passed, gay with *Epilobium latifolium, Oxytropis campestris, O. Lamberti* and *Dryas Drummondii,* and the wild roses were rapidly coming into flower.

About midway between the Dease and Frances a small river enters from the south-westward, which has been called the Rancheria River, but of which I do not know the native name. It appears to debouch by several mouths when in flood, and apparently rises in the eastern *Rancheria River.*

slopes of the Cassiar Range. A few miles above this, on the opposite side of the river, a small lake, reputed to be well stocked with fish, is reported. About seven miles below the mouth of the Frances, on the south west bank, is an old Indian camping place, which is said to be frequented at certain seasons by the Tahl-tan Indians for purposes of trade. It is reached by these people by some overland route which crosses the Cassiar Mountains to the north of the Dease River.

Confluence of Liard and Frances.

The Liard is full of islands at its confluence with the Frances, rendering it difficult to estimate the relative importance of the two streams, but they appeared to carry about an equal quantity of water. The Liard is, however, evidently more subject to freshets; Frances Lake doubtless serving to regulate the flow of the Frances River, the water of which is a clear, pale, amber color, and does not thoroughly mingle with the yellowish, turbid water of the Liard for some miles. Above the confluence, the Liard valley is seen to trend off in a south-westerly direction for ten miles or more, after which it again turns to the north-westward, and, from the scanty information available concerning it, seems to flow along the eastern side of the northern continuation of the Cassiar Range, from which it receives most of its water.

Sayyea Creek.

On comparing the statements of the few miners I have seen who have ascended this river, it appears that Sayyea Creek, which is an inconsiderable stream, flows in from the west about fifty-five miles above the mouth of the Frances. Good gold "prospects" were found on this creek in 1875, a number of pieces worth ten dollars having been obtained, but little work has ever been done. Of a party of miners who spent the winter of 1874-75 in its vicinity four died of scurvy. Of the other tributaries of the Liard, which must be numerous, I have been unable to ascertain anything authentic.

Names of Liard and Frances Rivers.

Respecting the names of the Liard and Frances rivers, it should be mentioned that Campbell called that which is now known as the Liard the "Bell River," after Mr. J. Bell, of the Hudson Bay Company. Under this designation it appears on Arrowsmith's map of 1854, the name Liard being applied to the branch now known as the Frances. Usage has, however, changed the first nomenclature, and it is undesirable to attempt to revert to the original names, as, irrespective of the question of relative size, the physical characteristics of the Liard below the confluence are undoubtedly continued on the west rather than on the east branch above that point. The Indian name of the Frances is identical with that of the Dease, being Too-tsho-toon', or "Big Lake River."

Rocks above the Cañon.

Rocks like those of the Lower Cañon are seen at intervals for about two miles above its head, beyond which, for about three miles, stratified gravels and sands only appear in the banks. Six miles from the cañon

Tertiary clays of whitish and grey colours, and associated with impure
lignite, are first met with, and these continue to appear here and there
along the river as far as the Frances. The thickest bed of lignite Lignite.
observed was about three feet, four miles below the Frances. The
lignite is generally impure and often very distinctly laminated. It
resembles in character the lignites of the Miocene of British Columbia,
and the associated clays and soft shales are similar in character to
those of that formation. Numerous boulders of basalt are found along Basalt.
this part of the river, and the basalt was observed to form a mural
cliff, at a height of about 300 feet above the river, at a place just
below the mouth of the Rancheria River. This rock evidently overlies the lignite-bearing beds. The shaly clays and lignites show evidence of considerable disturbance, and dip in some places at rather
high angles. This may be due to the action of old land-slides along
the banks of the river, but appears to be rather too constant to be
satisfactorily accounted for in this way.

Near the mouth of the Frances the white silts again become a pro- White silts.
minent feature, though scarcely seen lower down the river. They
overlie the Tertiary rocks and hold concretions of various forms here
and there. They are capped by the usual stratified sands and gravels,
which generally have a yellowish or rusty colour.

The gravel bars and the shores of this part of the Liard are almost Gold.
half composed of rolled quartz pebbles, which have evidently been
derived from veins traversing relatively soft schistose rocks like those
of the cañon. The great quantity of such vein material present in this
district may be regarded as a favorable indication in respect to mineral
development. Some small bars have paid to work along this part of
the river, and gold is also found in some layers of the gravel deposit
which overlies the older rocks along the cañon and above it, where
" wages " at $4 a day can be made. The amount of cover which it
soon becomes necessary to remove in following the paying layers,
has prevented extensive mining, but probably these gravels might be
advantageously worked as a whole, by sluicing or by the hydraulic
method.

No general view of the country can be obtained from the river, General
owing to woods and the depth of the valley, but from high points of appearance of
banks above the river, near the Frances, a large area may be over- the country.
looked. Thus seen, the country is found to be a wide, rolling plateau,
with an average elevation of about 500 feet above the river, or say
2700 feet above the sea. It rises here and there, however, in broad,
rounded swells, or flat-topped higher plateaux with steep edges, and a
considerable part of this higher ground is at an elevation of about
1000 feet above the river. The plateau is everywhere wooded, except

where intersected by grassy or mossy swamps of small area. There is a large triangular region of country of this kind between the Upper Liard and Dease, which is bounded to the westward by the front of the Cassiar Range, the sharp, rocky peaks of which carry a considerable quantity of snow and run along the horizon line for many miles, but which, with the exception of a few outlying summits, is at a minimum distance of about twenty-five miles from the mouth of the Frances. The same low country runs in a north-north-westward direction, without apparent limit, forming the upper part of the Liard valley. To the eastward it is bounded, at a distance of about ten miles, by a comparatively low range of rounded mountains and hills, which, from the Indian name of one of its salient points to the northward, may be called the *Tses-i-uh Range*. The part of this range nearest to the confluence of the Frances and Liard has an elevation estimated at about 3500 feet above the sea. Like other main features of the country, it runs in a north-north-west by south-south-east direction, but dies out completely before reaching the Upper Liard River, which, if continued, it would do at the Lower Cañon. It is probable, indeed, that the cañon is produced by the river cutting across the extension of the same ridge of rocks which produces these hills. The general uniformity of the plateau appears to be largely due to the Tertiary rocks, which doubtless underlie almost its entire area. The appearance of some of the flat-topped hills above alluded to is suggestive of the occurrence of sheets of basalt overlying the softer rocks. The forms of the Tses-I-uh Mountains show that they are not thus composed, but Tertiary rocks may again occur beyond them, in the valley of the McPherson or Highland River, which is not far off.

Cassiar Range.

Mountains to the east.

Tertiary plateau.

FRANCES RIVER.

Mouth of Frances to Middle Cañon.

The general direction of the Frances, for nine miles from its mouth, is north-north-west. It then bends to the north-eastward, and in four miles the lower end of the Middle Cañon is reached. For the first few miles above its mouth the Frances is extremely tortuous, so much so that the distance following the actual course of the river to the foot of the cañon is twenty-two miles. This river, like the Liard, was at a medium stage near the end of June, 1887. Marks along the banks showed that it had been about six feet higher in the spring, and that it had since been falling. Its average width in this part is about 600 feet, and the rate of the current, at the medium stage above referred to, about four miles and a-half an hour.

Terrace.

The highest land immediately bordering on this part of the river is a terrace at a height of about 150 feet above it, the surface of which is in some places composed of almost pure sand, upon which open woods of *Pinus Murrayana* grow. Larch was observed to be moderately abundant in damp, shady localities and the banks were in some places diversified with flowers, of which *Potentilla fruticosa* and *Primula mistassinica* were specially noted.

Numerous small exposures of Tertiary shales and clays, of grey, blackish and yellowish tints, occur along this part of the river. Lignite is strewn in great quantities over some of the bars, and though thin seams occur in places in the banks, it is probable that thicker ones exist in the bed of the river. The lignite often holds drops of fossil resin or amber. The Tertiary rocks are very generally covered by silts, like those already several times alluded to. In a bank near the mouth of the river, which gives a complete section from the top of the terrace above described, the lowest deposit consists of roughly stratified gravel and clay, with some glaciated boulders. This is followed by the silts, which are again in turn covered by stratified sands and gravels. The lowest deposit probably represents the boulder-clay, and resembles that of the Upper Pelly River, subsequently described. *Exposures in the banks.*

Quartz is not so abundant a constituent of the gravel of the river-bars on this part of the Frances as it is on the Liard below, and no basalt blocks or boulders were observed here.

The *Middle Cañon*, as it may be called for the purpose of distinguishing it, is about three miles in length, the river being hemmed in by broken, rocky cliffs of 200 to 300 feet in height for the greater part of this distance. We took our boats up along the south-east bank, making four short portages of part of the stuff, and two of both boats and load, across narrow, rocky points. One portage of greater length, on the opposite bank, would overcome all the really bad water, but the banks on that side are rougher, and the whole force of the current sets against the cliff in one place in a dangerous manner. The total fall in the cañon is estimated at about thirty feet. *Middle Cañon.*

This cañon is evidently produced by the southern extremity of a second range of mountains parallel to the Tses-ı̄-uh Mountains, but to the west of that range. This southern spur, though submerged in the Tertiary and drift materials by which the general surface of the country is covered, nevertheless presents a rocky barrier to the passage of the river, and in this place constitutes the eastern margin of the Tertiary basin, no beds referable to which are seen further up the Frances. The range of mountains here referred to may, for convenience, be named the *Simpson Mountains*.

The exposures in the lower part of this cañon show limestones, some of which are moderately pure, but others are nearly half composed of small, more or less rounded fragments of siliceous and schistose rocks. *Rocks of the Cañon.*

These weather to rough surfaces, and have a very peculiar aspect, as an intense pressure appears to have flattened the contained fragments parallel to a single direction. These limestones are associated with several varieties of calc-schists, with hard, greyish-blue, cherty quartzite, with schistose breccia, which appears to have been originally of volcanic origin, and with some pretty evident volcanic agglomerate. Further up, the rocks have been completely shattered and variously changed in appearance by solfataric or some similar action, some parts being bleached, while others are reddened by the deposition of iron, forming cliffs of a remarkably varied appearance. The upper gate of the cañon is composed of white cliffs of marble and quartzite, all much shattered. The marble and limestones are in places associated with red shales, resembling those found in a similar association on the Dease, near the eastern edge of the Cassiar Range, and the rocks of this part of the section are probably like those, of Carboniferous age. Specimens of *Fusulina*, with polyzoa, etc., are found in some of the limestones on microscopical examination. Stratigraphically, the rocks seen in the sections are all much confused and broken, and the angles of dip are very varied, though the strike may, in a general way, be given as north-north-west. The Simpson Mountains which are upon this line of strike are doubtless composed of rocks of the same character.

Above the Middle Cañon, the general course of the river is again north-north-westward for about twelve miles. It is here usually bordered by quite low land on both sides, and the valley between the southern end of the Simpson Mountains and northern part of the Tses-i-uh Range is about three miles in width. The wide, uniform plateau country is now, however, left behind, and we enter a generally mountainous region, though the highest summits in this immediate vicinity scarcely exceed 3000 feet above the river. Their forms are rather rounded and flowing, and the slopes of those on the east bank are nearly bare of trees, while the opposite range is generally wooded, but evidently with trees of small growth. The river itself is wide and deep, with a rather slack current. A single exposure only, composed of grey-green, silvery schist, was seen along this part of the river.

Near the end of this reach of the river, two considerable streams enter on the west side, and on one or other of these, at no great distance from the river, Simpson Lake of McLeod and Campbell is situated. As the Indians who had accompanied us from the mouth of the Dease had deserted before we reached this place, I was unable to ascertain any definite particulars respecting the lake, though it is reported to be a good one for fish. The position of Simpson Lake, as indicated by broken lines on the map, must therefore be regarded as quite uncertain. The same doubt applies to the Indian names of several rivers tributary to the Frances above this point, for although Tributaries of
the Frances. one of the local Indians had made for us, upon a sheet of canvas used as a boat cover, an elaborate charcoal drawing of the whole system, it proved to be extremely difficult to recognize the features represented. The Indian map, such as it is, serves to show that the streams tributary to the Frances River rise in a number of lakes, some of which are reported to be of considerable size, and offer a most attractive field for further exploration. We were told, however, that none of the lakes in this region are equal in size to Frances Lake, for which we were heading, a statement borne out by the circumstance that both this and Dease Lake are known in their respective districts as Too-tsho, or "big lake," while the Frances and Dease rivers are, as already mentioned, both similarly named Too-tsho-tooa', or "big lake river."

From the point just noted, the direction of the river changes to north-east, cutting across the direction of the Tses-I-uh range, which terminates at the edge of the river in low, wooded hills. The current is moderately swift throughout, and in one place the river is bordered False Cañon. on both sides by low, rocky banks, but no rapids are met with. This we named the *False Cañon.* One or possibly two streams enter from a valley which runs to the east of the range just mentioned, but they are not of large size. Greyish-green, quartzose mica-schist and greenish silvery schists were seen in one or two places, and in the low rocky banks above alluded to, blackish argillites and grey quartzites, of a less altered appearance than usual, but from which no fossils were obtained, occur.

From the end of this reach the general course of the stream again be- River above
False Cañon. comes north-north-west for about thirteen miles, running for the greater part of this distance parallel to, and a mile or two miles from the base of a mountain range, which comes in to the east of the Tses-I-uh Range. The country to the west of the river is here either flat or characterized merely by low, rounded and wooded hills for many miles back, the eye ranging across this country to the continuation of the Simpson Mountains, which, with generally rounded forms and no striking summits, reach elevations of 6000 to 6500 feet. These mountains do not form a strictly connected range, but appear rather as a series of mountainous areas, separated by wide, low passes. The Indian map above referred to shows three or four lakes in this region, supplying a Lakes. stream named *Too-tshi-too-a*, which flows into the Frances, reaching it probably just above the Upper Cañon. None of these lakes were visible from any point reached by us. On the opposite side, one stream of considerable size joins the Frances. This is supposed to be the *Agä-zĭ-za* of the Indians, and, if so, is represented as rising in a chain of small lakes, some of which drain in an easterly direction to the Macpherson (*Eg-is-e-too'-a*) River. The valley occupied by these lakes is a travelled route employed by the Indians.

Granitic rocks. The current is swifter in the upper than in the lower portion of this part of the Frances, and there are numerous islands in the river, but no rock-exposures occur. The mountains to the east of the river are high, but have blunt, rounded forms. Much bare rock shows in their sides, but there is no appearance of stratification, and this, with their form and color, and the great abundance of that material found in the streams in this vicinity, renders it nearly certain that they are composed of granite.

Character of the mountains. The mountains so far met with in the vicinity of the Frances form rather isolated ranges or masses, which rise somewhat abruptly from generally low country, or are separated by wide valleys, the appearance being that of a mountain system partly buried in later deposits; though no Tertiary rocks, either in place or as loose fragments, are met with above the Middle Cañon. The granitic mountains last referred to form an outlying spur or buttress of the most important range of the district, the axis of which is here about twelve miles east of the river. This it is proposed to designate the *Too-tsho Range.** The southernmost high summit observed was named, from its form, *Tent Peak*. It is situated in latitude 60° 52' 45", and has an altitude of 7860 feet above the sea.

Upper Cañon. The river next makes an abrupt turn to the west for four miles, a mile and a-quarter of this distance being occupied by a series of rapids, which are rocky and rather strong, and have a total fall of about thirty feet. The banks rise steeply from the river to heights of 100 to 200 feet, though the rocky cliffs along the water are of inconsiderable height, scarcely anywhere exceeding fifty feet. This place may be named the *Upper Cañon*, and is the last serious impediment to the navigation of the river. We found it necessary to make several short portages, but with a large boat and at a good stage of the river, it is probable that one portage of about 1000 feet in length, on the south bank, would overcome all the dangerous water, while the boat might be tracked up light. A stream, with moderate current at the mouth and about fifty feet wide, enters a short distance below the cañon, coming from the mountains to the north of Tent Peak. The rocks of

Rocks of Upper Cañon. the Upper Cañon comprise black, glossy calc-schists, black quartzite or chert, bluish limestone, and some green-grey, silvery schist. Similar rocks are seen again a couple of miles up the river, above the cañon, where a rapid occurs. The dips are all low, and so far as observed, uniformly in a northerly direction. Some of the schists are highly

---

* From the native name of Frances Lake. I was unable to ascertain the Indian name of this range, if indeed it has any such.

silicified by action subsequent to their deposition, and parts of all the rocks, including the limestone, are reticulated with narrow quartz seams. Near the upper part of the cañon some hard conglomerates occur, holding schistose fragments, as well as limestone pebbles, in which crinoidal joints are observable. It is not improbable that two unconformable series of rocks occur here, but I was unable to find means of distinguishing them in the sections.*

From the Upper Cañon to Frances Lake, a distance of twenty-one miles and a-half in a straight line, the river maintains a northerly direction with considerable uniformity. It is deep, with a moderate current, for about eight miles, or to *Moose Island*, above which for ten miles the current is again swift, averaging from four and a-half miles to five miles an hour. It again becomes slack for a short distance below the lake. Some portions of this part of the river are much broken up by islands and gravel bars. The river-valley averages about ten miles in width, extending to the slopes of the Too-tsho Range on the east, and being bounded to the westward by a series of rounded mountains, which diverge to the northward from the direction of the first-mentioned range, and run to the west of Frances Lake. These I propose to name the *Campbell Mountains*, for Mr. R. Campbell, whose initial exploratary trip through this country for the Hudson Bay Company is elsewhere referred to at length. Upper Cañon to Frances Lake.

The valley is partly occupied by terrace-flats, and partly by wooded hills or ridges with rounded or flowing forms but which rise in some places to heights of several hundred feet. The Too-tsho Range is here very compact and regular, and runs due north-and-south, the higher summits reaching 6500 to 7000 feet, and carrying some snow, though nothing like true glacier-ice was anywhere seen. The lower slopes of the range toward the river-valley are singularly uniform and light. Two or three streams of some size enter the river from the eastward in this part of its course. All that could be gathered respecting these is shown on the map. The furthest north was named Tyer's River by Campbell, and is known to the Indians as *Pas-ka'*. The exact position of its mouth was not definitely ascertained. Too-tsho Range

On approaching the lake, low ridges and irregular mounds begin to appear in the vicinity of the river, projecting through the lower terraces and suggesting the existence of morainic deposits. Large boulders also become abundant in the river-bed. No rock-exposures whatever were seen along this part of the river. Morainic ridges.

Our actual working time on Frances River, from its mouth to the lake, was sixty-seven hours and a-half. The difference of level between Travelling time on Frances River.

---

* If so, the rocks here noted may represent the Cretaceous to which they are lithologically similar.

Frances Lake and the mouth of the Dease is 477 feet. By assigning ninety feet of this to the fall in the three cañons, and dividing the remainder by the total length of the river (less the aggregate length of the cañons), we obtain an average rate of descent very slightly exceeding three feet to the mile, which is about what might be anticipated from the current met with in the river, as compared to that of other streams in the district.

FRANCES LAKE AND VICINITY.

Frances Lake. The elevation of Frances Lake above the sea, as determined by a series of barometer observations extending from the 8th to the 16th of July, is 2577 feet. Three miles from its lower end, the lake bifurcates, forming two approximately equal and nearly parallel arms, with lengths of about thirty miles. The two arms are about eight miles apart, and are separated by a group of low, rounded mountains, the culminating point of which, with an elevation of 5230 feet, was named Simpson's Tower by Campbell, the lake itself receiving its name at the same time in honour of Lady Simpson. The eastern side of its east arm is bordered by the Too-tsho Range or hills attached to it, while the country to the west of the west arm rises more gradually to the bases of the Campbell Mountains, some miles distant. Though so far referred to as a single lake, this body of water is in reality entitled to be considered as a group of lakes. The upper end of the west arm, with a length of five miles and a-half, is separated from the main portion of the same arm by a river-like constriction over a mile in length, while the east arm is entered by a narrow and inconspicuous opening with a strong current flowing out, and the real extent of this arm is seen only after passing, for about seven miles, through a series of irregular basins and small lake-like expansions connected by narrows, in which a very perceptible current is found. It appears best, however, to retain Campbell's original name for the whole body of water, rather than to multiply names for which there is no immediate call.

Character of its valley. Except in its bifid form, for which there are several parallels, and which results merely from the convergence of two valleys of similar character, Frances Lake closely resembles a large number of lakes in the mountainous regions of British Columbia, and has the long narrow parallel-sided outline characteristic of lakes which occupy old valley-excavations, the drainage of which has become interrupted in various ways. In this case, as in a number of others, there can be little doubt, that the lake is held in by morainic accumulations. The great number of boulders near its outlet has already been referred to, and the lumpy, irregular mounds and ridges composed of detrital matter, on the lower

seven miles of the east arm, as well as on the corresponding portion of
the west arm, appear without doubt to represent moraines in a
more or less degraded condition. The average width of the upper portions of both arms, above these interruptions, is pretty uniformly maintained at about a mile and a-half, such irregularities as occur being
produced by gravelly and sandy flats a few feet above the water-level,
which have been formed at the mouths of entering streams. The
extent and uniformity of these points, is such as to show that the lake
must have remained, during a long period, approximately at its present
level. The most important of these low points is that which separates
the upper part of the west arm, already referred to, and is due to the
Finlayson River.* The next is produced by a second stream which
enters on the same side five miles and a-half below. This stream is
somewhat smaller than the Finlayson, and is known to the Indians as
the *Il-es-too'-a.*

Except along the upper part of the eastern side of the east arm, the
mountains do not slope down abruptly to the shores of the lake. Elsewhere, the lake is almost continuously bordered by a terrace-like plateau,
which is widest to the west, and has an average elevation of about
300 feet. This resembles the low country found about Dease Lake,
though even more uniform and less sloping in character, and is not far
from the same actual elevation above the sea in both cases. The
streams entering the lake generally cut down through the edges of this
plateau-like margin, in deep narrow gorges, the sections in which show
that it is composed largely of rock, though levelled up to some extent
by the addition of superficial gravelly deposits. This fact appears
to indicate that the lake or the drainage level of the country was
maintained for a very prolonged period at or near the height of this
plateau before the base-level of erosion was so lowered as to permit
of the excavation of the lower valleys in which the lake now lies. There
is, in addition to this, a second lower terrace, not so well marked, and
not often of great width, at an elevation of ninety feet above the lake.
This is seen on both arms, and is composed of gravel and other detrital
deposits. It is specially conspicuous about the mouths of the entering
streams, and marks a later stage at which the water of the lake stood,
for a relatively short time, subsequent to the glacial period.

Few lakes which I have seen surpass Frances Lake in natural beauty,
and the scenery of the east arm, bordered on the east by the rugged
masses of the Too-tsho Range, is singularly striking. The mountains of
this range are very varied in form, and a number of points surpass
7000 feet in height, while one was found to attain an elevation of about

---

* So named by Campbell after Chief Factor Duncan Finlayson, afterwards a member of the
H. B. Co. Board of Directors.

FIG. 6.   OUTLINE SKETCH OF PART OF THE TOO-TSHO RANGE, FROM WEST SIDE OF FRANCES LAKE, AT ITS OUTLET.

(*The figures placed above the various summits are true bearings.*)

9000 feet. This is named *Mount Logan*, for the late Sir W. E. Logan.
Heavy masses of snow rest in some of the valleys, but no true glaciers
are produced, a fact indicating a comparatively small snow-fall. The
broken outlines of this range contrast strongly with the rounded forms
of the mountains to the west of the west arm, with which Simpson's
Tower and associated hills, separating the two arms, also conform.

The west arm terminates in a nearly circular basin about a quarter of
a mile in diameter, at one side of which a fair-sized river, easily navigable for boats, flows in. The east arm was not followed to its head,
though its termination in low land was seen. Here also, according to
Campbell's sketch, a considerable river, which he has named Thomas
River, enters. *Terminations of the lake.*

The two valleys, the lower parts of which are occupied by the east
and west arms of the lake, run on far beyond the heads of these arms.
Each of the rivers flowing in these valleys (according to the Indian
sketch already referred to) eventually bifurcates, and all four streams
thus formed rise in lakes. The river flowing into the head of the west
arm is named *Yus-sez'-uh*, and the lake on its western branch is known
as *Us-tas'-a-tsho*. No name was obtained for the lake on its eastern
branch, which is evidently, however, Macpherson Lake of Campbell. *Upper parts of tributary valleys.*

Henry Thibert, who made a prospecting expedition up the west arm
of Frances Lake and far up the river in question, some years ago, has
kindly supplied me with some notes on it. He estimated the river,
from the head of the arm to Macpherson Lake, to be about thirty-six
miles in length, while Macpherson Lake is ten miles long. The first
distance was, however, intended to include the windings of the stream.
He did not visit Us-tas'-a-tsho, which, however, from the termination
tsho (=big) is probably large. Us-tas is the name of the mythical
culture-hero of the Tinné. The Indian name of Thomas River is
Too-tlas', the lake in which its eastern branch rises being named *Tus-
tles-to*, the source of its western branch *Til-é-i-tsho*. These lakes and
connecting rivers are indicated by broken lines on the map, from
Thibert's account and the Indian sketch of the country, combined with
the observed positions of several of the mountain ranges.

The mountains to the north in which these rivers rise, were too distant to enable us to fix them with any great accuracy from points occupied by us on Frances Lake, but the whole country in that direction,
from such views as were obtained of it, appeared to be rugged and high.
It was with great regret that we were obliged to abandon the idea of
exploring these rivers further, but the summer was already so far ad-
vanced, that this was impracticable, in view of the journey still before us. *Mountains to the north.*

The water of Frances Lake is clear and of a pale, brownish tint, and
the lake is evidently very deep in its upper portions, though rather

Rock exposures shallow where encumbered by the morainic accumulations already alluded to. Rock exposures are, as a rule, quite unfrequent along its shores, which are generally composed of gravel and sand. At the time of our visit it was about six feet below its extreme high-water level, and it does not appear to be subject to very great fluctuations. Drift-wood is very abundant along some parts of the shores, particularly in the west arm, and it is probable that much of this is brought down by the river entering at the head of this arm. Lake-trout, white-fish, pike and suckers were found in the lake in considerable abundance.

Old Hudson Bay post. The site of the old Hudson Bay post is just above the narrow entrance to the east arm, on the edge of the bank, facing westward. Though Mr. Campbell had given me an accurate description of its position, it was so completely overgrown with bushes and small trees, that it was discovered with difficulty. The outline of the old stockade, with bastions at the corners, is still visible, though all traces of the structure itself has disappeared. This post has been abandoned since 1851.

Forest. All the lower country about Frances Lake is well wooded, and the mountains are also covered with forest, save where exceptionally steep and rocky, to a height of at least 1500 feet above the lake, while trees of smaller growth extend in the valleys considerably higher. The most abundant tree, here as elsewhere in the region, is the white spruce (*Picea alba*). It frequently attains a diameter of two feet, growing tall and straight on low ground and in sheltered places. The black spruce (*Picea nigra*) is also abundant. The larch (*Larix Americana*) is characteristic of damp, cool, northern slopes, and birch (*Betula papyrifera*) is moderately abundant, though not large. The shores, and particularly the delta-flats at the mouths of streams, are characterized by groves of cottonwood (probably all referable here to *Populus balsamifera*) and black pine (*Pinus Murrayana*).

Burnt country. Large tracts of country have been burnt over, many years ago, and extensive recent fires have swept the western side of the upper part of the east arm. Where a second growth has had time to spring up, it consists generally of mixed spruce, aspen and birch. Alders are common, but scarcely arboreal, along the borders of the lake. In the middle of July thickets of wild roses were seen in many places in full bloom.

General aspect of country. Taken as a whole, the growth of the forest and appearance of the country is remarkably pleasing, considering the high and northern position of the lake. The only characteristic difference of the woods here, as compared with those of the interior of British Columbia about the 54th parallel, is the great abundance and depth of the soft, mossy and lichenous floor which is everywhere found in them. The trees are also often well bearded with moss, affording evidence of a continuously moist atmosphere, to be accounted for by the almost daily occurrence of light showers and the great prevalence of clouded skies, which was found throughout this part of the country. As before noted, however, the snow-fall cannot be great, nor is there any indication that the total annual precipitation is very considerable.

The infrequency of rock exposures along the shores rendered it difficult to obtain any connected idea of the geology of the lake, both arms of which appear, however, to occupy valleys excavated along the strike of comparatively soft black and greyish glossy schists, which are often calcareous and frequently interbedded with bluish limestone. In lithological appearance these rocks resemble those of the Cambro-Silurian, in which graptolites were found on Dease River, though no fossils were obtained here. The strike is parallel, so far as observed, to the directions of the arms, the prevailing dips being westward on the west arm, eastward on the east arm. The character of the harder and doubtless older rocks which occupy the centre of the anticlinal thus formed and compose Simpson's Tower and connected hills, was not ascertained.

Geology of shores.

The high rugged central parts of the Too-tsho Range are composed largely or entirely of grey granite, pebbles and boulders of which are everywhere abundant, and particularly so along the beaches of the east arm. There is, too, a notable abundance of quartz along all the beaches of the lake, this material being derived from innumerable veins which traverse the schists in all directions, though most often found parallel to the bedding-planes, and generally assuming forms more or less lenticular. The largest of these are often several feet in width, and those seen in the cañon of the Finlayson, near its mouth, are of workable dimensions, if only moderately rich in gold. Specimens of quartz veins, containing some iron and copper pyrites, from the east side of the east arm about midway up it, were found to contain traces of gold on assay by Mr. Hoffmann.

Quartz veins numerous.

In general appearance the rocks of Frances Lake very closely resemble those from which the rich placer gold deposits of Dease Lake are derived, and they are probably of about the same age. Several "colours" to the pan were obtained from surface gravel at the mouth of Finlayson River, which struck me as specially promising in aspect and there seems to be no reason why some of the streams flowing across the schistose rocks into the lake or in its vicinity should not prove to be richly auriferous. This entire district well deserves careful prospecting. After my return to the coast, in the autumn, I ascertained from Charles Monroe that he and some other miners had actually done some prospecting in the vicinity of the lake at the time when the Cassiar mines were yielding largely, and the more enter-

Prospects for gold mining.

prising men were scouring the country in search of new fields. He reached the lake from Cassiar by the same route we had followed. On comparing notes we found that he had worked for a short time at the mouth of the Finlayson, where he found the gravel to pay at the rate of from $8 to $9 a day.

COUNTRY BETWEEN FRANCES LAKE AND PELLY RIVER.

We reached Frances Lake on the morning of the 8th of July, and had we been able to find any local Indians to serve as guides and assist in carrying over our stuff, we should have proceeded at once to the best point for that purpose and continued our journey overland toward the Pelly. As it was, it became our first object to endeavour to find the trail used many years previously by the Hudson Bay Compay, of which a general description had been furnished by Mr. Campbell. This necessitated a careful examination of the west shore of the west arm to its head, which enabled us to identify, with tolerable certainty, the stream which Campbell had named the Finlayson. It was supposed that the Indians might have employed the same route in the periodical journeys which they were known to make from the Pelly down the Frances to the little trading post at the mouth of the Dease; but though the remains of an old log *cáche* of the Hudson Bay Company were eventually found, together with the nails and iron work of a large boat which had evidently been burnt on the beach near it, no sign of a trail could be discovered. It thus appeared very doubtful whether we should be able to make our way across to the Pelly, with sufficient provisions and the necessary instruments for the continuation of our survey in the Yukon basin.

In order to exhaust the possibility of obtaining further assistance before making the attempt, I made a light trip in one of our boats round into the east arm, which was known to exist from Campbell's report, but the narrow entrance to which had not even been observed on our way up the lake. This also enabled me to sketch the east arm, but no Indians were found ; in fact, we discovered traces of only a single camp which had been made during the same summer, most of the Indian signs being two or more years old.

All that now remained to be done was to make the best of our own resources. We, therefore, went carefully over all our stuff, separating out everything which was not absolutely essential, and making up the remainder in packs, together with as much food as could be carried. This done, we stowed a great part of our camp equipage, together with some provisions, in a strong log *cáche*, which was constructed for the purpose in the bay immediately south of the mouth of the Finlayson, and moved round to the north side of the delta of that stream, to what we believed to be the best point from which to start. We then hauled out our two boats, and on the 17th and 18th of July carried our remaining stuff to a point some miles up the Finlayson and above the cañon and cascades, which render its lower part utterly impassable. Here *Difficult land carriage.* we set up the Osgood canvas boat, which we had also carried over. Into this a portion of our stuff was put, and two of our Coast Indians were instructed to endeavor to track it up the shallow and winding stream, while the rest of the party found their way as best they could along the valley, with heavy packs. The walking was extremely fatiguing on account of the deep moss, alternating with brush and swamps, and as in addition, the weather was very warm and the mosquitoes innumerable, our rate of progress was slow. On arriving at the forks of the stream we unfortunately took the wrong branch for several miles, leading to some loss of time, but we eventually reached a lake which we recognized as Finlayson Lake, on July 24th. The canvas boat did not arrive till the evening of the next day, as great difficulty was met with in getting it up the shallow stream, which was badly blocked with fallen trees. In the meantime, observations for latitude and time were taken, and a raft was constructed on which the stuff might be floated to the head of the lake, which lay in the general direction of our route.

The lake proved to be nine miles and a-half in length, and near its *Reach Finlayson Lake* head we again found the ruins of a Hudson Bay *cáche*, but no appearance of a trail. Having selected the most promising looking place from which to continue our journey, we took out the raft-sticks, in order that they might remain dry and serviceable for our Indians on their return, and made a second small *cáche* of provisions. The Osgood boat being almost worn out by its hard usage on the Finlayson, and being besides quite too heavy to carry overland in addition to our other stuff, was also drawn up and abandoned.

Soon after leaving the lake we fell upon small streams which evi- *Reach the Upper Pelly.* dently drained toward the west, and about noon on the 29th of July we had the satisfaction of reaching the bank of the Pelly River. From this place our five Coast Indians were sent back with instructions to take back to Mr. Reed, at Dease Lake, the articles left in the *cáche* on Frances Lake, and this duty, we subsequently learned, they faithfully performed.

Having constructed a canoe from the canvas brought over for that purpose, we began the descent of the river on the 1st of August.

The above is a summary of our proceedings from Frances Lake to *Probable better route.* the Pelly. I now feel convinced, that if we had had Indian guides, we might in all probability have shortened the land carriage and possibly have found a travelled Indian trail, by following up the waters tributary to the west arm of Frances Lake. It remains to give some notes of the country actually traversed.

Mountains.

Though the region between Frances Lake and the Pelly may be described as a mountainous one, no very high summits were seen, the elevations being, as a rule, rounded and regular in outline, and forming broad, plateau-like areas above the timber-line in some places. The Too-tsho Mountains, which run along the east arm of Frances Lake nearly due north, appear to turn more to the westward beyond the head of the lake, but the line of travel followed toward the Pelly still diverged rapidly from this, the culminating range of the district, and the general direction of the principal ridges in the vicinity of the Finlayson River is not far from east-and-west.

General character of the country.

It is probable that the general character of the country here met with fairly represents that of a wide belt to the west of the Frances River and north of the Liard, including the Campbell and Simpson Mountains and their vicinity. The mountains are about equal in altitude to those last mentioned, averaging from 5000 to 6000 feet. The country is traversed by wide, wooded valleys, of which that occupied by the Finlayson is here the principal. The climate evidently becomes less moist as Frances Lake and the vicinity of the Too-tsho Mountains are left, and dry, gravelly terrace-flats, with *Pinus Murrayana*, are not uncommon on the upper part of the Finlayson. Larch was observed in places for about half the distance up the river toward Finlayson Lake, but was not seen further west. White spruce is still the most abundant tree, and grows as large as along Frances Lake. The black spruce also, however, occurs, and *Abies subalpina* becomes the common and characteristic tree near the upward limit of forest growth on the mountains, which here occurs at about 4200 feet. Grassy swamps are found in a number of places, and a good growth of grass is also met with, where areas have been denuded of forest by successive fires, so that should it ever become desirable to use horses on this portage, they might be maintained without difficulty.

Character of Finlayson River.

The lower part of the Finlayson for about four miles, near its mouth, forms a series of rapids and small cascades in a narrow, rocky gorge, making in this distance a total descent of 300 feet to the lake. Above this cañon it is rapid for several miles, with gravelly bars, and quite shallow, but further up it becomes a narrow and often deep stream, flowing between muddy or sandy banks. At twenty-two miles from its mouth it divides into two nearly equal branches, the northern of which comes from *McEvoy Lake*, the southern from Finlayson Lake. Each of these streams, at their confluence,

is from twenty-five to thirty feet in average width and about two feet
deep. The northern branch, however, soon becomes shallow, rapid
and stony, while that coming from Finlayson Lake is extremely
crooked, winding in all directions in a flat valley about a mile in width,
and is besides, as already mentioned, very badly blocked by fallen
trees.

From the summit of an isolated, bare-topped hill, which occupies the *View from a mountain.*
angle between the two streams, and rises about 1200 above the val-
leys, an excellent view of the surrounding country was obtained. To
the north-eastward, broken masses of high, rugged mountains, patched
with snow, limit the horizon. These are evidently connected with
the Too-tsho Range, but appear to form an irregular western spur,
which is not continued to the west of north. The intervening district,
as well as the whole country to the south, is occupied by bare-topped,
rounded mountains and ridges of less elevation. Amid these hills the
round or flat-bottomed valleys of the streams extend, showing here and
there the paler green of a patch of meadow. The most remarkable
feature is, however, a tract of low, level country, in which McEvoy
Lake and the head of Finlayson Lake lie. This runs nearly due east-
and-west, and appears to continue in the former direction till it inter-
sects the northern continuation of the valley of the west arm of
Frances Lake, and is also observable to the west of the head of Finlayson Lake. It is intersected throughout by numerous small lakes or
ponds and swampy meadows.

Finlayson Lake (*Tle-tlan'-a-tsoots* of the Indians) is nine miles and *Character of Finlayson Lake*
a-half in length and rather irregular in form. Its elevation above sea-
level is 3105 feet, as determined by our barometer readings, and it may
be regarded as occupying the summit of the watershed between the
Mackenzie and the Yukon, as no stream of any importance enters it.
The country about it is all rather low, but is diversified, to some extent,
by wooded ridges and hills, which rise highest near its upper end. The
water is apparently shallow throughout, and had, in consequence, a
much higher temperature than that of Frances Lake. It is well
stocked with white-fish and lake trout, and also, no doubt, with the other
species found in Frances Lake. A dead amia, eighteen inches
long, was also found on the shore.

The immediate shores of the lake are generally quite low and often
swampy, and the country is covered with small, poor timber, much of
which has been killed by fire. A pretty well marked terrace, at 100 to
150 feet above the water, runs nearly all round the lake, and at the head
are irregular, low, lumpy ridges and islands, which evidently represent moraine accumulations. No rock-exposures were anywhere seen
along the lake-shore.

The water-shed.

The distance from the head of the lake to the nearest point on the Pelly, in a straight line, is about fifteen miles, but the low tract of country already referred to runs some miles to the south of such a line for the greater part of the way. The actual watershed in this low country is probably not fifty feet above the lake, but there is no evidence that the lake ever discharges toward the Pelly. Its height above sea-level is about 3150 feet. Small streams rising to the west of the lake, flow together to form a respectable brook about half way across. This occupies a wide, terraced valley, the ridges bordering which gradually diverge as the Pelly is approached, and the river itself is bordered by undulating terrace-flats several miles in width.

Country west of Finlayson Lake

On ridges west of the head of Finlayson Lake *Abies subalpina* becomes moderately abundant, but the white and black spruce are still the characteristic trees, and the former is well grown in sheltered valleys. No larch or black pine were seen on this part of the portage. The western yellow pond-lily (*Nuphar polysepalum*) was observed in great abundance in a small inlet of Finlayson Lake, and on the hills beyond *Polymoneum pulchellum* and *Mertensia paniculata*, with *Potentilla fruticosa*, were noted as specially abundant flowering plants. The vegetation in the vicinity of the Pelly was much further advanced than any we had yet seen, and the climate of the valley is evidently more favorable than that of the watershed region. The soil of the river-terraces is a fine, silty material, which, judging from the luxuriance of plant growth, must be very fertile.

Geological notes.

In consequence of the width of the valleys and the mantle of drift deposits, few rock-exposures were met with along the whole route from Frances Lake to the Pelly, and those examined consisted wholly of schists or schistose argillites, associated with cherty quartzites in some places, and generally of blackish or grey colors. The gravel wash in the various smaller streams and the rock *débris* met with on slopes of hills and elsewhere, consisted also predominantly of similar materials, and it would appear that the whole of this country is underlain by rocks resembling those described on Frances Lake and part of the river of the same name. A reddish argillite was noted as locally abundant in some streams entering the Finlayson on the south. Pebbles and small boulders of grey granite are not uncommon, but all appear to have been transported from a distance. In addition to the

Rocks of Finlayson Lake

rocks above described, the gravel beaches on Finlayson Lake show numerous fragments of grey-blue limestone, some of which contain obscure fossils. Green serpentine, like that of the vicinity of Dease Lake, and exhibiting minute veinlets of serpentine-asbestos, also a few pebbles of reddish serpentine, were also noted here, and fragments of a peculiar white quartz-porphyry are not uncommon. Large pieces of the same stone were afterwards found on the hills to the west of the lake, but it was not anywhere seen in place. Quartz-vein-stuff is everywhere very abundant, and on the terrace overlooking the Finlay- Massive quartz. son, on the north side, three miles below the lake, a large mass of quartz occurs in place. The extent of this mass of quartz could not be ascertained, as it protruded from the soil only in isolated spots over an area several hundred feet in length and breadth. A few specimens were collected, but on assay proved to contain neither gold nor silver.

One of the most notable features of this watershed region is the Superficial great quantity of detrital material or drift with which the whole is deposits of the covered. On the lower part of the Finlayson, irregularly bedded, watershed. clayey, gravel deposits, containing large glaciated stones and resembling boulder clay, were seen; but elsewhere stratified gravels and sands are generally shown in any scarped banks which occur. Well rounded gravel was found scattered over the very summit of the isolated mountain at the forks of the Finlayson, above referred to, at a height of 4300 feet above the sea, the material being of varied origin and including granite. No distinct terraces were found on this mountain, but terraces were noted further down the valley on the slopes of higher hills, at a height equal to, or greater than, that of this place. The evidence appears to be conclusive that a body of water in later glacial times extended quite across the Pacific-Arctic watershed in this region, standing at a level more than 1000 feet above it. Glacial striation, in a bearing parallel to that of the valley, was noted on the surface of the quartz mass previously alluded to, but the direction of motion of the ice could not be determined.

UPPER PELLY RIVER.

Our first camp on the Pelly was situated in lat. 61° 48′ 52″, long. Upper Pelly 131° 01′ 06″, the height of the river being at this place, as approxi- River. mately determined from the mean of a number of barometer observations, 2965 feet. The river is here 326 feet wide, with a current slightly exceeding two miles and a-half an hour, and a middle depth of seven feet. An approximate estimate of the discharge placed it at 4898 cubic feet per second. The river had evidently fallen very considerably since the early summer and was probably at or below its mean stage. The water is here nearly clear, with a light brownish tinge. From explorations made at the time of the existence of the Hudson Bay post, as well as from Indian report, the river is known to be navigable by boats for a considerable distance above this point, and to rise in two lakes, the position of which is approximately indicated on the map, according to

Mr. Campbell's sketch. Our camp was about two miles above the mouth of the stream which has already been mentioned as rising on the portage near Finlayson Lake, at the angle between which and the Pelly the old post named "Pelly Banks" was situated. We saw no trace of the buildings which formerly existed, though the old site might, no doubt, have been determined by a little search, had we thought it worth while to devote the necessary time to it.

"Pelly Banks" to Hoole Cañon.

Appearance of the country.

From our initial point, above mentioned, to Hoole Cañon and Cañon, is a distance of thirty-one miles in a straight line, the direction of which is a few degrees north of west. The river, however, forms a wide curve to the south of this line, and is besides very tortuous in detail, the actual distance, following its course, being fifty miles. The main orographic river-valley is here not confined, as is so often the case, between parallel ranges of mountains. There is on the contrary a wide tract of irregularly hilly country, which is bounded to the south by a well-defined mountain range at a distance of ten to twelve miles. This range is crowned by a series of square-outlined pyramidal peaks, which are probably composed of stratified rocks. It is proposed to distinguish it as the *Pelly Range.* To the northward, no definite boundary to the low hilly region can be seen. The actual trough in which the river meanders, however, is scarcely more than a mile in average width, and is generally bordered by terraces a hundred feet or more in height.

Hoole River.

Thirty-three miles, by the course of the river, below our starting point, a tributary comes in from the mountains to the southward, about fifty feet wide by one deep, and very rapid. This is identified as Hoole River.* Its water is bluish in tint, and clearer than that of the Upper Pelly, which by this time has become slightly turbid from material derived from its soft, silty banks. The river, between our first camp and Hoole River, has a rather moderate current, scarcely exceeding four miles and a-half an hour, though with several little "riffles" or small rapids.

Rapid.

Just below the mouth of Hoole River is a rapid about 600 feet long, with a total fall estimated at about ten feet. There is an easy portage on the right or north bank, but a fair-sized boat might run through without danger at most stages of the water. As a precautionary measure, we lightened our canvas canoe, of the behavior of which

---

* So named by Mr. Campbell after his interpreter. Mr. Campbell, on his original sketch and on Arrowsmith's map, in the construction of which it was used, has named a number of the tributaries of the Pelly. It has been found difficult to identify some of these, but all have been placed on the accompanying map, after a careful comparison.

in bad water we had had at the time no experience. From this rapid to Hoole Cañon the water is swift, and there are several little rapids.

The banks and benches of the Pelly above Hoole River, are generally silty or muddy, though the strength of the current is sufficient to produce well-washed gravel-bars in mid-stream. Below that point the banks and beaches are also as a rule gravelly, in conformity with the swifter flow of the stream.

The banks along the south side of this part of the river, are for the Vegetation. most part densely wooded, and where shady and damp the growth of timber is small and scrubby, with much black spruce. The banks on the opposite side are very different in appearance. Those above Hoole River show numerous open, grassy patches, and below that place grassy slopes preponderate over the wooded area, the grass having the characteristic growth and dry, tufted appearance of "bunch-grass." The trees are similar to those found along the rivers previously described, except that *Pinus Murrayana* and larch do not occur, and but a single white birch was noted, near the mouth of Hoole River. Groves of cottonwood of medium size cover some of the flats. In one Frozen soil. or two banks into which the river was cutting, and where the surface was covered with a dense, mossy growth, frozen soil was observed. The depth to which it extended could not be ascertained, as it went below the water-level of the stream.

Above the mouth of Hoole River the rock exposures are few and Rocks represented. inconsiderable. Near the mouth of Campbell Creek a yellowish-weathering irregularly silicified dolomite was observed in several low outcrops, together with green-grey, slightly lustrous schists, and similar schists were seen in one or two other places on this part of the river. The composition of the gravel of the river-bars may be accepted as indicating in a general way the character of the formations of the drainage area of the upper river. These include fragments of schists, quartzites and argillites of the same kind as before described on the Frances, with grey, fine-grained limestone, some pieces of coarse white marble, and occasional small pebbles of the same peculiar quartz-porphyry seen on Finlayson Lake. There are also represented several varieties of granitoid rocks, the most abundant of which has a coarse gneissic lamination, with whitish or greenish mica and large, white, porphyritic felspar crystals, round which the layers of the rock bend. This peculiar granite or gneiss is probably derived from the head-waters of the main river, and often occurs in large boulders, which can scarcely have been carried by the stream, and have probably been transported during the glacial period.

Basaltic area.

At the rapid at the mouth of Hoole River low bluffs of dark-brown basalt appear, and the same rock crops out in several places further down the river, extending probably to within two miles of Hoole Cañon, though the lower exposures have rather a dioritic appearance, somewhat different from those first noted. The horizontal extent of this local development of basalt is approximately indicated on the map, but as the country to the north is here all low, its limit in that direction is entirely hypothetical. This is probably the first occurrence of basalt on the river, as no basalt pebbles were seen above this place. The basalt is often amygdaloidal or vesicular, and contains chalcedony, calcite and some fibrous zeolite, but is scarcely at all columnar.

Scarped banks.

Above the mouth of Hoole River, frequent scarped banks exhibit white or grey bedded silts, associated with or underlain by stratified gravels, with a dark-grey, earthy matrix. These latter deposits often hold large boulders, and observations made further down the river appear to show that they represent the boulder-clay.

Between Hoole River and the cañon, the silts are scarcely seen in the banks of the Pelly, being replaced by gravelly and coarse sandy deposits.

Hoole Cañon to Ross River.

Hoole Cañon.

At Hoole Cañon, the river makes a knee-like bend to the north-eastward, and is constricted between rocky banks and cliffs about a hundred feet in height. These render it impracticable to use the line, and as the water is very rough and dangerous, it was found necessary to carry not only all our stuff, but the canoe as well, to the lower end of the cañon. The distance by the river is about three-quarters of a mile, by the portage half a mile, the highest point being one hundred feet above the river. The portage is on the south side of the river, and we found traces on it of skids which had been laid by the Hudson Bay Company many years ago, but no sign of its having been employed by the Indians, who in all this district generally travel by land, making rafts when they are obliged to cross any of the larger rivers.

Ross River.

Sixteen miles and a-half below the cañon in a straight line, or twenty-three miles by the course of the Pelly, is the mouth of a river which is identified as the Ross River of Campbell.[*] This stream, which comes from the north-eastward, is to all appearance as nearly as possible equal in volume to the Pelly, having a width of 290 feet, with a current of four miles and a-half an hour. Its water is turbid and milky, and colder than that of the Pelly, leading to the belief that it is not derived from lakes like that stream, or that if lakes do

---

[*] So named after Chief Factor Donald Ross.

occur on its upper waters, they are much less in area than those of the Character of county. Pelly. Its size would indicate that it may rise in the same distant range with the Pelly, but no long view was obtained up its valley, which is narrow and bordered by high, steep hills at its mouth. Midway between the cañon and the Ross, Ketza River,* a swift stream, about forty feet by one foot, joins from the south. Like other streams from that direction, it carries clear, blue, mountain water, and brings down quartzites, argillites and schists of the usual character, together with a great abundance of quartz-gravel.

The Pelly, between the cañon and Ross River, is swift throughout, Rocks. with numerous little rapids. To the south of the river there is still a wide extent of low, wooded country between it and the continuous range before referred to as the Pelly Mountains. To the north the view is more limited, particularly near the mouth of the Ross River, owing to the existence of a long, steep ridge, parallel to the course of the Pelly, and from 600 to 800 feet in height above it. The southern face of this ridge, which is cut through by the Ross River, is more than half, open grass land, and would afford excellent pasturage.

The rocks of Hoole Cañon and its vicinity are chiefly white marble, associated and interbedded with grey and black cherty-looking quartzites, which are often thin-bedded and sometimes rather schistose, and precisely resemble the Cáche Creek quartzites of southern British Columbia. Further down the river are occasional exposures of greenish and grey schists and schistose argillites. The rocks along this part of the Pelly strike nearly parallel to its main direction, or about north-west by south-east, and are either nearly vertical or have dips to the south-westward. Stratified gravels are seen in a few places in scarped banks, but silts are not here specially characteristic.

Ross River to Glenlyon River.

From the mouth of Ross River to the Glenlyon River, the general course of the Pelly is almost direct, on a bearing of N. 50° W., the distance being sixty-four miles. In consequence of the number of minor flexures in the stream, this is, however, increased by the river to eighty-two miles. Ten miles below the Ross, following the river, a stream, *Lapie River*,† sixty feet wide by one foot deep, and resembling in its general Lapie River. character and colour of water Hoole and Ketza rivers, comes in from the south. Twenty-three miles from the same point a smaller tributary joins from the north, which is supposed to be the Orchay of Orchay River.

---

* So named by Campbell, after one of his faithful Indian companions ; not Kelzas, as shown on Arrowsmith's map of 1854.

† This stream was not named by Campbell. I call it Lapie River, after one of his Indians, he having given the name of the other (Ketza) to a neighboring tributary.

Campbell. This is about twenty feet wide by six inches deep, and carries clear, brownish water, doubtless derived from a lake or lakes. Ten miles further, on the same side, is a valley running to the north, which probably brings in a moderate sized stream. But this falls into a slough, behind islands, and was not seen.

Features of the country.

All the way from the Ross to the Glenlyon the Pelly is closely bordered on the north by ridges and hills of considerable height, which become mountains of 4000 to over 5000 feet before the last-mentioned stream is reached. These entirely preclude any outlook over the country on that side. To the south, the important and well-marked Pelly Range is continued to a point opposite the Orchay River, where it appears to terminate in a group of mountains lower than those of its eastern part, but still from 5000 to 6000 feet in height. These are situated at a distance of about six miles back from the river, the intervening country being occupied by lower, wooded hills and broken country. The forms of the mountains are rather bold, consisting of steep crests and ridges, with intervening narrow, V-shaped gorges, and they appear to be grassed or covered with low, herbaceous growth, giving them a general greenish tint. There are few bare, rocky summits, and the whole appearance is that of a range shaped by normal processes of denudation from schistose or other crumbling rocks of a stratified character and nearly uniform hardness. They still carried a few patches of old snow on the 4th of August. The higher portions of this range to the eastward, present a rougher and almost serried outline, but there are not even there any exceptionally high points, and the slopes of the peaks are extremely uniform. Beyond the western termination of this range, for a distance of about twenty miles, no mountains were seen to the southward from the river-valley. From the fact that evidences of a more humid climate were found along the corresponding length of the river, it is highly probable that a somewhat important gap occurs in this direction, of sufficient width to admit the entrance of the moisture-bearing winds. The greater humidity of this part of the valley is particularly marked by the densely wooded character of the slopes on the north side of the river.

Pelly Range.

Gap to the southward.

Beyond the gap above referred to, a low mountain-range appears on the south side of the river, not in line with that last described, but quite close to the river, which here, for a number of miles, flows in a valley between two mountain axes.

Notes on the river.

The Pelly, for rather more than half the distance between the Ross and Glenlyon, continues to be pretty swift, and is much divided among islands and gravel-bars; the remaining part is comparatively tranquil, with the exception of the rapids in the immediate vicinity of the Glenlyon. The forest growth throughout is much like that previously

described, save that the birch is now moderately abundant, and the Black pine.
black pine (*P. Murrayana*) appears, coming in first on dry northern
slopes thirteen miles eastward from the Glenlyon. Cottonwood, aspen,
alder, spruce and willows are the prevailing trees on the river-flats,
which are usually about ten feet above low-water level. Frozen soil
was again seen in several places along the shady side of this part of Frozen soil.
the river, extending from about eighteen inches below a mossy and
peaty sod to the water-level, with a depth of ten feet or more. Some
of these banks were being rapidly undercut by the water, which
thaws the soil wherever it comes in contact with it, and causes large
masses, with the superincumbent sod and trees, to fall into the stream.

The rapids above alluded to as near the Glenlyon are two in number. Rapids.
The first occurs in an S-shaped bend about two miles east of the Glenlyon; the second just below the mouth of that stream. The upper
rapid is wide and rather shallow, with some rocky impediments. It
is easily run with a canoe, but at low stages of the river, doubtfully
passable for a steamer, unless of light draft. The current in the second
rapid strikes full on the face of a rocky bank on the right of the river,
and forms a heavy confused wash in consequence, but is otherwise
unimpeded and deep.

The rocks seen along the Pelly, between the Ross and Glenlyon, Geological
while resembling in a general way those previously described, differ features.
in their greater alteration and in the evident importance in their composition of products originally of volcanic origin. The most abundant
are blackish-grey and greenish quartzites and schists, often more or
less micaceous, and in places passing into true mica-schists. Three
and a-half miles west of the Ross River, on the left bank, are exposures
of massive, dark, leek-green serpentine, associated with green serpen-
tinous and quartzose schists, and a spotted white and green rock, which
may be a much decomposed diabase or diorite. One portion of the
bank shows at least a hundred feet in thickness of nearly pure serpentine, but no asbestos veins were seen here. Thirty-six miles west of
the Ross a very peculiar purplish felsite was noted. It is schistose and
slightly micaceous in the division planes, besides being porphyritic
with irregular white felspar masses. Four miles east of the Glenlyon,
a close-grained, banded, white-and-grey felsite occurs, in a much shattered exposure, and is probably a fine, altered volcanic ash. All these
rocks evidently form members of a single series, and though with
numerous local irregularities, strike in a general way parallel to the
course of the river. The circumstances tend to show that they are on
the whole stratigraphically higher than those seen further up the river,
but it is not certain that the dips are normal.

Laramie or Cretaceous rocks.

The most interesting fact developed on this part of the Pelly is, however, the occurrence of rocks of Laramie or Cretaceous age. These were noted in a single low exposure on the south side of the river, twenty-seven miles and a-half west of the mouth of Ross River. They consist of black carbonaceous or possibly plumbaginous shales, rather hard, and interbedded with grey-brown sandstones, the whole dipping nearly due south at an angle of forty-five degrees. But this single occurrence of rocks of this character was found, and no rocks are seen for several miles up or down the stream, so that the area characterized by the formation to which they belong is uncertain. Sir William Dawson writes as follows of the fossils obtained here:—"The few specimens examined are full of impressions of dicotyledonous leaves, much crushed and imperfect. One has the venation of *Corylus Mac-Quarrii* (Forbes). Another seems to be a *Juglans*, near to *J. acuminata* (Braun). Both of these species are said by Heer to occur at English Bay, Alaska, and also on Mackenzie River. The determinations cannot, however, be considered as certain."

Fossil plants.

Superficial deposits.

Fine sections of the drift deposits frequently occur along this part of the Pelly River, forming scarped banks from eighty to a hundred and fifty feet in height, and at times a quarter of a mile or more in length. The stratified gravels, with grey or brownish earthy matrix, which have previously been described, were seen just above the mouth of Ross River to be interbedded with and overlain by silts of the usual character. A few miles below the Ross they were first seen in association with indubitable boulder-clay, and thence down stream, the earthy or clayey gravels and boulder-clay form the lower portion of most of the scarps, being capped by bedded silts, which in some places are fifty feet in thickness. The stratified earthy gravels and boulder-clay are interchangeable and may be considered as constituting a single formation. These gravels are sometimes interbedded with rude layers of boulder-clay, while in other sections they occur in the bottom of the bank, with massive-looking boulder-clay above them, and in yet other instances these conditions are reversed, and the gravels pass above into the bedded silts, which everywhere constitute the upper member of the glacial series. When the matrix of the gravels becomes clayey, they closely resemble boulder-clay in composition, but do not often hold such large stones as the latter occasionally does. The stones of both the gravel and the boulder-clay are more or less completely water-rounded, and striated stones were seldom seen along the river. The gravels above referred to are quite distinct from the old river-valley gravels, which also occur at various levels, sometimes as the highest member of the section in scarped banks, in other cases forming the substratum of river-flats. With the appearance of

Peculiarities of boulder-clay

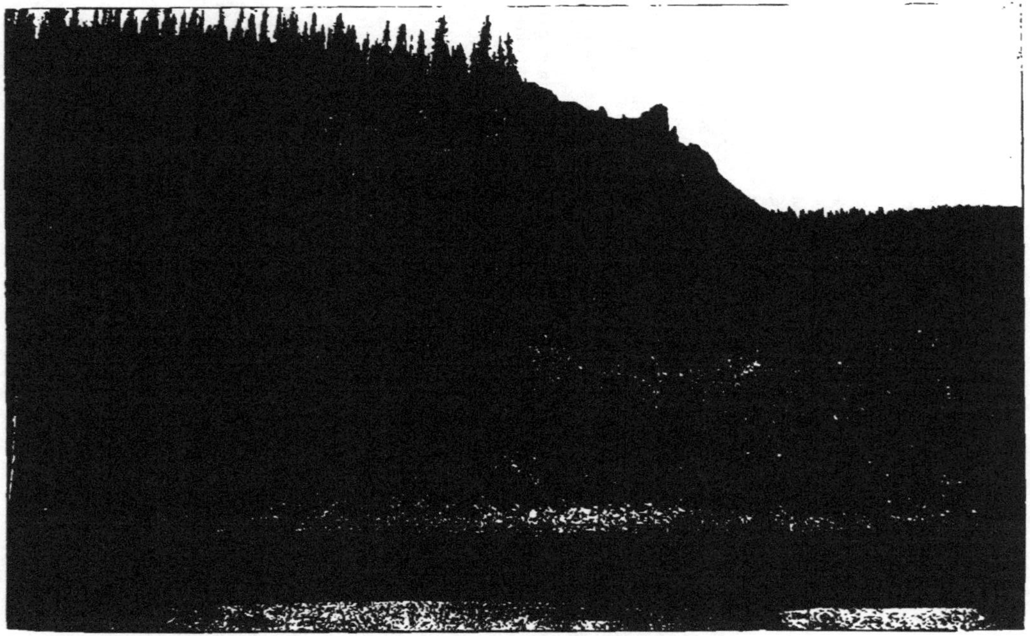

G. M. DAWSON, PHOTO.

DRIFT BLUFF, UPPER PELLY RIVER, AT MOUTH OF LAPIE RIVER

Lower part of bluff boulder-clay, irregularly overlain by earthy stratified gravels, these followed in ascending order by stratified silts.

the boulder-clay the scarped banks begin to assume a characteristically
castellated appearance, standing often in series of nearly vertical
buttresses and pillars, with deep intervening gullies.

Glenlyon River to Macmillan River.

For the purpose of description, the next convenient length of the
Upper Pelly which may be taken, is that extending from the Glenlyon to
the Macmillan River.*   This again naturally sub-divides itself into two
parts, the first with a general bearing of N. 53° W., twenty-eight miles
and a half, in continuation of the general course of the upper river, the
second about N. 77° W. thirty-three miles.   The total distance,
following the course of the river, from the Glenlyon to the
Macmillan, is ninety-one miles.   The tributary streams in this Tributary
distance, again measuring by the course of the Pelly, down stream, streams.
are as follows :—Glenlyon River, forty feet by one foot.   Eight miles
and a-half below, stream on the north, sixty feet by six inches.   Twelve
miles, tributary from the south, twenty feet by three inches.   Seventeen miles, on the south, dry torrent bed.   Twenty miles and a-half,
on the south, ten feet by three inches.   Thirty miles on the north,
thirty feet by six inches; the Earn River of Campbell.   Forty-seven
miles on the south, thirty feet by three inches; probably the Tum-
mel River of Campbell.   From this point to the Macmillan no tributary streams were observed, the country to the northward evidently
draining toward the last-named stream, and that to the south, at no
great distance, being in all probability within the drainage-basin of
the Lewes.

The above estimates of the sizes of the streams refer to the date at
which we saw them, in August, when most appeared to be at or near
their lowest stages.   For about twenty miles below the Glenlyon
River, the Pelly is more than usually free from abrupt bends, and few
islands are met with.   It is bordered to the south by a range of
mountains, which may be named the *Glenlyon Mountains*, the highest Glenlyon
points of which somewhat exceed five thousand feet.   Lower Mountains.
irregular hills border the north bank, and these, as usual, show
extensive grassy slopes on the southern exposures.   At the distance
just mentioned from the Glenlyon, the river turns abruptly to the
northward, making an S-shaped bend, and cutting completely through
the ridge which has previously bounded it on that side.   After a The Detour.
sinuous course of about fifteen miles (about midway in which it
receives the Earn River), to the north of the ridge, it turns again with
equal abruptness to the southward, rounding the west point of the

---

* Of Campbell, named for Chief Factor Macmillan.

ridge, which here dies away. This peculiar flexure is distinguished on the map as *The Detour*. To the south of the ridge is a wide valley, which lies in the general direction of the river, and which, though now apparently floored by drift deposits, doubtless represents a pre-glacial valley of the Pelly. The distance from bend to bend of the river, through this disused valley, is eight miles and a-half, and the height of its floor above the water-level was estimated at about two hundred feet. As far as the lower end of The Detour the current is rather swift and there are a number of little riffles, some of which might be called rapids, though none are of a character to impede navigation.

Approach to Macmillan River. From The Detour to the Macmillan, the Pelly has a current averaging not more than three miles an hour, though attaining four miles in a few places. The country begins to open out to a greater extent than found anywhere on the upper river, and is diversified only by comparatively low and irregular hills. About fifteen miles eastward of the Macmillan is a wide low gap opening to the north, by which the Indians evidently cross over to the valley of that river, as several large rafts were seen here on the north bank. Between this place and the mouth of the Macmillan, the river becomes again rather strictly confined between ranges of hills, but just below its confluence it turns sharply to the north and is broken up into several channels among a number of low, wooded islands.

Confluence of the rivers. The Macmillan and the Pelly valleys coalesce at an acute angle at the western point of the range of hills which alone has separated them for some distance, and the two streams must run nearly parallel for many miles above their junction. The Macmillan is bordered to the north by a well defined range of low mountains, which continues to the westward for about ten miles as the bordering range of the united streams. At the confluence, the Pelly appeared evidently to be somewhat the larger river at the time of our visit, and it is probably so at all properly comparable stages of water. The inequality in size can not, however, be very great. The width of the Macmillan, just above its mouth, was found to be 455 feet, the rate of the current, which is greater than that of the Pelly at the same place, was 2·7 miles per hour. The Macmillan water is much more turbid than that of the Pelly, and of a yellowish colour. The temperature of both rivers was identical on the ninth of August, being 54° F. It may probably be assumed from this circumstance that the origin of the rivers is similar, and that the Macmillan, like the Pelly, rises in or flows through considerable lakes, in which the water is warmed to a like extent. The suspended matter of the Macmillan may be entirely due to the washing away of silty banks, which is the usual cause of the turbidity of streams in this district. The upper part of the Mac-

G. M. DAWSON, PHOTO., AUG. 8, 1887.

G. E. DESBARATS & SON, ENGRAVERS & PRINTERS, MONTREAL.

ON UPPER PELLY RIVER, NINETEEN MILES ABOVE MACMILLAN.

millan has never been explored, but its size would indicate that it may rise as far to the eastward as the Pelly, and probably, like it, in mountains representing the western ranges of the Rocky Mountains. We do not, however, know to what extent this river shares with the Stewart the drainage of the comparatively low country to the northward. I afterwards met a couple of miners (Messrs. Monroe & Langtry) who had ascended the Macmillan for several days in a boat, but not finding encouraging "prospects" had returned. They reported the existence of a large area of low land with good soil, and had met with no impediments to navigation as far as they had gone. *[Macmillan River.]*

Ten miles above the mouth of the Macmillan we encountered a couple of Indians, father and son, working their way up the Pelly with a small dug-out canoe. They were the first human beings we had met with in the country since leaving the mouth of the Dease River, forty-three days previously, but as we were totally unable to communicate with each other except by signs, it was impossible to obtain any definite information from them. They were evidently quite at a loss to know whence we had come, and evinced a peculiar interest in examining our little canvas canoe. *[Meet Indians.]*

The Glenlyon Range appears to be throughout granitic. Its base does not touch upon the river, but the general aspect and uniform grey colour of its higher parts is that of the granitic mountains of this region. Its composition is also indicated by the character of the material brought down by the Glenlyon River and other rapid streams which rise on its slopes or in its valleys. This is largely, and in some cases almost exclusively, composed of granite of very uniform lithological character, grey in colour and generally hornblendic. The same rock is met with in place on the Pelly, about half way from The Detour to the mouth of the Macmillan, beyond the termination of the range itself, but precisely in the continuation of the line of its axis.* The rocks exposed along the Pelly itself, between the mouth of the Glenlyon and the granitic exposure just alluded to, and which may be regarded as a whole as occupying the northern flank of this granitic range, are more varied in character than those met with on the upper part of the river. Nothing can be said as to their order of superposition, for while the river nearly follows the main direction of the strike, the locally observed attitudes of the strata of the several isolated places where they were noted are very irregular. This is particularly the case in the vicinity of The Detour. The rocks comprise greenish and blackish schists and schistose quartzites, of varied aspect, generally somewhat more altered in appearance than usual. These are interbedded at the east end of The Detour with finely-banded white *[Geological features.]*

---

* See Appendix V. (Upper Pelly, No. 53).

9

marble and quartzite; and at ten miles west of The Detour, are somewhat extensive exposures of blackish and bluish-grey, rather flaggy and little altered limestones, in which, however, no fossils could be found.

Second range of granite. The range of hills which has been referred to as bordering the Pelly on the south, near the mouth of the Macmillan, is likewise composed of granite, which appears in several places on the river. This is of greyish and greenish-grey colours, and similar to that of the Glenlyon Range, though it apparently forms a distinct though parallel granitic axis. The rocks which immediately border this granitic axis to the north, though not seen in actual contact with the granite, have a more highly altered aspect than almost any of those seen further up the river, but the impression gathered from their examination is that they owe this alteration to the influence of the granite rather than that their character is an evidence of greater age. They comprise several varieties of rough, micaceous schists, which are highly quartzose, and evidently of clastic origin, as well as a much silicified, coarse grauwacke, and a pale-grey, speckled, silvery mica-schist, which breaks into thin laminæ. The last-mentioned rock is found on the north bank immediately below the Macmillan. Some distance further down, the river turns sharply to the south, and cuts across the whole width **Granite Cañon.** of the second granitic axis in *Granite Cañon*, presenting exposures of grey hornblendic granite for several miles, which, near the lower end of the cañon, becomes much shattered by jointage-planes.*

Drift deposits. The drift deposits along the part of the river between the Glenlyon and Macmillan, resemble those previously described, the only marked change being in the substitution, in some sections to a considerable extent, of sands for the silts before so characteristic. Stratified clayey gravels and boulder-clay occur, with relations similar to those noted on the upper river, but in some sections gravels and sandy silts are interbedded, the bedding at times being flexuous, and even contorted in character. All these materials are below the ordinary valley-gravels and sands of post-glacial age.

Glacial striation. Six miles below the Glenlyon, the first distinct case of glacial striation and ice-rounded rock-surfaces met with on the Pelly was noted, and below this place similar evidences were found in a number of localities. The direction of striation in all cases closely accords with that of the main depression of the river-valley, though cutting across it obliquely where it turns north towards the Macmillan. The form of the surfaces is such as to show that the sense of the movement of ice was westward or down stream.

---

* See Appendix V. (Upper Pelly, No. 57.)

Macmillan River to Lewes River.

From the mouth of the Macmillan to the confluence of the Upper Pelly Tortuous part
of the river. and Lewes rivers is a distance, in a straight line with a general bearing a few degrees south of west, of forty-six miles. A considerable portion of this part of the river is, however, extremely tortuous, and in consequence no doubt of the generally low character of the country, its flexures are not merely short, sharp bends from side to side of a trough-like valley, like those usually met with further up, but lax irregular curves of greater dimensions. The distance from the Macmillan to the mouth of the Lewes measured along the course of the stream is seventy-four miles.

Four miles below the mouth of the Macmillan, on the north bank, is a small log-cabin, the first sign of habitation we had seen. We afterwards ascertained that two miners had lived here during the winter of 1886-87. At five miles and a-half below the Macmillan the Pelly was found to be 754 feet in width, with a current of 2·3 miles per hour; a few miles below this the river turns south-westward and then nearly due south, entering Granite Cañon at thirteen miles from Gran te Cañon. the Macmillan. The rocks met with in the cañon have already been alluded to. The cañon is about four miles in length, with steep, rocky, scarped banks and cliffs, 200 to 250 feet in height. In the cañon are several little rapids, but the water is deep, and with the exception of some isolated rocks, the navigation would be quite safe for steamers, even at a low stage of water. As the river is much confined, however, it is probable that pretty rough water may be found here during floods. Just beyond the cañon, or sixteen miles and a-half below the Macmillan, a small stream, about ten feet by three inches, enters from the south-eastward. The bed is wide, and it appears at seasons of flood to become a formidable torrent. At thirty-six miles from the Macmillan another small stream was observed on the south side, but with this exception, the river receives no further tributaries before meeting the Lewes. Judging from Campbell's sketch, this otherwise insignificant stream must be that flowing from Tatlmain Lake, which was probably a source of supply of fish for Fort Tatlmain Lake. Selkirk while that post was maintained.

After passing the ridge which is cut through by Granite Cañon, the Low country. country on both sides of the river for about fifteen miles is quite low. No mountains or high hills are in sight on any bearing to the westward, and wide terraces run far back from the river at heights of 150 to 200 feet above it. These are often lightly wooded, largely with aspen, and are clothed with a good growth of grass presenting a very attractive appearance. The soil is good, and at the time of our

Appearance of the country.

visit the country was very dry. *Anemone patens* was seen here for the first time since reaching the Yukon basin, and *Elœagnus argentea* was also noted, both species characteristic of a rather dry climate. For the remaining distance to the mouth of the Lewes, the river is more closely bordered by low hills and ridges, which seldom exceed a height of 400 feet. At one place the stream is confined between high and somewhat rocky banks, but no rapid is met with. The southern slopes of the hills are generally open and grassy, and would afford excellent pasturage. The northern exposures are still pretty thickly wooded. Just above its confluence with the Lewes, the Pelly makes an abrupt turn to the south, and runs for several miles along the eastern base of a scarped cliff of basalt. From Granite Cañon to the confluence, the current scarcely exceeds two miles and a-half an hour.

Rock exposures

For a number of miles below Granite Cañon, no rocks are met with along the river, but lower down there are frequent exposures, extending for some miles, of highly crystalline schists, which strike nearly east-and-west, parallel to the main direction of the river, with general high northward dips. These rocks differ considerably from any before seen, including dark, wholly-crystalline schists, holding hornblende or hornblende and mica. With these are associated considerable exposures of a peculiar dark-green chlorite rock, containing large mica crystals.

This rock is interbedded with white, coarsely crystalline marble, in some places, and is quite evidently the alteration-product of some stratified material which has doubtless, however been of volcanic origin. Nine miles above the confluence, by the course of the river, a

Serpentine,

great mass of impure serpentine comes out on the bank, and six miles and a-half above the same place, grey granite of the usual character is again met with,* and appears to constitute the hills to the east of the river for the remaining few miles of its course.

Basalt bluffs.

The basalt, which forms a plateau from 200 to 250 feet in height in the angle to the west of the Pelly at its junction with the Lewes, consists of several superposed flows, not always distinctly separable at a distance. It forms a mural cliff, with a long talus of angular fragments sloping down to the river-level, and though not very distinctly columnar where it fronts on the Pelly, becomes so below the confluence. The rock is brown in colour and often vesicular.

Superficial deposits.

The bedded silts were seen above Granite Cañon, but are scarcely represented below it. Boulder-clay was noted in one place below the cañon, and the old stratified gravels in several places. The scarped banks along this lower part of the river are, however, chiefly composed

---

* See Appendix V. (Upper Pelly, No. 61.)

of well rolled valley- or river-gravels, which become much more important than before, and often constitute entire terraces up to forty feet in height.

A remarkable layer of fine white volcanic ash, which overlies the glacial deposits all along the Upper Pelly valley, as well as in that of the Lewes, has already been described on page 43 B.

Volcanic ash.

General Notes on the Upper Pelly River.

The total length of the Upper Pelly, following the course of the river, from the point where we first reached it at the west end of Campbell's Portage to its confluence with the Lewes, is 320 miles. The elevation at the first-mentioned point is about 2965 feet, that at the confluence 1555 feet, giving a total fall of 1410 feet or 4·4 feet to the mile, a considerable portion of which, however, occurs in the numerous little rapids and riffles of its course. In Hoole Cañon the estimated fall is about twenty feet. Two hundred and eighteen islands were counted in the river, without including such gravel bars as are submerged at high water, and are consequently without vegetation. The general course of the river is remarkably direct, and it embraces two main directions, the first bearing N. 55° W., the second, N. 87° W. These are parallel to the principal orographic features respectively of the upper and lower parts of the country traversed, and appear to indicate the main slopes of the general surface of the region.

Length and fall of the river

With the exception of Granite Cañon, where warping might have to be resorted to at one place, the river would be easily navigable for stern-wheel steamers as far up as the mouth of the Macmillan, and the latter stream is also navigable for a considerable though unknown distance. Above the Macmillan, I believe, no serious difficulty would be met with in taking a small stern-wheel steamer of good power up to the mouth of Ross River, and possibly as far as the foot of Hoole Cañon. A line might have to be carried ashore at a few of the stronger rapids, but the chief difficulty to be encountered would be from shoal water at low stages. Where the river is widely spread and swift, a depth of three feet could scarcely be found across some of the gravelly bars. The Ross River is a navigable stream at its mouth, but its upper part is quite unknown. Hoole Cañon is, of course, quite impassable for a steamer of any kind, and the rapid met with seventeen miles east of it, at the mouth of Hoole River, might prove to be a difficult one to surmount by warping, its fall being estimated at about eight feet. Above this point, the river is again, however, an easily navigable one

Navigability.

for small steamers to the furthest point seen by us, and possibly as far as the lakes.*

Tributaries from the south.

All the streams and small rivers flowing into the Pelly from the south and rising in or beyond the Pelly and Glenlyon mountains, are notably swift, and most of them are evidently subject to heavy freshets.

Timber.

Some notes have already been given respecting the character of the timber along the Upper Pelly. On the lower part of the river there are numerous groves on or not far from the banks, with good spruce up to two feet in diameter. Spruce of the same size is found also on the whole upper part of the river, but is relatively less abundant there.

Quartz.

As in the case of the Upper Liard and Frances rivers, quartz derived from veins is an abundant constituent of the gravel-bars of the Pelly, and numerous small quartz veins were observed in the rocks in many places. Where the granites are approached, the veins are found to cut all the rocks except these, and it appears that the development of the quartz veins is due to the same period of disturbance which has given rise to the uplift of the granite axes or their extrusion.

Gold.

Small "colours" of gold may be found in almost any suitable locality along the river, and "heavy colours," in considerable number, were found by us as far up as the mouth of Hoole River, in the bottom of a gravel-bed there resting on the basalt. The river has been prospected to some extent by a few miners, but no mining of importance has yet been done on it. Thomas Boswell, whom we met on the Lewes, informed me that he had found and worked for a short time, a bar which paid at the rate of $18 per diem. This was on a tributary which, from his description, is probably identified as the Ross River. Two miners only, Messrs. Monroe and Langtry, were at work on this river in 1887, and their operations were confined to the part below Granite Cañon, where they made on a couple of bars from $10 to $20 per diem to the hand. The headwaters of the Macmillan and Ross, and those of the Pelly itself yet remain unprospected, as well as the very numerous tributary streams of these rivers, in some of which "coarse" gold may yet be found.

Coal.

From observations subsequently made on the Lewes, coal may be looked for in the Laramie or Cretaceous rocks near the river at the locality described on page 126 B.

---

* Dall, in his Alaska and its Resources, 1870, p. 278, gives a hypothetical itinerary of the Pelly River, making it head in Frances Lake. The Pelly, as shown on the map which accompanies the work, is evidently in part after Arrowsmith, and where it differs, (as in regard to the connection of Frances and Finlayson lakes with the Pelly), becomes misleading. It is difficult to understand why this part of Arrowsmith's map, bearing intrinsic evidence of proximate accuracy, should not have been followed throughout in the compilation of later maps, particularly as the Pelly had not been farther explored since Campbell's time.

CONFLUENCE OF THE LEWES AND UPPER PELLY.

The country about the confluence, is generally speaking low, with Comparison of the rivers. extensive terrace-flats running back to the bases of rounded hills and ridges, of which none in sight probably exceed 1000 feet above the river. The moderate current which has been described as characteristic of the Upper Pelly for some distance above the confluence, continues to its mouth, but the Lewes is much swifter, and though at the point of junction divided among wooded islands, is evidently the larger stream, carrying a volume of water considerably greater than that of the Pelly, though probably less than twice as great (p. 18 B). It does not, however, necessarily follow from this that the Lewes is to be considered the principal head stream or continuation of the Yukon. The question of nomenclature and that of the position of the furthest sources of the Yukon, have, however, been referred to at greater length in another portion of this report. (p. 14 B).

The water of the Lewes is of a bluish, slightly milky cast and is easily distinguished from the brownish muddy colour by which the Pelly is characterized below its junction with the Macmillan. The temperature of the water in both rivers was found to be practically Temperature. identical, on the 17th and 18th of August, at 7 p.m., being 59° F.

The river below the confluence of the Pelly and Lewes averages Volume of united rivers. about a quarter of a mile in width, and though its appearance is placid and there is no rough water. it is uniformly swift. An approximate cross-section made by Mr. Ogilvie showed the river to be, at the point in question, 25·76 chains wide, from bank to bank. Of this width about two-thirds had an average depth of ten feet, with a surface velocity of four miles and three-quarter an hour. The remaining third was occupied by shallow bars and slack water. Using the same formula as before (see p. 98 B) the volume of the flow is found to be approximately 66,955 cubic feet per second. Traces of the passage of flood-water in the preceding spring were found on the river-flat, about ten feet above the low-water level, which, with a velocity no greater than that above stated and assuming the banks to be vertical, would give a flood discharge of at least 167,400 cubic feet per second. It may be, however, that the water-marks observed were caused by the damming back of the river by an ice-gorge.

The ruins of Fort Selkirk, formerly a post of the Hudson Bay Com- Ruins of Fort Selkirk. pany, stand on a partly open flat, on the south side, at a short distance back from the river, and about a mile and a-half below the confluence of the Pelly and Lewes. One chimney, built of basalt blocks which must have been brought across the river, and cemented with clay which has been baked almost into brick by the combustion of the ruins of the fort, still stands erect and uninjured. The lower part of a second is near it, and the fragments of several others strew the ground, which is partly overgrown by small aspens. These, and the traces of a couple of excavations which have probably been cellars, are all that now remain to mark the site of the buildings which were pillaged by Indians from the coast in 1852.

DISCOVERY AND EXPLORATION OF THE LIARD AND PELLY.

Hudson Bay
Company
explorers.

Fort Selkirk, of which the ruins alone now exist, was at one time the most important post of the Hudson Bay Company to the west of the Rocky Mountains in the far north, and with the exception of Fort Yukon, it was the farthest permanent post ever maintained by the Company to the north-west. On previous pages of this report, frequent mention has been made of the former establishments of the Company in the Liard and Yukon region, and as Fort Selkirk is the last of these with which our route brought us in contact, a note as to the operations of the Hudson Bay Company may appropriately be given here. When we call to mind that our knowledge of the geography of the region described in preceding pages has been up to the present time almost wholly due to the explorations carried out by the officers of the Company in connection with these establishments, it becomes evident that the history of these explorations and the facts respecting the several posts are well worthy of record.

McLeod.

The circumstances attending the discovery of the Dease and Upper Stikine have already been given on page 83 B. Mr. J. McLeod, whose explorations in that quarter are there referred to, appears in the same year in which he reached the Stikine (1834), to have ascended the Liard as far as Simpson Lake, and to have brought back the information according to which the river was represented on Arrowsmith's map

Campbell.

of 1850. It was to the energy of Mr. Robert Campbell, however, that the exploration of the Upper Liard and Yukon is almost entirely due. The only published account of Mr. Campbell's work, so far as I know, is that which appeared in the Royal Reader, Fifth Book, Toronto, 1883, p. 435, and which was reprinted, with slight alterations at Winnipeg in 1885, as a small pamphlet entitled " Discovery and Exploration of the Youcon (Pelly) River." From this source and from additional facts furnished by Mr. Campbell in answer to questions addressed to him, as well as from allusions in the unpublished journals of Chief Factor James Anderson, which have kindly been placed at my disposal by his son, the following brief account is drawn up.—

After the abandonment of Dease Lake post in 1839, Mr. Campbell was, in the spring of 1840, commissioned by Sir George Simpson to explore the "north branch" of the Liard to its source, and to cross the height-of-land in search of any river flowing to the westward, especially the head waters of the Colville, the mouth of which on the Arctic Ocean had recently been discovered by Messrs. Dease and Simpson.

Mr. Campbell writes:—"In pursuance of these instructions, I left Fort Halkett [on the Lower Liard] in May, with a canoe and seven men, among them my trusty Indians, Lapie and Kitza, and the interpreter, Hoole. After ascending the stream some hundreds of miles, far into the mountains, we entered a beautiful lake, which I named Frances Lake, in honor of Lady Simpson. * * * Leaving the canoe and part of the crew near the south-west [sic] extremity of this [the west] branch of the lake, I set out with three Indians and the interpreter. Shouldering our blankets and guns, we ascended the valley of a river, which we traced to its source in a lake ten miles long, which, with the river, I named Finlayson's Lake and River." From this point, Mr. Campbell struck across to the Pelly, which he then named in honor of Sir H. Pelly, a Governor of the Company. *Expedition to the Pelly.*

" After reaching the actual bank of the river, we constructed a raft, on which we embarked and drifted down a few miles on the bosom of the stream, and at parting we cast in a scaled tin can, with memoranda of our discovery, the date, etc."

During Campbell's absence the remainder of the party built a house at the point between the two arms of the lake, which was then named " Glenlyon House," but was afterwards known as Frances Lake House or Fort Frances. Returning down the river, they met a trading outfit which had been despatched for them, at Fort Halkett, and turned back with it to Frances Lake, after sending out a report of their proceedings. *Establishment of Fort Frances*

The Company now resolved to follow up these western discoveries, and in 1842 birch bark, for the construction of a large canoe to be used in exploring the Pelly, was sent up from Fort Liard. In the same year Fort Pelly Banks was constructed, or its construction begun, and early in June, 1843, Campbell left that place in the canoe which had been made, accompanied by Hoole, two French-Canadians and three Indians. *Exploration of the Pelly.*

They saw only one family of Indians ("Knife Indians") till they reached the mouth of the river which Campbell called the Lewes. Here was a large camp of " Wood Indians," and these, after recovering from their surprise at the sight of the party, so discouraged Campbell's men by their stories of the number and ferocity of the people on the lower river, that he was obliged to turn back.

For some years afterwards the operations of the Company did not extend beyond " Pelly Banks," though during the summer, hunting *"Pelly Banks."*

parties were sent down the Pelly to collect provisions, and in that way information was received respecting the river and the Indians inhabiting its vicinity.

Establishment of Fort Selkirk. In the winter of 1847-48 boats were built at Pelly Banks, and early in June following Campbell set out to establish a fort at the confluence of the Pelly and Lewes rivers. This was named Fort Selkirk, and was at first situated on the extreme point of land between the two rivers, but this point being found subject to floods during the disruption of the ice, the post was in the spring of 1852 moved to a site a short way below the mouth of the Lewes, on the left bank. The inner work of the new buildings was still unfinished at the time of the Indian raid, noticed further on.

Exploration of Porcupine River. Meanwhile an entry was being made into the Yukon basin from another direction. Mr. J. Bell had already in 1842 reached the Porcupine or Rat River, and had descended it for three days' journey. He was in 1846 in charge of the Hudson Bay post on Peel River, near the mouth of the Mackenzie, and was instructed again to cross the mountains and to further explore the Porcupine River. In pursuance of these instructions, he in that year reached the mouth of the Porcupine and saw the great river into which it flows, which the Indians informed him was named the Yukon. In 1847 Fort Yukon was established at the mouth of the Porcupine by Mr. A. H. Murray.

Identity of Pelly and Yukon shown. It still remained, however, for Campbell, in 1850, to prove that the Pelly and Yukon were identical. This he did by descending the river from Fort Selkirk, to Fort Yukon, after which he ascended the Porcupine, crossed the mountain-portage, and returned to Fort Simpson by the Mackenzie.* One result of this journey was to show that the route from Fort Selkirk by way of the Porcupine River to the Mackenzie was preferable to that originally discovered. The navigation of the Liard was both arduous and dangerous and several lives had been lost in boating on that stream. Added to this was the length of the land transport from Frances Lake to the Upper Pelly and the fact that great difficulty had been found in maintaining the posts in that district.

---

* Mr. Campbell states that when again on his way down the river from Fort Selkirk to Fort Yukon, in 1851, he found that a great number of the Indians had been carried off during the previous winter by some virulent disease.

He has further informed me, in answer to my enquiries on the subject, that the Stewart River was so named after his "dear and gallant friend and assistant-clerk, James G. Stewart, son of the late Hon. John Stewart, of Quebec." Stewart was sent out in the winter of 1849 to follow the Indian hunters in quest of meat. He found them some distance north of this river, which he crossed on the ice.

White River, Mr. Campbell named on account of its milky color. Of the other streams entering between Forts Selkirk and Yukon he says, " Antoine River " was named after the interpreter at one time at Fort Yukon, a son of his interpreter Hoole ; " Forcier River," after his guide, Baptiste Forcier; " Lolique River," for Forcier's wife; and " Ayonie's River," below the White River, was named after the natives of that quarter.

In 1849, the post at Pelly Banks, with the exception of the men's house, was accidently burnt. In 1850 it was finally abandoned, and in the spring of 1851 Fort Frances was likewise abandoned.*   The abandonment of these posts was not due to any hostility of the natives, who were on the contrary most friendly, but in consequence of the circumstances above noted, and the fact that while these establishments were very expensive to maintain, they merely bought furs which would otherwise have been carried by the Indians themselves to other posts, if these particular, and to them more convenient ones, had not been in existence.

The several ruined chimneys of Fort Selkirk still to be seen, with other traces on the ground, are in themselves evidence of the important dimensions and careful construction of this post. The establishment consisted, I believe, in 1852, of one senior and one junior clerk and eight men. The existence of this post in the centre of the inland or "Wood Indian" country had, however, very seriously interfered with a lucrative and usurious trade which the Chilkoot and Chilkat Indians of Lynn Canal, on the coast, had long been accustomed to carry on with these people; acting as intermediaries between them and the white traders on the Pacific and holding the passes at the head-waters of the Lewes with all the spirit of robber barons of old. In 1852, rumours were current that these people meditated a raid upon the post, in consequence of which the friendly local Indians staid by it nearly all summer, of their own accord. It so happened, however, that they absented themselves for a couple of days and at that unlucky moment the Coast Indians arrived. The post was unguarded by a stockade and yielding to sheer force of numbers the occupants were expelled and the place was pillaged, on the 21st August. Two days afterward Campbell, having found the local Indians, returned with them and surrounded the post, but the robbers had flown. Being now without means of support for the winter, Campbell set off down stream to meet Mr. Stewart and the men who were on the way back from Fort Yukon. He met them at the mouth of White River and after turning them back with instructions to arrange for wintering at Fort Yukon, set out himself in a small canoe up the Pelly River, crossed to Frances Lake, descended the Liard and arrived at Fort Simpson with the tidings of the disaster, amid drifting ice, on the 21st of October.

Being anxious to obtain Sir George Simpson's permission to re-establish Fort Selkirk, Campbell waited only till the river froze, when he left Fort Simpson on snow-shoes and travelled overland to Crow Wing in Minnesota, where he arrived on the 13th of March. On the

----

* Forts Frances and Pelly Banks are erroneously stated in Dall's Alaska and its Resources, to have been burnt and pillaged, p. 115, foot-note and p. 508.

18th of April he reached London but was unable to obtain from the directors of the company the permission he desired. A short account of this remarkable journey appeared in the Perthshire Advertiser and Inverness Courier, but I do not know the precise date of the publication.

News from Fort Selkirk. In the autumn of 1853, one of Campbell's hunters arrived at Fort Halkett on the Lower Liard by way of the Pelly and Frances. This is the last traverse of Campbell's Portage of which I can find any record, though it may doubtless have been used by the Indians subsequently. From this man it was learnt that the buildings at Fort Selkirk had been all but demolished by the local Indians for the purpose of getting the iron-work and the nails. He also stated that the Chilkats, being unable to carry away all their plunder in the preceding year, had taken merely the guns, powder and tobacco. They had cached the heavier goods, which were afterwards found and appropriated by the local or wood Indians. At a later date the ruins of the post must have been burnt, as their present appearance indicates.*

The United States and Fort Yukon. Fort Yukon, at the mouth of the Porcupine, was continuously maintained till 1869, when the Hudson Bay Company was expelled by the United States Government as represented by Capt. Charles W. Raymond, Corps of Engineers, U. S. Army; he having ascertained by astronomical observations that the post was situated to the west of the 141st meridian. He describes his proceedings as follows.—" On the 9th of August, at 12 m., I notified the representative of the Hudson Bay Company that the station is in the territory of the United States; that the introduction of trading goods, or any trade by foreigners with the natives, is illegal, and must cease; and that the Hudson Bay Company must vacate the buildings as soon as practicable. I then took possession of the buildings and raised the flag of the United States over the fort." † The fort was afterwards abandoned and allowed to go to ruin.

Pioneers of the Hudson Bay Company. The utmost credit must be accorded to the pioneers of the Hudson Bay Company for the enterprise displayed by them in carrying their trade into the Yukon basin in the face of difficulties so great and at such an immense distance from their base of supplies. To explorations of this kind performed in the service of commerce, unostentatiously and as matters of simple duty by such men as Mackenzie, Fraser, Thompson and Campbell, we owe the discovery of our great north-west . country. Their journeys were not marked by incidents of conflict or bloodshed, but were accomplished on the contrary with the

* Of Reid House, shown on Arrowsmith's map of 1854, near the Stewart River and to the north of Fort Selkirk, I have been unable to learn anything. Mr. Campbell never heard of it, and if it had any existence it was probably a temporary outpost of Fort Yukon.

† Report of a Reconnaissance of the Yukon River, 1871, p. 16.

friendly assistance and co-operation of the natives. Less resolute men would scarcely have entertained the idea of utilizing, as an avenue of trade, a river so perilous of navigation as the Liard had proved to be when explored. So long, however, as this appeared to be the most practicable route to the country beyond the mountains, its abandonment was not even contemplated. Neither distance nor danger appear to have been taken into account, and in spite of every obstacle a way was opened and a series of posts established extending from Fort Simpson, on the Mackenzie to Fort Yukon. Fort Simpson may itself be regarded, even at the present day, as a post very far removed from the borders of civilization, but this further route, which nearly half a century ago became familiar to the Company's voyageurs, stretched out beyond it for over a thousand miles. Mr. James Anderson, in 1853, writes thus of the Liard River : " You can hardly conceive the intense horror the men have to go up to Frances Lake. They invariably on re-hiring endeavour to be exempted from the West Branch [Liard]. The number of deaths which have occurred there is fourteen, viz. three in connection with Dease Lake and eleven in connection with Frances Lake and Pelly Banks, of these last three died from starvation and eight from drowning." Dangers of the Liard.

At the time of the establishment of Forts Yukon and Selkirk, and for many years afterwards, the "returns" from these furthest stations reached the market only after seven years, the course of trade being as follows : *Goods.*—1st year, reach York Factory ; 2nd year, Norway House ; 3rd year, Peel River, and were hauled during the winter across the mountains to La Pierre's House; 4th year, reach Fort Yukon. *Returns.*—5th year, reach La Pierre's House and are hauled across to Peel River ; 6th year, reach depot at Fort Simpson ; 7th year reach market. The "returns."

LEWES RIVER.

Our proceedings at the mouth of Lewes River and our meeting there with Mr. Ogilvie have already been noted. We finally left the confluence and began the ascent of the Lewes on the 18th of August, and arrived at Lake Lindeman, where the portage to the coast begins, on September 16th. We were during this time on the one travelled route of the country, and every few days fell in with small parties of miners, generally on their way out, up the river. A few men were still found working on bars, and six or eight passed down stream with the purpose of wintering at or near Forty-mile Creek. Meeting with Mr. Ogilvie.

Though my own observations did not extend below the mouth of the Lewes, Mr. W. Ogilvie sent out by the last party of miners met by him on their way to the coast, a small collection of rocks from places further down the river, as far as Forty-mile Creek. The general character of these has already been noted in the introductory part of this report (p. 34 B). They are not further described here, as they will be referred to by Mr. McConnell in connection with his geological examination of the portion of the river from which they were derived.

Discovery of the Lewes. The Lewes River * was discovered and named by Mr. Campbell in 1842, as already stated. It is indicated in an approximate manner, according to information supplied by this gentleman, on Arrowsmith's map of 1854. Mr. Campbell informs me that he was well aware of the existence at its head of a portage to the sea by which the Chilkat Indians came inland to trade. This route he had the intention of exploring, but the question of supplies and other difficulties prevented him from doing so. Communication was occasionally had by this route with the Hudson Bay steamer which traded along the coast, and it was thus that the Honolulu paper mentioned as received in 1848 by Sir. J. Richardson, on the Mackenzie, was sent inland. Such communication was, however, only accomplished by travelling parties of Indians.

First exploration. In 1867, Frank E. Ketchum, of St. John, New Brunswick, and Michael Labarge, of Montreal, explorers in the employ of the Western Union Telegraph Company, ascended the Pelly or Yukon from Fort Yukon to the mouth of the Lewes, returning down the river. In the same year, Michael Byrnes, also an explorer of the Telegraph Company, reached the Hotolinqu (of Telegraph Survey map, not the river subsequently so called by miners) which is now known to be one of the furthest if not the most remote source of the Lewes. This he did from the direction of the Stikine, but was recalled before he had, by descending the river, proved its relation to the Lewes. †

Incursion of miners. As elsewhere stated, in connection with the history of gold mining in the Yukon basin, (p. 178 B) the head-waters of the Lewes River were first reached from the head of Lynn Canal about 1878. Between the date of the explorations of the Telegraph Company and this time, the Lewes may have been visited by traders ascending from the Lower Yukon, but of this we have no record. Previous to 1883, however, the river and some of its tributaries had become well known to a number

---

* So named by Campbell after Chief Factor, John Lee Lewes.

The name of the Lewes given to me by the Tagish Indians was Ta-hi-ne-wat (=Big Salmon River) but I am doubtful whether this applies to the whole stream or to some special part of it.

† See Dall's Alaska, p. 277. A statement in a subsequent paragraph on the same page would appear to indicate that Messrs. Ketchum and Labarge reached Lake Labarge of later maps, but I can find nothing to bear this out. Whymper, in his travels in Alaska and on the Yukon (p. 229) also limits their journey at Fort Selkirk. Dall in consequence of the imperfection of the map of the Telegraph Survey with which he was supplied, in his work and on the map accompanying it, continues the head-waters of the Taku River into the Hotolinqu River, making them tributary to the Lewes, but in an addendum, at the end of the book, notes and corrects this error.

of miners and prospectors, and when Lieut. Schwatka, in the last Surveys by Schwatka. mentioned year, crossed the Chilkoot Pass and descended the Lewes, he merely followed in their footsteps. To Lieut. Schwatka is, however, due the credit of having made the first survey of the river, a survey which Mr. Ogilvie's work of 1887, has proved to be a reasonably accurate one, in so far as its main features are concerned. This being the case it would be an ungracious task to criticise in detail, either Lieut. Schwatka's map or the various accounts which he has given of his journey. As, however, he is not sparing in his condemnation of the inaccuracy of the compilers of the maps made before the results of his journey were available, I need have no hesitation in stating my belief, that his desire to affirm that he had started at the source of the Yukon and followed it to its mouth, caused him to fail to observe that Lake Lindeman is not even on the main source of the Lewes, and to change the name of the Lewes which had already appeared on the maps for about thirty years to that of Yukon, a quite arbitrary and unjustifiable proceeding. (See p. 16 n.) In addition to this he has completely ignored the names of many places already well known to miners, throughout the country, substituting others of his own invention, some of which even differ in the different versions of the map of his route which he has published. Strict justice might demand the exclusion of all these new names on the definitive maps now published, but to avoid an appearance of arbitrary action in the matter, and more especially in view of the scientific eminence of some of the names which he has selected, it has been decided to retain as many as possible of these.

While the general course of the Upper Pelly is remarkably straight, Pelly and Lewes contrasted. that of the Lewes makes several important and well marked bends and is besides interrupted by lakes and otherwise irregular. These irregularities are to be accounted for by the fact that the Lewes, instead of following a direction parallel with the main orographic features of the country, runs for a considerable part of its course diagonally across the principal ridges and valleys.

In describing the Lewes and the main geological features met with Distances. along it, the site of Fort Selkirk is taken as an initial point and the distances are given as measured on the map, up the mid-channel of the river. The distances thus arrived at will not be found to correspond exactly with those given by Mr. Ogilvie in his preliminary account of his survey of the river,* Mr. Ogilvie's distances being those instrumentally measured from station to station of his survey.

---

* Contained in the Annual Report of the Department of the Interior for 1887. See also Report of Proceedings of Association of Dominion Land Surveyors, 1883, p. 61.

Fort Selkirk to Rink Rapid.

Character of
the river.

From the site of Fort Selkirk to Rink or Five-finger Rapid, the course of the river is nearly straight, the bearing being about S. 50° W. and the distance, measured by the stream, fifty-five miles. The current of this part of the river is swift throughout, averaging about four miles and a-half an hour and seldom being under four miles. At a point six miles below Rink Rapid, where the course of the river was uninterrupted by islands and its velocity and width about normal, the rate of flow was found to be 4·8 miles per hour, the width 732 feet. There are numerous islands, which differ from most of those met with on the Pelly in frequently occupying positions in mid-channel instead of being merely portions of river-flats cut off by lateral sloughs. A few miles above the mouth of the Lewes, these islands are particularly numerous, for a distance of about five miles, and the total width of the stream from bank to bank, is increased to nearly a mile. This group has been named Ingersoll Islands by Schwatka.

Terraces.

The terraces and flats immediately bordering the river, are at first quite low, but in ascending, increase in height till they stand often at 100 to 200 feet above it before reaching Rink Rapid. They are for the most part composed of rolled river- or valley-gravels like those of the Pelly at a similar distance above the confluence. Boulder-clay first occurs in the scarped banks about six miles below Rink Rapid.

Character of
the valley.

The river-valley is generally wide and somewhat ill defined, the ridges and low hills bounding it seldom exceeding 1000 feet in height. Near the mouth of the river these are irregularly disposed, but further up, those on the north-east bank become more uniform and run parallel to the stream like the hills on that part of the Pelly near the Macmillan. In a few places the slopes of the hills run down to the water's edge, and it is generally only at such points that rock exposures occur. Hooche-koo Bluff is situated thirty-five miles above the old fort, on the north-east bank, and is formed by the abrupt face of an isolated hill, against which the river washes. With the exception of Tatshun River, a mile and a-half below Rink Rapid, the tributaries of this part of the Lewes are merely small brooks. This stream is about 30 feet wide by 6 inches deep, with clear brownish water.

Rink Rapid.

Two miles below Rink Rapid, the Lewes makes a right-angled bend to the south-westward. The rapid itself is caused by the occurrence of several bold rocky islands which obstruct the river, and is only a few yards in length, where the water flows swiftly between them. The channels are deep and unobstructed, and at low stages of water might, I believe, be ascended by a steamer of good power even without the assistance of warping. At high-water this rapid would, of course, be more formidable, as the velocity of the stream would be increased. It is pretty evident that a fall has at one time existed here, but the barrier of conglomerate which has produced it has now been cut completely through by the river. Below the main rapid there is a second "riffle" or minor rapid which appears to be somewhat stony, but which would not be a serious impediment to a properly constructed steamer.

The general appearance of the country along this part of the river is pleasing and resembles that of the corresponding part of the Pelly. It is usually wooded, but the southern exposures of some of the hills are partly open, and dry, grass-covered terrace-flats are frequent. The trees are of the same species before mentioned and birch is moderately abundant. *Eleagnus argentea* was noted on dry banks. Fine country.

On this part of the Lewes, rock-exposures are unfrequent and it is consequently impossible to give any connected account of the geology. About five miles above the old fort, on the west bank, are outcrops of basalt, which appear to indicate an outlying patch of this rock. Just below these on the river, is a dark greenish rock which seems to be a bedded diorite and to have a high south-west dip. On the other side of the basalt, a massive, coarsely crystalline, black, hornblende-rock occurs, which is followed by hornblendic granite. The granite, in some places, contains large porphyritic crystals of pink felspar, in addition to the more abundant white triclinic felspars. It continues for some miles, near the Ingersoll Islands, and probably connects with the exposures on the Pelly to the north-east. The few exposures examined between the granite and Hoo-che-koo Bluff, consist of greenish and greenish-grey rocks, being altered volcanic materials, probably with the lithological composition of diabase. In one place a distinct volcanic agglomerate was seen. Geology.

Hoo-chee-koo Bluff consists of a grey, slightly porphyritic, felspathic rock which is apparently interbedded with a fine-grained, nearly black argillite, but the rocks are everywhere very much fractured and jointed. The south end of the bluff shows a pretty evident, altered agglomerate of a similar felspathic material. The jointage planes often contain seams of calcite and show copper-staining. Specimens of the copper-stained portions of the rock proved, on assay by Mr. Hoffmann, to contain minute traces of gold, with ·088 oz. of silver to the ton. Hoo-chee-koo Bluff.

The rocks along the Lewes so far described, with the exception of the granites, may be referred to the Palæozoic.

For about twelve miles above the Hoo-chee-koo Bluff no rocks were seen, after which, for eight miles, or to Rink Rapid, there are frequent exposures of rocks of a different series, of much less altered appearance and all probably referable to the Cretaceous. These include coarse, hard, dark grauwacke-sandstones, with softer shaly sandstones, passing Rocks above Hoo-chee-koo.

10

Cretaceous rocks.

into dark sandy shales, all more or less calcareous. Just below Rink Rapid, on the south-east bank, are brownish evidently tufaceous rocks, the materials of which also, however, include well-rounded quartz pebbles. These pass by easy stages into grauwacke-sandstones and are interbedded with coarse conglomerates containing pebbles of granite and of greenish altered volcanic rocks, like those of the older series seen lower down the river. Carbonaceous streaks and pieces of dark-coloured fossil wood are included in some of the beds ; and a couple of layers two to three feet thick, were observed, which are so carbonaceous that they might almost be called coal. The dip is here N. 20°, W. < 40°, but elsewhere in this vicinity is varied and confused.

Conglomerates and sandstones.

The rock of the islands and banks of the actual rapid is coarse con-glomerate which often contains boulders of granite up to eighteen inches in diameter and is interstratified with irregular beds of yellowish sandstone, the appearance of the conglomerate being much like that of the conglomerate of Jackass Mountain on the Fraser River, though somewhat less altered. Immediately above the rapid, on the south-east side of the river, grey and blackish shales, with thin beds of sandstone and of limestone, appear from below the conglomerates. These were found to contain fossils in considerable abundance, though represent-ing but a few species.

Cretaceous fossils.

The fossils have been examined by Mr. Whiteaves, who states that of four determinable species, all but one appear to be new, but that the occurrence of a *Schlœnbachia* apparently identical with a species from the lower part of the section in the Queen Charlotte Islands, would seem to show that the rocks may be of corresponding age, or about the lower part of the Middle Cretaceous.

The species are as follows :—*

> *Discina pileolus*, N. sp.
> *Cyprina Yukonensis*, N. sp.
> *Schlœnbachia* (*propinqua ?* var.) *borealis*.
> *Estheria bellula*, N. sp.

Fossil plants.

Sir J. Wm. Dawson has examined the fossil woods found at the same place, and writes of them as follows :—" Two species of fossil coniferous wood. One of these shows large wood-cells with one to two rows of discs and long narrow medullary rays. It is not improbably the wood of a species of *Sequoia*. The other has thick-walled wood-cells with one row of discs and spiral lines, the medullary rays being short and few celled. It has the characters of a taxine wood, and is not unlike that of *Salisburia*. Another specimen from this place is a small and badly preserved branchlet, with short and apparently thick curved

---

* To be described and figured in Part II. Contributions to Canadian Palæontology.

subulate leaves. It is probably coniferous, and it is not unlike *Sequoia ambigua* and *S. concinna*, of Heer, from the Cretaceous of Greenland. It is, however, quite obscure, and might be a species of the Mesozoic genus *Pachyhyllum*."

The constituents of the gravel found along the Lewes River differ con- Gravels of the Lewes. siderably in appearance from those of the Pelly gravels. Granite of various kinds is abundant, and there is a notable profusion and variety of green and greyish-green altered rocks of volcanic origin in association with which are found occasional pebbles of more or less pure jade, which appear to pass by insensible gradations into green rocks of the kind above mentioned. Quartz vein-stuff is much less important as a constituent of the river-gravels than it is on the Upper Pelly, Upper Liard and other streams to the eastward.

Rink Rapid to Little Salmon River.

From Rink Rapid to the mouth of the Nordenskiöld, the general bearing of the river is nearly due south, the distance in a straight line being twelve miles. From this point the general bearing is about south-east for eighteen miles and a-half, when it turns abruptly to a north-east direction round Eagle's Nest Rock, and in five miles reaches the mouth of the Little Salmon River. The total distance from Rink Rapid to the last-named place, measured by the stream, is fifty-three miles, though the through distance, on a straight line (which would have a south-east bearing) drawn between the two terminal points is twenty-seven and a-half miles only.

The Nordenskiöld is a small swift river with clear bluish water, Nordenskiöld River. which enters the Lewes on the west side. It was estimated as eighty feet wide by six inches deep, a couple of hundred yards above its mouth, on the 23rd of August, when it was evidently near its lowest stage. Its valley is not a wide or important one, it being in fact difficult to decide from which direction the stream comes a few miles back from the Lewes. The Little Salmon (or Daly, as re-christened by Schwatka) joins the Lewes on the opposite side, and was estimated to carry about twice as much water as the Nordenskiöld. It is about one hundred feet wide with an average depth of three feet. The water is clear and brownish in tint, and the current not rapid at the mouth.

The valley of the Lewes, between Rink Rapid and the Little Salmon Lewes valley. River, is in general somewhat irregular and not very wide, but a few miles before reaching the Little Salmon, the river turns into a wide valley which runs north-east and south-west and appears to be continuous with that of the Little Salmon in the first mentioned direction. The hills, in the vicinity of the river, seldom exceed 800 feet in height, till near the Little Salmon, when they attain 1000 or possibly 1500 feet.

No mountains are in sight from this part of the river. Terraces rising to 200 feet are frequent and often run back at about that level to the bases of the hills. Near the mouth of the Nordenskiöld, the river is extremely crooked, and the current is everywhere swift. The southern slopes of the hills and terraces are generally in large part open and grassy, no difference such as might indicate a climate more humid than that of the region about old Fort Selkirk being met with. Several magpies were seen, for the first time, on this part of the river.

Gold bars.

The first spot observed by us in ascending the river where bars have been worked for gold, is situated six miles above the Nordenskiöld.

Thick Cretaceous series.

The rocks along this portion of the river, like those last described, belong to the Cretaceous series, but their attitudes are too varied to enable anything like a complete section to be gained from the isolated exposures met with, though the impression was received that the total thickness represented must be very great. The rocks consist generally of sandstones, grauwackes, coarse grits and conglomerate which not unfrequently have a general reddish appearance on weathering, probably in consequence of local dolomitization. A few localities, however, show features worthy of special mention.

Beds of coal.

One of these is found five miles and a-half above Rink Rapid, where a high bluff shows a series principally composed of sandstones, shales and shaly clays, poorly exposed in consequence of the sliding character of the bank, which is being washed away by the river at its base. These have a south-eastward dip, at low angles, and the thickness of beds represented must be several hundred feet. This exposure includes, within sixty feet of the base of the bluff, at least three coaly beds, of which the lowest is about three feet thick. This and the other beds contain some good looking coal, of which a thickness of about a foot sometimes occurs, but the greater part of the material is so sandy and impure as to be useless. The highest of these beds is underlain by a layer of dull purplish-grey, finely granular and porphyritic trachyte from six to eight feet in thickness, and evidently representing a contemporaneous flow of volcanic matter. Its upper surface is somewhat broken up and mixed with carbonaceous matter, and passes into black, carbonaceous sandstone, about a foot thick, above which is the upper impure coal before referred to, overlain by shales and sandstones of the ordinary character.

Wide synclinal

The condition of all the beds in this vicinity is remarkably unaltered, as compared with those seen lower down the river, and would appear to show that if (as assumed) they form a connected series, these represent its upper part. The dip of these beds, taken in connection with that of those near Tantalus Butte and the horizontal appearance of the strata in the hills to the south-westward, indicates the existence

of a synclinal five or six miles in width, running in a south-west by
north-east direction. The relatively high position of these beds is
further shown by the occurrence, about two miles further up the river,
of fossil plants referable to the Laramie. These were found in a hard,
white, shaly rock, which has apparently been permeated by waters
charged with silica about the time of its formation. Sir J. Wm. Dawson Fossil plants.
states that the following species are represented :—

> *Taxodium Tinajorum*, Heer.
> *Glyptostrobus Europæus*, Heer.
> *Sequoia Langsdorfii*, Heer (doubtful).

The thin coal-seams here actually seen cannot be considered as of Composition
economic value, but are important as indicating the existence of a coal- of coal.
bearing horizon which may prove to contain thicker beds elsewhere
and might become an important point in connection with the navigation of the river. The coal has been examined by Mr. G. C. Hoffmann
who describes it as a lignite-coal, with the following composition.—

Hygroscopic water	6·03
Volatile combustible matter	36·92
Fixed Carbon	49·03
Ash	8·02
	100·00

About a mile below Eagle's Nest Rock, are exposures of coarse con- Conglomerate.
glomerate, with inter-bedded sandstones precisely like those of Rink
Rapid. The included stones are well rounded, and often a foot in
diameter, and consist of granites and various green and grey hard,
altered, volcanic rocks. This is probably the same conglomerate bed
with that of the rapid. The dip here is N. 13° W. < 40°.

Frequent exposures of true boulder-clay occur along this part of the Drift deposits.
river, particularly above the Nordenskiöld, where they often form castellated bluffs, in consequence of their considerable induration. The boulder-clay generally shows traces of bedding more or less distinct, and is
sometimes very stony and includes large boulders, a few of which were
observed to be striated. The pebbles are, as a rule, well rounded and
even superficially polished. Clayey gravels with silty layers are
in places associated with the boulder-clay in the manner already
described on the Pelly. In some places the boulder-clay also appears
to be overlain by silty deposits, but on the Lewes thus far up, these
are not extensive or well marked.

Little Salmon to Big Salmon River.

The river and its valley.

From the Little Salmon to the mouth of the Big Salmon River or D'Abbadie, the general bearing of the Lewes is about east-south-east, and the sinuosities of the river are not nearly so great as in the portion last described. The distance by the stream between these tributaries is thirty-four miles. A considerable portion of this part of the river is not so swift as usual, and for eight or ten miles, midway between the Little and Big Salmon rivers, both the river and its valley are more than usually narrowed. Beyond this, the valley begins to widen rapidly and for some miles before the mouth of the Big Salmon is reached, is notably wide, between the bases of the limiting hills. At the mouth of the Big Salmon, the Lewes turns abruptly to the south, while the main valley is continued in a south-easterly direction, becoming there the valley of the Big Salmon. From the confluence of the rivers, the main valley can be seen running on for a distance of about fifteen miles, bordered by low hills to the northward, and by higher hills to the south. These last are the Seminow Mountains of Schwatka. The Lewes cuts through this range, which is continued also for some miles westward, forming the south-west side of the Lewes valley. The hills are rounded in form and wooded, and rise to heights of 1500 to 2000 feet above the river.

Geological features.

Few rock-exposures occur along this part of the Lewes, and in consequence, nothing very definite can be said as to its geological structure. Thirteen miles above the Little Salmon, greenish, grauwacke-sandstones, and green, highly calcareous conglomerates were found, the latter containing pebbles of limestone or marble, granite, various schistose rocks and green altered volcanic rocks. The greater part of the hills in this vicinity seemed to be composed of similar materials, which are evidently newer than the altered volcanic series, and therefore in all probability Mesozoic, and very possibly even Cretaceous. For some distance below the Big Salmon, numerous fragments of lignite-coal and of soft, shaly materials, like those previously described as occurring with the coal, are found on the bars, but cease to appear above the confluence of the Big Salmon, leading to the belief that Cretaceous or Laramie rocks attain a considerable development in the valley of that stream. It would require, however, a detailed survey to separate the various formations in this region, and the result of such an examination would probably be to place in the Mesozoic series a much larger area than would, at first sight, appear probable. At the mouth of the Big Salmon a grey-green, crystalline rock which is apparently a diorite, occurs. It appears to be bedded, and dips southward at an angle of 25°.

Nine miles below the Big Salmon is the first extensive display met Bedded silts.
with on the Lewes of the bedded silty deposits. Scarped banks and cliffs
one hundred feet in height are here composed of these white silts with
some interstratified sands and gravels.   The silts contain numerous
nodular layers and sheets of calcareous concretionary matter, and are
hard and fine-grained toward the base, where they may be seen, in some
places, resting on boulder-clay.

Several bars which had been worked on for gold were seen along this Gold.
part of the Lewes.

Big Salmon River.

The Big Salmon* has been re-named by Schwatka, the D'Abbadie Appearance of the river.
River, a name which has the merit of being more distinctive than that
previously in use, but the miners who (with the exception of the
Indians) alone travel through the country, refuse to know it by any but
the old name.   It is much more important than any of the tributaries
joining the Lewes further down, being 347 feet wide, with a depth of
five feet for about one-third of its width, and a current of about two
miles an hour.   The water is clear and of a bluer tint than that of the
Little Salmon, and the discharge was estimated at 2726 cubic feet per
second, when probably rather below its mean stage.   It might, no
doubt, be navigated by a small stern-wheel steamer for many miles.

I was afterward so fortunate as to meet a party of four miners who had, Notes on upper part of river.
spent a part of the summer of 1887 in prospecting this stream, and from
one of them, Mr. John McCormack, obtained some particulars respecting it, together with a sketch of its course.   Thirty-two miles from the
Lewes, the Big Salmon is said to be joined by a smaller stream, which
McCormack calls the North Fork.   For about a mile and a-half below,
and a short distance above the mouth of this branch, the river is very
rocky and rapid. Half a mile above it there is an Indian salmon-fishing
place.   For some distance beyond this the river is sluggish, and at
sixty-six miles from the Lewes, the South Fork branches off.   This
fork occupies a wide valley and comes from the south-eastward.   Above
it the water is swifter and the valley of the river is narrow, with high
mountains on both sides, but particularly on the north.   Granite and
mica-schist were seen along this part of the river.   At a supposed distance of one hundred and five miles from the Lewes, another stream
joins from the south-east, and this also occupies an important valley,
though not so wide as that of the South Fork.   Above this point the
river turns to a northerly bearing for about fifteen miles, the current
being, in general, slack.   It then reverts to an easterly bearing, and ·

---

* Ta-tlin-hi-ni of the Tagish.

Lakes at head of river. after passing a rapid, at one place, Island Lake is reached at 190 miles from the Lewes. This lake is four miles long, and has two arms at its upper end, from the southern of which a river leads, in eight miles, to a second lake two miles and a-half long. A stretch of river, a mile and a-half long, joins this to the highest lake, which McCormack named Quiet Lake, and of which he estimates the length at twenty-four miles. At the outlet of the lake is an Indian fishing place. The country to the south of these lakes is mountainous, granite being a common rock, and several streams run from these mountains into Quiet Lake. The north-east side of the lake is bordered by lower ridges, and from its head, McCormack travelled about eight miles, through a low country, to the bank of the Tes-lin-too, which he found here flowing from north to south.*

Gold. These miners found "fine" gold all along the river, but no good paying bars. They were in search of "coarse" gold, but did not discover any. A small specimen of pyrites and quartz, from veins met with on one of the streams flowing into Quiet Lake, given to me by Mr. McCormack, was found by Mr. Hoffmann to contain very distinct traces of gold with a trace of silver.

Salmon. According to the Indians, the salmon run up this river to its source, and the same is reported of the Little Salmon and the Tes-lin-too.

Big Salmon River to Tes-lin-too.

The river and river-valley. As already noted, the bearing of the Lewes becomes nearly due south, at the mouth of the Big Salmon. Though crooked in detail, it preserves this general bearing to the mouth of the Tes-lin-too, a distance by the river of thirty-one miles. Both the valley and the river itself are unusually narrow where the Seminow Hills are cut through, the width of the range being about five miles, and the river continues narrow and deep, with a swift current, beyond this point, though, the valley widens and permits the stream to resume its flexuous character. The actual width of the river, at a point nine miles below the mouth of the Tes-lin-too, was ascertained to be 483 feet, the current being at the rate of 4·84 miles per hour. These figures may be taken as representing the general character of this part of the stream. A short distance south of this point, the river again begins to widen and to resume its usual aspect. The hills bounding the valley on the south of the Seminow range seldom exceed a height of 800 feet till the vicinity of the confluence of the Tes-lin-too and Lewes is reached, when they gradually increase to 1000 or 1500 feet.

* The above estimates of distance are probably all in excess, and include the minor sinuosities of the stream. The actual distances from point to point are shown on the map as well as it has been possible to estimate them.

A number of auriferous gravel-bars have been worked along this part Cassiar bar.
of the Lewes, including Cassiar Bar, which has so far proved the richest
on the river.   Limited areas of the river-flats have also been worked
over, where the alluvial cover is not too deep.

The valley near the mouth of the Tes-lin-too is again narrower Lewes and
than usual, singularly so for the point of confluence of two im- Tes-lin-too
compared.
portant rivers.   The valley of the Tes-lin-too is evidently the main
orographic depression which continues that occupied by the Lewes below the confluence.   The Lewes flows in through a narrow gap, closely
bordered by high hills and nearly at right angles to the lower course of
the river.   On the map accompanying Lieut. Schwatka's report, the
width of the Tes-lin-too is shown as about half that of the Lewes, the
actual fact being precisely the reverse and all the main features of the
lower river being contained by the Tes-lin-too; while the other branch,
both in its irregular mode of entry, the nature of its banks, the colour
of its water and its very rapid current, presents, at first sight, all the
appearance of a tributary stream of new character.   To such an extent
is this difference observable, that Mr. Ogilvie and the members of his
party, as well as most of the miners on the river, were of the opinion
that the Tes-lin-too actually carries much the greater volume of water.
As this appeared to be a question of some importance, we stopped a day
at the confluence for the purpose of investigating it, cross-sectioning each
river and ascertaining the rate of the current at distances of about half
a mile from the junction, where the circumstances were favourable.
It was thus ascertained that the rivers possess the following dimen- Volumes of
rivers.
sions :—

	Lewes.	Tes-lin-too.
Mean width	420 feet.	575 feet.
Maximum depth (near left bank)	12 " (near right bank)	18 feet 4 inches.
Sectional area	3015 "	3800 feet.
Maximum velocity	5·68 miles pr. hr.	2·88 miles pr. hr.
Discharge per second	18,664 cubic feet.	11,436 cubic feet.

In connection with these measurements it may be stated that the Water of the
two rivers.
Lewes showed evidence of having risen about a foot above its lowest
summer level, while the Tes-lin-too was probably near its lowest summer
stage.*   If we subtract the volume of water represented by this extra
foot in depth, the discharge of the Lewes at the summer low-water
stage may be approximately stated at 15,600 cubic feet.   The water of
the Lewes has a blue, slightly opalescent colour, much resembling that
of the Rhone where it issues from the Lake of Geneva, while that of the
Tes-lin-too is brownish and somewhat turbid.   The temperatures of the
Lewes and Tes-lin-too were respectively 54° and 53·5° F. on the evening

---

* All the rivers in this country reach their actual minimum toward the end of the winter.

of August 31st.   A considerable part of the water of the former stream must be derived from the glaciers and snows of the Coast Ranges, but the existence of large lakes on both streams doubtless accounts for their proximate equality in temperature.

Rocks.   From the few exposures which occur on that part of the Lewes which cuts across the Seminow Hills, the range would appear to be composed of greenish, altered volcanic rocks, probably diabase, interbedded with grey or whitish marble.   Rocks of this character are those which have supplied the material for the conglomerates described before (p. 146 B) and are evidently much older than these and doubtless referable to the Palæozoic.   At another place, south of the Seminow Hills, felsite, schistose diabase and dark fractured argillite were noted in association, and at about a mile and a-half below the Tes-lin-too, purplish and greenish amygdaloid, with calcareous filling, was seen.   The exposures on this part of the river are few and unconnected and that last mentioned shows less sign of alteration than usual, and may be referable to a period newer than the Palæozoic.

Drift deposits.   Clayey and earthy gravels, like those often associated with the boulder-clay, were noted in some places along this part of the Lewes. These are overlain by nearly white, bedded silts, which often form entire banks of considerable height.   A mile and a-half below the mouth of the Tes-lin-too, the first glaciated rock-surfaces seen in ascending the Lewes, were noted.   The direction of glaciation is N. 4°, E.   The glaciation is here well preserved on surfaces a few feet above the river, and consists of wide, shallow, straight grooves and flutings, quite evidently the work of a glacier.

Tes-lin-too or Newberry River.

Notes on the river.   The Tes-lin-too River is named the Newberry or Tess-ol-heena* on Schwatka's map, and is evidently the same which is sketched on the U. S. Coast Survey map of Alaska, etc., (1884) as the Nus-a-thane.   By the miners who pass along the Lewes, it is known as the Hootalinkwa or Hotalinqu, in consequence, as it proves, of a misapprehension.   The Hotilinqu, which has appeared on the maps for many years, was traversed in its upper part by Byrnes in the course of his exploration already mentioned.   I have ascertained that one or more of the miners who first descended the Lewes knew Byrnes and were familiar with his work, and, naturally enough, on finding this

---

* This is doubtless a version of Tes-lin-hl-nl, *hin* (or in combination *hi-nl*) being Tagish for river. Tes-lin-too is the name given to me by the Tagish Indians, the termination being the Tinné equivalent for *hin*. This is, however, not the only case of such use of Tinné words by the Tagish. Nas-a-thane is doubtless Ni-sutlin or Ni-sutlin-hl-nl, the name of the river above the great lake. Krause names this river, on an Indian sketch attached to his map, Tis-lin-hin.

river, they jumped to the conclusion that it was the Hotalinqu of
which he had told them.

This river still remains to be explored and mapped, and as it drains River not yet mapped.
a country with a rather dry climate, the area of its basin is probably
very considerable. It has been prospected to some extent by a few
miners, but it is difficult, from the accounts which they are able to
give, to ascertain much of a definite character respecting it. At the
mouth of the river we met Mr. T. Boswell and two other miners who
had spent most of the summer on it, and from Boswell's description,
together with sketches subsequently obtained from Indians, the following notes are drawn up.

The general tread of the Tes-lin-too appears to be south-eastward, Tes-lin Lake.
and Boswell estimates its length, to the great lake, at one hundred miles.
There are no rapids or falls in this distance, but the water for sixty or
seventy miles from the mouth is moderately swift, the remaining distance to the lake being quite slack. The lake is represented as being
at least one hundred miles in length, but accounts differ as to the existence of a large tributary river at its head, some affirming that
there is merely a small unimportant stream. Be that as it may,
the main continuation of the Tes-lin-too is found at the head of
an arm ten or twelve miles long, on the east side of the lake.
This river, known to the Tagish Indians as Ni-sutlin-hi-ni, must The upper river
come from a north-easterly direction in the first instance, and it is
represented as circling completely round the head of the Big Salmon
River and rising between that river and the Upper Pelly. At a distance
variously estimated at from eighty to one hundred and twenty miles
from its mouth (and said by the Indians to be two days travel down
stream), the river forks, the west fork being the larger and that of
which the course has just been described. The east fork is swift and
full of rapids and rises in a mountainous country, which no doubt
represents a portion of the northern continuation of the Cassiar Range.
The Indians travel several days up this fork and then cross mountains
to tributaries of the Upper Liard and descend by these to the little
trading post at the confluence of the Liard and Dease. Between the
mouth of the main river and the forks above mentioned, the navigation
is fairly good and no heavy rapids occur.

The great lake above mentioned, into which the Ni-sutlin-hi-ni Features near the lake.
discharges, is said by the Indians to be the largest known to them.
It is named Tes-lin by the Tagish Indians, and is bordered to the
westward, at a distance of several miles, by a high range of mountains,
while a similar range, but of inferior height, runs along its east side
and, further north, separates the Tes-lin-too from the Big Salmon.
Near the head of the lake is an Indian trail by which, it is said, the head

Pass to Taku.   of canoe navigation on the Taku River may be reached in two long days packing. Enquiry seems to show that the distance from point to point by this trail is about sixty miles, and that it crosses a range of mountains, but not at such a height as to pass entirely out of the timber. It is stated that a miner named Mike Powers, with eight or nine other men, crossed from the Taku to the lake in 1876 or 1877. These men built three boats on the lake, but do not appear to have done much prospecting and came out by the same route by which they had entered.

Gold.   There are two Indian salmon-fishing stations on the Ni-sutlin-hi-ni above Tes-lin Lake. Mr. Boswell and his partners found fine gold all along the Tes-lin-too and also on the Ni-sutlin-hi-ni. They worked in different places along the river and appear to have done fairly well.

Tes-lin-too to Lake Labarge.

From the mouth of the Tes-lin-too or Newberry to the lower end of Lake Labarge the distance by the Lewes is twenty-seven miles and a-half. The river is very crooked and for the first six or seven miles very rapid, averaging probably six miles an hour. Large boulders occur in its bed in some places, but it is believed that a stern-wheel steamer of good power might ascend without difficulty. The current becomes slack three or four miles before reaching the lake. The river does not follow any well marked or important valley, but an irregular depression among lumpy inconsequent hills, none of which probably rise over 1000 feet above it. No rocks were found exposed on the river, but some of the hills are evidently composed in large part of pale, grey limestone. Scarped banks, about a hundred feet high, show boulder-clay overlain by white silts, which on the lower part of this reach of the river form about one-third of the height of the bank. The lakes above evidently prevent the occurrence of heavy floods on this part of the river, the sod coming down quite to the edge of the water in a manner not found on the lower part of the Lewes or on the Tes-lin-too where seen near the mouth.

Lake Labarge.

Nomenclature of the lake.   This lake, through which the Lewes River flows, is undoubtedly that named for Mike Labarge on the older maps, though Schwatka names it Kluk-tas-si which is, no doubt, an attempt at its Tagish Indian name Tloo-tat-sai'. Krause calls it Tahiniwūd, which is evidently the name given to me as that of the Lewes River. (See p. 142 B).

The lake is a little over thirty-one miles in length. It lies nearly Size of the lake. north-and-south, but is somewhat irregular in outline and does not present the parallel-sided form and constant width of most of the mountain lakes. About six miles of its lower end averages two miles and a-half in width. It then maintains a pretty constant width of a mile and a-half, for nine miles, after which it again increases in size and attains a width of five miles near Richtofen Island. (Named Richtofen rocks and shown as a peninsula on Schwatka's map). Its elevation above sea-level is approximately 2100 feet. It appears to maintain its level pretty constantly, the total rise and fall as indicated by the shores being about four feet only. It was about a foot above its low-water stage at the time we passed early in September.

The lake is bordered nearly everywhere by hilly or mountainous Country about the lake. country, but two important valleys occur which require special mention. The first of these evidently forms the continuation of the hollow occupied by the lake itself, and runs on from its north or lower end in a north-westward direction, while the river, where it leaves the lake, turns to the north-east and breaks through the ranges of hills on that side. The greater part of this valley, which I propose to name the *Ogilvie valley*, appears to drain from the lake in a north-westerly direction and probably to White River, as it is seen to be blocked by terrace-flats about 200 feet above the lake, at a distance of a few miles from it. The second valley begins in a tract of low land to the west of Richtofen Island and runs parallel to the first, being like it, one of the main orographic valleys of the region. A small river appears to enter the lake from this valley. The mountains on the south-west side form a well characterized range, but appear scarcely to exceed 2500 feet in height above the lake. They carried, however, some patches of old snow, the first seen by us since leaving the upper part of the Pelly River.

The hills along the lower part of the lake on the east side are quite Mountains. remarkable in their abrupt forms and have white limestone summits. They rise from 300 to 1000 feet above the lake and no higher mountains were seen behind them. Further up the lake, on the same side, similar limestone mountains attain a height of about 2000 feet at a short distance back, but are not so remarkable in form. On the west side of the lake, north of the Richtofen valley, the hills slope gradually back from the shore and in a few places reach a height of probably 2000 feet above it, at some miles inland. The outlines of these hills are monotonous and they are wooded nearly to the summits. South of the Richtofen valley the *Miner's Range* * approaches the lake at an oblique angle, but decreasing in altitude. The mountains forming this range are more varied in form than those just described.

* I name this for the miners met by us along the river, good fellows all of them.

Survey of the shores.

Mr. Ogilvie's measured line was carried down from point to point along the west shore of the lake, a few points only having been fixed on the east shore by triangulation. In order to complete the outline of the lake I decided to make a track-survey of the east shore, connecting this by bearings with known points on Ogilvie's survey. We had not time to circumnavigate the lake and nothing was known to point out one side as better than the other for the purpose of geological examination. The lake is reputed to be a very stormy one, the prevailing winds being from the south in summer, and often so strong that miners have been detained in camp for many days. We lost almost the whole of one day, owing to wind, on our way up the lake. Though local evidence of

Climate.

a more humid climate was noted on the Lewes near the Seminow Hills, these are soon lost after passing that range, and along Lake Labarge, southern slopes of terraces and hills are often grassy and open. *Anemone patens* was noted as abundant in many places.

Two series of rocks.

The rocks bordering the east side of Lake Labarge evidently represent two distinct series, of which the older is for the most part composed of grey limestone; which, in some places, nearly approaches marble but in others becomes rather flaggy and argillaceous. Resting unconformably on this, is a series composed of conglomerates, which pass into hard grey and greenish grauwacke-sandstones, and hard, dark, calcareous shales which occasionally become nearly black, impure, flaggy limestone. The two series are folded together, the strike of both being north-north-west and meeting the shore of the lake very obliquely. The direction of dip is generally westward at high angles or vertical. The conglomerates are chiefly composed of greenish, grey and purplish altered volcanic rocks, together with limestone of various kinds, and the same constituents in a more comminuted form enter into the composition of the grauwackes. At a point opposite Richtofen Island, black, argillaceous and calcareous beds are charged with numerous angular fragments of the older limestones, the occurrence of which and of the pebbles of altered volcanic rocks elsewhere associated with the limestones, constitute the evidence of unconformity, as the two series are too closely folded together to admit the observation of an angular unconformity. The good exposures found along this shore of the lake are important as indicating the intimate manner in which the rocks of differing age are associated in this region. They show that their separation on the map can be accomplished only by means of a detailed survey. No characteristic fossils were found in the older limestone series which may, however, be regarded from analogy as probably of Carboniferous age. The newer series is evidently Cretaceous and very probably of the horizon of Series C., the Lower Shales and Sandstones of the Queen Charlotte Islands. A few fossils were obtained at the point already referred to, opposite Richtofen Island, on which Mr. J. F. Whitcaves supplies the following note.—

"The fossils collected at this locality appear to be somewhat as follows, though they have only been subjected, so far, to a preliminary and by no means exhaustive examination. 1. A single specimen of a small sponge, and, (2.) several badly preserved corals, one with compound and very slender corallites. 3. Several small lamellibranchs apparently referable to three genera, two of which are represented by mere fragments, while the other may be a form of *Pleuromya lævigata*. 4. A mould of part of a spiral gasteropod, which may be referable to *Nerinæa* or to the genus *Pseudomelania* of Pictet and Campiche. 5. A piece of a phragmocone of a small belemnite.

"These fossils, though somewhat obscure, appear to be of Cretaceous age and possibly of about the horizon of Series C., of the Queen Charlotte Islands."

Of the rocks on the opposite or west side of the lake nothing certain can be said. Limestone is, however, not a prominent feature in the hills near the lake, though apparent in some of those seen behind the first range. It is not improbable that the Mesozoic rocks are here more extensively developed.

Terraces were noted on the lower part of the lake at about 200 feet above it and at various lower levels, and near the head of the lake they were seen at an elevation estimated as being at least 400 feet above it. The rocks along the lake-shore frequently show glaciated surfaces, the bearing being in general parallel to that of the lake and the sense of the movement of ice from south to north. The limestone hills are channelled, planed and fluted along their sides and over their summits in such a way as to indicate the former existence of very heavy ice pressure. Two miles from the lower end of the lake, at the water-level, the glaciation points directly down the valley through which the river now runs, or N. 24° E., while two miles further on, the summit of a limestone hill 300 feet high is crossed by heavy glaciation running N. 8° W. The latter may be accepted as that of the main direction of motion, the divergence met with being not greater than that frequently found in tracing the course of the ice of the former Strait-of-Georgia glacier on the coast, where it has passed over rugged country,* and it would appear that in this case the main mass of ice moved into the wide Ogilvie valley, while part of the lower portion of the mass was pressed through the smaller valley by which the lake itself now discharges. Where the limestone hills have recently been stripped of their covering of soil, the sloping glaciated surfaces are still so smooth that it is difficult to walk over them.

* See Annual Report Geol. Sur. Can., 1886, p. 100 B.

Origin of the lake.

No definite indication of the mode of origin of the lake was obtained. The observation just cited shows that the valley through which it now discharges existed in glacial times, but it may probably have been of less importance and it is not impossible that before the glacial period the river flowed out by the Ogilvie valley which may since have become blocked by morainic or other drift deposits.

Lake Labarge to Tahk-heena River.

The valley.

Beyond the head of Lake Labarge, the valley of the Lewes continues equally wide, and runs in a general southward direction like that of the lake. At the head of the lake, the valley is occupied by swampy flats nearly at the water-level and by low terrace-flats, which, where cut in the river banks, are seen to be composed of stratified fine sands, which are often iron-stained and a few miles up the river are found to rest upon the white silts, showing that they are valley deposits of post-glacial date. The limestone range which has bordered the east side of Lake Labarge, runs on in a southward direction, forming the east side of the wide valley. Eleven miles and a-half from the head of the lake the Tahk-heena River flows in from the west, making a right angle with the main river and at thirteen miles further (still measuring along the

The river.

river), the foot of White Horse Rapid is reached. The current of the Lewes is rather slack for eleven miles from the lake, and the bed and banks are clayey or sandy. Above this point, the river becomes swift, averaging about four miles an hour, and gravel banks and bars re-appear. For about two miles below the White Horse Rapid, the current is very swift, and though the latter may be designated as the head of possible steamer navigation, it would scarcely pay to endeavour to force a steamer up to th every foot of the rapid.* No rock exposures what ever were seen along this part of the Lewes, the scarped banks, which are often a hundred feet in height, consisting almost entirely of white silts with a widely undulated bedding.

Tahk-heena River.

Size of the river.

The Tahk-heena† River is a considerable stream and is wide and slack at its confluence with the Lewes. At about 200 yards from the Lewes, where it has attained its normal size, it was ascertained to be 237 feet wide, with a depth of ten feet for about one-third of this width,

---

* Several small stern-wheel steamers have, for some years, ascended each summer the Lower Yukon, in Alaska, but so far as I know, none of these have yet gone further up than the mouth of the Stewart : it would, however, be quite practicable to ascend to the point here indicated.

† Named the Yukon at its outflow from " west Kussooa Lake " at its head, on Krause's map. The orthography of the published maps is here retained. The name would probably be more correctly rendered Ta-hi-ni.

and a current estimated at two miles an hour.   The discharge may be roughly estimated at 3600 cubic feet per second, and appeared to be about half that of the Lewes above the junction or one-third of that below the confluence.   The hills which border the south side of this river at its mouth, rise to high rugged mountains at about fifteen miles to the west, and these have the appearance of being largely composed of granite.   The water of this river is very turbid as compared with that of the Lewes, and the temperature of both rivers was found to be 52° F. on the 6th of September.

The principal sources of the Tahk-heena are shown by Dr. A. Krause's exploration to be at a distance of forty to fifty miles from the head of the west branch of Lynn Canal, and the river was formerly much employed by the Chilkat Indians, whose chief place is on that arm, as a means of reaching the interior.   It is not used by the miners, and now only to a small extent by the Indians themselves, on account of the long and difficult carriage from the sea to its head, but the lake at the head of the river once reached, the voyage down stream is reported to be easier than that by the main river, the rapids being less serious.   A sketch of the course of the Tahk-heena River, probably based on Indian accounts, is given on map No. 20 which accompanies the U. S. Coast Survey Report for 1867.   This sketch has, however, not been employed on the map of of 1884, it being probably supposed at that time that the Indian information on which it had been drawn referred to the upper part of the Lewes.

Upper part of
the river.

The Cañon.

The White Horse Rapid and Miles Cañon form together the most formidable obstacle to the use of the Lewes as a route into the interior, constituting an interruption to navigation of two and three-quarter miles in total length.   White Horse Rapid is three-eights of a mile long. *   The worst rapid is at the lower end of the White Horse, where the river scarcely exceeds a hundred feet in width, with low basaltic banks, and the force of the water is very great.   In the upper part of the White Horse, the water flows between low basalt cliffs scarcely exceeding twenty feet in height, but sufficient to render tracking precarious and difficult, while the occurrence of numerous rocks in mid-channel makes the rapid dangerous to run.   The portage is on the west bank and it is usual to carry both boats and cargo over it.

White Horse
Rapid.

Between the White Horse and the foot of the cañon the river is very swift, and at one place, a mile above the former and three-quarters of a mile below the latter, the set of the stream is so strong round a rocky

---

* The distances here given are those measured by Mr. Ogilvie.

11

The cañon.

point as to render it advisable to make an additional short portage of 130 feet. A third portage of five-eights of a mile is necessary at Miles Cañon. This portage is on the east bank, and at the lower end, a very steep ascent has first to be overcome. Here a sort of extemporized windlass has been rigged up by the miners for the purpose of hauling up their boats. The cañon is cut through a horizontal, or nearly horizontal, flow of basalt and is not more than about a hundred feet in width, with vertical cliffs averaging about fifty feet, and never exceeding one hundred feet, at the sides. It opens out into a species of basin in the middle, but the river is elsewhere inaccessible from the banks. Terraced hills rise above the basalt walls on each side of the valley, but are particularly abrupt on the west bank. The river flows through the cañon with great velocity, but is unimpeded in its course, and it is therefore not very risky to run with a good boat. The White Horse Rapid is, however, much more dangerous, and though some of the miners have run through it—generally accidently—it should not be attempted.

Basaltic rocks.

The basaltic rocks of the rapid and cañon are not seen for any distance above or below these points, and appear to represent a local effusion of no great area, which is probably confined to the bottom of the valley. A second wide valley runs behind *Cañon Hill*, to the east, and it is possible that this may represent a pre-glacial channel of the river. The basalt is itself evidently older than the glacial deposits. It is grey in colour and often vesicular, the cavities being in some places filled by a radiating zeolitic mineral.

Miles Cañon to Lake Marsh.

Lewes River and valley.

The great structural valley which is occupied by Lake Labarge and by the river above it up to this point, runs on above the cañon as a wide, important depression, bearing nearly due south, and appears to be uninterrupted till it joins the lower end of Bennett Lake, thirty-two miles distant. The course of the river, however, diverges to the south-east, in which direction also a wide valley runs, and in twenty-three miles (following the stream) the lower end of Lake Marsh is reached. This valley, though extensive between its limiting slopes, is not regularly bounded by parallel ranges, like that first mentioned. The current of the river to within five or six miles of the lake is moderate, not exceeding three miles an hour, and the immediate river-trough is narrow, being rather closely bordered by terraces of a hundred feet or more in height. Above this point, to the lake, the current is quite slack; the terraces gradually retreat toward the bases of the hills, and wide, swampy flats occur. The water above the cañon is quite clear and blue, showing that its turbidity further down is entirely due to the washing away and falling in of the high banks of silt. The turbidity of the Tahk-heena is probably also due to the same cause.

Anemone patens and *Elæagnus argentea* are common on dry banks, and slopes covered with bunch-grass and *Artemisia frigida* still occur, evidencing a dry climate. The black pine (*Pinus Murrayana*) is now very abundant, much more so than on the lower river, and it was here observed that this tree began to assume a more branching and less rigid form than it has to the north. Large numbers of salmon were found dead or dying along the banks for a few miles above the cañon, and the grass along the shores was trodden down by bears attracted here by this circumstance. No salmon were found so far up as Lake Marsh, and the Indians state that this is their limit. It would appear that after their long journey from the sea, those which get so far, exhaust their last remaining strength in ascending the cañon.

There are some very fine exposures of stratified white silts, often interbedded with sands, along this part of the river, but no boulder-clay was seen; neither are there any exposures of rock in place. Basalt is seldom found as a constituent of the gravels above the cañon, and then only in small pebbles. Rounded pieces of greenish, jade-like rocks and impure jades, which were abundant below the Tes-lin-too, here again become common.

Lake Marsh.

Lake Marsh, so named by Schwatka, in honour of Prof. O. C. Marsh, is known to the miners as "Mud Lake." It is twenty miles in length, with an average width of about two miles, pretty uniformly maintained. The valley of which this lake occupies the centre, is notably wide, and the country in the immediate vicinity of the lake is quite low, consisting of terrace-flats, or low rounded or wooded hills and ridges. Conspicuous mountain summits, however, occur at a distance of some miles inland on both sides of the lake. A moderately well defined range, of which Michie Mountain* 5540 feet in height is the most elevated point, bounds the view on the east side of the lake, from which it diverges in a south-easterly direction. To the west is an irregular and broken mass of mountains in which several notable gaps occur and which occupy the country between Lake Marsh and the Watson valley, previously referred to. The highest points of these, *Mounts Lorne* and *Lansdowne*, were ascertained to have approximate elevations of 6400 and 6140 feet respectively. The diversified forms of the mountains in view from this lake render it particularly picturesque,

---

* So named by Schwatka.

and at the time of our visit, on the 10th and 11th of September, the autumn tints of the aspens and other deciduous trees and shrubs, mingled with the sombre greens of the spruces and pines, added to its beauty.

The lake and its tributaries.

The shores of the lake are generally rather shoal, and in some places the beach-gravel was found to rest on mud or clay, but these peculiarities are not so striking in themselves as to warrant the application of the name "Mud Lake." The mouth of the M'Clintock River, which enters the lower end of the lake from an important valley, was not examined closely. It appeared, however, to be a small stream, and the greater part of the country to the east of the lake probably drains to the Tes-lin-too. A second stream joins the lake at the south-east angle at its head.

Track-survey.

As in the case of Lake Labarge, Mr. Ogilvie's measured line was here carried along the west shore and in order to complete the outline of the lake, I travelled up the opposite side, making a track-survey of it, which has been embodied on the map.

Rocks.

The rocks seen at the lower end of Lake Marsh, and on the island, may be taken as representing the composition of the range which borders the Lewes on the north-east for some distance below. They consist of greenish and purplish altered volcanic materials, probably all diabase in composition, and are bedded, the strike being approximately parallel to the run of the range just mentioned.* Further up the lake on the same side, similar rocks were noted in several places, together with some which might be taken to represent the grauwacke-sandstones of the newer series described on Lake Labarge. The higher mountains off to the eastward appear to be, at least in part, composed of limestone. At the head of the lake are considerable exposures of black and dark-grey, hard, slaty argillites, finely cleaved and traversed by numerous small quartz veins. The strike of the cleavage is S. 30° E., with a high easterly dip.

Glaciation.

The rock surfaces along the lake are heavily glaciated, the direction being, in general, parallel to that of the main valley. The evidence is such as to show, however, that at least the subjacent part of the ice of the former great glacier, bifurcated at the north end of the lake, one branch taking the valley of the Lewes, the other that of the M'Clintock River. In the same way, at the south end of the lake, a great part of the ice has been delivered through the wide valley which comes from the south-east between *Jubilee Mountain*† and *Mount White.*‡

---

* See Appendix V. (Lake Marsh, No 86) for note on one of these rocks.

† 1887 being the year of Her Majesty's Jubilee.

‡ So named in honor of the late Hon. Thos. White, to whose initiative the despatch of the expedition to which this report refers was largely due.

Tagish, Bennett and Lindeman Lakes.

The upper end of Lake Marsh is connected with Tagish Lake by a Connecting wide tranquil reach of river five miles in length. The current is here river. very slack, and the depth, according to Ogilvie, from six to twelve feet. The river is bordered by low terraces, which are particularly wide on the west side, and are covered with open woods, chiefly consisting of white spruce and cottonwood. To the east, the long irregular ridges and slopes which culminate in Jubilee Mountain begin to rise a short distance back from the river. A mile above Lake Marsh, on the Indian names. east bank of the river, are two roughly built houses belonging to the Tagish Indians. These are the only permanent houses seen along the whole course of the Lewes, and here the Tagish people who roam over this part of the country, reside during the winter months.

From the description just given, it will be seen that the navigation, Navigable waters. by steamers, from the head of the cañon through Lake Marsh and to Tagish Lake would offer no difficulties, while the tranquil character of the connecting river between the two lakes last mentioned, is such as to practically render Lake Marsh the lower portion of an extensive system of still-water navigation which includes not only Tagish Lake but also Lake Nares, Lake Bennett and possibly other connected waters and which will prove of the greatest utility at no distant date in facilitating the opening up and development of the mineral resources of the tract of country in their vicinity.

The through distance, from the lower end of Lake Marsh to the head of Lake Bennett, measured along the central line of the various lakes and connecting waters, is about seventy miles, made up as follows.—

Marsh Lake	20	miles.
River	5	"
Tagish Lake	16·6	"
Lake Nares	2·7	"
Bennett Lake	25·8	"
	———	
Total	70·1	

The still-water navigation, however, includes also the West Arm of Bennett Lake, about twelve miles; Windy Arm of Tagish Lake, eleven miles; Tako Arm of same lake, (of which some notes are given below) at least twenty miles; making a grand total of at least one hundred and thirteen miles.

Taken as a whole, these lakes constitute a singularly picturesque Scenery. region, abounding in striking points of view and in landscapes pleasing in their variety, or grand and impressive in their combination of rugged mountain forms.

Height above sea-level.

The elevation of this remarkable system of lakes above the level of the sea, as approximately ascertained by the mean of about eighteen barometric observations extending over several days, (all taken in triplicate on as many different aneroids,) is 2150 feet. The mean of the barometer readings was compared with that of those taken during the same days at Haines' mission, on Lynn Canal, and the resulting height as above given, is probably a near approach to the truth.

Position relatively to Coast Ranges.

The inner or north-eastern edge of the Coast Ranges is not here very well defined, but Tagish and Bennett Lakes, with their several arms, may be described as lying upon this border and as in part penetrating the outskirts of the range. The lower part of Tagish Lake occupies the continuation of the same wide valley in which Lake Marsh lies, and the valley of the Tako Arm may also be included as a part of the same depression. To the west of this, the upper part of Tagish Lake and Bennett Lake must be considered as lying among the mountains of the Coast Ranges, and the height as well as the abrupt and rugged character of the mountains increase in that direction, their slopes and summits holding large areas of permanent snow, even late in the summer.

Connection of the lakes.

The lower part of Tagish Lake is very generally bordered by terrace-flats or by low land of the nature of terraces, and the valley runs through to the lower end of Bennett Lake, with a nearly uniform width, as measured between the bases of the mountains, though the lake is somewhat constricted between Tako and Windy arms by the extension of the low land from the north side. A similiar projection of low alluvial land separates Lake Nares from the west end of Tagish Lake, a river-like current being distinctly observable in the narrows. The same occurs at the narrows known as the Caribou Crossing which separates Nares from Bennett Lake, but here with the addition of a number of irregular sand-hills, with which the low land in question is covered, and which also extend round a considerable part of the north end of Bennett Lake.

Arms of the lakes.

The Windy Arm of Tagish Lake, together with the upper part of Bennett Lake and its West Arm are comparatively narrow mountain-walled inlets, with all the characters of true fiords. The Windy Arm terminates in low, hilly land, from which a couple of small brooks come, but no important stream; and it would appear that the drainage which might be expected to enter here is cut off by a transverse valley which holds a lake and flows out toward the Tako Arm.

The West Arm of Bennett Lake was not explored to the head, but terminates in a mass of wild, rugged and bare mountains, of which the outline sketch given on p. 167 B may give some idea. The upper part of the main lake lies, as a narrow water-way, between beetling granite ranges which rise almost perpendicularly to heights of 3000 and 4000

LAKE NARES, LOOKING EASTWARD FROM CARIBOU CROSSING.

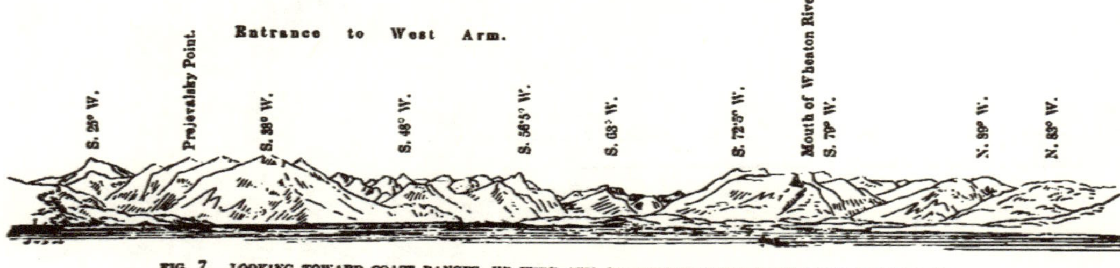

FIG. 7. LOOKING TOWARD COAST RANGES, UP WEST ARM OF BENNETT LAKE, FROM EAST SIDE OF LAKE.

(*The figures placed above the various summits are true bearings.*)

feet above it. Many of the summits beyond the heads of these fiords and in the vicinity, attain heights of 6000 to 7000 feet above the sea, and the region is in every sense an alpine one, though no dominating peaks of great altitude occur.

Climate and vegetation.

In consequence of the position of this country, in the lee of the higher crests of the Coast Ranges, and notwithstanding its considerable altitude, the climate appears to be equally dry with that met with about the site of old Fort Selkirk, and no very striking difference is met with in the character of the vegetation. The southward-facing slopes of some of the mountains, to a height of a thousand feet or more above the lake, are grassy and open, a circumstance particularly observable on the north side of the west part of Tagish Lake and on Lake Nares. The *Amelanchier* was seen on the lower part of Tagish Lake, this being the most northern station observed, and *Anemone patens* continues abundant, locally. Somewhat more alpine conditions are, however, indicated by the occurrence of *Picea subalpina*, which was noted as abundant at the water-level on Windy Arm, and on the upper part of Bennett Lake forms entire groves, growing to a considerable diameter, but tapering rapidly and very rough and knotty. Several places were, however, noticed where miners had built boats on Bennett Lake, and it was here that Mr. Ogilvie constructed a large scow for the transport of his provisions and bulky freight down the river.

Tako Arm.

The Tako Arm, which has already been alluded to, really constitutes the main continuation and upper part of Tagish Lake. It is narrowed at its entrance to a width little exceeding a mile, by a promontory from its west side, but further on, maintains pretty uniformly, for ten miles or more, a width of a mile and a-half to two miles. It is bordered on the west by a uniform, bare and wall-like range of limestone mountains, between which and the edge of the lake, however, a certain width of lower slopes intervenes. The east side is similarly bordered by mountains which also appear to be in the main composed of limestone, but the forms of these were not so well seen, as they were continuously covered by clouds and mists while we were near them. This arm was not explored and with its connected waters yet remains to be properly delineated on the map. It runs in a south-eastward direction for a distance estimated at ten miles, beyond which it turns more nearly south, and its length and other features connected with it can only be given on the authority of Indian reports and sketches. A long way up this arm, possibly twenty miles or more, a considerable river enters from the east. This is the main continuation of the Lewes and is reported to be a tranquil stream of no great length, resembling that between Marsh and Tagish lakes. It flows out of the west side of an-

other very long lake which lies nearly parallel to Tahko Arm. This
lake, near its south end, receives several feeders, one of which, entering
at its extremity, I suppose to be the Hotalinqu River of the Telegraph
Survey, already mentioned, though the Tagish Indians informed me
they named it Yil-hī-nī.   It is probably the south end of this lake *Connection with Taku River.*
which was reached by Byrnes in 1867, and its connection with the
Tako Arm and the remarkable system of lakes just described, would
explain the statement made to Byrnes by the Indians, viz. that it was
three days good paddling in a canoe to the lower end of the lake. The
length of the portage from the head of this lake to the Indian houses on
the Taku was variously stated by Indians at from two to four days.
The trail is said to be good, and to run through low country except at
one place where it follows along the mountain to avoid swampy land.
The name of this lake was given by one Tagish Indian as *A-tlin*, by
another as Tā-koo-shok and again Sik-i-ni-kwan, the last being said to
be the Taku Indian name. The first-mentioned name is adopted on
the map.

It is certain that the greater part of the water constituting the *Main source of Lewes River.*
Lewes River enters by the Tako Arm.   This is rendered apparent in
comparing the stream which flows out of Tagish Lake with that entering it by the narrows from Lake Nares, where the discharge is probably not much over one-fourth of the volume of that of Tagish Lake.
The brooks entering Tagish Lake (exclusive of Tako arm) are quite
insignificant.

The Indian name of the lake here named Tagish Lake, is Ta-gish-ai *Names of the lakes.*
(Tagīschä of Krause).   It is commonly known by the miners as Tako
Lake, and Schwatka adopts this name on his map.   It appears, however, admissible to revert to the proper Indian pronounciation of the
name, as is here done.   I am obliged, by the facts of the case, to include Bove Lake, of Schwatka, as part of Tagish Lake, but in order to
preserve the name, propose to attach it to the large island in the mouth
of Windy Arm.   Lake Nares is known to the miners as "Moose Lake,"
Lake Bennett as "Boat Lake."   In these cases, though not without
some doubt as to the propriety of so doing, I retain Schwatka's later
names.   The Tagish Indian name of Lake Bennett is Koo-soo-wā'.   It is
the East Kussooā Lake, of Krause. Its west arm is called Noo-koo-tahk.
The name of the island on Bennett Lake is Ketle-di-kā'-te.   I did not
ascertain the Indian name of Lake Nares. The islands on Tagish Lake,
of which Bove Island is one, are named In-te'-i.

It will be observed, on comparing Lieut. Schwatka's map with that *Observations by Schwatka.*
now published, that he names the west arm of Bennett Lake (though
nearly two miles wide at the mouth) "Wheaton River."   To the
river which enters near this arm from a valley parallel to the Watson

valley, I propose to apply this name. In the same way, Windy Arm is put down as "Bove Bay and probably river," and the great Tako Arm is shown as "Tako River," and described as a stream of inconsiderable dimensions. I can offer no reasonable explanation of these errors.

Geology of the Lakes.

General character of the rocks.

The eastern edge of the granitic rocks of the Coast Ranges, is found to cross Bennett Lake obliquely, and probably runs northward along the Wheaton valley. The rocks exposed on the lakes to the east of this line, may be described as belonging, in so far as ascertained, to a single great Palæozoic series, of which the sub-division cannot yet be attempted, but in which the only fossils found by us are of Carboniferous age. It is the same to which the older rocks on the Lewes belong, and closely resembles, both lithologically and in its fossils, the typical area of the Câche Creek series on the Thompson and Fraser. The series, as a whole, here consists of massive limestones, with a great thickness of green and green-grey diabase and felsite rocks, representing altered volcanic materials, and dark- or light-colored cherty quartzites and argillaceous or calcareous schists. The order of superposition is uncertain, but the limestones appeared probably to constitute an upper member of the series, and to be closely associated with the more important masses of contemporaneous volcanic material, while the cherty quartzites and schistose or slaty beds may follow respectively in descending order beneath the limestone. Volcanic materials are, however, found in greater or less quantity in all parts of the series.

Schists.

Black argillaceous schists and grey, silvery calc-schists were found on the east side of Tagish Lake, between the lower end and the entrance of Tako Arm, and again at the head of Windy Arm, in considerable force. At the latter place, the argillite is finely cleaved, forming a true slate. It contains quartzite pebbles, which have been remarkably sheared by pressure acting at right angles to the cleavage-planes and doubtless the same which has produced these. The great

Limestone.

mass of limestone occurs in the ranges bordering Tako Arm on both sides and in the mountains between this arm and Windy Arm. It is generally in the state of marble, and usually rather fine grained, many specimens being very handsomely and curiously marked with grey and black lines or spots. Some beds contain a good deal of silica, and weather rough, occasional layers are more than half composed of cherty matter. Numerous crinoidal remains are often visible, and a microscopical examination of thin sections, prepared by Mr. T. C.

Weston, proves some parts of the stone to be largely composed of the Fusulina.
remains of *Fusulina.**

To the west of this great limestone belt and between it and the edge Altered
of the granites, most of the rocks consist of altered volcanic materials, as volcanic rocks.
previously described. Some distinct amygdaloids were observed among
these, but no minute lithological examination of them has been made.†

The eastern edge of the granites is reached at about ten miles up Edge of
Bennett Lake, on the east side.   Granites continue thence, on the same granites.
side, for about five miles and a-half; when they are replaced for five
miles by an included belt of stratified rocks, chiefly quartzites, but
including also some hornblendic schists.   This belt crosses the lake
very obliquely in a nearly north-and-south bearing, and appears to represent a detached portion, more highly altered, of the Palæozoic rocks
before described.

The quartzites are here much shattered and pyritized, weathering to
rusty surfaces and causing the red appearance of some of the mountains.   The same rocks were seen from a distance in the mountains to
the west of the lake, but the greater part of the mountains on the west
side is evidently granite.

The granites seen along the shores of Bennett Lake are generally Character of
rather coarse-grained and hornblendic, though an abundance of black granites.
mica is also developed in some places.   The felspar is not uncommonly
of two kinds, a pink (probably orthoclase) which is often in large porphyritic crystals, and a white triclinic variety.   The general tint of
the rock is grey, and it closely resembles those described from
the vicinity of Vancouver Island in the Annual Report for 1886.   No
gneissic structure was observed, and the micaceous and hornblendic
schists locally developed at the junction with the stratified series, are
no doubt the result of the extreme alteration of volcanic portions of
that series.

Glaciation was observed in many places in this system of lakes.   It Glaciation.
is unnecessary to specify these, but it may be stated that conclusive
evidence is afforded that glacier-ice moved northward, down Tako
Arm, Windy Arm and Bennett Lake, as well as eastward, nearly at right
angles, in the east-and-west part of the lake between Windy and Tako
arms.   This eastward motion was, however, probably subordinate and
local, for no great number of granite boulders is found about the lakes
till the lower end of Bennett Lake is reached, a circumstance which

---

* The *Fusulina* found here are often remarkably large. The largest actually observed in the
few slices prepared for microscopical examination has a transverse diameter of 0·25 inch.
Fragments occurring in the same slides, however, indicate the existence of much larger individuals. No critical examination of these fossils has yet been made, but they appear referable
to *Fusulina robusta* (Meek), found in California. Palæontology of California. vol. i., p. 3.

† In Appendix V. (Tagish Lake, No. 93), some notes on a felsite from Windy Arm are given.

show that the main mass of ice passing down the Bennett Lake valley continued on to the north by the Watson valley. Well marked and extensive terrace deposits occur on the mountains on the north side of Tagish Lake, at an elevation estimated at 1000 feet above it, or about 3100 feet above the sea-level.

Valleys of the lakes.

A glance at the map will show that the lakes of this system occupy a portion only of a still more extensive system of wide valleys, which are probably of great antiquity, and the pre-glacial direction of drainage in some of which can only be conjectured. All these valleys are now, to a great extent, filled with detrital deposits, probably due for the most part to the glacial period. No appreciable deepening of drainage levels is going on, and the action at present in progress is constantly tending toward the filling up of the lake-basins. It may be presumed, here as elsewhere, that the lakes of this region now occupy the place of the last tongues of the great glacier, which in the end disappeared so rapidly that their beds had not time to become filled with detritus.

Lake Lindeman.

Lake Lindeman, occupies the continuation of the same valley in which Lake Bennett lies, but is separated from that lake by a small rapid stream, three-quarters of a mile in length. This stream falls about twenty feet between the two lakes and is rough and rocky. The portage is on the east side, and after carrying the greater part of our stuff overland, no difficulty was experienced in bringing the boat up the rapids. Lake Lindeman (Ti-tshoo-tah-min' of the Tagish Indians Schütlüchroä Lake of Krause) is five miles in total length, with an average width of about half a mile. It is the extreme head of navigation in this direction. The lower end is shallow, and the occurrence there of many large boulders, may show that it is moraine-dammed. Its shores are rough and rocky along both sides, high rough mountains rising on its north bank, while lower country, consisting of rocky hills, extends to the south-eastward, as far as the White Pass. A stream joins the head of the lake from the west, in which direction the main valley runs, but bifurcates at a distance of about three miles, the branches running off among high granite mountains. A second stream of some size, which shows evidence of being a formidable torrent at certain seasons, flows into the lake about a mile from its head, on the south side. It is the valley of this stream which is followed by the trail by which the Coast Mountains are crossed. The scenery about this lake is wild and fine, though solitary and alpine in the extreme. The rocks everywhere about the lake are granites of the kind just described.

As a number of miners had preceded us, on their way to the coast, we found several boats drawn up on the shore at the mouth of the stream above mentioned. We were also so fortunate as to find a small party of Tagish Indians camped there, but as most of the men had

LAKE LINDEMAN, LOOKING UP FROM OUTLET

already gone over the portage with some of the miners, we were obliged
to wait two days for their return, before we could obtain the requisite assistance to carry over our stuff. Meanwhile we put our boat in a place of
security, and occupied ourselves in eliminating everything which was
no longer of value from our "outfit."

GENERAL NOTES ON LEWES RIVER.

The total length of the route by the Lewes River from "the Land- Length of route
ing" on Lake Lindeman to the site of Fort Selkirk is 357 miles. From
the outlet of Lake Labarge, to the same point, is a distance of 200
miles, in which the total descent is 595 feet, or at the rate of 2·97 feet
to the mile.

The information obtained respecting the dates of opening and Opening and
closing of the river in spring and autumn is very fragmentary. It closing of rivers
would appear, however, that the rivers generally throughout the region
open early in May, while they may be expected to freeze over, in slack-
water reaches, any time after the middle of October, on the occurrence
of a few consecutive days of hard frost. Loose ice sometimes begins to
run in the rivers as early as September 20th, but this generally pre-
cedes the actual closing of the rivers by a couple of weeks. In some
seasons the rivers do not freeze over till well on in November. The
ice, however, remains much longer unbroken upon the lakes, the lakes
on the course of the Lewes thus generally preventing the descent of
that river by boats till June. In 1887, some of the lakes were not
open for navigation till June 10th, but as already mentioned the season was an unusually late one. The Tes-lin-too could be crossed in
places on ice-jams as late as May 22nd in the same year, but was open
throughout within a day or two after that date.

Miners entering the Yukon district by the Chilkoot Pass and Lewes Travel on the
River, frequently leave the head of Lynn Canal in April, and after river.
crossing the pass,—for which fine weather is essential,—continue on
down the lakes on the ice, and then, if necessary, wait at some convenient point for the opening of navigation, and build their boats.

In ascending the river, much depends on the build of the boat employed and skill of the men in poling, as well as on the occurrence, or
otherwise, of head-winds on the lakes. The whole distance from Forty-
mile Creek to Lake Lindeman has been made once or twice in so short
a time as thirty days, and I believe that even this record has been sur-
passed by a couple of days on one occasion, but under very exceptional
circumstances.

Our actual travelling time, from the mouth of the Lewes to the Travelling time
lower end of Lake Labarge, deducting all stoppages, was 121 hours, 15

minutes. From the head of Lake Labarge to the lower end of Lake Marsh, deducting stoppages as before, and not including the time occupied on the portages (at White Horse Rapid and Miles Cañon) 25 hours 55 minutes. Much, however, depends on the stage of water in the river, as when it is unusually high, the current is not only stronger but many of the bars and beaches are covered, and the poling and tracking is much worse. The time occupied in traversing the lakes is not included in the above statement.

Timber.   Timber suitable for building boats can scarcely be found in the vicinity of Lake Lindeman, but no difficulty is met with in obtaining trees of fair size on Bennett and Tagish lakes. Below these lakes, the country is generally wooded, and there is an abundance of spruce of fair quality, growing tall and straight in sheltered localities, but seldom attaining a diameter of two feet.

Chilkoot or Taiya Pass.*

Cross Chilkoot Pass.   On the 19th of September we set out with four Indian packers, crossed the summit, and reached a point in the valley of the west slope near what is known as Sheep Camp, the same evening. On the evening of the 20th we arrived at the head of tide-water on Taiya Inlet, and were hospitably received by Mr. J. Healey, who has established himself at that point for purposes of trade with the Indians and miners. We had at this time just completed our fourth month of arduous and incessent travel from Wrangell, at the mouth of the Stikine River, by the rivers, lakes and portages of the interior described in the foregoing pages, the total distance traversed being about 1322 miles. No serious accidents had befallen us by the way, and though, like the miners, we came back to the coast with a deplorably ragged and uncouth aspect, we had with us, intact, our collections, instruments, survey-records and notes. It was not the least pleasing moment of the entire journey when, from a distance of some miles, we first caught sight of the sea shining like a plate of beaten bronze under the rays of the evening sun.

The Pass.   The length of the mountain portage from Lake Lindeman to Healey's house, is twenty-three miles and a-half, the summit of the pass being at a distance of eight miles and a-half from Lake Lindeman, with an elevation of 3502 feet.

The valley on the north or inland side of the summit contains several little lakes which are evidently true rock-basins, with lumpy bottoms and irregular contours. The trail is rough and crooked, and entirely

---

* Known as Chilkoot Pass by the miners, named Perrier Pass by Schwatka. (1883). Dejäh Pass of Krause (1882) of which Taiya is merely an alternative rendering adopted for the sake of conformity with published charts.

without attempt at improvement of any kind.   It follows the stream in Character of
the route. one place, for about a mile, through a narrow rocky defile, which has evidently been cut out since the glacial period.   Where it crosses wide areas of shattered rocks, it requires the closest attention to follow it, and this can only be done, in the absence of guides, by noting the slightly soiled appearance of the grey stones from one to another of which the Indians step.   Some of the valleys to the north of the summit, and near it, are deeply filled with perennial snow, over which the trail runs by preference, to avoid the rocky slopes.   The small lakes highest in the pass were, at the time we crossed, about two-thirds covered with new ice, which showed little sign of melting, even under the bright sun which prevailed.   Hard frosts were evidently occurring here in the mountains every night at this season.

From seven to eight miles of the highest part of the pass may be Timber-line said to be entirely destitute of timber, even of a stunted growth such as might be used for firewood.   The nature of the ground is, however, so rocky that it does not afford a proper criterion of the normal height of the timber-line.

At the actual summit, the trail leads through a narrow, rocky gap, Summit. and the whole scene is one of the most complete desolation, the naked granite rocks rising steeply to partly snow-clad mountains on either side.   The slope of the pass on the north side is rather gradual, and the total ascent from the lake not very great, being but 1334 feet. To the south, on the contrary, it is at first abrupt and even precipitous, South slope. being accomplished over huge masses of fallen rock, which alternate here and there with steep, slippery surfaces of rock in place; but the travelling here is after all not so bad as that met with lower down the valley, where the trail goes through the woods along the steep, rocky and often boggy hillside, leading up and down the sides of several deep, narrow gullies.   Two small detached glaciers occupy hollows in the slope of the mountains on the west side of this valley, and from these a considerable part of the water of the stream is derived.   The "Stone house," or stone houses, and "Sheep camp" are points noted in this part of the pass, the first consisting of several natural though inconvenient shelters, beneath great masses of rock which have rolled down from the mountain, where the Indians often stop over night; the second being the point where arboreal vegetation of fair growth first begins.

At six miles from the head of the inlet, the stream followed down The Forks. from the summit is joined by another which has been dignified by the name of the Nourse River.   A short distance up the valley of the latter, are somewhat extensive glaciers and high snow-covered mountains. Both the valley of this stream and that coming from the pass, are narrow and V-shaped, but from their point of junction, a wide flat-bottomed valley runs due south between high mountain walls and is continued further on in that occupied by the inlet itself. This valley is largely floored by gravel-flats and is evidently subjected at times to heavy floods. The little river formed by the confluence of these streams may be ascended with difficulty by canoes, for some miles, when the water is not low, but at the time we passed this was scarcely practicable. It is, however, easy to walk along the gravel-flats, the only discomfort being the necessity of fording the ice-cold and very swift water several times *en route*.

Taiya River.

In the early summer, when the valleys on both sides of the summit are deeply filled with hard snow for a number of miles, the Indians secure a less abrupt grade (particularly on the south slope) by travelling on the snow and altogether avoiding the rough sides of the valley. This was the state of the pass when Mr. Ogilvie made his way inland over it in June. His greatest difficulty was found in connection with the Indians, who are untrustworthy and extortionate to a degree. He and his men were in consequence obliged to pack over a great part of their stuff themselves, and in so doing most of the party became snow-blind. He had with him two Peterborough boats, intended for use in his survey, and in safely transporting them across the Coast Ranges, accomplished a feat hitherto not attempted.

Spring travel.

The rocks met with on the Chilkoot Pass are practically all granites, generally hornblendic and grey, though varying in coarseness of grain, and often porphyritic with pink orthoclase. The granite is cut in places by dark grey-green dykes, probably diabase. Near the actual summit it assumes a brecciated or shattered appearance, and here a considerable mass of coarse, black, and probably intrusive diorite occurs. In the valley south of the summit similar granites prevail, but in some places include rocks with pretty evident gneissic lamination, which were observed locally to pass into mica-schists. The gravel in the valley is also almost entirely composed of grey granite, though some specimens weather red on account of the quantity of pyrites they contain. Below the Forks, on the east side of the valley, the summits of several mountains show rocks evidently stratified, dipping at high angles. These are probably gneiss or schist, like those seen in the valley of the pass.

Rocks.

Many rock-surfaces on both sides of the summit and up to the highest level of the pass were observed to be glaciated, and though no very certain evidence on this point could be obtained, it seemed probable that the ice had moved southward through the gap at the summit. The probable great accumulation of snow and ice on the north slope of the range might account for the parting-axis of the glacier lying to the north of the present actual water-parting.

Glaciation.

Scrubby hemlock (*Tsuga Pattoniana*) in a prostrate form occurs not Vegetation.
far below the actual summit on both slopes. Below the "Stone house"
this tree begins to become arboreal, and a few miles further down the
valley, grows tall and straight, forming entire groves. Menzies spruce
(*Abies Sitchensis*) also appears, a short distance below "Sheep camp," together with cottonwood (probably *Populus balsamifera*). Here also elder
and birch were first seen on the south slope. The devil's club (*Fatsia
horrida*) comes in about a mile above "Sheep camp." *Pinus contorta*
was not seen till the Forks was reached.

The "Stone house" is named To-hīt by the Indians. The Indian name Indian names.
of the Taiya River of the maps, is Dal-ē'. Nourse River is named Kīt-
lī-koo-goo-ā', the stream followed southward from the summit of the
pass Sī-tīk'. These rivers are named Katlakúchra and Ssidrajīk on the
map of Dr. A. Krause.

<h2 style="text-align:center">THE WHITE PASS.</h2>

Having heard reports of the existence of a second pass from Taiya Character of
Inlet to the lakes on the head-waters of the Lewes, Mr. Ogilvie sent the pass.
Capt. W. Moore to make an examination of it, with instructions to re-
join the party to the east of the mountains. This pass Mr. Ogilvie has
named White Pass in honour of the late Minister of the Interior. It
leaves the coast at the mouth of the Shkagway River* five miles
south of the head of Taiya Inlet, and runs parallel to Chilkoot Pass at
no great distance from it. Though the land carriage is somewhat
longer by this pass, it appears to present less difficulty to the construction of a practicable trail or road. Some account of this pass, based on
Capt. Moore's notes, is given in Mr. Ogilvie's preliminary report,† and
additional particulars have since been obtained by correspondence with
Capt. Moore. The distance from the coast to the summit is stated as
seventeen miles, of which the first five miles is level bottom-land,
thickly timbered. The next nine miles is in a cañon-like valley where
heavy work would be encountered in constructing a trail. The remaining distance of three miles, to the summit, is comparatively easy. The
altitude of the summit is roughly estimated at 2600 feet. Beyond the
summit a wide valley is entered and the descent to the first little lake
is said to be not more than one hundred feet. The mountains rapidly
decrease in height and abruptness after the summit is passed, and
the valley bifurcates, one branch leading to the head of Windy Arm of
Tagish Lake, the other (down which the water drains) going to Tako
Arm of the same lake.

---

* So named on chart in U. S. Coast Pilot, Schkague River of Krause.
† Annual Report of the Department of the Interior, 1887. Part ii, p. 64. See also Report by
Moore to Chief Commissioner of Lands and Works of British Columbia, dated April 25th, 1888.

Other routes.   The Chilkat Pass has already been noticed (p. 161 b). There is still another route into the interior, which the Indians occasionally employ in winter when the travelling is good over the snow. This leaves the Nourse or west branch of the Taiya and runs west of the Chilkoot Pass to the head of Lake Lindeman.

EXPLORATION AND PROSPECTING ON THE LEWES, AND GOLD MINING IN THE UPPER YUKON BASIN.

Various maps.   The discovery and naming of the Lewes River by Campbell has already been referred to, (p. 138 b) but the information respecting the river obtained by the officers of the Hudson Bay Company during their short occupancy of Fort Selkirk, as embodied on Arrowsmith's map of 1854, was very incomplete, consisting merely of the fact that it divided into two main streams when followed up, and that large lakes existed on these. A considerable improvement is found in the delineation of the river on the map accompanying Dall's work on Alaska. (1870) in which information collected by the explorers of the Telegraph Survey is embodied, but the Lewes is there still merely outlined from report, and no approach to a reasonably correct map of its course existed up to the date of Schwatka's expedition in 1883. The first map of the Chilkoot and Chilkat passes and their vicinity is due, as mentioned further on, to Dr. A. Krause.

Indian jealousy   The passes connecting the coast with the interior country, from the heads of Lynn Canal to the upper waters of the Lewes, were always jealously guarded by the Chilkat and Chilkoot Indians of the coast, who carried on a lucrative trade with the interior or "Stick" Indians, and held these people in a species of subjection. Though the existence of these routes to the interior were known to the traders and prospectors, the hostility of the Chilkats and Chilkoots to the passage of whites long prevented their exploration.

Fables.   In the Alaska Coast Pilot (1883, p. 278) it is stated on the authority of Captain J. C. Carroll, that the first transit of the Lewes River and Chilkoot Pass, by a white man, was accomplished in 1864 or 1865 by an employee of the Hudson Bay Company, who started from Fort Selkirk and was delivered by the Chilkoot Indians to Captain Swanson, then in command of one of the Company's steamers. This story is repeated and amplified in a work by Mrs. E. R. Scidmore, where the adventurer is designated as "a red-headed Scotchman" who " forced his way alone through the unknown territory to Chilkoot Inlet."*

I have endeavoured to verify this tale, but quite unsuccessfully, and while it is possible that some deserter from the Company's posts in

---

* Alaska, its Southern Coast and the Sitkan Archipelago. Boston, 1885, p. 119.

the interior may thus have reached the coast, it is more probable that the story is entirely apochryphal. Enquiry made on the ground among the miners and others fails to substantiate it. Fort Selkirk had been in ruins for twelve years at the date referred to, and officers of the Hudson Bay Company who were on the coast at the time do not believe in its authenticity. It may, however, not improbably have grown out of the circumstance that a gun and some other articles which had belonged to Campbell's people at Fort Selkirk were, shortly after the raid upon that post, obtained from the Coast Indians by servants of the Company.

I have been able to find no reference to the discovery of gold in any part of the Yukon waters earlier than that given by Mr. F. Whymper, who writes in 1869: "It is worthy of mention that minute specks of gold have been found by some of the Hudson Bay Company's men in the Yukon, but not in quantities to warrant a 'rush' to the locality." * Discovery of gold.

The first white man who crossed from the coast to the head-waters of the Lewes appears probably to have been one George Holt†, who did so with the object of prospecting the country.‡ Holt.

The date of Holt's journey was, I believe, 1878. He was accompanied by one or more Indians, and crossed by the Chilkoot or by the White Pass to the head of the Lewes. He followed the river down to the lower end of Lake Marsh and walked over the Indian trail thence to the Tes-lin-too, returning to the coast again by the same route. On his return, he reported the discovery of "coarse gold." but none of the miners who afterwards prospected the region mentioned, have been able to confirm his statement in this particular. In the Alaska Coast Pilot the date of Holt's journey is given as 1875, and in the addendum to the same work as 1872§ in Mrs. Scidmore's book, already quoted, as "1872 or 1884." The date and route above assigned to Holt are, however, probably correct, being the result of enquiry among miners who knew him, followed his route through the country, and came in contact with the Indians whom he had met.

Some years later, in 1880, a prospecting party of nineteen men was organized at Sitka under the leadership of one Edward Bean. Amicable

---

* Travels in Alaska and on the Yukon. London, 1869, p. 227.

† Afterwards murdered by Indians at Cook's Inlet in 1885. Shores and Alps of Alaska, H. W. Seton Karr, London, 1887.

‡ U. S. Coast Pilot. Alaska, 1883, pp. 200, 278.

§ Other extraordinary journeys assigned to Holt in Mrs. Scidmore's book are, according to the miners, altogether incorrect. Holt appears to have been a romancer with considerable inventive powers, but it is possible that he made more than one journey. In May 1876, Messrs. Rath Bros , of Victoria, and Mr. Bean, of California, set out to cross by the Chilkoot Pass for the purpose of prospecting, but were not allowed to go inland by the Indians. Morris, Report upon the Customs District, etc., of Alaska, 1879, p. 97.

First prospecting party, 1880. relations were established with the Chilkats and Chilkoots through the kind offices of Capt. Beardslee, U.S.N., and the Chilkoot Pass was crossed to Lake Lindeman. The party had, by this time, increased to twenty-five in number.* Boats were built on Lake Lindeman, and on the 4th of July the prospectors set out down stream. The Tes-lin-too was reached and was then, for the first time (and as it proves, erroneously,) recognized as the Hotalinqu. Before returning, the Tes-lin-too, was ascended and prospected for some distance. From George Langtry who was a member of the original party, and R. Steel, who joined it later, the facts, as above given, are derived.† No encouraging "prospects" were met with at this time, though Steel states that he found bars yielding at the rate of $2·50 a day in a small stream which joins the Lewes fifteen miles above the cañon.

This large party was closely followed by two miners known as Johnny Mackenzie and "Slim Jim," who reached Lake Lindeman on July 3rd. It is possible that other parties as well may have entered the country in this year, but if so I have been unable to trace them.

1881. In 1881, a party of four miners, including G. Langtry and P. Mc-Glinchey again crossed the Chilkoot Pass. These men got as far as the Big Salmon River, which they called the. Iyon, by which name it is marked on the U. S. Coast Survey map of 1884. They ascended the Big Salmon, according to their estimate, about 200 miles, finding a little gold all along its course and meeting with some remunerative river-bars. This may be characterized as the first discovery of paying placers in the district. According to the U.S. Coast Pilot, already quoted, some account of this expedition is given in the New York Herald, of Sept. 21st, 1881, to which I have been unable to refer.

1882. In 1882, a number of miners entered the Yukon country by the Chilkoot Pass, and probably during this season, but certainly not before,‡ two prospecting parties ascended the Pelly to Hoole Cañon and some of the men appear to have even gone some distance further up.§

Exploration by Krause. Dr. Arthur Krause, engaged in an expedition on behalf of the Bremen Geographical Society, in May and June, 1882, made an explora-

---

* It had increased to twenty shortly after leaving Sitka. See Report by Capt. Beardslee. 47th Congress, 1st Session, Senate, Ex. Doc. No. 71, p. 65. In the same report, the names of the nineteen original members of the party are given and some account of its organization, etc.

† The account of the further wanderings of the party given in the U.S. Coast Pilot, Alaska (1883) p. 278 is incorrect.

‡ According to miners who were in the country at the time, the statements which have been published of earlier prospecting along the Upper Pelly are erroneous.

§ Through the kindness of Mr. François Mercier, I have obtained from Mr. D. Bertrand, who was a member of one of the parties above referred to, the names of the men composing both, as follows :—Thomas Boswell, John Dougan, Robert Robertson, D. Bertrand, Frank Densmore, John Riley, P. Cloudman, Robert Fox, Thomas Curney. The date, as above given is from Mr. Bertrand. Mr Boswell, whom we met on the Lewes in 1887, was understood to say that he had been prospecting up the Pelly in 1884 or 1885, but this statement probably referred to a subsequent expedition.

tion of the Chilkoot and Chilkat passes, reaching Lake Lindeman and the sources of the Tahk-heena River respectively. His work is embodied in maps published by the Bremen and Berlin Geographical Societies, and it is worthy of special note on account of its conscientious accuracy.*

In 1883, some mining was again in progress, but details respecting it have not been obtained. It was in this year that Lieut. Schwatka crossed the Chilkoot Pass and descended the Lewes and Yukon to the sea.† In 1884 a little mining was done on the Pelly and on the Teslin-too, and possibly also on the Lewes. In 1885, mining was begun along the Stewart River, and in the following year, the greater part of the mining population was engaged on that river. Cassiar bar, on the Lewes, twenty-seven miles below the Tes-lin-too, was discovered in the spring of 1886, and actively worked during the same summer. _{Schwatka's journey.}

Late in the autumn of 1886, " coarse gold " was found on Forty-mile Creek (Cone-hill River of Schwatka) still further down the main river than the Stewart, and the announcement of the fact drew off nearly the entire mining population to this place in 1887. In the attempt to bring out the news of this discovery, a miner named Williams was frozen to death on the Chilkoot Pass in January, 1887. _{Gold found on Forty-mile Creek.}

Taking a general view of the gold discoveries so far as made in the Upper Yukon country, we find that, though some small bars have been worked on the upper part of the Lewes, and "prospects" have been obtained even in the stream flowing into Bennett Lake, paying bars have been found on this river only below the mouth of the Tes-lin-too. The best of these are within a distance of about seventy miles below this confluence, and the richest so far has been Cassiar Bar. This is reported to have yielded, in some cases, at the rate of $30 a day to the hand, and gold to the value of many thousand dollars has been obtained from it, chiefly in 1886. In 1887 only three or four men worked here. All along the Lewes below the Tes-lin-too, many bars occur which, according to the reports of prospector's, yield as much as $10 a day, and the same is true of the Tes-lin-too itself, both below and above Tes-lin Lake. Bars of this kind are, however, considered scarcely remunerative at present. _{Lewes and Tes-lin-too.} _{Cassiar Bar.}

Gold has also been found for a long distance up the Big Salmon River, and on the Upper Pelly as far as it has been prospected. The Teslin-too, Big Salmon and Pelly have each already afforded some good paying ground, but in consequence of the rush to Forty-mile Creek only about thirteen miners remained in 1887 on the first-named river, four _{Salmon and Pelly.}

---

* Deutsche Geographische Blätter Bd. v. Heft. 4, 1882. Zeitschr. des Ges. für Erdk. zu Berlin Bd. xviii, 1883.

† See Science vol. iii, 1884, also Report of a Military Reconnaissance in Alaska, Washington Government, 1885. Along Alaska's Great River, New York, 1885.

on the second, and two on the Pelly. On the Stewart River, as much as $100 a day to the hand was obtained in 1885 and 1886, and probably over $100,000 worth of gold has already been obtained along this stream. It has been prospected for a distance of 100 to 200 miles from its mouth, (according to varying statements) and the gold found furthest up is said to be somewhat "coarser" than that of the lower part.

Character of Forty-mile Creek.

Forty-mile Creek is reported to be a river of some size, but more rapid than most of those in the district. It has, according to miners, been prospected for about a hundred miles from its mouth, gold being found almost everywhere along it as well as in tributary gulches. The gold varies much in character, but is quite often coarse and nuggety, and very large amounts have been taken out in favourable places by individual miners. Few of the men mining here in 1887 were content with ground yielding less than $14 a day, and several had taken out nearly $100 a day for a short time. The amount obtained from this stream in 1887 is reckoned by some as high as $120,000, but I believe it would be safe to put the entire output of the Upper Yukon region for the year, at a minimum of $75,000, of which the greatest part was derived from this stream.

Miners.

The number of miners in the whole Upper Yukon country in 1887 may be stated at about 250; of these, 200 were on Forty-mile Creek, and it was estimated that at least 100 would winter on the creek to be ready for work in the spring.

Forty-mile Creek is what the miners term a "bed-rock creek" i.e., one in which there is no great depth of drift or detrital deposits below the level of the actual stream. It is so far the only locality which has been found to yield "coarse gold," but from the extremely wide distribution of "fine gold," it may safely be predicted that many more like it remain to be discovered.

General features of mining.

Mining can scarcely be said to have begun in the region more than five years ago, and the extent of country over which gold has been found in greater or less quantity is already very great. Most of the prospecting has been confined to the banks and bars of the larger rivers, and it is only when their innumerable tributary streams begin to be closely searched, that "gulch diggings" like those of Dease, Mc-Dame and other streams in the Cassiar district, and possibly even on a par with Williams and Lightning creeks in Cariboo, will be found and worked. The general result so far has been to prove that six large and long rivers, the Lewes, Tes-lin-too, Big Salmon, Pelly, Stewart and White, yield "fine gold" along hundreds of miles of their lower courses. With the exception of the Lewes, no part of the head-waters of any of these have yet been prospected or even reached by the miners, and scarcely any of their innumerable tributaries have been examined. The developments made up to this time are sufficient to show that when means of access are improved, important bar-mining will take place along all these main rivers, and there is every reason to anticipate that the result of the examination in detail of the smaller streams will be the discovery of much richer auriferous alluviums. When these have been found and worked, quartz mining will doubtless follow, and the prospects for the utilization of this great mining field in the near future appear to me to be very promising.

I must not, however, omit to state that great difficulties and hard- ships have to be overcome by the miners now entering this country. The traverse of the Chilkoot Portage is itself a formidable obstacle, and over this pass most of the provisions and requisites for the miner must be carried. There is at the present time a trading post belonging to Messrs. Harper, McQuesten & Co., (established in the spring of 1887) at the mouth of Forty-mile Creek, but the supplies are brought to this point by small stern-wheel steamers which ascend the whole length of the Yukon. Goods do not arrive by this route till late in the summer, and any accident or detention may prevent their arrival altogether. The winter in the country is long and severe, and the sea- son of low-water suitable for working on river-bars is short. It is also found that beneath its mossy covering, the ground is often frozen, pre- senting difficulties of another character to the miner, which have pre- vented the working of many promising flats and benches. This, how- ever, is likely to be remedied before long by the general burning off of the woods and moss in the mining camps. Frozen ground was found in the same way in the early days of the Cassiar mines, (see p. 82 B) but the destruction of the timber has now almost everywhere allowed the summer heat to penetrate to the lower layers of the soil. It is not likely that this great inland country will long want some easy means of connection between the coast and its great length of navigable lake- and river-waters, and when this is afforded, there is every reason to believe that it will support a considerable mining population.

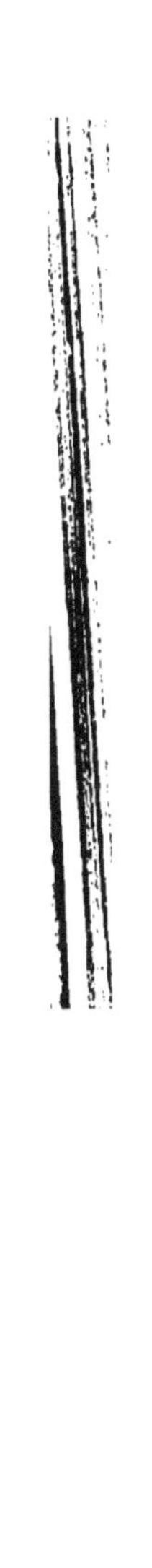

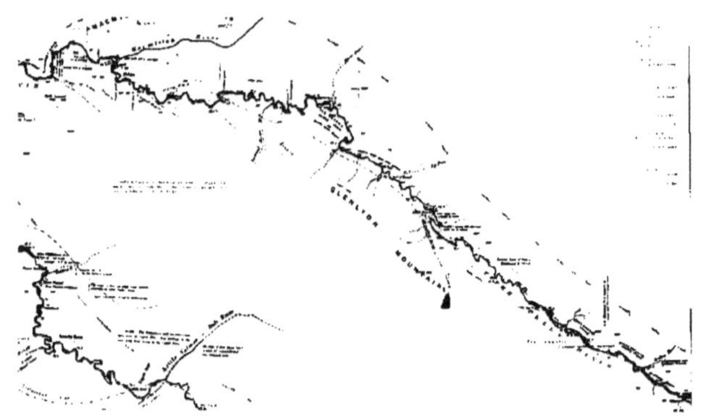

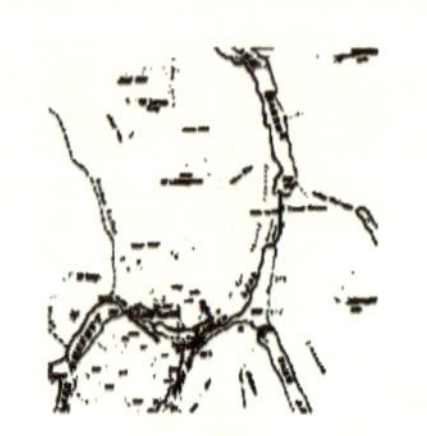

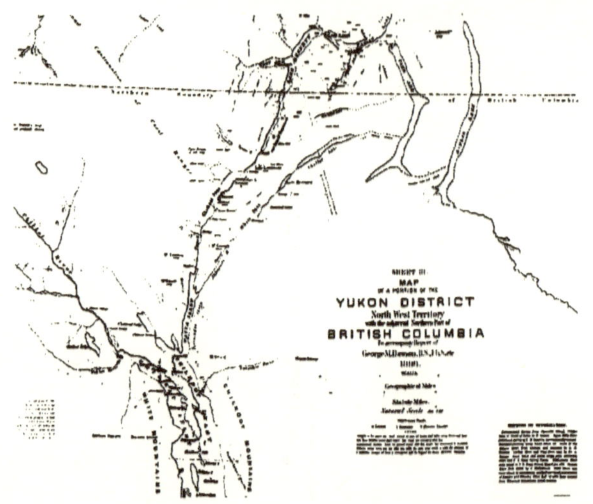

SHEET III
MAP
OF A PORTION OF THE
YUKON DISTRICT
North West Territory
with the adjacent Northern Part of
BRITISH COLUMBIA
To accompany Report of
George M. Dawson, D.S. J.L. Note
1889.
Scale
Geographical Miles
Statute Miles
Natural Scale

APPENDIX I.

NOTES ON THE DISTRIBUTION OF TREES AND OF CERTAIN SHRUBS IN THE YUKON DISTRICT AND ADJACENT NORTHERN PORTION OF BRITISH COLUMBIA.*

Some observations on the trees and plants noticed during the progress of the exploration here reported on, have been given in the preceding pages in connection with the localities described. In this note the general results obtained are presented in a connected form. A list by Prof. Macoun, including the names of all the species recognized, forms Appendix III.

The various lines traversed in the course of the exploration are included between 56° 30' and 63° north latitude, the 128th and 138th meridians of west longitude. This area embraces the extreme northern part of British Columbia and adjacent regions of the North-west Territory, together with part of the "coast strip" of Alaska. Observations by the writer on the distribution of trees in the more southern portion of British Columbia, are contained in previous reports of this survey, particularly in that of 1879–80, which is accompanied by a map showing the limits of some of the more important species.

As already more fully stated, the region above defined is drained by the Stikine and other rivers, which flow through the Coast Ranges to the Pacific, by the Liard, a great tributary of the Mackenzie, and by several branches of the Yukon, but the several drainage basins do not mark out regions of diverse floras. The main division, from this point of view, is found as between the humid and comparatively uniform climate of the coast and the relatively dry and extreme climate of the interior, the first constituting the northern extension of the botanical region of the British Columbian coast, the second that of the interior of the same province. The dividing line is found along the higher ranges of the Coast Mountains.

The considerable altitude of the interior region also has its influence on the flora, but within the limiting parallels above stated, difference of latitude produces a comparatively small effect, in consequence of the fact that the country as a whole becomes lower to the northward or north-westward.

The chief facts to be recorded with respect to the distribution of trees are those connected with the northern limits of the well-known West Coast species, the total number of arboreal forms represented so far north being quite restricted.

Trees of the interior.

In the interior, which may be treated as a whole, the Douglas fir (*Pseudotsuga Douglasii*), Engelmann's spruce (*Picea Engelmanni*), the hemlock (*Tsuga Mertensiana*) and the red cedar (*Thuya gigantea*), all common and characteristic trees a few degrees of latitude to the south, are nowhere found. The white and black spruce (*Picea alba* and *P. nigra*), balsam-fir (*Abies subalpina*), aspen (*Populus tremuloides*) and cottonwood (*Populus trichocarpa*, probably with *P. balsamifera*), are found in suitable localities over the whole region east of the Coast Mountains, the two first-mentioned trees constituting probably half the entire forest covering of the country.

Ubiquitous species.

The white spruce, along the rivers and in sheltered valleys and low ground, everywhere forms fine groves to the furthest northern point reached, many trees attaining a diameter of two feet, tall and well grown. It affords lumber of very fair quality,—the best to be obtained in the country. It is found, with *Abies subalpina*, at the highest limit of timber,—about 4200 feet,—on the inland mountains. The black spruce has scarcely received mention in previous notes on the distribution of trees in British Columbia, but is now known to be abundant locally on high plateaux about the region of the Upper Fraser, and in the country here specially described, grows, mingled with the white spruce, in swampy situations and along cool, shady and damp river-banks. It attains a considerable height, but is never large enough to afford good lumber. *Abies subalpina* was found wherever the upper limit of trees on the mountains was approached, but was not observed near the rivers, except on Bennett Lake (2150 feet), near the head-waters of the Lewes River, in latitude 60°, where it becomes very abundant. The aspen is specially characteristic of second-growth woods and of dry, open, grassy hill-sides facing to the southward, of which there is a great extent on the Upper Pelly and Lewes. The cotton-wood here represented is, so far as the specimens brought back can be determined, *Populus trichocarpa*, but there is little doubt that the balsam-poplar also occurs. Specimens six feet in diameter were seen on the Stikine River near the Coast Mountains, but further in the interior the tree is rarely large enough for the manufacture of dug-out canoes, or, say, three feet in diameter.

Greater interest, from a botanical point of view, attaches to the trees of which the ranges are more restricted. The black pine (*Pinus Mur-*

rayana), perhaps the most common and characteristic tree of the whole Black pine. interior of British Columbia, is also pretty widely distributed in this northern region. It is found in abundance on the Stikine, near the Little Cañon, on the eastern side of the Coast Mountains, and thence inland, in suitable localities. It was observed on the Dease and Upper Liard, and from the mouth of the Dease (according to specimens sent back by Mr. R. G. McConnell) extends down the Liard to Devil's Port- age, some miles east of the range which appears to represent the northern continuation of the Rocky Mountains proper. Beyond this point the Banksian pine becomes characteristic of the great valley of the Mackenzie, which is here entered, but this tree does not extend to the west of the Rocky Mountains. On the head-waters of the Liard *Pinus Murrayana* reaches nearly to Finlayson Lake, its most northern source, but does not occur on the Upper Pelly, on descending which it was first met with in long. 133° 30′. From this point down the Pelly and up the whole length of the Lewes to its sources at the base of the Coast Mountains, it was constantly noted, becoming quite abundant near the Lewes head-waters. Mr. W. H. Dall gives the mouth of the Lewes (lat. 62° 47′) as the northern limit of this tree. * Cones were brought back from this place by Ketchum, of the Telegraph Survey party, which were sent by Mr. F. Whymper to Sir J. Hooker, who determined them. (Under the name of *P. contorta*, from which *P. Murrayana* was not at that date separated.)

My own observations did not extend to the north of this point, down the river, but Mr. McConnell, who has since examined the lower river, states that this tree does not occur at Forty-mile Creek, and that he did not observe it till he reached the vicinity of old Fort Selkirk, in ascending the stream, thus confirming Mr. Dall's remark.

The known range of the common larch (*Larix Americana*) has, by Larch. the observations here reported on, been carried to the west of the Rocky Mountains. This tree extends westward on the Dease River to a point twenty-two miles above its mouth, and along the Liard and Frances rivers spreads northward nearly to Finlayson Lake, reaching latitude 61° 35′. Between the limits thus defined it is quite abundant, and characteristic of cold, swampy tracts and northern slopes, where it grows with the black spruce. It was looked for all along the Pelly, but nowhere found either on this river or on the Lewes. It appears quite probable, however, that this tree will eventually be proved to characterize the sub-arctic country, further to the north, from the Mackenzie valley nearly to the shores of Behring Sea, as Dall refers to the presence of a larch in several places on the Lower Yukon (under

---

* Alaska and Its Resources, pp. 441-692.

the names *L. microcarpa?* and *L. Davurica?*),* which can scarcely be any other than this species. *Larix Lyallii*, which, about the 49th and 51st parallels in the Rocky Mountains, is the most characteristic tree at the timber-line, was not anywhere seen in the region now in question, and would therefore appear to be a relatively southern mountain species.

Birch.

The birch (*Betula papyrifera*) was first seen on leaving the coast by the line of the Stikine, near Kloochman Cañon, thirty miles below Telegraph Creek, some trees here being two feet in diameter. It was also seen on the Dease River, and on the Liard head-waters northward to Frances Lake, where it is abundant, but does not occur on the Upper Pelly till a point a few miles beyond the 131st meridian is reached. Below this, along the Pelly, it is found with increasing frequency, and also occurs here and there on the Lewes, though its limit toward the head-waters of this stream was not noted. The birch never in this region forms extensive groves, but grows singly or in small groups among other trees. It is also found on the Yukon far below the confluence of the Porcupine.

Dwarf birch.

Betula glandulosa, though only a shrub, may be mentioned here, and probably occurs throughout the entire region. It was first noted on the trail between Telegraph Creek, on the Stikine, and Dease Lake.

Juniper.

The juniper (*Juniperus Virginiana*) was observed as a small tree, with trunk six inches in diameter, in the dry country in the lee of the Coast Mountains at Telegraph Creek on the Stikine, (540 feet), but is not elsewhere arboreal.

Alder.

The alder, (probably *Alnus rubra*) and one or more species of willows, become small trees along some of the rivers of the interior. The alder was noted as specially abundant and large on the Upper Pelly.

Service-berry.

The service-berry (*Amelanchier alnifolia*), as a low shrub, was also noted in the vicinity of Telegraph Creek, and was there in full flower on May 24th. It was again seen, to the east of the Cassiar Mountains, in the valley of the Dease (about 2400 feet), on June 22nd, somewhat more advanced than at the first-mentioned locality, but still, in the stage of growth to which it had attained at this date, indicating a comparatively retarded summer in this locality. It does not occur on the Upper Liard or the Pelly, and was only once again observed, on Tagish Lake (2150 feet), at the head of the Lewes; here also in the dry lee of the Coast Ranges. It is here in latitude 60° 15', which is believed to be the furthest northern point from which this species has been recorded to the west of the Rocky Mountains. From observations made in the Peace River region, and elsewhere in British Columbia, it appears that the northern range of this species nearly coincides with that of

* Alaska and its Resources, pp. 29-441.

the growth of wheat, and it is interesting to note, in connection with its appearance at Telegraph Creek, that wheat can actually be grown and ripened there, under the 58th parallel. *Elæagnus argentea* was also noted at Telegraph Creek, but was not again seen till near the mouth of the Lewes, on the Pelly River. In ascending the Lewes it was observed in several places, and always indicates a rather dry climate.

As already stated, the timber-line, or upper limit of the growth of forest, on the mountains of the interior, in the vicinity of the watershed between the Liard head-waters and those of the Pelly in lat. 61° 30′, was found to be at about 4200 feet. At a similar distance from the Pacific Coast, in the corresponding range of the mountains, in lat. 51° 30′, the same line is found at about 7000 feet, showing a descent to the north of 2800 feet in ten degrees of latitude, or about 280 feet in each degree. Timber-line.

It is generally stated that the influence of the warm waters of the Pacific Gulf Stream, striking the northern part of the West Coast and flowing southward along it, is such as to produce a nearly similar climate and flora from the Straits of Fuca far to the north. While this is true in a general way, it is a mistake to suppose that no effect is produced by the increasing latitude. The most marked change of climate, as indicated by the arboreal vegetation, nearly coincides with Dixon Entrance, on the 54th parallel. The forest north of this point is generally inferior in growth, and the quantity of marketable timber is much smaller. The red cedar (*Thuya gigantea*) is not found in any abundance north of the latitude of the mouth of the Stikine River, and though closely looked for along the coast in the vicinity of Lynn Canal, no single specimen of it was detected there. It is confined to the mouth of the Stikine River, and does not follow up this low valley for any distance inland. The yellow cedar (*Thuya excelsa*) scarcely reaches Sitka, and is not anywhere found among the inner islands near the entrance to Lynn Canal. The alder (*Alnus rubra*) forms groves along the shore at least as far north as latitude 59°. The western crab-apple (*Pyrus rivularis*) occurs here and there as far north as Lynn Canal. The broad-leaved maple (*Acer macrophyllum*) may reach latitude 55° on the Alaskan coast, as stated by Prof. Sargent,* but was not observed by me, and must be quite rare. North of the Prince-of-Wales Archipelago, eight-tenths of the entire forest of the coast region consists of the single species, Menzie's spruce (*Picea Sitchensis*). *Pinus contorta* was noted at the head of Lynn Canal and elsewhere along the coast. Here also, in the valley of the stream on the south side of the Chilkoot Pass, by which the Coast Mountains are crossed, *Tsuga Pattoniana* grows to a fair size. It is found also within a few hundred

Change due to latitude on the coast.

Northern limits of certain trees.

---

* Report on the Forests of North America, U. S. 10th Census, p. 47.

feet of the summit of the pass, at an altitude exceeding 3000 feet, in a prostrate form, but still frequently bearing cones. *Abies amabilis* (?) was noted in the valley of the west slope of the pass, and occurs along Lynn Canal and elsewhere on the coast.

The devil's-club (*Fatsia horrida*), a plant most characteristic of an atmosphere saturated with moisture, is not anywhere seen in this part of the interior country, but was met with in the valley to the west of the Chilkoot Pass, and ascends the Stikine valley to a point a few miles above the Kloochman Cañon.

NOTE.—The approximate limits of several species of trees, etc., are indicated on the Index Map attached to this report.

APPENDIX II.

NOTES ON THE INDIAN TRIBES OF THE YUKON DISTRICT AND ADJACENT NORTHERN PORTION OF BRITISH COLUMBIA.

Such information as I have been able to obtain during our journey respecting the Indian tribes of the extreme northern portion of British Columbia and the adjacent Yukon District, are given in the following pages. Between the northern edge of the ethnological map of British Columbia prepared by Dr. Tolmie and myself in 1884,* and the known portion of the area of Mr. W. H. Dall's similar map of Alaska and adjacent regions,† a great gap has existed, which I had proposed to endeavor to fill in connection with the work of the Yukon Expedition. While this intention has been very imperfectly executed, owing to various causes not necessary here to particularize, but especially to to the fact that during a great part of our journey we met with neither Indians nor whites from whom information might have been obtained, it is felt that any facts on the Indians of the district possess some value, not alone from a scientific point of view, but also in their bearing on the Indian question from an executive standpoint. *[Region included.]*

Throughout the more southern portion of British Columbia, a difference of the most marked kind is everywhere found as between the maritime Indians of the coast and the inland tribes. While this difference is largely one of habit and mode of life, it is also almost everywhere coincident with radical differences in language; the natural tendency to diversity as between coast-inhabiting fishermen and roaming hunters being intensified and perpetuated by the great barrier of the Coast Ranges. Only upon certain routes of trade which have existed between the coast and the interior is this striking diversity to some extent broken down. The Fraser, the Skeena, the Nass and—in the region here specially referred to—the Stikine and the passes at the head of Lynn Canal, constitute the most important of these routes. *[Inland and Coast Indians.]*

From Dixon Entrance northward, with the exception of certain small outlying colonies of the Haida on Prince-of-Wales Island, the *[Thlinkit.]*

---

* Comparative Vocabularies of the Indian Tribes of British Columbia, 1884.
† Contributions to North American Ethnology, Vol. i.

Coast Indians are undoubted Thlinkit, forming a series of contiguous and more or less closely allied bands or tribes, between which the diversity in language is small. The inland Indians, on the contrary, belong to the great Tinné family. On the Stikine, as explained below, a certain overlapping of these two races has occurred; and to the north, the Tagish, a branch of the Thlinkit, extend a considerable distance inland into the basin of the Lewes, as now first ascertained. The interior Indians are collectively known on the coast as "Stick Indians," and the fact that this name is also applied to the Tagish, in consequence of their situation and habits being like those of the Tinné, explains the circumstance that they have heretofore been confounded with that people.

Tinné.

Respecting the Thlinkit of the coast I am unable to add anything of value to what has already been published. In what follows regarding the inland Indians, the several tribes are taken up in the order in which they were met with on our line of travel.

The region included between the Coast Ranges and the Rocky Mountains, to the south of that here reported on, and in which are the head-waters of the Skeena, Fraser and Peace rivers, is inhabited by two great divisions of the Tinné people, designated on the map before referred to, as Takulli and Sikani. These main divisions comprise a large number of small tribes or septs. Since the publication of the map, I have ascertained that these divisions are known to the people them-selves as Tah-khl and Al-ta'-tin respectively. The division of the Tinné met with on ascending the Stikine is named Tahl-tan, and consists of the Tahl-tan people proper and the Taku. These Indians speak a language very similar to that of the Al-ta'-tin, if not nearly identical with it, and, so far as I have been able to learn, might almost be regarded as forming an extension of the same division. They appear to be less closely allied by language to the Kaska, with which people they are contiguous to the eastward.

Tahl-tan Indians.

The Indian village near the Tahl-tan or First North Fork of the Stikine, is the chief place of the Tahl-tan Indians, and here they all meet at certain seasons for feasting, speech-making and similar pur-poses. The Tahl-tan claim the hunting-grounds as far down the Stikine, coastward, as the mouth of the Iskoot River, together with all the tributaries of the Iskoot and some of the northern sources of the Nass, which interlock with these. Their territory also includes, to the south, all the head-waters of the main Stikine, with parts of adjacent northern branches of the Nass. Eastward it embraces Dease Lake, and goes as far down the Dease River as Eagle Creek, extending also to the west branch of the Black or Turnagain River. It includes also all the northern tributaries of the Stikine, and the Tahl-tan River to its sources.

Their territory.

The Taku form a somewhat distinct branch of the Tahl-tan, though Taku Indians. they speak the same dialect. They are evidently the people referred to by Dall as the Tăh'-ko-tin'-neh.* They claim the whole drainage-basin of the Taku River, together with the upper portions of the streams which flow northward to the Lewes; while on the east their hunting-grounds extend to the Upper Liard River, and include the valleys of the tributary streams which join that river from the west-ward. They are thus bounded to the south by the Tahl-tan, to the west by the coast Taku ('Thlinkit), to the north-west by the Tagish, and to the east by the Kaska.

The territorial claims of the Tahl-tan and Stikine Coast Indians Rights of coast and inland ('Thlinkit) overlapped in a very remarkable manner, for while, as tribes. above stated, the former hunt down the Stikine valley as far as the Iskoot, and even beyond that point, the latter claimed the salmon-fishery and berry-gathering grounds on all the streams which enter the Stikine between Shĕk's Creek (four miles below Glenora) and Telegraph Creek, excepting the First South Fork, where there is no fishery. Their claim did not include Telegraph Creek nor any part of the main river; nor did it extend to the Clearwater River or to any of the tributaries lower down. In whatever manner the claim to these streams may have been acquired, the actual importance of them to the Coast Indians lay in the fact that the arid climate found immediately to the east of the Coast Ranges enabled them to dry salmon and berries for winter provision, which is scarcely possible in the humid atmosphere of the coast region.

The strict ideas entertained by the Indians here with respect to ter-ritorial rights is evidenced by the fact that the Indians from the mouth of the Nass, who have been in the habit of late years of coming in sum-mer to work in the gold mines near Dease Lake, though they may kill beaver for food, are obliged to make over the skins of these animals to the local Indians. Thus, while no objection is made to either whites or foreign Indians killing game while travelling, trapping or hunting for skins is resented. In 1880 or 1881 two white men went down the Liard River some distance to spend the winter in trapping, but were never again seen, and there is strong circumstantial evidence to show that they were murdered by the local Indians there.

On the Stikine, as in the case of other rivers and passes forming Trade between coast and routes between the coast and the interior, the Coast tribes assumed the interior. part of middle-men in trade, before the incursion of the miners broke up the old arrangements. The Stikine Indians allowed the Tahl-tan to trade only with them, receiving furs in exchange for goods obtained on the coast from the whites. The Tahl-tan, in turn, carried on a

* Contributions to North American Ethnology, vol. i.

similar trade with the Kaska, their next neighbors inland. The right to trade with the Tahl-tan was, in fact, restricted by hereditary custom to two or three families of the Stikine Coast Indians.

Houses. With the exception of the houses already referred to as constituting the Tahl-tan village, and some others reported to exist on the Taku, the residences and camps of these people are of a very temporary character, consisting of brush shelters or wigwams, when an ordinary cotton tent is not employed. We noticed on the Tahl-tan River a couple of square brush houses formed of poles interlaced with leafy branches. These were used during the salmon-fishing season. At the same place there were several graves, consisting of wooden boxes or small dog-kennel-like erections of wood, and near them two or three wooden monumental posts, rudely shaped into ornamental (?) forms by means of an axe, and daubed with red ochre.

Chief's name. On attaining the chieftaincy of the Tahl-tan tribe, each chief assumes the traditional name Na-nook, in the same manner in which the chief of the Coast Indians at the mouth of the Stikine is always named Shĕk or Shake.

Superstitions. The Tahl-tan Indians know of the culture- or creation-hero Us-tas, and relate tales concerning this mythical individual resembling those found among the Tinné tribes further south, but I was unable to commit any of these to writing. Amongst many other superstitions, they have one referring to a wild man of gigantic stature and supernatural powers, who is now and then to be found roaming about in the summer season. He is supposed to haunt specially the vicinity of the Iskoot River, and the Indians are much afraid of meeting him.

Character of wars. Between the Tahl-tan and the Indians inhabiting the Upper Nass* there has been a feud of long duration, which is even yet outstanding. There is much difficulty in settling such feuds when life has once been sacrificed, as they assume the character of a vendetta, a strict account being kept, which must be balanced by the killing of an equal number on each side before lasting peace is possible. The account of the feud here referred to is derived from Mr. J. C. Callbreath, who has been at some pains to ascertain the circumstances. It may serve to illustrate the nature of the intertribal "wars" carried on in the sparsely inhabited region of the interior.

---

* We are unfortunately without precise information as to the tribal divisions of the Indians of the Nass. According to the late Dr. Tolmie, who had long resided at Fort Simpson, in the vicinity of the Nass, the people about the mouth of the river are named Niska (sometimes written Naskar), while further up the river are the Nitawöllk (Tinné?). (Comparative Vocabularies, p. 113 B.) It is probably the people so designated who come in contact with the Tahl-tan, but in the meantime I prefer to call them merely Nass Indians. The statement above quoted, however, does not tally with that made to G. Gibbs by Celestine Ozier, a Tshimsian half-breed, i.e., that to the northward of the tribe inhabiting the Nass was a tribe named Nis-kah. (Contributions to North American Ethnology, vol. i, p. 143.)

For a long period preceding 1856 there had been peace between the Tahl-tan and Nass Indians, but in or about that year the latter, following up one of the branches of the Nass River into Tahl-tan territory, killed two individuals of that tribe, who happened to be men of importance. Two or three years later, the Tahl-tan found an opportunity of killing in retaliation four of the Nass. In 1861, the year preceding the first gold excitement on the Stikine, a peace having been meanwhile concluded, the Nass Indians induced some of the Tahl-tan to visit them in their own country, a short distance from the recognized boundary, at a place named Yak-whik, which is the furthest up fishery of the Nass Indians, and at which they have a large house. The Nass people then persuaded two of the Tahl-tan men to return some distance into the Tahl-tan country, ostensibly that they might bring their friends to engage in a peace talk and dance, two of the Nass Indians accompanying them. The Nass, however, killed both Tahl-tan Indians the first night out, and then turned back. When they arrived at the house, the remaining Tahl-tan men were killed and their women (seven in number) and children (three boys) were made prisoners. Two of the women, with one of the boys, however, escaped and eventually found their way back to their friends. Another of the women was afterwards brought up the Stikine and redeemed by her people. Two more have since died in the Nass country, and one still remains there as a slave. The last event in connection with this feud occurred in 1863 or 1864, when the Tahl-tans raided into the Nass country and waylaid a man and woman with three children. The adults, with two of the children, were left for dead, but the man afterwards recovered consciousness and managed to get home. One of the children was not harmed and has since grown to manhood, and is known to be meditating revenge on the Tahl-tan people.

Notes on the Tahl-tan Indians by Mr. J. C. Callbreath.

The following account of the principal characteristics of the Tahl-tan Indians has been kindly drawn up at my request by Mr. J. C. Callbreath, who has spent many years among these people. The general order followed is that of the Circular of Enquiry issued by the Committee of the British Association on the North-western tribes of the Dominion of Canada. In transcribing Mr. Callbreath's notes some unimportant verbal alterations only have been made.

Maximum stature about 5 feet 7½ inches. Maximum girth about the chest 37 inches. Legs and thighs well muscled. Arms rather light. As a rule full chested. Heads, unlike the coast tribes, small. Feet and hands generally small, as are also the wrist and ankle, especially in the women. We sell more No. 2 women's and No. 6 men's shoes than any other size [representing a length from toe to heel of 8⅝ inches and 10 inches respectively]. In hats for the Indian trade we take nothing above No. 7 [equal to circumference of 22 inches].

The trunk is generally long and the legs short,—the former nearly always straight, with small waist and broad hips, the latter usually curved or crooked, a circumstance which appears to be due to too early walking and carrying packs by the children. Brain-capacity small, head round, forehead low and bulging immediately above the eyes, but generally broad.

Half-breeds.

The half-breeds are more like the father, and three generations where the father is in every case white, seem to obliterate all trace of Indian blood. If the case were reversed and the male parent in all cases an Indian, the result might be different. Have never seen or heard of an albino among them.

Diseases.

Their most common ailments are pulmonary consumption and indigestion. The former caused by careless and unnecessary exposure, the latter by gorging and drinking at their periodical feasts. They have other diseases peculiar to themselves, induced, as I believe, by imagination or through fear of the medicine-men or witches.

Acuteness of senses.

Their acuteness of sight, hearing and smell are great, but I do not believe racial. Practise and training as hunters, render them proficient in these respects. Their eyes fail early, and are even more liable to disease than those of whites. It is rare to meet a man of fifty among them with sound eyes. Snow and sun together, with smoky dwellings, probably explain this. The children are cunning and clever when young, more so than those of the white race, but grow dull as they age.

Language.

I have never seen anything like gesture-language among them, and will not attempt a description of their common tongue, except to say that I can see no similarity in it to that of the Chinese, with whom I have had intercourse to a considerable extent for the past forty years.

Stone implements.

They reckon time by moons, and now seem to rely more on what the whites may tell them as to the coming of winter or spring, than on their own knowledge. The stone age is now scarcely more than a tradition, though they know of the time when they had no iron, axes, knives, guns or the like. Stone knives, adzes, and sledges or hammers, have been found by the miners from time to time, and it is said that the sledges were used for killing slaves on certain occasions, as well as for braining bears in their hibernating dens.

Weaving.

I cannot learn that these Indians ever used copper before its introduction by the whites. Yarn is spun from the wool of the mountain goat (not the mountain sheep or big-horn) and is woven into excellent

. blankets which are highly coloured and ornamented. The process of
boiling water with hot stones in baskets or wooden bowls was formerly
common.

The dances of the Tahl-tan are tame affairs compared with those of Dances.
the Coast tribes. Masks representing birds or bears are sometimes
worn on these occasions. Their musical propensities and capabilities
are, however, considerable. In their dances they use the common
Indian drum, known all over the continent. No athletic games are
practised. Kinship, so far as marriage or inheritance of property Kinship.
goes, is with the mother exclusively, and the father is not considered a
relative by blood. At his death his children inherit none of his property, which all goes to the relatives on his mother's side. Even though
a man's father or his children might be starving, they would get none
of his property at his death. I have known an instance where a rich
Indian would not go out or even contribute to send others out to search
for his aged and blind father who was lost and starving in the mountains. Not counting his father as a relative, he said,—"Let his people
go and search for him." Yet this man was an over-average good
Indian. They seem to have no inherent good qualities which will
overcome the vicious and unnatural rules and customs of their tribe.
Although the son thus, in many cases, seems to have no regard for his
father, the latter generally has a parent's love for the son, and desires
to see him do well.

The whole tribe is divided into two casts, *Birds* and *Bears*. A man Totems.
who is a Bird must marry a Bear and his children belong to the Birds,
but the Bears, his mother's people, inherit all his effects. The right to
hunting-grounds is inherited. A Bear marrying a Bird may go to the
Birds hunting-ground, that is to the hunting-ground belonging to the
particular family of Birds into which he has married, or he may stay
on his own hunting-ground belonging to his particular Bear family,
which he inherited from his mother. His children, however, by his
Bird wife or wives, after becoming adult, cannot resort to his hunting-
ground. His children, both male and female, being Birds, must marry
Bears. They might, if males, marry his full sister, who being a Bear
is not counted a relative, and thus, through her, inherit a right to her
father's old hunting-ground. In some cases, when such proprietary
rights are valuable, and the father is anxious that his son should be
able to claim the old homestead or hunting-ground, such an arrangement is made. The son may be eighteen and his father's sister (his
aunt) may be fifty, but such disparity in age is of no consequence at all.
The son's wish is to secure his title. He may forthwith take another
young wife to please his fancy.

Marriage.

A man's female children are as much his property as his gun and he sells them to whom he pleases without consulting their feelings at all. The vendor sometimes gets his pay at once, sometimes by installments, and if the installments are not paid, he may take back his daughter with her children as well. If, however, the husband pays for his wife in full, the vendor is held strictly to his bargain in respect to supplying a wife, and should the first die and he have any more eligible daughters, one of these must take her place, and that without any additional compulsory payment. Thus, for instance, a man of fifty may buy a young wife of fifteen (a not uncommon occurrence) and pay for her in full. Ten years afterward the young wife may die, and if there be another unsold sister, that sister, according to their laws, must take her place without any compensation, unless it be voluntary. The husband always evinces a high regard for his wife's parents and never tires, if able to do so, of making them presents.

Chieftaincy.

A chief's son has no right to his father's title or any claim to rule by virtue of his being the son of the chief, although the tribe may choose him as their chief. A chief's brother (full or half) or his sister's child, is the legal heir, but his right must be sanctioned by a majority of the tribe, and the office frequently passes to whoever has most property to give away.

Customs and laws.

All the Indians are very miserly, and they often go hungry and naked for the purpose of saving up blankets, guns, etc., with which to make a grand " potlatch " (donation feast) to their friends. This secures them consideration and a position in the tribe. Practically very few of the men have more than a single wife. When a man has two wives, the younger, if she be sound and lively, is the head. Separation and divorce is easy and requires no formal act, but if a man should send away his wife, on whose hunting-grounds he may have been staying, he must leave her inherited hunting-ground, unless he has another wife who has a right to the same ground. These hunting grounds are extensive and are often possessed in common by several families.

The laws are based on the principle that any crime may be condoned by a money payment. If a man should kill another, he or his friends must pay for the dead man—otherwise he himself or one of his friends must be killed to balance the account.

The vicious and unnatural practices of these people appear to be traceable in all cases to the teaching of their medicine-men or witches, in whom they believe implicitly. Their religious belief was simply what their medicine-men might lay down for them from time to time, the idea of a Supreme Being, being very obscure, if not altogether wanting.

They have no war chiefs, and I cannot find that they ever had a general war with any other tribe. Some families have had and are yet having trouble with families of other tribes whom they claim encroach on their hunting-grounds. These families fight it out among themselves by waylaying and murdering each other, but there it ends without producing any inter-tribal war.

Gratitude and charity seem to be foreign to the natures of these people. A man often gives away all he has to his friends, but it is for purposes of personal aggrandizement, and his father, mother or sister may be sick, freezing or starving within sound of his voice. His presents bestowed upon those who are strong and above want bring him distinction, which is his only object. The young Indians are, however, more humane and charitable than the aged.

The Tahl-tan Indians have no totem-poles, although they preserve the family lines, and observe them as strictly as do the salt-water tribes. They have no fear of death except from dread of the pain of dying, and this is very much lessened if they have plenty of goods to leave to their friends. They are very stoical, and not emotional, in any sense. I have never seen one of them tremble or quake with fear or anger. There is a belief propagated by their medicine-men or witches that the otter gets inside of their women and remains there until death, sometimes causing death by a lingering illness unlike anything I have ever seen, in other cases allowing the woman to live on till she dies from some other cause.

The name Kaska (from which that of the district Cassiar is derived*) is applied collectively to two tribes or bands occupying the country to the eastward of the Tahl-tan. I was unable to learn that this name is recognized by these Indians themselves, and it may be, as is often the case with names adopted by the whites, merely that by which they are known to some adjacent tribe. It is, however, a convenient designation for the group having a common dialect. This dialect is different from that of the Tahl-tan, but the two peoples are mutually intelligible and to some extent intermarried. The Kaska are still more closely allied by language and marriage to the Indians of the Lower Liard, who are commonly referred to as the " Hudson Bay Indians," from the circumstance that they trade with that company. Practically the whole of the Kaska trade either at McDame Creek or at the little outpost at the mouth of the Dease. The entire number of Indians re-

---

* Mr. J. W. McKay states, in answer to a question addressed to him on that subject, that Cassiar is a corrupt spelling of the word Kaska. Mr. McKay further adds that he has a suspicion that the word Kaska is connected with that *kaska-met* used by the Stuart Lake Indians to designate dried beaver meat, though he has been unable to confirm this.

sorting to the first named place is 70. That at the mouth of the Dease 94, made up of 23 men, 18 women, and 53 children. The aggregate number of the Kaska, who inhabit a vast territory, is thus very small.

Boundaries. To the westward, the Kaska are bounded by the Tahl-tan. They hunt over the country which drains to the Dease east of McDame Creek; but north of the sources of streams reaching the Dease, they wander seldom, if at all, to the west of the Upper Liard. They also hunt over the basin of the Black or Turnagain River, southward, but not to the head-waters of that stream, as the country there is claimed by the Al-ta'-tin ("Siccanie") of Bear Lake region, who have lately returned to it after having abandoned it for a number of years. Eastward they claim the country down the Liard to the site of Old Fort Halkett, and northward roam to the head of a long river (probably Smith River) which falls into the Liard near this place, also up the Upper Liard as far as Frances Lake, though it would appear that not till recent years have they ventured so far in that direction.

Composed of two tribes. The two cognate tribes here referred to collectively as the Kaska are named respectively, by themselves, Sa-zē-oo-ti-na and Ti-tsho-tī-na. The first occupy the corner between the Liard and Dease, above referred to, as well as the country southward on Black River, where they meet the Bear Lake Indians, named by them Sat-e-loo'-ne. The Ti-tsho-tī-na claim the remaining eastern half of the Kaska country, and call the Indians further down the Liard, below Fort Halkett, A-tsho-to-tī-na.* These are no doubt the tribes referred to by Dall (following a manuscript map by Mr. Ross, of the Hudson Bay Company) as the Achē'-to-tin'-nch and Dābo'-tenä' respectively.† The latter are, however, I believe, distinct from the "Siccanie" or Al-ta'-tin proper. The number stated for the Indians trading at the mouth of the Dease, probably includes some individuals properly referable to the tribe just mentioned. The Indians from Pelly River also sometimes come to the same place to trade, but are not included in the enumeration, and occasionally a few Taku or Tagish wander so far, following the trail eastward from Lake Marsh on the Lewes.‡

Names of the tribes. The Ti-tsho-tī-na call the Pelly River people Ta-koos-oo-ti-na and designate those beyond there again by the term Ai-ya'-na.

Characteristics. The Kaska have the reputation of being a very timid people, and they are rather undersized and have a poor physique. They are lazy and untrustworthy. We met practically the entire tribe of the Ti-

---

* Erèttchi-ottinè or Ndu-tchó-ottinè (?) of Petitot in Bul. Soc. Geog., 1875.

† Contributions to North American Ethnology, vol. i.

‡ Mr. Campbell, in answer to my enquiries, states that there were no leading tribes, under chiefs, in his time on the Upper Liard, but scattered family bands only. These included the " Bastard " tribe or family, the " Thlo-co-chassies " and the " Nahanies of the Mountains," the last-named trading indifferently on either side of the mountains, but being quite a different race from the Nahanies of the Stikine (Tahl-tan).

tsho-tī-na at the little post at the mouth of the Dease, and their
curiosity proved to be very embarrasing. Mr. Egnell, who was in
charge of the post, excused it by explaining that they had never seen
so many Whites together before, the number being nine in all, including our party, Mr. Egnell himself and Mr. McDonald, of the Hudson
Bay Company. Of these Indians, only two had been as far west as
Dease Lake, and none had ever seen the sea. They are, however, fairly
well off, as their country yields abundance of good furs. They visit the Migrations.
trading post only once in the course of the year, spending the remainder of their time moving from camp to camp in isolated little family
parties, hunting and trapping; each one traversing a very great extent
of country in the course of the twelve months. Some of their traps or
household goods are packed on dogs, but the greater part of their im-
pedimenta is carried by themselves on their backs, canoes being seldom
employed. Rivers and lakes are crossed in summer by rafts made for
the occasion. They generally bring in only the fine furs, as bear-skins
and common furs are too heavy to transport. They evidenced great
curiosity with regard to our equipment, being particularly struck by
a canvas boat and an air pillow. These and other objects, I have no
doubt, furnished subjects of conversation round many camp fires for the
ensuing year.

The Kaska form a portion of the group of tribes often referred to
by the Hudson Bay Company's people as the Nahanie or Nahaunie,
and so classed collectively by Dall in the absence of more definite information.*

For the northern district, drained by the Pelly, Stewart and other Indians of
rivers, I am unfortunately unable to give much detailed information northern
district.
respecting the Indians, a circumstance due to the fact that we scarcely
met any of these Indians, nor did we proceed far enough down the main
river to meet the traders, from whom something might doubtless have
been obtained.

The name of the Indian tribe inhabiting the Upper Pelly valley was Indians of
given to me by the Indians at the mouth of the Dease as Ta-koos-oo- Upper Pelly.
ti-na, by Indians met by us near the site of Fort Selkirk as Na-ai'. The
territory of this tribe includes also the basin of the Macmillan and that
of the Stewart as far down as the mouth of the Beaver, or " First
North Fork," a very extensive region. I believe, however, that the
names above noted either refer to local sub-divisions of the tribe, or are
terms applied to them by neighbouring tribes and not recognized by
themselves. Dall in his article already cited (following Ross) gives
Abbáto-tenä' as the name of a tribe inhabiting the Upper Pelly and
Macmillan, while Petitot places the name Esbá-ta-otinnè in the same

region. Campbell again states that the Indians met by him on the Pelly were " Knife Indians," and I think there can be very little doubt that the true name of this tribe is Es-pā-to-ti-na, formed by the combination of the word Es-pā-zah (meaning knife in the neighbouring Kaska language) and ti-na. This is again evidently the same with the name rendered to me as Spo-to-ti-na by a trader in Cassiar and said by him, to be a Kaska name for the tribe to the north of their country.

From the Indians above mentioned as having been met with at the site of Fort Selkirk, who were travelling with miners, the following information was obtained :—

Tribes below Fort Selkirk.

A tribe or band named Klo-a-tsul-tshik' (-otin ?) range from Rink Rapid and its vicinity on the Lewes to the head of the east branch of White River, where they go at the salmon-fishing season. These people probably also range down the river as far as the mouth of the Lewes, or further. They are the Gens des Bois or Wood Indians of the fur-traders. It will be observed that their name does not terminate in the usual way, but of this no explanation could be obtained.*

The To-tshik-o-tin are said to live about the mouth of Stewart River, and to extend up the Stewart as far as the Beaver River, meeting there the Es-pā-to-ti-na to whom they are or were hostile. They are no doubt the Tutchone-kutchin of Dall's map.

Near the mouth of Forty-mile Creek are the Tsit-o-klin-otin and a short distance below this point on the river, so I was informed, is a tribe named Ka-tshik-o-tin. These were said to be followed by the Ai-yan', below which come the O-til'-tin, the last tribe occupying the vicinity of the mouth of the Porcupine and extending some way up that river.

It was further stated that the people of the above mentioned tribes, with others, making seven in all, were collectively classed as Ai-yan'. This agrees sufficiently closely with the name Ai-ya'-na, given to me as a general name of Indians beyond those of the Pelly River by those found at the mouth of the Dease.

Number.

According to Schwatka the entire number of Indians along the main river from the mouth of the Lewes to the Porcupine is about 250. I can make nothing, however, of the local names given by him, with respect to which indeed he appears to have been himself in doubt.

The Indians inhabiting the whole basin of Peel River, were said, by my informants at Fort Selkirk, to be named Sa-to-tin. A tribe named

---

* Mr. Campbell informs me that in his time while a very few families of the " Knife Indians" inhabited the region of the Upper Pelly, the Indians were very numerous and divided into bands, under chiefs, along the river from Fort Selkirk to Fort Yukon. The " Wood Indians" numbered several hundreds. Below them on the river were the " Ayonais " as well as other tribes, of which Mr. Campbell was unable to learn the names.

San-to-tin' was further said to occupy the territory about a lake on Tanana River Indians. White River and westward to extend down the 'Tanana River to a point nearly opposite the head of Forty-mile Creek. Below this people, on the Tanana come the Sa-tshi-o-tin' or "Bear Indians," Lieut. Allan* gives the names of tribes or bands along the Tanana, from its head down (though on doubtful authority) as Nutzotin, Mantototin, Tolwatin, Clatchotin, Hautlatin, the second and fourth of which seem to represent the names given to me.

From the above information, such as it is, I think it probable that Conclusions. the Ai-ya'-na or Ai-yan people may be said to consist of the following tribes : Klo-a-tsul-tshik, To-tshik-o-tin, Tsit-o-klin-o-tin, Ka-tshik-o-tin, O-til'-tin, San-to-tin, and Sa-tshi-o-tin'. The name Ai-yan may be that of a premier tribe or of a meeting place common to the various tribes. The Ai-ya'-na would thus extend from the lower part of the Lewes to the mouth of the Porcupine, and include the basin of White River, together with the greater part or all of that of the Tanana.

The term Kutchin as a general suffix to the names of tribes, re- "Kutchin." placing *tinné*, *tina* or *otin* has, I believe, been carried much too far westward in this region on ethnological maps, being properly referable only to certain tribes situated to the north of the Ai-ya'-na and Es-pä-to-ti-na and lying between these and the Eskimo. Docking off this gratuitous termination from the names Han-kutchin and Tenän'-kut-chin applied as tribal names by Dall on the main river above the mouth of the Porcupine and along the Tanana River respectively ; we may, with some probability, consider Han and Tenan as versions of Ai-yan. Differences such as this and others previously referred to in the rendering of Indian words—which are never clearly pronounced by the people themselves—are, as I think any one who has had some experience in endeavouring to reduce them to writing will admit, very easily explained.

A grave was seen on the Upper Pelly, near the mouth of the Mac- Graves. millan and others near the site of Fort Selkirk. There were the usual coffin-boxes, surrounded by pickets, and near them tall poles were set up, bearing streamers of cloth.

The Tagish Indians, occupy the greater part of the valley of the Tagish Indians. Lewes above the mouth of the Tes-lin-too, as well as the last-named river as far as to its efflux from Tes-lin Lake, the lake itself being in the Taku country. To the Tagish belong the group of lakes of which Tagish-ai or Tagish Lake is the principal. They may be said to be separated from the coast tribes by the water-shed ridge of the Coast Mountains on Chilkoot Pass, though the line of division is not apparently well drawn, and they likewise probably reach the head-

---

* Report of an Expedition to the Copper, Tanana and Koyukuk Rivers, etc., 1887.

waters of the Tahk-heena branch of the Lewes. The name of this stream evidently means Tagish River, and though I follow the usual orthography, this is incorrect. The precise line of demarcation between this tribe and the Taku, in the valley which connects A-tlin Lake with the Taku River, is not known. One of the Tagish people informed me that they claim also the head-waters of the Big Salmon River, and Lieut. Schwatka (who calls these people Tahk-heesh) in his report mentions having found some of them temporarily in occupation of a spot not far above the mouth of the Lewes. I believe, however, that this party may have been merely on a trading expedition and feel doubtful also of their extension to the Salmon, unless temporarily on some such errand. Their principal place is upon the short reach of river connecting Tagish Lake with Lake Marsh, where two rough wooden houses, somewhat resembling those of the Coast Indians, are situated. Here the greater part of the tribe congregates during the winter.

So far as I was able to judge, the Tagish in their mode of life and habits are identical with the Tinné Indians. They are classed with those as "Stick Indians," by the coast tribes, and have been assumed to be Tinné, but their language very clearly shows that they are in reality a Thlinkit people. Most of their words are either identical or very nearly so with those of the Thlinkit, while a few appear to resemble those of the Tinné. Till of late, they have been effectually dominated by the Chilkats and Chilkoots of Lynn Canal and have thus been kept poor both in goods and in spirit. From time immemorial they have been in the position of intermediaries in trade between the Coast and the Tinné Indians, without being sufficiently strong to levy a toll. On the question as to whether the blending of characteristics which they appear to show physically, as well as in other respects, has resulted only from intermingling of the two peoples, or may be regarded as preserving evidence of the actual derivation of the Thlinket from the Tinné, or its converse, I can offer no definite opinion. The question is, however, a very interesting one for further investigation, and may eventually throw light on the connection between these peoples, first, I believe, pointed out by my friend, the late Dr. W. F. Tolmie.*

The Tagish tribe is a very small one, and includes about fifteen families only, all told,—representing possibly seventy or eighty individuals. Their snow-shoes, together with their travelling and hunting equipment generally and their mode of camping, are identical with those of the Tinné, so far as I was able to observe.

---

* Comparative Vocabularies of the Indian Tribes of British Columbia.

At the lower end of Lake Marsh we found several graves which, no Graves.
doubt, belonged to the Tagish.　One was a small tent-shaped erection
covered with calico, another a box wrapped in spruce bark and piled
round with neatly cut pieces of wood and logs, held in place by
pickets.　A third, a similar box, on which billets of wood and finally
rough branches and rubbish had been piled.　The boxes were too small
to contain the corpses of adults, even if placed in the constrained pos-
ture usual to Indians, and as the ground beneath and around each of
the deposits was thoroughly burnt, it appeared quite possible that the
bodies had been cremated and the ashes only coffined.

Respecting the Chilkat and the Chilkoot tribes of Lynn Canal, I can Chilkat and Chilkoot Indians.
add little or nothing to what is already known.　Lieut. Schwatka, in
his report already referred to, speaks of these people as constituting
divisions of a single tribe under the general name of Chilkat. They are
certainly very closely allied, though in times past they have not always
been at amity.　Schwatka further states that "the Chilkats, proper,
have three permanent villages, which are situated in the immediate
neighbourhood of Pyramid Harbour, and at no great distance from
each other.　The Chilkoots, the other division of the tribe, have one
village, situated permanently in the Chilkoot Inlet."　These people are
of course, in all respects, typical Thlinkit.　They number, in all,
according to Lieut. Symons, U.S.N., 981.　Schwatka says they call the
Tagish, in some connection, Si-him-e-na.

Mr. J. C. P. De Krafft* says that he was informed of the Chilkat,
Chilkoot and neighbouring interior tribes, that they are all of the
general classification Thlinkit, and name the whole region inhabited
by them Kunana, the inhabitants Kunääni.　That one group of tribes
named Alitch (being their name for people) consists of six small tribes
viz., Tagosh (living nearest the coast), Kluhtano, Netlatsin, Tahtlin,
Klukha, and Tahho.　Of the above names, most are recognisable as those
of places in the Tagish country, and they may refer to the hunting-
grounds of various families, but there is evidently some confusion
respecting the names, which are quoted here chiefly with the object of
suggesting further enquiry.

The subjoined table, giving a census of the Indian population of the Hudson Bay Company's census.
Mackenzie River District, and including the Yukon region so far as
known to the Hudson Bay Company in 1858, is of interest, as showing
the tribal sub-divisions as recognized by the Company, and as throwing
some light on the questions discussed above.　The table is due to the
late Chief Factor, James Anderson, and has been communicated to me
through the kindness of his son.

---

* U. S. Senate Doc. 1 Session, 47th Congress, vol. iv, p. 100.

	Married.		Adults.		Children.		Total.		Total Males and Females.	
	Male.	Female.	Male.	Female.	Male.	Female.	Male.	Female.		
Fort Simpson and Big Island.										
Slaves, Dog Ribs and Hares.	124	129	96	20	159	130	379	279	658	
Nahanies	13	14	35	....	12	13	60	27	87	—745
Fort Rae.										
Dog Ribs and a few Slaves and Yellow Knives..... }	123	131	91	25	145	142	359	298	657	—657
Peel R. and La Pierre's House..										
Loucheux (Koochin).	81	92	21	7	83	53	185	152	337	—337
A few Esquimaux occasional visitors.										
Yukon.										
Loucheux of six tribes......	135	156	121	75	218	137	474	368	842	—842
These are all that resort to the fort.										
Fort Liard.										
Slaves	45	47	38	14	84	53	167	114	281	
Sicannies or Thicannies	12	16	7	....	16	27	35	43	78	
Nahanies.	9	9	2	....	11	7	22	16	38	—397
Fort Resolution.										
Chipewyans and Yellow Knives, with a few Dog Ribs and Slaves .... }	98	149	....	....	119	103	217	252	469	—469
Fort Good Hope.										
Hare Indians..............	76	78	68	23	80	39	224	140	364	
Loucheux and Batard Loucheux .... }	23	22	18	3	17	12	58	37	95	
Nahanies.	1	1	3	3	....	....	4	4	8	—467
Fort Norman.										
Slaves	19	19	10	2	20	14	49	35	84	
Hares	23	25	17	....	27	11	67	36	103	
Dog Ribs	22	24	21	9	28	29	71	62	133	
Nahanies	8	9	....	....	18	8	26	17	43	—363

	MARRIED.		ADULTS.		CHILDREN.		TOTAL.		Total Males and Females.	
	Male.	Female.	Male.	Female.	Male.	Female.	Male.	Female.		
Fort Halkett.										
Sicannies or Thicannies.....	17	19	7	5	14	11	38	35	73	
Mauvais Monde, Batard Nahannies and Mountain Indians. All tribes of Nahannies	63	63	19	9	57	48	139	120	259	—332
										4609
RECAPITULATION.										
Slaves, Dog Ribs, Chipewyans and Yellow Knives, who are all of the same race, and speak — with slight variations — the same dialect of the Chipewyan language........	530	602	341	93	662	521	1533	1216	2749	
Nahanies or Mountain Indians, who speak a very corrupt dialect of the Chipewyan	94	06	59	12	98	76	251	184	435	
Sicannies or Thicannies, who also speak a dialect of the Chipewyan language	29	35	14	5	30	38	73	78	151	
Loucheux or Koochin and Batard Loucheux (half Hare, half Loucheux). Only some words of this language are understood by the Slaves	239	270	160	85	318	202	717	557	1274	
	892	1003	574	195	1108	837	2574	2035	4609	

SHORT VOCABULARIES OF THE TAHL-TAN, TI-TSHO-TI-NA, AND TA-GISH OBTAINED IN 1887.

The alphabet employed is identical with that of the "Comparative Vocabularies of the Indian Tribes of British Columbia," and is as follows:—

Vowels.

a	as in English		*fat.*
ă	"	"	*father.*
e	"	"	*met.*
ē	"	"	*they.*
i	"	"	*pin.*
ī	"	"	*marine.*
o	"	"	*pot.*
ō	"	"	*go, show.*
u	"	"	*nut, but.*
y	"	"	*year.*
ai	"	"	*aisle.*
ei	"	"	*vein.*
oo	"	"	*pool, fool.*
eu	"	French	*peu* (seldom used).
ow	"	English	*now.*

The distinction of long and short vowels (following Gibbs) is noted as far as possible, by the division into syllables,—the consonant that follows a vowel being joined immediately to one intended to be pronounced short, while a long vowel is left open, being followed by a hyphen. When this is insufficient, or a nicer distinction is desirable, the usual long and short marks are supplied.

Explosive or klicking sounds are represented by the letters *k*, *t*, etc., in combination with an apostrophe, thus—'*k* '*t*.

An acute accent (') at the end of a syllable indicates its accentuated character, when this is very distinct. In some cases certain syllables are run very hurriedly over and almost whispered, and though really forming a part of the word, might easily be omitted by a careless listener. Where this has been noted it is indicated by the use of smaller type. Strongly guttural syllables are printed in small capitals, thus,—*law*-KH. A nasal sound is denoted by a small letter above the line, thus—ⁿ.

English.	Tahl-tan.	Ti-tsho-ti-na.	Ta-gish.
Man	den'-e	skel-ĕ'-nă	tah-kŭ'-ne
Woman	e-ga-tĕn'	is-tshī-yong	ug uh-tĕ'-na
Boy	etŏ-nĕ'	is-tshī'-ma	too-nī'-na
Girl	'tĕ'-la	is-too'-ū	ti-tshoo-tlug'-a-tĕ-na *(little woman)*
Infant	——	——	is-too'-ū
My father	e-te'-uh	a-ta'-a	e-tūh'
My mother	o-tlī	en-ū'	ah-mā'
My husband	es-kuh-lĕ'-na	sine-ske-lĕ-nă	uh-hoh'
My wife	es-tsi-yă'-na	sine-is-tshī-yong	us-sa-wut-tŏ
My son	es-tshī-me	sine-is-tshī'-ma	uh-hī-yit'-e
My daughter	es-too'-eh	sine-is-too'-ū	——
My elder brother	es-tī-uh	kut-ĕ'-uh	——
My younger brother	es-tshīt'-le	ĕ-tshī'ala	——
My elder sister	e-tā'-ta	a-tad-ĕ	——
My younger sister	es-tĕ'-juh	a-tad'-zuh	——
An Indian	dī-den'-e	den'-uh	tshut-lĕk'
Head	es-'tsi	es-sĕ'	ka-suh
Hair	es-tsī-gŭ'	es-tsĕ-ga'	ka-sha-hū-oo
Face	es-snĕ	es-enĕ'	ka-guh'
Forehead	es-tsĕ'-ga	es-tsī'-ge	ka-kok'
Ear	es-thĕs'-botl	sus-pă'-luh	ka-kook'
Eye	es-tă'	es-tă'	ka-wok
Nose	es-tshī'	es-tsī	ka-tlooh
Mouth	es-săt'-a	es-zū-de	'kŏh
Tongue	es-sū'	es-zū-de	ka-tloot'
Teeth	es-gooh'	es-ĕyuh'	ka-ŏh'
Beard	es-stane'-gun	es-ton-o-kh'	ka-kuh-tad-zai'
Neck	es-kŏs'	es-'kŏs	ka-hloo-tih'
Arm	es-sī-tluh	es-kā'-nuh	ka-tshīn
Hand	es-sluh'	es-sitā'	ka-tshīn
Fingers	es-sluh' *or* slus-sĕ-guh	es-sitā'	ka-tlĕ-uk
Thumb	slus-tshŏ'	slas-tshŏ'	ka-koosh'
Little finger	slus-tshed'-le	——	——
Nails	is-lŭ-gun'-a	sla-kun-ū'	ka-hak_{wh}
Body	es-hīu'	es-zī'	ka-kĕ-sin'
Chest	es-tshān	es-tzonḡ	ka-hāt-ka'
Belly	es-bĕt	es-pĕt	ka-yoo-kuh'
Female breasts	ma-tŏ'-ja	es-tŏ'-ja	too-tlā
Leg	es-tsĕn-a	es-tsut'-za	kā-kud'-ze
Foot	es-kuh'	es-'kiă'	ka-kŏs
Toes	es-kus-tshŏ' *(probably great toe)*	es-kuh-gau'-da'	ka-tlĕ-uk
Bone	es-tseⁿ'	es-tsun'-uh	tsăk

English.	Tahl-tan.	Ti-tsho-ti-na.	Ta-gish.
Heart	es-tshĕa′	es-tzi-ū	ka-teh′
Blood	e-ted-luh	e-til-uh′	sheh
Village	kĕ-yĕ′	kon′-a	ai-ĭ-i-tĭ (?)
Chief	tin-ti′-na	tin-a-tĕ′-yuh	an-kow′
Warrior	e-ted′-etsha	——	——
Friend	es-tsĭn-ĕ	sū-za	yu-keh′
House	kĭ-mah′	es-kon′-a	hīt
Brush wigwam	tso-la-hīt′	es-kon′-a	hīt
Kettle	′kōtl	sīoo-sū′-a	kĭ-sha′
Bow	des-ūn	sĭ-te-uh′	tshoo-net′
Arrow	′k-ah	es-kū-ah	kū-kutl
Axe	tsĭ-tl	tsĕntl	shin-a-whū
Knife	pĕsh	es-pā-zuh	klĭ-ta
Canoe	ma-lā′-te	sa-la-ah′	yakw
Moccasins	e-tshil-e-kĕh′	es-kuh′	tītl
	(skin shoes)		
Pipe	t′	es-tzil-e-kĕ′-duh	tsik-ta-kĕt′
Tobacco	tsĕ-a-ĸɪɪ	tzid-a-too′-de	tsĕ-uk
Sky	ya-za	kŭs	tik-kĭ′
Sun	tshū	sŭ	ka-kun′
Moon	——	sū	itl-tĭs′
Star	sᴜɴᴍ	sᴜn	kwat-a-hin-a-ba
Day	zɕu-ĕs	do-te-dzuh	ha
Daylight	yĕ-kū′	——	——
Night	ih-klĕ-guh	kla-klĕ-ge	tūt
Morning	tshut-tshaw- tlunĕ′	e-klū-dzi	tsoo-tūt′
Evening	hĭh-guh′	tlah-kū-ha’	hū′-nū
Spring	tū-nĕ′	ta-tuna-kū-ga	ya-kunĕ-tshatl′
Summer	klĭ-we-guh′	ĭ-pah	kus-sĭ-at′
Autumn	tū-tla′	——	yes′k
Winter	ih-ha-yĕh	hat′-ya	——
Wind	it-tsĭ′	it-sĭ	nook
Thunder	it-ti-i-tshĭ′	it-tĭ-ji	in-dĭ-jeh′
Lightning	kun-ta-tsĕl	kun-tū-tzil′	soon-tsha′-na
Rain	tshū′	tshaⁿ	tsoo
Snow	zus	zus	klĭĕt
Fire	kŏn	kun	′kūn
Water	tsoo	too	hĭn
Ice	tenⁿ	tun	′t-ĭk
Earth, land	nĕn	nin	hoo-tĭ-tluk
Sea	ĕ-ĕtlŭ	ĕ-ĕtla	ĕ-′tl
River	too-dĕsᴎ	ta-kū′-koo-tsho (when large) too-za-za (when small)	hĭn

ENGLISH.	TAHL-TAN.	TI-TSHO-TĪ-NA.	TA-GISH.
Lake	mǒn	mǒn	āh
Valley	tä-gǒs'-ke	tsin-i-tla	yīn-a-tlet'-ki
Prairie	'klo'-ga	a-tega	tshoo'-kun
Hill	tah	hi-za-za	shūh
Mountain	his-tsho	tsutl	—
Island	ta-ĕ-too-e	ta-dŏ-a	kū'-tuh
Stone, rock	tsǒ	tsa	tĕh
Salt	ĕ-ŏtlä	—	ĕ-'tl
Iron	pos-te-zīn'	pĕ-zin	ki-ye'-tsuh
Forest	got-ĕ	—	shī-tī-hin-as (many trees)
Tree	tli-gĕ-gut'	tsoo	she-tlek'-as
Wood	tsot-tsh-tsĕlsh	tsutz	et-ka-whut'-ti
Leaf	e-tŭne'	a-tŏna	ke-ga-nl
Bark	ed-lä	se-tĕd-za	a-hloo-nl
Grass	klōñh	klō-ye	tshoo'-kun
Pine	gä-za	—	kletl *or* kaon-sĕ
Cottonwood	—	—	tīe
Flesh, meat	e-tsĕt'	a-tzun	tlī
Dog	klī	kli	kĕtl
Bear	shush	sus	hootz
Wolf	tshī-yō-ne	tshi-yŏ'-nuh	noos
Fox	nus-tsŏ'he	nis-tsū'	na-kat-sĕ
Deer	kīw-igana	—	—
Mountain-goat	—	—	tshen-oo
Mountain-sheep	—	—	tū-wĕh'
Caribou	ŏ-tsī'	goo-dzi'	but-sīh'
Beaver	tshä	tsa	tsi-go-di'
Rabbit, hare	guh	guh	kah
Fly	tsĭ-mĕh	tso-tsa'	ka-kon-a-wit'-se
Mosquito	tsĭ	tsi-a	tä'-ka
Snake	—	—	ti-koo-too'-da
Bird	tsĭ-mĕh	tih	koktl
Egg	ĕ-ga-zuh'	ĕ-ga'-zuh	et-kot'-ĕ
Feathers	tshŏsh	met-tshŏsa	a-kwat'-le
Wings	mĭ-ĭ-tsĕne	me-tzon-a	e-ki'-je
Goose	gän-jeh	gun-tsha	ta-wuk
Duck (mallard)	too'-deh	too'-dah	ka-whw
Fish	klew'-eh	hloo'-ga	nat
Salmon	klew'-eh	gĕs	tāh
Name	on-yŏh	toon'-ya	—
White	ta-'käd'-le	ta-kud'-za	klŏ-tuh'-uh-tĕ
Black	ten-es-klä'-je	ten-as-kluz'-e	too'-teh
Red	te-tsĭ-je	a-tul-a'	ka-nuh'-e-te
Blue	te-tlesh'-te	det-lĭs-da	ta-tlin-suh
Yellow	tsīm'-tlet	ten-a-tsĕ-a	tsoo-yuh-uh-ta

ENGLISH.	TAHL-TAN.	TI-TSHO-TĪ-NA.	TA-GISH.
Green	(same as yellow)	tsud-a-da-tsŏ'	(same as yellow)
Great, large	e-tsho	ta-etshŏ	a-tlin'
Small, little	ta-a-tsed'-le	ta-tzille'	ti-tshoo-tluh'
Strong	na-tī-yi	nun-tī	hli-tsin'
Old	es-tshăn	sa-ĭ	yoo-got
Young	es-kī-uh	ti-too	yis
Good	e-tī'-uh	e-tĕ'-uh	ya-kä'
Bad	tshā'-ta	koos-tsn'-tsa	kon-ai-a-oo
Dead	a-juh'	a-jah	yoo'-na
Alive	te-tshĭ'	goo-te'	kwa-gi-tī'
Cold	hos-tlĭ'	goos-tli or el-oo-goo	ye-tik
Warm, hot	hos-sitl	a-te-zulle'	yoo-tli-tik
I	shī-ni	nin'-e	hat
Thou	nīn-e	sin'-e	me-eh
He	a-yī-ge	i-ye	——
We	ta-hun'-e	——	——
Ye	kla'-tse	——	——
This	tĭ-te	di-di	——
That	a-yī-ge	i-ye'	——
All	sĕ-tse	ta-tĕ-da	ut-la-kut
Many, much	oo-tlaⁿ	nus-tloⁿ	shi-a-te-hen'
Who	ma-dai-e	——	——
Far	nī-sŭ-te	goo-din-e-sat'	na-hli
Near	hah'-ne	ha-nä	kwun-a-sī
Here	tis-tsik	——	
To-day	too'-ga	di-doo-den-e	ye-kī'-yi
Yesterday	kit-sŏ'-kuh	ta-tshoⁿ	tet-kuh
To-morrow	tsha-tshā'	ta-tshon	tsoo-tät'
Yes	ĕh	hoⁿ	a-huh
No	ti-wuh	in-too-uh	klĕk
One	tlī-geh'	e-tle'-ga	tshut-lĕk
Two	tla-kĕh	hlek-et-e-ta'	tĕh
Three	tä-tĕ'	ta-di-da	natz
Four	klen-teh'	hlen'-ta	ta-koon '
Five	klo-dläe'	klo-la'	kī-tshin'
Six	na-slikĕ'	uod-sli'-ga	kle-doo-shuh'
Seven	na-sla-kĕh'	nod-i-slik-a	tuh-a-doo-shuh'
Eight	na-stäe'	nos-ta-di-da'	natz-ka-doo-shuh'
Nine	na-sten-tĕh'	nos-ī-slen-e-ta	koo-shok'
Ten	tso-snū'-ne	tis-ĕnŭ-go-anzi-tli-ga'	tshin-kat
Eleven	tso-snä'-ne-tes-liheh	tis-ĕnŭ-go-anzi-la-kut-e-tla	tshin-kat-ka-tlah'
Twelve	o-dis-lŭ-kĕh'	tleh-gad-ih-no'	tshin-kat-ka-tĕh

TAHL-TAN.	TI-TSĪTO-TĪ·NA.	TA-GISH.
ten-tlā-dih-teh′	ta-tis-no	teh-tshin-kat
ta-tsos-nan	tlen-tad-es-no	nats-tshin-kat
klon-ta-tsos-nan	klan-tad-es-no	ta-koon-tshin-kat
tlo-tlāts-oos-nū-ne	hloo-lad-es-no	—
na-stlik′-is-oos-nū-ne	no-sli-gi-tis-no	—
na-slak-ets′-oos-nū-ne	no-sa-sla-kad-is-no	—
na-stā-o-tsoos-nū-ne	no-de-tad-es-no	—
na-stlin-tĭs-oos-nā-ne	no-slan-tad-es-no	—
klo-la-ten-ān-e-ta	tis-no-kin-e-ta′	tshin-kat-ka
—	—	—
etz-et-etz′	en-tsutz (?)	at-huh′
etz-oo-tān-en-e	too-in-to″′	too-nuh′
kīs-too-tshĕ′-ane	in-gulh′	klakw
en-dlĕ′	in-le′	kit-li-gatz′
en-tshīn	in-jīn	a-tshi′
nes-tĕtl′	sin-te′	tah
hun-tĕh	goo-din-tah′	yoo-kwa-tin′
nat-sī	guan-es-ta′	hle-tin′
na-is-tlook′	—	tloon-kut-la-tin (?
tsin-hia′	ze-hī	whā-tshuk
sīn-tuh′	sin-ta′	sī-tah′
nun-zit′	nun′-zut	git-a-han′
un-tlĕh′	had-in-tlelh	yuh-kŏt
a-nĕh′	a-nī	ha-koo
yes-shā′-dle	had-in-tle′	yoo-tin-a-kooh′
ho-ya-estluh′	kin′-hla	kloon-kut-tlai-yuh
en-a-ī	in-ī′	ha-ti-tih′
tse-es-tsīt′	toon-tsit′	skai-tli′-ilh
me-ga-nī-āh′	ta	ī-ka′-wha-te
na-es-tlook′	ted-in-tlooh′	a-tshook′
eh·tshih	en-tsal′	kāh

APPENDIX III.

———

LIST OF PLANTS COLLECTED BY DR. G. M. DAWSON IN THE
YUKON DISTRICT AND ADJACENT NORTHERN
PORTION OF BRITISH COLUMBIA IN 1887.

By Prof. J. Macoun, F.L.S.

Note.—References are also included to plants contained in a small
collection made by Mr. W. Ogilvie, D.L.S., during the progress of his
work on the Lewes River.

RANUNCULACEÆ.

1. *Anemone parviflora*, Mx.
   Cañon of Upper Liard River.
2. *Anemone deltoidea*, Hook.
   Dease Lake. Fl. June 8th. A rare and interesting species.
3. *Anemone Richardsoni*, Hook.
   Cassiar Trail twenty miles west of Dease Lake. A very remarkable species with yellow flowers.
4. *Anemone multifida*, DC.
   Frances River.
   Lake Bennett. (W. Ogilvie.)
5. *Anemone patens* L. var. *Nuttalliana*, Gray.
   Dease River, east of Cassiar Mountains; Upper Liard near
   Frances River; Upper Pelly River near its confluence with
   the Lewes.
6. *Ranunculus Flammula*, var. *reptans*, Meyer.
   "Pelly Banks;" Upper Pelly River.
7. *Ranunculus affinis*, var. *validus*, Gray.
   Cassiar Trail nine miles west of Dease Lake. Fl. June 5th.
8. *Ranunculus abortivus*, L.
   Cassiar Trail twenty miles west of Dease Lake. Fl. June 3rd.
9. *Aquilegia brevistyla*, Hook.
   Frances River.
10. *Delphinium scopulorum*, Gray.
    Hills west of Finlayson Lake.

11. *Caltha palustris*, L.
     Chilkoot Inlet.   (W. Ogilvie.)
12. *Aconitum Napellus*, var. *delphinifolium*, Sevinge.
     Finlayson River.   Very fine specimens.
13. *Actæa spicata*, var. *arguta*, Torrey.
     Telegraph Creek.   Fl. May 28th.

NYMPHÆACEÆ.

14. *Nuphar polysepalum*, Engelm.
     Finlayson Lake.

FUMARIACEÆ.

15. *Corydalis glauca*, Pursh.
     " Pelly Banks," Upper Pelly River.
16. *Corydalis aurea*, var. *occidentalis*, Gray.
     Telegraph Creek.   Fl. May 27th.

CRUCIFERÆ.

17. *Cardamine pratensis*, L.
     Frances River; Finlayson River.
18. *Cardamine hirsuta*, L.
     Hills west of Finlayson Lake.
19. *Arabis lyrata*, var. *occidentalis*, Watson.
     Cassiar Trail nine miles west of Dease Lake.   Fl. June 5th.
20. *Arabis Holbœllii*, Hornem.
     Stikine River above the cañon.   Fl. May 22nd.
     Telegraph Creek.   Fl. May 27th.
21. *Barbarea vulgaris*, var. *arcuata*, Hook.
     Finlayson River.
22. *Sisymbrium incisum*, Engelm.
     Telegraph Creek; Stikine River.   May 27th.
23. *Sisymbrium humile*, C. A. Meyer.
     Mouth of Lewes River.   Aug. 15th.
24. *Draba nemorosa*, var. *hebecarpa*, Lindb.
     Tahl-tan River.   Fl. May 31st.

VIOLACEÆ.

25. *Viola blanda*, Willd.
     Cassiar Trail 36 miles west of Dease Lake.   Fl. June 2nd.

CARYOPHYLLACEÆ.

26. *Silene Douglasii,* Hook.
     Dease River.
27. *Silene acaulis,* L.
     Lake Lindeman.   (W. Ogilvie.)
28. *Arenaria verna,* var. *hirta,* Wat.
     Mouth of Lewes River.
29. *Arenaria congesta,* var. *subcongesta,* Wat.
     Lewes River.
30. *Arenaria lateriflora,* L.
     Telegraph Creek.   Fl. May 27th.
31. *Arenaria physodes,* DC.
     Polly Banks; Mouth of Lewes River; Lake Lindeman.
32. *Stellaria longipes,* var. *minor,* Hook.
     Telegraph Creek, Fl. May 27th; Tahl-tan River, Fl. June 1st;
     Lewes River.
33. *Cerastium alpinum,* var. *Behringianum,* Regel.
     Hills west of Finlayson Lake.
34. *Cerastium trigynum,* Vill.
     " Polly Banks."   Very rare.

LINACEÆ.

35. *Linum perenne,* L.
     Upper Polly River.

SAPINDACEÆ.

36. *Acer glabrum,* Torr.
     Stikine River above the cañon. Fl. May 22nd. (The form
     with laciniate-lobed leaves.)

LEGUMINOSÆ.

37. *Lupinus Nootkatensis,* Donn.
     Upper Liard River ; Second North Fork of Stikine River. Fl.
     June 1st.
38. *Lupinus arcticus,* Watson.
     Upper Liard River. A very interesting species.
39. *Astragalus alpinus,* L.
     Forks of Liard and Dease rivers.
40. *Oxytropis campestris,* DC.
     Upper Liard River.
     Lewes River. (W. Ogilvie.)
41. *Oxytropis viscida,* Nutt.
     Dease River.

42. *Oxytropis Lamberti*, Pursh (?)
Dease River.

43. *Hedysarum boreale*, Nutt.
Frances Lake.
Tagish Lake.   (W. Ogilvie.)

44. *Hedysarum Mackenzii* Richards.
Telegraph Creek, Fl. May 27th ; Upper Liard River.

ROSACEÆ.

45. *Prunus Virginiana*, L. (?)
Telegraph Creek.   Fl. May 27th.   A very remarkable form, and seems to be the one referred to on p. 167 of the Botany of California, as distinct from *P. demissa*, and yet not true *P. Virginiana*.

46. *Rubus arcticus*, L.
Francis River.

47. *Rubus arcticus*, var. *grandiflorus*, Ledeb.
Dease Lake.   Fl. June 8th.

48. *Dryas octopetala*, var. *integrifolia*, Cham. & Schlecht.
Francis River, cool, shady bank, not seen in any other locality.

49. *Dryas Drummondii*, Hook.
Glenora, Stikine River.   Fl. May 25th.   (Common along river bars.)
Lewes River.   (W. Ogilvie.)

50. *Geum macrophyllum*, Willd.
Hills north of Finlayson Lake.

51. *Fragaria Virginiana*, Duchesne.
Telegraph Creek.   Fl. May 25th.   Abundant locally over the whole region.

52. *Potentilla Norvegica*, L.
Mouth of Lewes River.

53. *Potentilla Hippiana*, var. *pulcherrima*, Wat.
Telegraph Creek.   Fl. May 27th.

54. *Potentilla palustris*, L.
Lewes River.

55. *Potentilla fruticosa*, L.
Frances River.   Very common throughout district.
Lake Bennett.   (W. Ogilvie.)

56. *Poterium Sitchensis*, Wat.
Lake Lindeman ;   near the mouth of Lewes River.

57. *Rosa Sayi*, Schw.
Upper Liard River ; "Pelly Banks" ; Lewes River.   August 26th (second flowering).

58. *Pirus sambucifolia*, Cham. & Schlecht.
    Lake Bennett.
59. *Amelanchier alnifolia*, Nutt.
    Telegraph Creek. Fl. May 24.
    Dease River, east of Cassiar mountains.
    Tagish Lake.

SAXIFRAGACEÆ.

60. *Saxifraga nivalis*, L.
    Frances River.
61. *Saxifraga tricuspidata*, Retz.
    Telegraph Creek, Fl. May 25th; Dease River, east of Cassiar
      Mountains.
    Lake Bennett. (W. Ogilvie.)
62. *Tellima tenella*, Walp.
    Telegraph Creek. Fl. May 27th.
63. *Chrysosplenium alternifolium*, L.
    Dease River. Fl. June 7th.
64. *Parnassia palustris*, L.
    Lewes River, near the cañon. Common generally along the
      rivers.
65. *Ribes setosum*, Lindl.
    Glenora, Stikine River. Fl. May 25th.
66. *Ribes rubrum*, L.
    Head of Dease Lake. Fl. June 7th.
    Chilkoot Inlet. Fl. May 27th. (W. Ogilvie.)
67. *Ribes laxiflorum*, Pursh.
    Dease Lake. Fl. June 7th.
68. *Ribes Hudsonianum*, Richards.
    Glenora, Stikine River. Fl. May 25th.
    Telegraph Creek. Fl. May 27th.

CRASSULACEÆ.

69. *Sedum stenopetalum*, Pursh.
    Cañon of Lewes River.
    Tagish Lake. (W. Ogilvie.)

HALORAGEÆ.

70. *Hippuris vulgaris*, L.
    Lewes River.

ONAGRACEÆ.

71. *Epilobium coloratum*, Muhl.
   Lewes River.
72. *Epilobium augustifolium*, L.
   Common and generally distributed.
   Lake Bennett.   (W. Ogilvie.)
73. *Epilobium latifolium*, L.
   Common along rivers generally.
   Lake Bennett.   (W. Ogilvie.)

UMBELLIFERÆ.

74. *Selinum Dawsoni*, C. & R.
   Pelly River.
   Lake Labarge.   (W. Ogilvie.)
   A new and very interesting species described in Coulter's
      Botanical Gazette, Vol. XIII. p. 144, June 1888.
75. *Archangelica Gmelini*, DC.
   Chilkoot Inlet.   (W. Ogilvie.)

ARALIACEÆ.

76. *Fatsia horrida*, Benth. & Hook.
   Two miles from Kloochman Cañon, Stikine River, and in the
      valley on south side of Chilkoot Pass.   Not seen in interior.

CORNACEÆ.

77. *Cornus Canadensis*, L.
   Common generally.
78. *Cornus stolonifera*, Mx.
   Telegraph Creek, and common generally.

CAPRIFOLIACEÆ.

79. *Viburnum pauciflorum*, Pylaie.
   Telegraph Creek, and generally abundant throughout the entire
      district.
80. *Linnæa borealis*, Gronov.
   Common generally.

RUBIACEÆ.

81. *Galium boreale*, L.
   Upper Pelly River; Tagish Lake; Lake Bennett.
   Lake Labarge.   (W. Ogilvie.)

COMPOSITÆ.

82. *Solidago multiradiata*, Ait.
   Tagish Lake. (W. Ogilvie.)
83. *Solidago Virgaurea*, var. *alpina*, Bigel.
   Lewes River. (W. Ogilvie.)
84. *Aster occidentalis*, Gray.
   Lewes River.
85. *Aster Sibiricus*, L.
   "Pelly Banks;" Frances River; between Frances Lake and
      Pelly River.
   Lewes River. (W. Ogilvie.)
86. *Erigeron acris*, L.
   Lewes River.
87. *Erigeron acris*, var. *Dræbachensis*, Blytt.
   "Pelly Banks"; Lake Lindeman; hills south of Pelly Banks.
88. *Erigeron compositus*, var. *discoideus*, Gray.
   Telegraph Creek. Fl. May 25th.
89. *Erigeron cæspitosus*, Nutt.
   Pelly River in two localities (above and below Macmillan
      River).
90. *Erigeron glabellus*, var. *pubescens*, Wat.
   Near mouth of Lewes River.
91. *Antennaria plantaginifolia*, Hook.
   Lewes River.
92. *Achillea Millefolium*, L.
   "Pelly Banks."
   Tagish Lake. (W. Ogilvie.)
93. *Artemisia borealis*, var. *Wormskioldii*, Bess.
   "Pelly Banks."
94. *Artemisia Canadensis*, Mx.
   Pelly River.
95. *Artemisia vulgaris*, var. *Tilesii*, Ledeb.
   Francis Lake; "Pelly Banks."
96. *Artemisia dracunculoides*, Pursh.
   Pelly River.
97. *Artemisia frigida*, Willd.
   Telegraph Creek. Fl. May 27th; Upper Pelly River; Dease
      River to east of Cassiar Mountains.
98. *Petasites sagittata*, Gray.
   Second North Fork of Stikine River. Fl. June 1st.
99. *Arnica cordifolia*, Hook.
   Telegraph Creek. Fl. May 28th.

100. *Arnica latifolia,* Bong.
  Lake Bennett. (W. Ogilvie.)
101. *Senecio palustris,* Hook.
  Hills south of " Pelly Banks."
102. *Senecio lugens,* Richards.
  Upper Liard River; Frances River; hills west of Finlayson Lake.
103. *Senecio aureus,* var. *borealis,* T. & G.
  Dease River; Finlayson River; Telegraph Creek.   Fl. May 27th.
104. *Crepis elegans,* Hook.
  Upper Pelly River above the cañon.
105. *Taraxicum officinale,* var. *glaucescens,* Koch.
  Cañon of Upper Liard.

ERICACEÆ.

106. *Vaccinium uliginosum,* L.
  Frances River; Lewes River; head of Bennett Lake.
107. *Vaccinium ovalifolium,* Smith.
  Head of Bennett Lake.
108. *Vaccinium cæspitosum,* var. *cuneifolium,* Nutt.
  Dease River; Cañon of Upper Liard.
109. *Arctostaphylos alpina,* Spreng.
  Cassiar Trail twenty miles west of Dease Lake, Fl. June 3rd; also about height of land between Liard and Pelly, and on the Upper Pelly River.
110. *Arctostaphylos Uva-ursi,* Spreng.
  Telegraph Creek. Fl. May 27th.   Generally abundant.
111. *Loiseleuria procumbens,* Desv.
  Chilcoot Pass. (W. Ogilvie.)   Fl. June 10th.
112. *Ledum latifolium,* Ait.
  First seen on Cassiar Trail about thirty miles from Dease Lake. Abundant on Upper Liard and Pelly rivers.
  Tagish Lake. (W. Ogilvie.)
113. *Menziesia ferruginea,* Smith (?).
  Lake Lindeman, and west slope of Chilkoot Pass.

PRIMULACEÆ.

114. *Primula Mistassinica,* Mx.
  Francis River, in flower and quite common on river banks from which water had lately receded.
115. *Androsace septentrionalis,* L.
  Telegraph Creek, Fl. May 27th; Glenora, Stikine River, Fl. May 24th.

GENTIANACEÆ.

116. *Gentiana Amarella*, var. *acuta*, Hook.
     Finlayson River.
     Lewes River. ! (W. Ogilvie.)
117. *Gentiana glauca*, Pall. (?)
     On mountain near Finlayson River.

POLEMONIACEÆ.

118. *Polemonium cœruleum*, L.
     Finlayson River; quite abundant about the height of land be-
         tween Liard and Pelly rivers.
119. *Polemonium humile*, var. *pulchellum*, Gray.
     Telegraph Creek. Fl. May 27th; Glenora, Stikine River, Fl. May
         25th; very abundant and characteristic on south-east part of
         Cassiar Trail.

HYDROPHYLLACEÆ.

120. *Phacelia Franklinii*, Gray.
     Cañon of Lewes River.

BORRAGINACEÆ.

121. *Echinospermum Redowskii*, var. *occidentale*, Wat.
     Telegraph Creek, Fl. May 27th.
122. *Mertensia paniculata*, Don.
     Cassiar Trail thirty miles south-west of Dease Lake. Fl. June
         2nd. Common.
     Lake Bennett. (W. Ogilvie.)

SCROPHULARIACEÆ.

123. *Castilleia pallida*, var. *septentrionalis*, Gray.
     Lewes River.
124. *Collinsia parviflora*, Dougl.
     Glenora, Fl. May 25th; Telegraph Creek.
125. *Euphrasia officinalis*, L.
     Lewes River.
126. *Pedicularis hirsuta*, L.
     Finlayson River.
127. *Veronica alpina*, L.
     Hills west of Finlayson Lake; Finlayson River.

128. *Pentstemon confertus*, var. *cœruleo-purpureus*, Gray.
     Cañon of Lewes River.
     Tagish Lake.   (W. Ogilvie.)

LENTIBULARIACEÆ.

129. *Pinguicula villosa*, L.
     Frances River.

CHENOPODIACEÆ.

130. *Chenopodium capitatum*, Wat.
     Telegraph Creek, Stikine River, Fl. May 27th; " Pelly Banks."
     Lake Labarge.   (W. Ogilvie.)

POLYGONACEÆ.

131. *Polygonum viviparum*, L.
     Francis River.

ELÆAGNACEÆ.

132. *Elœagnus argentea*, Pursh.
     Telegraph Creek, near confluence of Pelly and Lewes Rivers,
        and in several places on latter river.
133. *Shepherdia Canadensis*, Nutt.
     In flower, abundant at Glenora and Telegraph Creek, May 23rd.

SANTALACEÆ.

134. *Comandra livida*, Richards.
     Frances River.

BETULACEÆ.

135. *Betula papyrifera*, Ait.
     Stikine River, May 22nd; Lewes River, near its mouth;
        Dease River. Occurs generally throughout the district, ex-
        cept along upper part of Pelly River.
136. *Betula glandulosa*, Mx.
     Abundant everywhere in suitable localities.
137. *Alnus rubra*, Bong.
     Frances Lake.
     Chilkoot Inlet.   May 27th.   (W. Ogilvie.)

SALICACEÆ.

138. *Salix speciosa*, Hook. & Arn.
    Upper Liard River.
139. *Salix cordata*, Muhl.
    Upper Liard River.   A singular form.
140. *Salix longifolia*, Muhl.
    Upper Liard River.
141. *Salix conjuncta*, Bebb, n. sp.
    Cassiar Trail twenty miles north-west of Dease Lake. June 3rd.
142. *Salix rostrata*, Rich.
    Telegraph Creek.   May 27th.
143. *Salix flavescens*, var. *Scouleriana*, Bebb.
    Stikine River above Little Cañon.   May 22nd.
144. *Salix reticulata*, L.
    Finlayson River.   Abundant in cold, mossy swamps about
        height of land between Liard and Pelly Rivers.
145. *Salix glauca*, L.
    Near mouth of Lewes River.
146. *Populus trichocarpa*, T. & G.
    Mouth of Lewes River, August 15th; "Pelly Banks"; Stikine
        River, above the cañon, May 22nd; Lake Francis; Dease
        River; Forks of Taiya River.
147. *Populus tremuloides*, Mx.
    Generally abundant.

CONIFERÆ.

148. *Juniperus Virginiana*, L.
    Telegraph Creek (arboreal); general elsewhere in a shrubby
        form.
149. *Pinus contorta*, Dougl.
    Common along the coast.
150. *Pinus Murrayana*, Balf.
    From the Little Cañon, on the Stikine, north-eastward to Devil's
        Portage, on the Lower Liard (McConnell); northward to
        Finlayson Lake; along Lewes River, from Lake Lindeman to
        mouth of, and up Pelly River to long. 133° 45'.
 51. *Pinus Banksiana*, Lambert.
    East of Devil's Portage, on Lower Liard (McConnell.)
152. *Picea Sitchensis*, Carr.
    The most abundant forest-tree along the coast and on the sea-
        ward slopes of the Coast Ranges.   Not found to the eastward
        of these mountains.
153. *Picea alba*, Link.
        15

The most abundant forest tree over the entire region east of the Coast Ranges.

154. *Picea nigra*, Link.

More or less abundant over the entire region east of the Coast Ranges.

155. *Tsuga Pattoniana*, Engelm.

Forming groves in Taiya valley and on the mountains, Chilkoot Pass. Probably characteristic of the higher parts of the Coast Ranges throughout.

156. *Abies subalpina*, Engelm.

Bennett Lake, and generally on the mountains in the vicinity of the timber-line.

157. *Larix Americana*, Mx.

Extends westward twenty-two miles up Dease River, and northward along Upper Liard to lat. 61° 35'. Nowhere seen along the Pelly or Lewes.

ORCHIDACEÆ.

158. *Corallorhiza innata*, R. Br.

Upper Liard River.

159. *Calypso borealis*, Salisb.

Cassiar trail, thirty-six miles south-west of Dease Lake.

160. *Cypripedium montanum*, Dougl.

Lewes River. (W. Ogilvie.)

LILIACEÆ.

161. *Disporum Oregana*, Watson.

Glenora, May 27th.

162. *Allium Schœnoprasum*, L.

Frances River; mouth of Lewes River.

Lake Labarge. (W. Ogilvie.)

163. *Veratrum viride*, Ait.

Lake Lindeman; south slope of Chilkoot Pass.

164. *Zygadenus elegans*, Pursh.

Cañon of Lewes River. (W. Ogilvie.)

JUNCACEÆ.

165. *Juncus Lescurii*, Bolander.

Lewes River.

166. *Juncus castaneus*, Smith.

Lewes River.

CYPERACEÆ.

167. *Eriophorum capitatum,* Host.
     Upper Pelly River, above the cañon.
168. *Carex siccata,* Dew.
     Upper Pelly River.
169. *Carex festiva,* Dew.
     Lake Lindeman.
170. *Carex leporina,* L., var. *Americana,* Olney.
     Stikine River, above the cañon, May 22nd; Telegraph Creek,
        May 27th.
171. *Carex atrata,* L.
     Frances River.
172. *Carex aurea,* Nutt.
     Upper Pelly River.
173. *Carex alpina,* Swartz.
     Lewes River.
174. *Carex acuta,* L.
     Lewes River.
175. *Carex ambusta,* Bailey.
     Frances River; Lewes River; "Pelly Banks."
176. *Carex podocarpa,* R. Br.
     Lewes River.

GRAMINEÆ.

177. *Hierochloa alpina,* Roem. & Schultz.
     Mountain near Finlayson River, alt. 4300 feet, lat. 61° 30′.
178. *Hierochloa borealis,* Roem. & Schultz.
     Telegraph Creek; Upper Liard River; Lewes River.
179. *Phleum alpinum,* L.
     Lake Lindeman.
180. *Agrostis scabra,* Willd.
     Lake Lindeman
181. *Cinna pendula,* Trin., var. *mutica,* Vasey.
     "Pelly Banks."
182. *Deyeuxia neglecta,* Kunth.
     "Pelly Banks," and confluence of Lewes and Pelly rivers.
183. *Deyeuxia neglecta,* var. *brevifolia,* Vasey.
     "Pelly Banks."
184. *Deyeuxia sylvatica,* Kunth.
     Lewes River; "Pelly Banks."
     Dease River.

185. *Deyeuxia Columbiana*, Macoun.   n. sp.
  Tagish Lake.
186. *Deschampsia cæspitosa*, Beauv.
  Lowes River, and " Pelly Banks."
187. *Trisetum subspicatum*, Beauv.
  Upper Liard River; " Pelly Banks;" Frances Lake; Finlayson
   Lake.
188. *Poa alpina*, Linn.
  Lake Lindeman; " Pelly Banks."
189. *Poa cæsia*, Smith.
  Lake Lindeman; Dease River; Frances River; " Pelly Banks."
190. *Poa cenisia*, All.
  Hills west of Finlayson Lake.
191. *Festuca ovina*, L.
  Lake Lindeman; " Pelly Banks."
192. *Festuca scabrella*, Torr.
  Frances Lake, and Finlayson Lake.
193. *Agropyrum violaceum*, Lange.
  Lake Lindeman; " Pelly Banks"; Lewes River.
194. *Hordeum jubatum*, L.
  Lewes River.
195. *Elymus dasystachys*, Trin.
  Dease River.

EQUISETAECÆ.

196. *Equisetum variegatum*, Schleicher.
  Upper Liard River.   June 2, 1887.

FILICES.

197. *Aspidium fragrans*, Swartz.
  On rocks, Frances River.
198. *Cystopteris fragilis*, Bernh.
  Telegraph Creek.

MUSCI.

199. *Splachnum luteum*, L.
200. *Webera nutans*, Hedw.
  Upper Liard River.   June 27, 1887.
201. *Marchantia polymorpha*, L.
  Upper Liard River.   June 27, 1887.

—

ZOOLOGY.

LIST OF DIURNAL LEPIDOPTERA BY JAMES FLETCHER, F.R.S.C., F.L.S.

1. *List of Diurnal Lepidoptera collected in the Yukon District and adjacent Northern Portion of British Columbia.*

Specimens in this list, not otherwise noted, were collected by Dr. G. M. Dawson and assistant, J. McEvoy, in 1887.

Papilio Machaon, L., var. *Aliaska*, Scud. Frances River, July 1 ; three miles below summit of Chilkoot Pass (from Mr. McDougall). July 15, 1886.

Papilio Turnus, L., June 28, 1887; three miles below Little Cañon, Lower Liard (long. 128° 13′), McConnell; Devil's Portage, Lower Liard (long. 126° 10′), July 15, 1887, McConnell; Frances River (lat. 60° 29′), July 1.

Pieris Nelsoni, Edw, Telegraph Creek, Stikine River, May 27.

Pieris Napi, Esper. Arctic form, *Bryoniæ*, Ochs. Dease Lake, June 6.

Pieris Napi, Esper. Arctic form, *Bryoniæ*, Ochs., var. *Hulda*, Ed.. West of Finlayson Lake (lat. 61° 45′, long. 130° 55′), July 28.

Pieris Napi (1) ; winter form *Venosa*, Scud. Dease Lake, June 17.

Pieris Napi (2) ; winter form *Oleracea-hyemalis*, Har. Frances River (lat. 60° 29′), July 1; Lewes River (lat. 61° 55′), August 27.

Anthocaris Ausonides, Bd. Cassiar Trail, ten miles west of Dease Lake, June 4; Telegraph Creek, Stikine River, May 29; Dease Lake, June 7.

Anthocaris Stella, Edw. Telegraph Creek, May 29.

Colias Christina, Edw. Upper Pelly River (lat. 62° 47′, long. 137° 20′) August 7; site of Fort Selkirk, August 17, Ogilvie.

Argynnis Chariclea, Schneid. Finlayson River (lat. 61° 40′, long. 130° 16′), July 22; Finlayson Lake, July 27 ; Upper Pelly River (lat. 61° 50′, long. 132°), August 3. Pelly or Yukon River, August 7, 1888. McConnell.

Argynnis Freya, Thunb. Cassiar Trail, ten miles west of Dease Lake, June 4; Dease Lake, June 5.

Phyciodes Tharos, Dru. Devil's Portage, Lower Liard (long. 126° 10'), July 15, McConnell.

Phyciodes Pratensis, Behr. Upper Liard River (lat. 60°), June 26.

Grapta Faunus, Edw. Fifty miles below Forty-mile Creek, Pelly or Yukon River, August 7, 1888, McConnell.

Grapta Progne, Cram. Lewes River (lat. 61° 55'), August 27.

Thecla Irus, Godt. Telegraph Creek, Stikine River, May 29; Cassiar Trail, twenty-two miles east of Telegraph Creek, June 1.

Chrysophanus Helloides, Bd. Upper Pelly River (lat. 62° 40', long. 134° 30') August 7.

Lycæna Sæpiolus, Bd. Devil's Portage, Lower Liard (long. 126° 10'), July 17, McConnell; Finlayson Lake, July 25.

Lycæna Couperii, Grote. Telegraph Creek, Stikine River, May 31; Cassiar Trail, thirty miles west of Dease Lake, June 2; Cassiar Trail, ten miles west of Dease Lake, June 4; Dease Lake, June 5; Devil's Portage, Liard River (long. 126° 10'), July 13, McConnell; Upper Liard River (lat. 60°), June 26; Frances River (lat. 60° 29'), July 1.

Lycæna Shasta, Edw. Upper Pelly River (lat. 61° 50', long. 132°), August 3; Lewes River (lat. 62° 20'), August 21.

Lycæna Pseudargiolus, Bd. Lec.; winter form (1) *Lucia*, Kirby. Dease Lake, June 4; Dease Lake, June 8.

Lycæna Pseudargiolus, Bd. Lec.; winter form (2) *Marginata*, Edw. Cassiar Trail, twenty miles west of Dease Lake, June 3.

Lycæna Pseudargiolus, B.-L., winter form (3) *Violacea*, Edw. Cassiar Trail, ten miles west of Dease Lake, June 4.

Lycæna Amyntula Bd. Devil's Portage, Liard River (long. 126° 10'), July 17, McConnell.

Nisoniades Icelus, Lint. Telegraph Creek, Stikine River, May 27.

Nisoniades Persius, Scud. Dease Lake, June 4.

Nisoniades Juvenalis, Fab. Cassiar Trail, ten miles west of Dease Lake, June 4.

2. *List of Diurnal Lepidoptera collected by Mr. W. Ogilvie on Mackenzie River in 1888.**

Papilio Machaon, L., var. *Aliaska*, Scud. Fort Macpherson (lat. 67° 20'), June 21.

Pieris Napi, Esper.; Arctic form *Bryoniæ*, Ochs., var. *Hulda*. Fort Macpherson (lat. 67° 20'), June 21.

---

* This and the following list do not come strictly within the limits of this report, but are included here to ensure publication.

Anthocaris Ausonides, Bd.   Mackenzie River, July 8.
Colias Christina, Edw.   Fort Good Hope (lat. 66° 15′), August 11.
Vanessa Antiopa, L.   Ninety miles above Fort Good Hope (lat. 65° 20′),
    July 19 ; Fort Smith (lat. 60°), August 24.

3. *List of Diurnal Lepidoptera collected by Mr. Fredk. Bell, at the instance
    of Mr. R. G. McConnell, at Fort Simpson, Mackenzie River
    (lat. 61° 52′), 1888.*

Papilio Turnus, L.   (Five specimens.)   June 24 to July 8.
Pieris Napi, Esper. (2) ; winter form *Oleracea-hyemalis*, Har. (Thirteen
    specimens.)   June 24 to July 8.
Colias Occidentalis, Scud.   July 17.
Colias Christina, Edw.   Male, July 17 ; female, July 25.
Grapta Progne, Cram.   (Two specimens.)   July 12.
Vanessa Milbertii, Godt.   (Eleven specimens.)   June 26 to July 20.
Limenitis Arthemis, Dru. (1) ; dimorphic form *Lamina*, Fab.   (Three
    specimens.)   July 23.
Erebia Discoidalis, Kirby.   June 25.
Lycæna Pseudargiolus, Bd. Lec. ; winter form (1) *Lucia*, Kirby. June 25.
Nisoniades Icelus, Lint.   June 26.

FISHES, DETERMINED FROM PHOTOGRAPHS, BY DR. T. H. BEAN, UNITED
        STATES COMMISSIONER OF FISH AND FISHERIES.

   Photographs were taken of some of the fishes met with, but no
specimens were brought back. The photographs have been kindly
examined by Dr. Bean, who enumerates the species represented as
follows :—
Salvelinus namaycush, Walbaum.
        Lake Trout. Frances River, July 2. Spent male, judging from
    great length of maxilla. "Much darker than the other lake trout,
    and with white instead of yellow flesh."
Salvelinus namaycush, Walbaum.
        Lake trout. Frances Lake, July 14. "Ordinary lake trout of
    the region."
Esox lucius, Linné.
        Pike. Frances Lake, July 12. Length, 3 feet 3 inches.
Coregonus Nelsoni, Bean.
        Nelson's whitefish. Frances Lake, July 16 ; also Lake Linde-
    man, September 18.
Catostomus catostomus, Forster.
        Northern sucker ; small-scaled sucker. Frances Lake, July 16.
Thymallus signifer, Richardson.
        Back's grayling. Finlayson River, July 19.

DESCRIPTION OF A NEW RED-BACKED MOUSE (EVOTOMYS DAWSONI) FROM THE HEAD-WATER OF LIARD RIVER, NORTH-WEST TERRITORIES.

BY DR. C. HART MERRIAM.

Of a few skins of birds and small mammals brought back, the only one of particular interest is that described below by Dr. J. Hart Merriam. *American Naturalist*, July, 1888. (The figure given with the original description, illustrating the dentition, is not here reproduced.)

"Dr. George M. Dawson, Assistant Director of the Geological and Natural History Survey of Canada, has kindly sent me for determination a red-backed mouse collected by him June 23, 1887, at Finlayson River, one of the northern sources of Liard River, in lat. 61° 30′ N., long. 129° 30′ W., altitude 3000 feet.

"So little is known of the small mammals of this remote and inaccessible region that it is not particularly surprising to find that the mouse collected by Dr. Dawson proves to be undescribed. In some respects it is intermediate between the circumpolar *Evotomys rutilus* and its more southern congener, *Evotomys gapperi*. But since it differs from both and no intermediate forms are known, it must be regarded as specifically distinct. Hereafter, should intergrades be discovered, it may be necessary to consider it a sub-species. It may be characterized as follows:—

EVOTOMYS DAWSONI, sp. nov.

Dawson's Red-backed Mouse.

"Type in Museum of Geological and Natural History Survey of Canada, at Ottawa. From Finlayson River, a northern source of Liard River, N. W. T. (lat. 60° 30′ N., long. 129° 30′ W., altitude 3000 feet). Size, about equal to that of *Evotomys gapperi*. Measurements from mounted specimen (apparently well mounted and not at all stretched): Head and body, 75 mm.; tail vertebræ, 28 mm.—pencil, 8 mm. (total, 36 mm.); ears, from crown, 7 mm. Tail shorter and thicker than in *gapperi*, but longer and slimmer than in *rutilus*, in this respect (but no other) agreeing with a specimen collected at Fort Liard by Kennicott (No. 4562, U. S. National Museum). The hind foot is intermediate between that of *rutilus* and that of *gapperi*, being thicker than in *gapperi*, but not so thick as in *rutilus*. The ears conspicuously overtop the fur, fully equalling those of *gapperi*. The tail is bicolor, the yellowish of the under part occupying a little more than half of the circumference. It is well haired, and the terminal pencil is nearly black above (and 8 mm. long). The red dorsal stripe begins just behind the

SHEET 2.
MAP
OF A PORTION OF THE
YUKON DISTRICT
North West Territory
with the adjacent Northern Part of
BRITISH COLUMBIA
To accompany Report of
George M. Dawson, D.S., F.G.S. etc.
1887.
SCALES
Geographical Miles
Statute Miles
Natural Scale
FRELL LAKES
MOUNTAIN

DESCRIPTION OF A NEW RED-BACKED MOUSE (EVOTOMYS DAWSONI) FROM THE HEAD-WATER OF LIARD RIVER, NORTH-WEST TERRITORIES.

BY DR. C. HART MERRIAM.

Of a few skins of birds and small mammals brought back, the only one of particular interest is that described below by Dr. J. Hart Merriam, *American Naturalist*, July, 1888. (The figure given with the original description, illustrating the dentition, is not here reproduced.)

"Dr. George M. Dawson, Assistant Director of the Geological and Natural History Survey of Canada, has kindly sent me for determination a red-backed mouse collected by him June 23, 1887, at Finlayson River, one of the northern sources of Liard River, in lat. 61° 30′ N., long. 129° 30′ W., altitude 3000 feet.

"So little is known of the small mammals of this remote and inaccessible region that it is not particularly surprising to find that the mouse collected by Dr. Dawson proves to be undescribed. In some respects it is intermediate between the circumpolar *Evotomys rutilus* and its more southern congener, *Evotomys gapperi*. But since it differs from both and no intermediate forms are known, it must be regarded as specifically distinct. Hereafter, should intergrades be discovered, it may be necessary to consider it a sub-species. It may be characterized as follows:—

EVOTOMYS DAWSONI, sp. nov.

Dawson's Red-backed Mouse.

"Type in Museum of Geological and Natural History Survey of Canada, at Ottawa. From Finlayson River, a northern source of Liard River, N. W. T. (lat. 60° 30′ N., long. 129° 30′ W., altitude 3000 feet). Size, about equal to that of *Evotomys gapperi*. Measurements from mounted specimen (apparently well mounted and not at all stretched): Head and body, 75 mm.; tail vertebrae, 28 mm.—pencil, 8 mm. (total, 36 mm.); ears, from crown, 7 mm. Tail shorter and thicker than in *gapperi*, but longer and slimmer than in *rutilus*, in this respect (but no other) agreeing with a specimen collected at Fort Liard by Kennicott (No. 4562, U. S. National Museum). The hind foot is intermediate between that of *rutilus* and that of *gapperi*, being thicker than in *gapperi*, but not so thick as in *rutilus*. The ears conspicuously overtop the fur, fully equalling those of *gapperi*. The tail is bicolor, the yellowish of the under part occupying a little more than half of the circumference. It is well haired, and the terminal pencil is nearly black above (and 8 mm. long). The red dorsal stripe begins just behind the

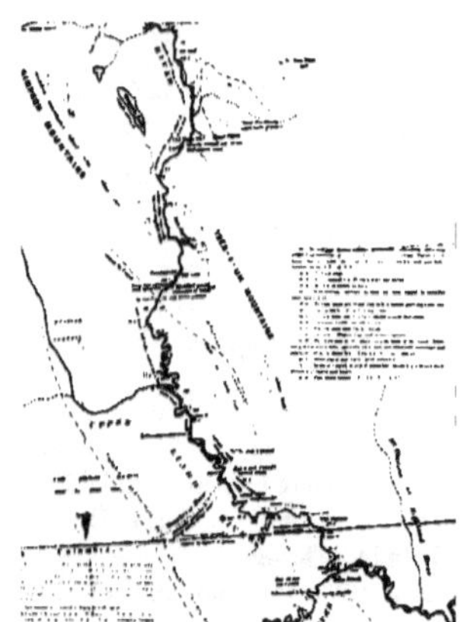

SHEET II.

YUKON DISTRICT & BRITISH COLUMBIA.

eye and extends to the root of the tail.   In color it is bright chestnut—
not far from ferruginous; the sides are tawny gray, and the belly is
strongly washed with ochraceous buff.   The admixture of black-tipped
hairs is as great as in *gapperi*, and it is very much more conspicuous,
owing to the lighter ground-color of the back and sides.   The result is
a sort of 'peppery' appearance not seen in any other representative
of the genus.   There is a tolerably well-defined whitish post-auricular
spot—an exaggeration of the pale blotch sometimes seen behind the
ear in *rutilus*.   The whiskers are black and white; they reach back to
the shoulders, instead of stopping at the occiput, as usual in the genus.
A blackish stripe, bordered below with fulvous, runs from the base of
the whiskers to the tip of the nose.   The projecting margin of the ear
is well covered with reddish hairs, brightest on the interior of the
auricle.

"*Cranial and Dental Characters.*—Unfortunately the skull was badly
smashed and part of it altogether wanting; hence no cranial characters can be made out.   The teeth, however, remain, and are represented in the accompanying cut [not reproduced].   Their most marked
peculiarity, compared with those of *gapperi*, consists in the openly-
communicating loops.   The upper molar series measures 4·5 mm. on
the crowns, 4·8 mm. on the alveolæ.   The lower molar series measures
4·4 mm. on the crowns, 4·6 mm. on the alveolæ.

"I take great pleasure in bestowing upon this handsome mouse the
specific name *Dawsoni*, as a slight recognition of the indefatigable zeal
of its discoverer, the distinguished explorer and geologist, Dr. Geo. M.
Dawson, who has added so much to the fund of knowledge relating to
North-western Canada."—*C. Hart Merriam.*

NOTES ON THE

LITHOLOGICAL CHARACTER OF SOME OF THE ROCKS COLLECTED IN THE YUKON DISTRICT AND ADJACENT NORTHERN PORTION OF BRITISH COLUMBIA.

By Mr. F. D. Adams, M.A.Sc.

———

(Of the rocks described below, Nos. 16, 25, 2, 4, 7 and 10 were collected by Mr. R. G. McConnell, "No. C." by Mr. W. Ogilvie, and the remaining specimens by Dr. G. M. Dawson.)

Stikine River, No. 16. (Near mouth of Clearwater River. See p. 55 B.)

Diabase Porphyrite.—A rock consisting of a fine-grained groundmass, through which crystals of plagioclase, augite and iron-ore are porphyritically distributed. The plagioclase individuals are well twinned and have good crystalline forms. The augite occurs in eight-sided crystals, both prinacoids being well developed, and the iron ore, which is ilmenite, partly decomposed to leucoxene. The groundmass is crypto-crystalline and microcrystalline. A good deal of chlorite and other decomposition products occurs disseminated through the rock.

Marsh Lake, No. 86. (North end of lake, near outlet. See p. 164 B.)

Diabase Porphyrite.—Resembles No. 16, but the porphyritic crystals are, as a general rule, smaller. The groundmass also, although for the most part microcrystalline, is in some places isotropic, consisting of glass.

Stikine River, No. 25. (Telegraph Creek. See p. 57 B.)

Diabase Tuff.—A somewhat fine-grained clastic rock a good deal decomposed, made up of irregular-shaped grains of plagioclase, pyroxene

and titanic iron ore, with a very little pyrite and some fragments of a
fine-grained porphyritic rock. The majority of the grains are plagioclase, showing polysynthetic twinning, a few untwinned felspar grains
are also present, some of which may be orthoclase. The plagioclase is
a good deal decomposed, many grains consisting almost entirely of a
cryptocrystalline or microcrystalline aggregate of calcite, kaolin and
other decomposition products. The pyroxene is clear and colorless,
being as a general rule less decomposed than the feldspar. It is
biaxial, and shows the usual pyroxene cleavages, with a high angle
of extinction on the clinopinacoid, which in one case reached
41°. It is sometimes decomposed to chlorite, a considerable quantity
of this mineral also occurring scattered through the rock. The fragments of titanic iron-ore are for the most part decomposed to leucoxene,
showing the characteristic cross-hatched structure. The fragments of
fine-grained porphyritic rock above mentioned have a fine-grained
groundmass, in which are imbedded lath-shaped crystals of plagioclase and crystals of augite, and are apparently pieces of a decomposed
diabase-porphyrite. Traversing the section are several bands or streaks,
much finer in grain and showing cataclastic structure, and which were
evidently lines of motion caused by crushing.

Dease Lake, No. 8. (About eight miles from head of lake, west shore.
See p. 78 B.)

A very fine-grained yellowish-green rock, with schistose structure
and somewhat talcose appearance. Under the microscope it is seen to
consist of an exceedingly fine-grained groundmass, almost opaque, in
which are a few strings and irregular-shaped segregations of calcite
and a number of porphyritic crystals of pyroxene. Under a very high
power, the groundmass is seen to be composed largely of little shreds
of a micaceous mineral, probably sericite, which are approximately
parallel in position and give to the rock an appearance resembling flow
structure. With this is associated a smaller quantity of a colorless
mineral polarizing in dull bluish tints and with somewhat undulatory
extinction, which resembles felspar, but does not show any lines of
twinning. The pyroxene crystals are colorless. Cross sections are
eight-sided, showing the development of both prism and pinacoids,
with cleavages parallel to both and extinction parallel to the latter.
It is biaxial, and longitudinal sections show a single set of cleavages,
sometimes intersected by tranverse cracks. The extinction direction
makes an angle with this cleavage, which in one case was as high as
34°. The crystals are short and stout, and are occasionally twinned,
they generally have good crystalline forms, but are sometimes broken.

A few grains of pyrite and a little chlorite are also present in the rock. As would be expected from the appearance of the hand specimen, the section shows that the rock has been subjected to a good deal of motion, two varieties of the rock differing somewhat in appearance, being irregularly mixed with one another. It is probably *some highly altered basic igneous rock;* the presence of the pyroxene crystals, retaining, as a general rule, their crystalline form, is however, somewhat remarkable.

Tagish Lake, No. 93. (Windy Arm. See p. 171 B.)

Felsite.—An exceedingly fine-grained rock, much crushed and altered. Small irregular-shaped segregations of calcite are scattered through the rock, and here and there little fragments of plagioclase can be seen. It is impossible by means of a section alone to determine its original character. Before the blowpipe it fuses easily to a black magnetic globule, and may provisionally be termed a *felsite.*

Cassiar Trail, No. 4. (Tooya River, at trail-crossing. See p. 70 B.)

Tuff?—An exceedingly fine-grained, red, somewhat schistose rock, holding numerous irregular-shaped cavities, filled with a light green chloritic mineral, mixed with calcite. The section is rendered nearly opaque by a dense impregnation with iron-oxide. It is also traversed by thin veins of calcite. Before the blowpipe the rock fuses to a black magnetic bead. It is probably an altered tuff.

GRANITIC ROCKS FROM THE COAST RANGES.

Wrangell, No. 2. (Wrangell Island. See p. 54 B.)

Biotite Granite.—A rather fine-grained gray granite, with very indistinct foliation. It is composed of quartz, orthoclase, plagioclase, biotite and epidote, with a very small amount of apatite and of an isotropic mineral, light brown in color, with high index of refraction, but without good crystalline form, and which is probably garnet. Almost every grain of quartz exhibits, between crossed nichols, an uneven extinction, showing that the rock has been submitted to pressure. Both the orthoclase and plagioclase are generally fresh. The epidote, which is present in considerable amount, is colorless, strongly doubly refracting, and is almost always associated with the biotite. It occurs in curiously corroded, somewhat elongated, prismatic crystals, with perfect cleavage parallel to the longest axis, the plane of the optic axes being at right angles to this cleavage. The mode of occurrence of this epidote is very similar to that found in the mica-diorite from Stony Point, on the Hudson River, and described by Dr. George Williams (*American Journal of Science*, June, 1888).

Stikine River, No. 4.   (Near mouth of river. See p. 54 B.)

A Porphyritic Biotite Hornblende Granite, approaching a Quartz Diorite in composition.—A medium-grained grey rock, with numerous small white porphyritic crystals. It is composed of quartz, plagioclase, orthoclase, biotite and hornblende. The porphyritic crystals are felspar, which is almost invariably plagioclase. They possess a zonal structure, and contain numerous colorless inclusions heaped up toward the centres of the crystals. Some of them also contain inclusions of muscovite, which is probably a decomposition product. The quartz generally shows an uneven extinction, owing to pressure. The plagioclase preponderates largely over the orthoclase, but some untwinned grains have been referred to the latter species. The biotite and hornblende are intergrown with each other. Two or three grains showing granophyr structure are also seen in this section.

Stikine River, No. 7.   (Moraine of Great Glacier. See p. 54 B.)

Biotite Hornblende Granite.—A rather coarse-grained grey granite, with very indistinct foliation. It is composed of quartz, orthoclase, plagioclase, biotite, hornblende, sphene and magnetite. The quartz shows a somewhat uneven extinction. Both feldspars often show zonal structure. The hornblende is about equal to the mica in amount, and only small quantities of sphene and magnetite are present. The latter is probably titaniferous.

Stikine River, No. 10.   (Little Cañon. See p. 54 B.)

Biotite Granite.—A coarse-grained grey granite, poor in mica. The orthoclase, of which there is a very large amount, often shows an indistinct zonal structure. A small quantity of magnetite, or more probably ilmenite, with which a little sphene is associated, is also present. A crystal of zircon was observed in one of the mica grains. Although the rock has no foliation, it shows very distinct cataclastic structure, induced by great pressure. The constituent minerals are seen to have been much squeezed and twisted, the larger grains being often, around their edges, broken up into a very fine-grained mass. The mica also, which is in part decomposed to chlorite, has been in many places pulled apart into shreds.

GRANITIC ROCKS FROM THE INTERIOR RANGES.

Upper Pelly River. No. 61. (Near mouth of river. See p. 132 ᴮ.)

Muscovite Biotite Granite.—A medium-grained grey granite, with very indistinct foliation. It is composed of quartz, orthoclase, microcline, plagioclase, muscovite, biotite and epidote, with small amounts of garnet, sphene, pyrite and calcite. The plagioclase is present in relatively smaller amount than in the granites from the Coast Ranges. The muscovite is more plentiful than the biotite. The epidote occurs in colorless corroded crystals, and has the appearance of an original constituent of the rock. The garnet is reddish, and occurs in a few irregular-shaped isotropic grains, usually much cracked. The sphene occurs in the usual wedge-shaped crystals. The calcite is seen in the section in a few large grains. The grains of quartz and orthoclase are somewhat cracked and broken, but beyond this, no distinct evidence of pressure is exhibited by the section.

Upper Pelly River, No. 57. (Granite Cañon. See p. 130 ᴮ.)

Biotite Granite.—A rather coarse-grained, much decomposed, massive grey granite. The feldspars are so decomposed that it is difficult to determine their character, but a considerable amount of plagioclase is present, and probably a still larger amount of orthoclase. The biotite is entirely decomposed to chlorite and epidote. A few small grains of hæmatite are present in the section. The quartz grains are much cracked, and show very uneven extinction, owing to the pressure to which the rock has been subjected.

Pelly or Yukon, " No. C." (Opposite Stewart River. See p. 34 ᴮ.)

Quartoze Biotite Gneiss.—A rather fine-grained red gneiss, showing very distinct foliation. It is composed of quartz, orthoclase, plagioclase, calcite, chlorite, ilmenite and a little pyrite. The plagioclase is present in rather small amount. The chlorite is a decomposition product, probably of biotite, and the calcite, of which there is a considerable quantity, is also a decomposition product. The ilmenite is partly altered to leucoxene. The cataclasic structure is distinctly seen in the section.

Upper Pelly River, No. 53. (Nine miles above Macmillan. See p. 129 ᴮ.)

Biotite Granite.—A rather coarse-grained, reddish-grey, massive rock, composed of quartz, orthoclase, plagioclase and chlorite, with a little ilmenite and pyrite.   Both feldspars are much decomposed, being in some places nearly opaque.   The plagioclase, which is not so plentiful as the orthoclase, is generally better crystallized, and frequently occurs in crystals penetrating this mineral.   The ilmenite is partly decomposed to leucoxene, and the chlorite is evidently a decomposition product of biotite.   The section is traversed by a little very fine grained granitic vein, showing a banded structure parallel to its walls.   The quartz has been much cracked, nearly every grain showing an uneven extinction.

APPENDIX VI.

METEOROLOGICAL OBSERVATIONS.

The Meteorological Observations here recorded are as follows:—

1. Observations made along the line of route, June 1 to September 19, 1887.

2. Observations at Telegraph Creek, Stikine River, by Mr. J. C. Callbreath, 1881–1886.

3. Observations at Laketon, Dease Lake, by Mr. J. Clearihue, 1878-1882.

4. Record of temperature at Laketon, Dease Lake, by Mr. Robert Reed, 1886–1887.

The observations included under Nos. 2, 3 and 4 are unfortunately very incomplete. They refer to the winter months only, and in general the minimum reading of the thermometer alone is recorded. The thermometers employed were, however, instruments of good class by well-known makers, and in view of the paucity of information bearing on the region, it has been considered useful to print them, I am indebted to Mr. Callbreath for the opportunity of extracting the observations made by him from his diaries, and to Mr. Reed for communicating the third and fourth series of observations. The observations forming the first part of this appendix were recorded by Mr. J. McEvoy during the progress of our journey.

G. M. D.

16

(1) METEOROLOGICAL OBSERVATIONS IN THE YUKON DISTRICT AND ADJACENT NORTHERN PART OF BRITISH COLUMBIA, JUNE 1 TO SEPTEMBER 19, 1887.

The barometer readings are those of a single pocket aneroid (Cary No. 859) checked at intervals by reference to the mercurial barometer and corrected according to a table of differences based on these comparison. Readings made on two additional aneroids and employed in the determination of elevations are not here included.

Temperature is stated in degrees Fahrenheit. Thermometers employed, Nos. 60,361 and 60,363, Kew Observatory.

The force of the wind is estimated according to Beaufort's scale. The proportion of the sky covered by clouds is estimated by a scale of 0 to 10, 0 being a cloudless sky, 10 a completely clouded sky. The character of the clouds is denoted by the usual letters or combination of letters refering to Howard's classification.

PLACE.	Date.	Hour.	Barometer corrected.	Ther. corrected.			Direction of wind.	Force of wind.	Amt. of cloud.	Kind of cloud.	Temperature of water.	Weather at time.	Weather during last interval.
				Air.	Max.	Min.							
Tahl-tan Bridge, Cassiar Trail, 10 ft. above river	June 1	5 00 a.m	29.86	34.5		30.5	W.	1	8	C & K.			Detached Clouds.
Wilson's	" 1	7.00 p.m		59.			W.	1	2	K.		Fair.	" " and blue sky.
"	" 2	5.00 a.m.	28.34	39.		30.5	Calm.		1	C.		"	Passing clouds.
Cariboo Camp	" 2	7.00 p.m.	27.89	51.			N. W.	3	7	K.		Showery.	Fair. Clear and passing showers.
"	" 3	5.20 a.m.	27.90	42.		37.	Lt. var.		9	C K.		Dull.	Showers. Detached clouds and overcast.
24-m. post	" 3	7.00 p.m.	27.97	51.5			N. E.	3	1	C.		Fair.	Passing showers.
" "	" 4	6.45 a.m.	28.08	49.		31.	N. E.	4	0				Clear.
Nine-mile Creek	" 4	7.00 p.m.	27.59	40.5			N. E.	3	0			Clear.	Clear. Very warm all day.
" "	" 5	4 40 a.m.	27.52	41.		28.	N. E.	2	0			"	Very light C. clouds.
Head of Dease Lake	" 5	7.00 p.m.	27.35	63.			S. E.	2	1	C.		Hazy.	Clear. Very warm.
" " "	" 6	7.00 a.m.	27.41	48.5		45.5	Calm.		0				Fair.
" "	" 6	7.00 p.m.	27.25	63.	76.		W.	3				Hazy.	{ " " Hot sun all day. / Open water 3 m. on lake.
" " "	" 7	7.15 a.m.	27.33	45.		35.	N. W.	1					Clear. Strong N.W. wind.
" " "	" 7	7.10 p.m.	27.86	63.	74.		S.	1				Hazy.	" Light breeze.
" " "	" 8	7.00 a.m.	27.27			32.	N.	1	1	C.		"	" Calm.
Dense Lake, 5 m. down	" 8	7.00 p.m.	27.14	61.			N.	1	1	C & K.			" Light N. airs.
" " "	" 9	7.00 a.m.	27.28			29.5	N.	2	1	C.			Cloudy. " "
" " "	" 9	7.00 p.m.	27.19	57.	68.		N. N. W.	1	8	K.			Clouds. S. wind 3. Hot sun.
" " "	" 10	7.00 a.m.	27.26	49.		35.5	N.	3	10	S.		Threatening.	Gloomy. Overcast.
" " "	" 10	7.00 p.m.	27.30	50.	63.		N. E.	2	9	C & S.		Raining.	Rain. Wind S. & E. 5. Showery p.m.
" " "	" 11	7.00 a.m.	27.31	41.5		37.5	Lt. var.		10	S & C.		Gloomy, ugly.	Overcast. Gloomy. Calm.

Locality	Date	Hour	Bar.	Temp.	Temp.	Temp.	Wind	Force	Cloud	Kind	Water	Sky	Remarks
Dease Lake, 5 m. down	11	7.00 p.m.	27.29	55.5	47.5	.	W.	1	1	K.			Light showers. Light N.E. airs.
"	12	7.00 a.m.	27.83	44.		28.	Calm.	..	8	K & C.		Hazy.	Light W. wind.
" 10 m. down	12	7.00 p.m.	27.21	53.			W.	1	1	C & K.			C. clouds. Light W. wind.
" "	13	7.00 a.m.	27.25	43.		32.	S.	2	1	C K.			Light S. Wind. Ice formed on pools.
" "	13	7.00 p.m.	27.18	52.5	63.		S.W.	2	10	S.		Gloomy.	Clouded over. p.m., strong S. wind for a while.
" "	14	7.20 a.m.	27.18	41.5		38.5	Lt. var.	..	4	S.		"	
" "	14	7.00 p.m.	27.12	46.5	52.		Calm.	..	10	S.		Clearing.	Raining all p.m.
" "	15	7.10 a.m.	27.19	49.		39.	S.	1	5	C K.		Breaking.	Overcast. Raining.
" "	15	7.40 p.m.	27.17	56.	59.5		S.	1	10	K S.		Threatening.	Detached clouds. Lt. sprinkle from S.
" "	16	7.00 a.m.	27.26	44.		40.7	S.	2	10	K S.		"	Overcast. Gloomy. S. wind 4.
" Laketon	16	7.00 p.m.	27.28				S.	3-4	5	K.		Showery.	Light showers. " 2.
" "	17	8.10 a.m.	27.24				S.	1	5	K.			
" "	17	7.40 p.m.	27.17				S.	1	7	K.		Showery.	Hail and rain showers. p.m., N. & var. wind.
" "	18	7.30 a.m.	27.12				Calm.	..	9	S.			Passing showers.
" Porter's Landing	18	7.00 p.m.	27.03	40.			N.	1	8	C S.		Showery.	Showery all day. Wind 3 var. N. & S.
" "	19	7.00 a.m.	27.22	45.		39	S.	1	10	K S.		Raining, foggy.	Heavy rain.
" River, 1st camp	19	7.00 p.m.	27.38	54.			S.W.	2	1	K.			Rainy morning. cleared up 9 a.m.
" "	20	6.30 a.m.	27.44	43		36.5	S.	2	3	C light.			Fair. C. clouds. Wind S.W. 2.
" McDame Creek	20	7.00 p.m.	27.51	64.			S.	1	10	K S.		Gloomy, ugly.	Overcast. Dull. p.m., wind S. 2.
" "	21	6.20 a.m.	27.60	48.		41.5	Calm.	..	10	S.		Dull.	Heavy rain during night. Wind 3.
" "	21	7.00 p.m.	27.51	61.				..	10	K S.	46.	Showery.	Detached clouds. W. air.
" "	22	6.30 a.m.	27.00	54.		44.5	S.S.W.	1	1	K.			Wind 4. Cleared off.
" "	22	7.00 p.m.	27.69	56.			S.W.	3	8	K & C K.	47.		Showers of rain and hail. Wind 2.
" "	23	6.30 a.m.	27.08	41.			S.W.	2	10	S & K S.		Gloomy.	Cold. Windy. River rose 15 in. during night.
Mouth of Dease River	23	7.00 p.m.	27.06	46.			S.W.	1	10	S.	45.5	Heavy Rain.	Cold heavy rain. River rising.
" "	24	8.15 a.m.	27.79	43		41.	W.	1	10	S.		"	Heavy rain. River fell 1 ft.
" "	24	7.00 p.m.	27.68	40.			W.	1	10	S.		Raining.	Steady rain all day.
" "	25	7.00 a.m.	27.79	45.		40.	W.	1	10	S & K S		Gloomy.	Showers last night. Clouds a little broken. River fell.
Liard River, foot of cañon	25	7.00 p.m.	27.76	51.			W.	1	10	S & K S.	45.	"	Showery. Generally overcast.
" "	26	6.00 a.m.	27.81	43.		41.	N.W.	1	9	K S.			Light showers. River fell 3 in.
" 6 m. above "	26	7.00 p.m.	27.67	48.			S.	1	5	K.	49	Fair.	K. & C. clouds. 2 to 8. sunshine.
" "	27	6.00 a.m.	27.69	50.		40.	W.	2	9	K S.		Gloomy.	Calm night. River fell 2¼ in.
" "	27	7.00 p.m.	27.66	61.5			W.	2	1	C.	52.	Hazy.	C. & K. clouds.
" "	28	6.00 a.m.	27.79	51.		44.5	Calm.	.	1	C.			Calm night. River rose 2 in.
" "	28	7.00 p.m.	27.73	51.5			W.	2	5	K S.	52.5		K. clouds. Showers. Warm day.
" "	29	6.00 a.m.	27.76	47.5		46.5	N.	1	9	S & K S.		Rainy, gloomy.	Dull. Light showers this morning. River rose 1 in.
Frances River	29	7.15 p.m.	27.63	57.			Calm.	..	1	K.	50.5		Warm day. K. clouds 3
" "	30	6.00 a.m.	27.63	45.		38.	"	..	2	C K.			Calm night.
" "	30	7.00 p.m.	27.65	54.			"	..	1	C & K.	48.5		p.m. S. 10. Lt. rain. Cleared off 5 p.m.
" "	July 1	6.00 a.m.	27.58	48.		39.	"	..	9	C K.		Gloomy.	Clear sunshine early this morning.
" head of 1st cañon	1	7.00 p.m.	27.43	59.			"	..	4	K.	48.5		Detached K. clouds.
" "	2	6.00 a.m.	27.38	49.		43.5	"	..	1	C.			Calm. K. 4.
" "	2	7.00 p.m.	27.25	55.5			S.	1	9	K & S.	49.	Gloomy.	Light passing showers. Wind S.
" "	3	6.00 a.m.	27.34	46.		44.5	S.	1	1	C.			Several showers during night. Wind S.
" "	3	7.00 p.m.	27.32	54.			W.	1	1	K.	47.		K. 5. Light S. wind.

PLACE.	Date.	Hour.	Barometer corrected.	Ther. corrected. Air.	Max.	Min.	Direction of wind.	Force of wind.	Amt. of cloud.	Kind of cloud.	Temperature of Water.	Weather at time.	Weather during last interval.
Frances River	July 4	6.30 a.m.	27.29	38.		27.	Calm.		10	S.		Gloomy.	Clouded over during night.
"	4	7.00 p.m.	27.16	52.			N.W.	1	5	K & S.		Showery.	Drizzling rain a m.: p m., showery.
"	5	6.00 a.m.	27.30	44.5		37.	S.	1	10	S & K S.			Two showers during night.
"　2nd cañon	5	7.00 p.m.	27.34	51.			N.W.	1	8	K.	46.5		Showery. Heavy K. clouds 6.
"	6	6.00 a.m.	27.39	49.		33.	N.	1	2	C & K.			Fairnight. K. 5.
"	6	7.00 p.m	27.38	50.			Calm.		8	K.	46.		K. clouds 1-6.
"	7	5.30 a.m	27.31	40.		36.	"		10	S.		Gloomy.	Overcast.
"　near foot of lake.	7	7.00 p.m.	27.81	42.5			S. W.	1	3	K.	45.		Showers. Hail in evening.
"　" "	8	6.00 a.m.	27.18	41.5		32.	S. E.	1	1	C.			K.&S. clouds. Ice ¼ in. River fell 1 in.
"　Lake	8	7.00 p.m.	27.11	51.			Calm.		8	C & K.	50.		Showery. Wind S. K. 1-8. Rather warm.
"	9	6.30 a.m	27.22	47.		36.	"		9	K & S.		Gloomy.	Showery this morning.
"	9	7.00 p.m.	27.26	52.			"		9	K & K S.	49.7	Gloomy.	Showery. N. wind 4. K. 1-8.
"	10	6.00 a.m.	27.33	47.		41.	S.	1	10	K & K S.			Calm. Overcast. K. S.
"	10	7.00 p.m.	27.32	49.			S.	1	10	K & S.		Raining.	Rain storms all day. 1st thunder of season.
"	11	7.00 a.m.	27.42			34.5	W.	1	3	K		Fair.	Showery.
"	11	7.00 p.m.	27.42	45.	63.		S. W.	1	8	K & K S	46.	Showery.	Showers all day. Wind W. Warm sun.
"	12	6.21 a.m	27.49	48.		29.	W.	1	6	K.		Fair.	Fair night. Clear.
"	12	7.00 p.m	27.34	51.	62.		S.	1	1	C.	47.5		Few showers. Wind S. 2. Lake fell 6 in. in 3 days.
"	13	6.00 a.m	27.24	41.		32.	N.	1	9	K & K S.		Raining.	Fair. K. 6　Clouded up this morn.
"	13	7.00 p.m.	27.17	58.	66.		Calm.		10	K & S.	51.		Showers. Lake fell 4 in.
"	14	6.00 a.m.	27.20	44			"		10	K & S.		Gloomy.	Rain all night.
"	14	7.00 p.m.	27.32	50.	58.		S.	1	8	C & S.	46.	Hazy.	Showers　Gloomy, Water fell 3 in.
"	15	7.00 a.m.	27.33	41.		4.	N.	1	10	S.		Raining.	Rained latter part of night.
"	15	7.00 p.m.	27.32	41.	58.		S.	1	9	C & S.	49.		Raining a.m : p.m. cleared.
"	16	7.00 a.m.	27.39	52.5		10.	Calm.		1	K & C.		Fair, clear.	Fair.
"	16	7.00 p.m.	27.35	61.	45.		"		1	K.			Sprinkle. K. 1-4. Little thunder.
"	17	6.00 a.m.	27.43	45.		29.	"		1	C.		Fair, clear.	Fair.
Finlayson River, 3 m. up	17	7.00 p.m.		65.5			E. N. E.	2	9	S & K.	50.		Clouded in p.m.
"	18	7.00 a.m	27.19	56.5		43.5	Calm.		6	S & K S.			Clearing during night.
"	18	7.00 p.m	27.17	61.			S.	1	2	K & K S	53.		Fair. Sunny.
"	19	6.0 a.m	27.20	52.		41.	W.	1	9	S & K S.		Gloomy.	Dull night.
"	19	7.00 p.m.	27.12	60.			Calm.		1	K.			Fair. K. 5.
"	20	6.10 a.m.	27.15	50.		31.	"		1	C.			Calm night.
"	20	7.00 p.m	27.00	61.			"		1	C S.		Fair.	Very warm day.
"	21	6.00 a.m.	27.08	48.		33.	"		1	C.			night. Skin of ice.
"	21	7.00 p.m.	26.93	65.			W.	1	5	K.	59.5		Warm day.

Finlayson River	July	22	6.70 a.m.	26.98	79.		41.	Calm.		1	K & C.		Fair	Fair. River fell 1 in.
East Branch Finlayson River	"	22	8.00 p.m.	26.81	58.5			N.W.		0			"	" Warm.
" " " "	"	23	7.00 a.m.	26.91	57.		40.	Calm.		1	K.		"	" night.
Finlayson River Valley	"	23	7.00 p.m.	26.51	72.			"		1	C & K.		"	" Very warm all day.
" " "	"	24	7.00 a.m.	26.60	67.		50.	S.	1	0			"	" night.
" Lake	"	24	7.00 p.m.	26.80	74			Calm.		0		64.		K. 1 greater part of day. Fair.
" "	"	25	7.00 a.m.	26.83	59.		41.5	"		0				Fair. S. wind 2 last night. Smoky.
" "	"	25	7.00 p.m.	26.81	74	78.5		"		1	C.	65.	Fair.	N. wind 2. Blue sky.
" "	"	26	6.30 a.m.	26.93	58.		52.	"		0			"	S. wind 1. Smoky. Fair.
" "	"	26	7.15 p.m.	26.79	72.			"		1	C S.	66.	Fair, smoky.	Fair. S. wind 1, a.m.; calm p.m.
" "	"	27	6.30 a.m.	26.72	58.		51.	E.	1	3	K S.		" "	" E. wind 1-2 all night.
Country west of Finlayson Lake	"	27	7.30 p.m.	25.81	70.			Calm.		1	K.			" K. 2-7.
" " " "	"	28	6.00 a.m.	25.74	50.		37.	"		0			Fair.	" K. 1-2.
" " " "	"	28	7.00 p.m.	26.46	69.			W.	1	1	C & K.		"	Smoky. K. 1-4
" " " "	"	29		26.54	40.		46.	Calm.					"	Fair.
Pelly River	"	29	7.00 p.m.	26.88	64			S.	1	4	C S.	61.	"	p.m. S. wind 2. Like rain.
" "	"	30	6.30 a.m.	26.93	55.		46.	Calm.		6	K & K S		Threatening	Fair. River fell 1 in.
" "	"	30	7.00 p.m.	26.87	55.	70.		"		10	S.	60.	"	Thunderstorm in evening. S. wind 1.
" "	"	31	7.00 a.m.	26.86	51.		45.	"		4	K.		Clearing.	Rain all night. Cleared 6 a.m.
" "	"	31	7.00 p.m.	26.84	55.5	62.5		S. W.	2	4	K.	59.	Fair.	Wind S.W. 2. K. 1-5.
" "	Aug.	1	6.30 a.m.	26.84	43.		29.	Calm.		9	K.		Threatening.	Fair. K. 2-5.
" "	"	1	7.00 p.m.	26.87	54.			"		10	K S.	59.	Gloomy.	Wind W. 2. Showery. K & K.S.
" "	"	2	6.00 a.m.	26.91	40.		40.	"		1	K & C.			Light sprinkle rain during night.
" "	"	2	7.00 p.m.	27.12	57.			Lt. var.		2	C & K S.	50.		Showers Wind W 2. K & K.S.
" "	"	3	6.00 a.m.	27.25	34.		28	Calm.		0				Fair night. River still falling.
" " Hooles Cañon	"	3	7.00 p.m.	27.28	49.			Lt. var.		9	K & S.	54.		" Clear. Wind N. 2.
" " " "	"	4	6.00 a.m.	27.22	50.		40.	N. E.	1	1	K.		Fair.	Clears off last evening. Wind 3.
" " " "	"	4	7.00 p.m.	27.42	51			N.W.	2	9	S.	53.	Gloomy.	Showers p.m. Wind N.W. 3, p.m.
" "	"	5	6.00 a.m.	27.45	44.		37.	W.	1	10	S.		"	Gloomy night. River fell 2 in. Wind N.W. 2.
" "	"	5	7.00 p.m.	27.62	54.			Lt. var.		10	K S	52.5	"	W. wind. 3 showers. Dull day.
" "	"	6	6.00 a.m.	27.70	47.		[illegible]	E.		1	K S.			2 showers in night. K.S. 10-2.
" "	"	6	7.00 p.m.	27.81	58.			Calm.		3	K.	54.	Fair.	Wind W. 2. Sunshine p.m.
" "	"	7	6.00 a.m.	27.88	36.			"		1	K.		"	Calm. Fair. K. 1.
" "	"	7	7.00 p.m.	27.83	64.			"		0		57.	Smoky.	Fair wind N. & N.E. 2 to-day.
" "	"	8	5.10 a.m.	27.63	51.		50.	W.	2	10	K & S.			K. & K.S. 0-6 p.m. River fell 1 in.
" "	"	8	7.00 p.m.	27.69	59.			W.	2	3	K.	57.	Fair.	Wind W. 2. Cleared up about 12 m.
" "	"	9	6.00 a.m.	27.99	45.		44.	Lt. var.		0			Very clear.	Wind W. 3.
" "	"	9	7.00 p.m.	28.19	58.			"		0		57.	Fair.	Showers. Wind 2. K. 0-6.
" "	"	10	6.00 a.m.	28.30	40.		34.	Calm.		2	C S.		Fog on river.	Fair.
" "	"	10	7.00 p.m.	28.28	60.			E.	1	9	K S.	56.	Gloomy.	S.C. 5. Light winds up & down river.
" "	"	11	6.00 a.m.	28.39	34.		33.	Calm.		1	C.		Fog on river.	K.S. 10-0.
Camp near Fort Selkirk	"	11	7.00 p.m.	28.43	62.			"		6	C S.	56.3	Fair.	C.K. 2-4. Light N.W. air.
" " " "	"	12	7.00 a.m.	28.46	50.		46.	E.	1	10	S & K S		Threatening	Hazy and calm.
" " " "	"	12	7.00 p.m.	28.35	64.	78.		W.	1	4	C K.	58.		C. & K.S. 0-9 Dull day.
" " " "	"	13	7.00 a.m.	28.38	50.		45.	S.	1	1	K S.			K.S. 8. Calm.
" " " "	"	13	7.00 p.m.	28.30	65.	75.5		Calm.		1	K.	57.		" 1. " River fell 1 in.
" " " "	"	14	7.00 a.m.	28.39	45.		38.	E.	1	1	K.			" 1. "
" " " "	"	14	7.00 p.m.	28.33	63.	71.		Calm.		3	C.	56.5		C.S. 1-4. "

PLACE.	Date.	Hour.	Barometer corrected.	Air.	Max.	Min.	Direction of wind.	Force of wind.	Amt. of cloud.	Kind of cloud.	Temperature of Water.	Weather at time.	Weather during last interval.
Camp near Fort Selkirk	Aug. 15	7.00 a.m.	28.26	48.		48.	Calm.		6	C K.	....	Threatening.	Gloomy. Calm. C S & K 5, River fell 1 in.
"	15	7.00 p.m.	28.24	70.5	81.5		"		3	C.	58.	Smoky.	Sultry. C. 1-4.
"	16	7.30 a.m.	28.35	52		40.	"		5	C K&C S.	.....	"	Calm. C S & K 4. Very thin clouds.
"	16	7.00 p.m.	28.31	62.	70.		"		3	C & K.	57.	"	" C & K 5 all day. River fell 1 in.
"	17	8.30 a.m.	28.34	59.		48.	"		3	K.	....	Fair.	Cloudy. C S & C K 4-6.
"	17	7.00 p.m.	28.29	69.	80.		S.E. Air.		0	......	59.	"	Fair. Clear.
"	18	6.30 a.m.	28.36	39.		38.	Calm.		1	C S	....	"	" Very clear night.
Lowes River	18	7.00 p.m.	28.13	65.			"		1	C.	59.	"	Wind 1 S. Clear p.m.
"	19	5.30 a.m.	28.24	47.		45.	"		1	K S.	.....	"	Overcast.
"	19	7.00 p.m.	28.27	56.			"		10	S & K.	56.	Rainy.	Rain from S. p.m.
"	20	5.45 a.m.	28.34	47.		42.	"		10	S.	.....	Foggy	Stopped raining last eve. Calm. Ugly.
"	20	7.00 p.m.	28.32	55.			"		0	......	56.	Fair	Overcast till 4 p.m. Wind S.E.1.
"	21	5.45 a.m.	28.41	35.		34.	"		0	......		Dense fog.	
"	21	7.00 p.m.	28.29	65.			"		5	C & K.	56.	Fair.	K. 3. Wind 1 S.E. Warm day.
"	22	6.00 a.m.	28.41	45.		44.	"		0	......		Fair, clear.	Light showers during night.
"	22	7.00 p.m.	28.32	56.			"		1	K.	46.	Fair.	Sunny. Wind S S.W.1.
"	23	6.00 a.m.	28.10	33.			"		0	......		Foggy.	
"	23	7.00 p.m.	28.09	59.			"		1	C.	56.	Fair.	Calm. C S 5.
"	24	6.00 a.m.	28.08	8.		31.	"		6	K.	......	Clear.	Clear. Wind S. 1.
"	24	7.00 p.m.	27.89	64.			"		0	......	56.		Hot day.
"	25	6.00 a.m.	27.95	52.		51.	"		10	K S.	.....	Drizzling.	Rainy, light.
"	25	7.00 p.m.	27.92	49			S.	1	10	K & S.	55.	Gloomy.	Clouded all day. Raining half time.
"	26	6.00 a.m.	27.91	46.		44.	S.E.	1	10	K & S.	.....	"	Showery. Wind S. 1.
"	26	7.00 p.m.	27.82	52.			"	1	10	K & K S.	54.	"	K & K S 10 all day. Cool wind S.E. 1.
"	27	6.00 a.m.	27.81	41.		37.	Calm.		9	K S.	.....	Fog.	K S 10. Calm.
"	27	7.00 p.m.	27.82	53.			"		4	K S	55.	Fair.	Showery. K. 5-6. Warm sun.
"	28	6.00 a.m.	27.93	43.		32.5	E.	1	1	C.	.....	Fog	K 4-0.
"	28	7.00 p.m.	27.80	46.			Calm.		1	K	54.	Fair.	Sunny. K. 3.
"	29	6.00 a.m.	27.92	30.		28.6	"		0	......		Fog.	Clear. Calm.
"	29	7.00 p.m.	27.86	55.			S.	1	6	K.	51.	Fair.	Fair wind S. 3. K S. 5-8.
"	30	6.00 a.m.	.....	36.		33.5	Calm.		8	S & C K	......	Fog.	C K & S 6.
mouth of Tes-lin-too.	30	7.00 p.m.	27.72	55.			S.W.	3	10	S & K S.	52.	Gloomy.	Showery. K & S 10. Wind S.3. Cold. " S & K S 10 " 3.
"	31	7.30 a.m.	27.70	54.		49.	S.	4	10	S & K S.	.....	Fair.	K S & C S 8. Wind S. 3 all day.
"	31	7.00 p.m.	27.72	57.	60.		S.	3	5	C K.	52.	Fair.	R S & C S 8. Wind S. 3 all day.
"	Sept. 1	5.30 a.m.	27.72	52.		49.5	Calm.		10	S.	......	Light rain.	Showery. Wind died out last night.

Locality		Day	Hour	Bar.	Temp.	Max.	Min.	Wind	Force	Cloud	Kind	Water	Weather	Remarks
Lewes River	Sept.	1	7.00 p.m.	27.03	57.			S. W.	2	8	S & K S.	52.	Fair.	Wind N.E. 1 a.m., S. 2 p.m.
"	"	2	5.30 a.m.	27.78	32.		30.	Calm.		0			Fog.	Fair. Clear.
Foot of Lake Laburge	"	2	7.00 p.m.	27.88	41.			"		3	K.	53.	"	K. 1-6. Wind S. 2.
" "	"	3	6.00 a.m.	27.92	33.5		27.5	N.	1	6	C S.		Fair.	Clear. Calm.
Lake Labarge	"	3	7.00 p.m.	27.71	54.5			S.	3	3	C.	51.5	"	C. & S. 1-5. Wind S. 3 all day. Hazy sunshine.
"	"	4	5.30 a.m.	27.83	39.5		36.	Lt. var.		10	C S & K.		"	C. 5. Wind died out early last night. C. clouds coming rapidly from W. p.m.
Near head of Lake Laburge	"	4	7.00 p.m.	27.60	56.			W.	2	5	K & S.	49.5	"	Showery a.m. W. wind 3 for 1 hour.
" " "	"	5	6.00 a.m.	27.88	44.		42.	W.	1	10	K S.		Light rain.	Fair. C. K. 3. Wind S. 1., p.m.
Lewes Riv., below Tahkheena R.	"	5	7.00 p.m.	27.87	53.			Calm.		3	C S.	54.	Fair.	
" "	"	6	6.00 a.m.	27.67	50.		49.	S.	3	10	S & K.		Gloomy.	S. 10 wind latter part of night.
" " White Horse Rapid	"	6	7.00 p.m.	27.54	53.			Calm.		3	K & C.	53.5	Fair.	K. C. 1-4. Wind S. 4.
" "	"	7	6.00 a.m.	27.72	42.		41.	"		9	K S.		"	Calm. K. 2-6. Light rain this a.m.
" " below cañon	"	7	7.00 p.m.	27.65	48.5			S.	2	10	S.	53.	"	K. 0-5. Wind S. 1.
" "	"	8	6.00 a.m.	27.67	44.		42.5	Lt. var.		6	K.		"	Fair. Wind S. W. 1.
" " head of "	"	8	7.00 p.m.	27.57	51.			S. W.	1	6	K S.	53.5	"	
" "	"	9	6.00 a.m.	27.49	38.		34.	Lt. var.		9	K.		Gloomy.	K. 2-0.
"	"	9	7.00 p.m.	27.54	18.			N. W.	2	10	S.		"	Wind p.m. N. W. Cool day.
Lake Marsh	"	10	7.00 a.m.	27.75	41.5		37.	Calm.		10	S.		Drizzling.	Rained a little. Calm. Snowed on mts.
"	"	10	7.00 p.m.	27.76	41.5			Lt. var.		10	S & K S.	52.	Gloomy.	Showery. Wind W. 1. Cool.
Tagish Houses	"	11	0.20 a.m.	27.83	39.		32.	E.	1	10	S & K S.		"	Overcast all night. Calm.
"	"	11	7.00 p.m.	27.69	42.			Calm.		1	K.	49.5	Fair.	K S & K 8-2, a.m.; p.m., Wind W. 2. C. clouds.
Tagish Lake	"	12	0.00 a.m.	27.60	29.		27.	"		10	S.		Gloomy.	K S 1. Calm. Clouded over this a.m.
Windy Arm	"	13	6.30 a.m.	27.69	36.		34.	Lt. var.		3	C S & K.		Fair.	Wind W. 3.
" "	"	13	7.00 p.m.	27.76	33.			"		1	K S.	48.5	"	K S 4-0. A.m. wind N. 1: p.m. calm.
"	"	14	6.00 a.m.	27.88	26.5		25.	Calm.		0			"	Clear. Calm.
Bennett Lake	"	14	7.00 p.m.	27.83	30.			N.	1	0		46.5	"	K. 1. Hot sun. Wind S. 2 all day.
" "	"	15	6.40 a.m.	27.83	29.		26.	S.	1	1	K.		Fair.	Clear. Calm.
"	"	15	7.00 p.m.	27.75	43.			N.	3	8	K.	45.5	"	K & C K 1 3. Low wind N. 2, high wind W.
Lake Lindeman	"	16	6.30 a.m.	27.75	40.5		39.	N.	1	10	K S.		Gloomy.	K. 8. N. 2 wind all night.
"	"	16	7.00 p.m.	27.75	40.			N.	1	10	K S.	45.	"	K S. 6-10. Wind S. 1, a.m.; N. 1, p.m.
" "	"	17	7.00 a.m.	27.74	41.		29.	S. W.	1	8	K.		Fair.	K. 10-6. Calm.
" "	"	17	7.00 p.m.	27.72	37.	58.		S.	1	1	K.	45.	"	K. 10-4. High wind N., low wind S. 1.
" "	"	18	7.00 a.m.	27.75	36.		19.	Calm.		0			"	Clear. Calm. Light fog on water.
" "	"	18	7.00 p.m.	27.71	32.	51.		N. E.	1	1	C.	45.	"	" all day. " var. wind.
" "	"	19	6.00 a.m.	27.75	21.		18.	N. E.	1	0			"	Fair; clear. " fog on water.

(2) OBSERVATIONS AT TELEGRAPH CREEK, STIKINE RIVER, B. C., DURING PORTIONS OF THE YEARS 1881 TO 1886, BY J. C. CALLBREATH.

Date.	Minimum Temperature. (°)	Remarks.
1881.		
Oct. 2	23	Coldest night yet.
3	....	Heavy frost last night.
8	12	
9	7	First ice running on river.
10	14	
11	22	
12	20	
13	....	Little frost last night.
14	....	No frost this morning.
15	24	
16	14	
17	10	
18	7	
19	10	
20	21	
21	30	
22	....	No frost last night.
23	....	Weather mild.
24	....	" "
25	....	" "
26	....	" "
27	....	" " 9 p.m., 45°
28	26	
29	25	
30	33	
31	23	
Nov. 1	20	
2	32	
3	26	
4	....	No frost last night.
5	32	
6	25	
8	31	
9	26	
10	29	
11	24	
12	10	
13	12	2 in. snow on range at Tahltan.
14	8	
15	-13	3 or 4 in. snow on range at [Tahltan.
16	-17	
17	-4	
20	....	Mild.
22	-7	
23	4	Mild all day.
24	8	8 in. snow on range at Tahltan.
25	32	
26	34	
27	20	
28	20	
29	15	
30	10	
Dec. 1	20	
2	20	
3	2	
4	0	
5	4	
6	12	
7	7	
8	3	
9	-2	
10	0	
11	-13	
12	-29	
13	-20	
14	-18	
15	-4	
19	6	
20	24	
1881.		
Dec. 21	2	
22	10	
23	-2	
24	-2	
25	15	
26	-2	
27	-2	
28	-2	
29	-7	
1882.		
Jan. 1	-4	
2	-17	
3	-4	
4	-13	
5	-2	
6	5	
7	6	
8	6	
9	8	
10	0	
11	8	
12	15	
13	....	Heavy thaw.
14	8	
17	30	
18	22	
19	22	
20	15	
21	7	
22	-4	
23	-15	
26	-26	
27	-30	
28	.	Mild.
29	27	
30	6	
31	13	
Feb. 1	19	
2	5	
3	8	
4	15	
7	-1	
8	-9	
9	-12	
10	-28	
11	-28	
12	20	
13	0	
14	0	
15	-27	
16	-32	
17	-20	
18	....	9 a.m., -2°
19	....	Thawing.
20	4	
21	30	
22	12	
23	-8	
24	-1	
25	-2	
26	0	
27	....	Mild.
28	5	
March 1	10	
2	-6	
3	-16	
4	-22	
5	-13	
6	10	

Date.	Minimum Temperature.	Remarks.
1882.	°	
March 7	30	
8	23	
9	—1	
10	—4	
11	—7	
12	22	
13	7	
14	6	
15	—6	
16	13	
17	—5	
18	—18	
19	—17	
20	—10	
22	—19	
23	2	
24	15	
25	22	
26		
27	15	
29	—8	
30	—12	
31	10	
April 1	14	
2	10	
3	29	
4	15	
5	14	
6	12	
7	12	
9	22	
10	28	
11	24	
13	24	
14	24	
15	25	
16	33	
17	34	
20	31	
21	9	
22	30	
23	16	
24	2	
25	16	
26	17	
27	19	
28	25	
29	25	
30	26	
May 1	27	
2	29	
3	34	
4	34	
5	33	
6	32	
7	26	
9	33	
10	42	
11	29	
13	31	
14	30	
15	30	
16	29	
17	35	
18	32	
19	28	
21	29	
22	29	
23	......	No frost.
24	"	"
Sept. 29	22	Coldest night of season, bright clear day.
30	20	Wind N,, bright and clear all day.
Oct. 1	24	Wind N.
3	19	

Date.	Minimum Temperature.	Remarks.
1882.	°	
Oct. 4	19	
6	......	Bright, fine day.
7	21	
8	30	Cloudy, light sprinkle rain a.m.
10	33	" raining a little all day.
11	34	
13	30	
14	24	
16	30	Fine, clear day, strong wind up river.
17	30	Cloudy and calm.
18	32	Rained hard in eve., drizzling all day.
19	35	
21	32	Snowing this morn., melting as it fell.
28	......	Mild and plasant.
31	12	Ice running in river for first time.
Nov. 1	14	
2	20	Wind up river since noon.
3	24	Fine, mild day.
5	15	Mild and pleasant; bright all day; less than 1 in. snow fell yesterday
6	12	
7	17	Mild and calm all day.
8	18	Overcast, light mist: little or no ice in river.
9	3	
10	2	Calm, mackerel-sky clouds moving up river.
11	22	Mild and calm all day.
12	23	Snowed a little.
13	19	Clear and calm all day.
14	21	Light floating clouds; calm and mild all day.
15	17	Commenced raining 2 p.m.
16	32	Rained all night; snowed for 1 hour after daylight; cleared off.
17	30	Mild and pleasant all day; wind up river.
18	25	Mild and pleasant; light snow in evening.
19	21	Bright, calm day.
20	11	Partly clear.
21	—5	Clear and calm.
22	—10	" " "
23	—6	Partly overcast a.m., p.m. mild, calm, overcast.
24	6	Lightly overcast, calm.
25	7	Snowed a little this a.m.
26	20	Lightly clouded all day, mild.
27	8	Overcast, snowing a little, mild all day.
28	7	Clear and mild all night.
29	3	Misty, began snowing from N.E. 4 p.m.
30	15	Snowed 3 in.; river nearly closed.
Dec. 1	6	Lightly overcast.
2	7	Mild day.
3	14	Light overcast, calm all day.
4	14	Hazy and calm.
5	14	" " "
6	—1	
7	0	Mild and calm.
8	1	Mild, overcast; lt. snow p.m.
9	11	Lightly overcast, mild and calm.
10	8	Partly clouded; snow squalls.
11	—7	Cold all day; wind down river.

Date.	Minimum Temperature.	Remarks.
1882.	°	
Dec. 12	—11	
13	—28	Cutting N. wind; not above —20° all day.
14	......	9 a.m., —16°; 5 in. fine snow all day.
15	—11	Snowed about 8 inches.
16	6	Little snow during night; growing warmer.
17	21	Overcast, wind E.
18	6	Overcast, as usual this mild weather.
19	—4	
22	......	This evening 33°.
23	20	
24	12	Mild and pleasant all day.
25	......	10 a.m., 34°.
26	23	Misty, sprinkle of snow, mild and calm.
27	12	Clear, mild and pleasant all day.
28	5	Clear; 15 in. snow on Tahltan range.
29	—10	Clear and calm.
30	—14	" " "
31	—4	Mild and calm.
1883.		
Jan. 1	4	" " "
2	0	
3	......	9 p.m., —3°.
4	......	8 a.m., —11°.
5	—16	Clear; wind N.
6	—20	Clear and calm.
7	—16	Mild all day; clear.
8	0	
9	—6	Overcast.
10	......	8 a.m., 5°.
11	8	
12	—11	Mild and calm all day.
13	—9	
14	......	8 a.m., 5°.
15	0	Calm.
16	—17	Clear and calm; cold all day.
17	—24	
18	—18	" " " growing milder.
19	—8	
20	2	Mild and calm.
21	17	Calm all day.
22	24	Lightly overcast, squally.
23	16	Mild and squally.
24	10	Misty overhead; calm.
25	5	Calm; lightly overcast.
26	—2	Lightly overcast and calm.
27	......	11 p.m., 0°.
28	0	Mild and calm.
29	10	" " " partly overcast.
30	—3	
Feb. 1	......	Weather milder.
2	......	10 p.m., —24°; clear.
3	......	11 p.m., —22°.
4	......	10.30 p.m., —16°; clear.
5	—13	Lightly overcast; cold and clear.
6	—10	Clear.
7	—4	
8	—3	Lightly overcast.
9	—2	Clear and calm.
10	—4	Clear; snowed a little.
11	12	Overcast a.m.; strong E. wind, clear and calm p.m.
12	0	Strong N.E. wind; clear.
13	—20	Clear; N. wind.
14	—23	Clear and calm.
15	—23	Lightly overcast and calm.
16	—10	" " sprinkling snow.
1883.	°	
Feb. 17	5	Overcast; a little snow.
18	10	Mild and calm; snowed 2 in. last night.
19	7	Calm.
20	—2	Clear and calm.
21	—3	Clear.
22	......	10 p.m., 5°.
23	—1	Calm and partly clouded.
24	9	Cloudy.
25	—1	10 a.m., thawing—first thaw of season.
26	39	Thawing; clear all day.
27	35	Thawed all night.
28	22	Bright and warm.
March 1	9	Clear.
2	......	Warm day.
3	25	Wind N.E.
4	11	Bright, clear.
5	11	Bright.
6	7	Clear.
7	15	Clear, warm day; thawing in shade.
8	21	Clear, bright; strong wind up river.
9	28	Clear.
10	18	Clear and warm.
11	12	
12	20	
13	26	
14	24	
Oct. 13	......	Weather mild.
14	......	" "
15	......	" " overcast.
16	......	Very mild.
17	......	Mild and calm.
29	......	About 12°; weather moderate; little ice running in river.
Nov. 1	—5	Coldest night of season; much ice in river.
2	5	9 p.m., 8°.
3	4	10 p.m., 32°.
4	27	Snowed 1 in.; mild day.
5	26	" 2 " last night.
6	27	
7	16	
8	10	
9	15	Snowing lightly a.m.; p.m. clear
10	—3	Lightly overcast.
11	6	Mild, hazy, calm.
12	......	8 a.m., —4°; clear, calm.
13	—12	Moderating; calm.
14	—3	Clear and calm.
15	10	Mild and calm,
16	12	Clear; wind down river.
17	......	8 a.m., 27°; river closing fast.
18	25	Mild and overcast.
19	26	
20	28	Clear.
21	......	8 a.m., 24°.
22	13	
23	—7	Clear; N. wind.
24	—16	" " "
25	—20	Clear and calm.
26	—25	" " "
27	—27	Clear and calm a.m.; p.m. hazy.
28	—12	Snowed a little last night; clear day.
29	—11	
30	—3	Mild; overcast all day
Dec. 1	14	Snowed and rained a little to-day.
2	31	

Date	Minimum Temperature	Remarks	Date	Minimum Temperature	Remarks
1883.	°		**1884.**	°	
Dec. 3	9	Hazy, calm.	Feb. 10	—18	Clear and calm.
4	9	Mild.	11	—18	" " "
5	10	Mild.	12	—17	" " "
6	—10	Calm, hazy, mild.	13	—15	" " "
7	......	8 a.m., 22°; snowed 1 in. last night.	14	—9	
8	13	Calm and clear.	15	—23	Calm.
9	16	Misty; snowed a little.	16	—19	Strong north wind; clear.
10	20	Wind S.	17	—21	Strong N.E. wind; lt. snow; overcast.
11	26	Clear and calm.	18	—20	Clear; N. wind.
12	21	Clear.	19	—30	Clear and calm; coldest night of winter.
13	7	Mild all day.	20	—25	Calm.
14	12	Snowed a little all day.	21	—25	Clear and calm; p.m. overcast.
15	......	9 a.m., 22°; snowed a.m.; rain p.m.	22	—5	Snowed a little.
16	......	9 a.m., 42°; clear: strong S. wind.	23	10	Lightly overcast; little snow.
17	......	9 a.m., 34°.	24	40	Strong S. wind; thawing.
18	......	9 a.m., 23°; little snow.	25	24	
19	14		26	35	Rained hard during night.
20	18		27	30	Little hazy.
21	9	Clear and calm.	28	12	
22	—1	Clear and hazy.	29	10	Clear, calm.
23	......	9 a.m., —1°.	March 1	15	" " "
24	......	9 a.m., —11°.	2	20	Clear.
25	—17	Clear and calm.	3	20	Overcast; strong N E. wind all day.
26	—14		4	—2	Clear; N. wind.
27	—9	Clear.	5	—7	
28	—26	Clear: N. wind.	6	—8	
29	—30	Clear and calm.	7	10	
30	—33		8	6	Clear and calm.
31	......	6 a.m., —1°; wind N.E.	9	—3	" " "
1884.			10	—4	" " "
Jan. 1	—6	Clear and calm.	Oct. 18	......	Ice commenced running in it.
2	—10	Clear.	19	12	
3	—14	Clear: N. wind.	20	......	Not much ice running to-day.
4	—20	Hazy all day: 10 p.m., —6°.	21	......	More
5	—6	Hazy; 10 p.m., —2°; lt. snow.	22	......	Ice running thick; little frost last night; thawed all day.
6	—15		23	......	Ice running thick; froze a little last night; thawing this a.m.
7	—6		24	......	Snowing this evening.
8	......	9 a.m., 5°.	26	......	Mild; snowing a little; river almost clear of ice.
9	......	" " 8°.	27	......	Mild; no ice running.
10	......	" " 16°; snowed 1 inch.	28	20	Cloudy; light snow.
11	......	" " 22°; hazy, calm.	29	13	Overcast; light snow; good deal of ice running.
12	15	Snowed a little last night.	30	12	Much ice running; mild to-day.
13	7		31	12	Dry, mild and clear.
14	20		Nov. 1	7	Clear; coldest night of season so far.
15	0		2	11	Lightly overcast; mild and pleasant.
16	37	Strong southerly wind; thawing.	3	16	Mild and pleasant day.
17	9	Clear and calm.	4	24	Snowing this a.m.
18	0	Hazy, calm.	5	30	Snowed 2 in. last night; thawing this morn.; snow at Thaltan range nearly 1 ft. deep.
19	—10	Clear and calm.	6	24	Clear.
20	0	Partly overcast.	7	22	
21	14	Mild and hazy; a little snow.	8	29	
22	20	Clear and calm.	9	10	
23	22	Mild all day.	10	30	
24	20	" " "	11	32	Snowing at noon; turned to rain and sleet.
25	23	Snowed about 2 in. last night.	12	38	Raining.
26	5	N.E. wind.	13	34	Clear; no ice in river.
27	—17	Clear and calm.	14	24	Clear and calm.
28	—20	" " "	15	14	
29	—21	Clear; wind up river.	16	16	Overcast.
30	—5	Thawing all day; 10 p.m., 30°.	17	20	Misty and calm; snowed a little in evening.
Feb. 1	—5	Snowed 4 in. last night; strong N.E. wind.			
2	—19				
3	—21				
4	—8				
5	—7	Clear.			
6	—5	" and calm.			
7	—7	" strong wind down river.			
8	—15	" and calm.			
9	—3	" " "			

Date	Minimum Temperature	Remarks
1884.	°	
Nov. 18	32	Clear.
19	22	A little snow during day.
20	21	Overcast, calm.
21	11	Hazy and calm.
22	13	Mild " "
23	16	Clear.
24	14	Hazy and calm.
25	20	Snowed about 2 in. last night.
26	26	Nearly clear.
27	20	Hazy.
30	40	Rained hard all day.
Dec. 1	31	Clear a.m.; clouded and raining p.m.
2	....	8 a.m., 34°; 1 p.m., raining; 3 p.m., cleared.
3	30	Clear.
4	24	Snowed about 2 in. this eve.
5	24	Clear.
6	20	Misty and cloudy: wind S.W.
7	.....	10 a.m., 42°.
8	30	Clear and calm.
9	21	Lightly overcast.
10	21	Clear.
11	12	Clear; wind down river.
12	7	Clear.
13	3	Lightly overcast.
14	3	Clear; N. wind.
15	−15	Clear; N. wind: below −12° all day.
16	−16	Clear.
17	−4	Strong easterly wind.
18	−8	Clear: strong wind down river; crossing on ice to-day.
19	−12	Clear: N. wind.
20	−15	" "
21	−20	Strong; N.W. wind a.m.; calm p.m.
22	−20	Little wind.
23	−10	Overcast.
24	−5	Clear.
25	−15	"
26	−22	Clear, strong north wind.
27	−22	
28	−3	Clear.
29	−20	Clear and calm.
30	−14	" "
31	−7	Lightly overcast.
1885.		
Jan. 1	−3	Calm and hazy.
2	−3	Lightly overcast.
3	5	Partly clear.
4	−6	Overcast; snowing.
5	17	
6	.....	Mild and calm.
10	.....	Snowed 4 in. last night; light snow to-day.
11	.....	Clear and colder this morning.
12	.....	10 p.m., −14°: below zero all day.
13	−22	
14	−30	Clear.
15	−32	" N. wind.
16	−32	" and calm.
17	−22	" " "
18	−28	" " "
19	−5	Hazy; light snow last night.
20	3	Calm. misty.
21	10	Snowed about 3 in. last night; clear and calm.
22	−6	Hazy, calm.
23	6	" "
24	10	" "
25	16	Rained all p.m.
28	.....	Mild.

Date	Minimum Temperature	Remarks
1885.	°	
Jan. 30	.....	Light snow.
31	.....	Mild and calm.
Feb. 1	19	
2	22	Calm
3	25	Lightly overcast.
4	30	Overcast, calm.
5	11	" "
6	10	Cloudy: E. wind.
7	−2	Clear and calm.
8	−9	" " "
9	−15	. " " "
10	−5	Calm and overcast.
11	10	" " misty.
12	10	Clear and calm.
13	13	Hazy " "
14	14	" " " lt. snow in eve.
15	20	Clear
16	.....	10 p.m., 15°.
17	4	
18	−9	Clear and windy.
19	−16	" " calm.
20	−15	" " "
21	−5	Overcast.
22	19	Thawing in shade at noon.
23	29	Heavy thaw all day.
24	20	Clear and calm.
25	20	Clear: thawing all day.
26	27	" " " "
27	12	Wind N.E.
28	32	Sleet this p.m.
March 1	30	Clear: maximum temp. 40° in shade.
2	26	Clear and calm.
3	20	Clear all day.
4	10	Clear and calm.
5	10	Lightly overcast: clearing.
6	22	Overcast, calm: snowing at 2 p.m.
7	38	Raining hard.
8	34	Overcast. calm.
9	16	Murky. calm.
10	16	Snowed a little this evening.
11	21	Clear: strong S.W. wind.
12	26	Snowing all day.
13	24	8 in. snow fell yesterday: last night clear and calm.
14	26	Clear.
15	34	Clear: heavy thaw.
16	22	Clear and calm.
17	12	" " "
18	12	" " "
19	.....	" " "
20	20	" " "
21	.....	10 p.m., 28°.
22	10	Clear and calm.
23	16	" " "
25	32	
26	25	
30	.....	No frost last night: cloudy; strong wind up river.
31	31	Clear: wind up river.
April 1	30	Warm: S. wind all day.
2	23	Overcast in morning; raining p.m.
3	.....	Rained and snowed most of night: 2 in. went off this p.m.: bright.
4	.....	Frost last night.
5	35	Clear.
6	18	"
7	22	Cloudy.
8	.....	No frost last night: strong S.W. wind.
9	30	

DATE.	Minimum Temperature.	REMARKS.
1885.	°	
April 10	28	Clear: strong wind up river,
11	31	
12	31	High winds.
13	30	Little wind: some snow squalls.
14	......	Not much wind to-day.
15	25	
16	16	
17	10	
18		Hard frost.
19	......	No frost last night.
20	27	
23	29	
Nov. 4	20	
7	26	Strong S.E. wind.
8	22	First ice running in river.
9	5	Clear: good deal of ice running.
10	20	Calm.
11	22	Calm; spitting snow; cloudy.
12	19	Calm and clear.
13	14	Clear: snowed a little last night.
14	19	A little ice running.
15	22	Calm.
16	18	Overcast, calm.
17	22	"　　"
18	16	Calm: snowing a little.
19	14	Clear.
20	12	
21	7	Clear.
22	6	Clear: river open yet: very little ice running.
23	15	Hazy, calm.
24	21	River entirely free of ice: hazy.
25	13	Hazy.
26	10	Hazy p.m. clear.
27	12	Clear and calm.
28	10	Hazy and calm.
29	31	Snowing 9 a.m., p.m. thawing.
30	28	9 in. snow fell during night.
Dec. 1	7	Clear, calm.
2	—2	
5	......	Snowing a little.
6	22	Cloudy.
7	20	Overcast.
8	12	Clear.
9	—8	Clear and calm.
10	—18	"　　"　　"
11	0	Snowed a little.
12	8	Hazy, calm all day: snowed little in evening.
13	10	Snowed 5 in. last night.
14	20	
15	14	Hazy, calm.
16	12	Clear.
17	3	Clear and calm.
18	3	"　　"　　"
19	—6	Clear.
20	—10	Clear: river closing from edges.
21	—16	
22	4	Clear and calm.
23	—4	"　　"　　"
24	......	8 a.m., —1°.
25	0	
26	10	Thawing; raining in evening.
27	38	
28	28	Cloudy.
29	13	Cloudy; snowed 1 in.: wind up R.; wind down R. in eve.
30	—6	Clear (?): snowing a little all day.
31	—13	Clear.
1886.		
Jan. 1	—4	Snowed 2 in.: strong wind up R.

DATE.	Minimum Temperature.	REMARKS.
1886.	°	
Jan. 2	18	Snowed 2 in.
3	—2	Wind N.E.
4	—9	Snowed 2 in.
5	—26	Clear.
6	—32	Clouded up p.m.: snowed 2 in.
7	—10	Clear.
8	—0	Calm.
9	4	Clear.
10	6	Overcast: snowed a little in evening.
11	16	Snowed about 2 in.
12	20	Snowed 1 in.; calm and clear.
13	—6	Clear and calm.
14	—17	"　　"　　"
15	......	8 a.m., —10°; clear; wind N.W.
16	—14	
17	......	8 a.m., 20°; clear.
18	—8	Very clear.
19	—14	N.E. wind all day; clear.
20	—23	Very clear: N. wind.
21	—26	Clear.
22	—30	Clear and calm.
23	......	9 a.m., 14°.
24	—16	Blew a gale all night.
25	—31	
26	—36	Hazy.
27	—22	"
28	—6	
29	—10	Snowed 2 in.
30	—12	Clear.
31	—6	Clear and calm.
Feb. 1	—10	
2	—2	Overcast: a little snow.
3	0	Snowed about 4 in.
4	—2	"　a little.
5	22	"　2 in.
6	34	Rained all night: snow in eve.
7	22	Clear.
8	18	misty.
9	20	Blowing a gale: snowed 6 in.; drifting badly.
10	—2	Clear: evening snowing.
11	......	8 a.m., 12°: snowed a little: clear.
12	—2	Lightly overcast.
13	—10	
14	—10	Clear and calm.
15	—2	Snowed 2 in.: rained a little p.m.
16	......	9 a.m., 28°: max., 42°: much rain.
17	34	Strong S.W. wind; much rain
18	......	8 a.m., 36°; raining hard most of night and to-day.
19	......	6 a.m., 36°.
20	38	Max. 44°: cloudy and raining.
21	36	Rained nearly all night; clear to-day.
22	27	Overcast: snowed a little.
26	......	10 p.m., 9°; very clear.
27	0	Clear and calm.
28	0	
March 1	8	Clear.
2	18	Overcast; p.m. snowing.
3	28	Cloudy.
4	20	Overcast.
5	14	Hazy and calm; eve. clear.
6	8	Clear.
7	......	10 p.m., 22°.
8	18	Cloudy and calm.
10	24	Thawing all day.
11	20	Clear.
12	30	Cloudy most of day.
13	24	

Date.	Minimum Temperature.	Remarks.
1886.	°	
Mar. 14	30	Heavy thaw.
15	27	Wind N.E.: snowed 1 in.
16	4	Clear: wind N.E.
17	−4	
18	16	
19	12	
20	10	
23	8	Cloudy most of day.
24	12	
25	18	Clear; freezing in shade.
26	20	Strong N.W. wind: thawing.
27	26	Wind up river: thawing.
29	......	No frost: cloudy.
30	28	Calm.
31	24	
April 1	30	Overcast.
2	......	No frost: overcast and foggy.
3	......	No frost.
5	20	
1886.	°	
April 6	18	
7	20	
8	30	
9	31	Clear.
10	30	
11	......	No frost.
12	27	
13	28	Clear.
14	......	No frost.
15	20	Clear.
16	30	Clear; clouded up in evening.
17	......	No frost.
14	......	" "
20	......	Frost last night.
21	......	No frost last night.
22	......	Finished ploughing.
23	......	Pack-train off to range.
24	......	Canoes arrived to-day.

(3) OBSERVATIONS AT LAKETON, DEASE LAKE, B.C., DURING PORTIONS OF THE YEARS 1878 TO 1882, BY MR. J. CLEARIHUE.

Date.	Minimum Temperature.	Direction of Wind.	Remarks.
1878.	°		
Nov. 1	0	S.W.	Mild and cloudy.
2	0	S.W.	Mild and clear.
3	18	S.W.	Raining.
4	22	N.W.	Heavy snowfall.
5	0	S.	Mild and clear.
6	0	S.	Mild and cloudy.
7	20	S.	Mild; sunshine.
8	14	S.	" "
9	0	S.	Rain in afternoon.
10	0	S.	Heavy snowfall at night.
11	14	N.W.	Bright and clear.
12	10	N.W.	" " "
13	10	N.W.	" " "
14	12	N.W.	Cloudy, stormy afternoon.
15	10	N.W.	Bright and clear.
16	14	N.W.	Light snowfall.
17	18	N.W.	" "
18	19	S.W. strong.	Drifting all day.
19	0	S.	Cloudy; mild in p.m.
20	0	S.	Snowing.
21	20	S.	Cloudy.
22	18	N.W.	Snowing.
23	10	N.W.	Cloudy.
24	20	S.W.	Heavy snowfall.
25	10	S.W.	Mild, cloudy.
26	18	S.W.	" "
27	8	W.	Cloudy.
28	10	W.	Bright and clear.
29	10	W.	" " "
30	12	W.	" " "
1	12	S.W.	Snowing p.m.
2	20	S.W.	Mild, bright and clear; heavy snow at night.
	10	S.W.	Bright and clear.
1878.	°		
Dec. 4	12	N.W.	Bright and clear.
5	0	N.W.	Cloudy.
6	0	N.W.	"
7	12	N.	"
8	8	N.	Lake frozen in front of town.
9	1	N.W.	Bright and clear: skating on ice.
10	−8	N.W.	First arrival from McDames and Thibert Cr. on ice.
11	12	S.W.	First arrival from head of lake on ice.
12	16	S.W.	Cloudy.
13	18	S.W.	Heavy snow p.m.
14	20	S.W.	" " last night.
15	4	W.	Bright and clear.
16	−4	N.W.	Snow.
17	−1	N.W.	Bright and clear.
18	14	S.W.	Cloudy.
19	24	N.	Very mild, bright and clear.
20	20	S.	Heavy thaw; lake open in places.
21	12	W.	Cloudy.
22	6	W.	"
23	−2	N.W.	Bright and clear.
24	−4	N.W.	" " "
25	−8	N.W.	" " "
26	−4	N.W.	" " "
27	−6	N.W.	" " "
28	−7	S.W.	" " "
29	−4	S.W.	" " "
30	−8	N.W.	" " "
31	−10	N.W.	" " "
1879.			
Jan. 1	−4	N.W.	" " "

Date.	Minimum Temperature.	Direction of Wind.	Remarks.
1879.	°		
Jan. 2	−1	N.W.	Bright and clear.
3	−4	N.W.	"
4	6	N.W.	Bright and clear; light snow last night.
5	10	N.W.	Bright and clear.
6	6	N.W.	" "
7	0	N.W.	Snowing.
8	8	N.W.	"
9	−22	N.W.	Bright and clear.
10	−26	N.	" " "
11	−32	N.	" " "
12	−30	N.	Snowing; at noon, −12°.
13	−30	N.	Bright and clear.
14	−22	N.	Snowing; at noon, −4°.
15	6	N.	Cloudy.
16	0	N.	Bright and clear.
17	1		
18	−2	N.	Snowing; very stormy.
19	−6	N.	Bright and clear.
20	−4	N.	" " "
21	−5	N.	Cloudy; stormy p.m.
22		N.	Stormy all day.
23		N.	Strong drifting.
24	−18	N.	Bright and clear.
25	−24	N.	" "
26	−20	N.	Cloudy.
27		N.	Bright and clear.
28	10	N.	Cloudy.
29	12	N.	Bright and clear.
31	12	S.	Bright and clear; snow last night.
Feb. 1	10	N.	Bright and clear.
2	−11	N.	" " "
3	−11	N.	" " "
4	6	N.	Storming.
5	16	N.	Storming; heavy snow last night.
6	10	N.	Bright and clear.
7	−4	N.	" " "
8	−27	N.	" " "
9	−29	N.	" " "
10	−18	N.	" " "
11	−27	N.	" " "
12	−26	N.	" " "
13	−24	N.	" " "
14	−23	N.	" " "
15	−29	N.	" " "
16	−10	N.	" " "
17	−10	N.	" " "
18	−17	N.	Stormy.
19	−20	N.	Bright and clear.
20	−15	N.	Stormy, drifting.
21	−25	N.	Bright and clear.
22	−26	N.	" " "
23	−10	N.	Stormy, drifting.
24	−24	N.	Bright and clear.
25	−30	N.	" " "
26	−10	N.	Snow last night.
27	−10	N.	Heavy storm, snowing, drifting.
28	−8	N.	Snowing and drifting.
Mar. 1	−4	N.	Heavy wind, drifting.
2	4	N.	Storming.
3	0	N.	"
4	−12	N.	Bright and clear.
5	−5	N.	" " "
6	−12	R.	Cloudy, drifting.
7	6	N.	Bright and clear.
8	−6	N.	" " "
9	−4	N.	Bright and clear; strong wind.
10	−18	N.	Bright and clear.
11	−16	S.E.	" " "
12	−20	N.	" " "

Date.	Minimum Temperature.	Direction of Wind.	Remarks.
1879.	°		
Mar.13	−20	N.	Bright and clear.
14	4	N.W.	Stormy.
15	−9	N.W.	Bright and clear.
16	−10	N.W.	" " "
17	2	N.W.	" " "
18	−4	N.W.	" " "
19	2	N.W.	" " "
20	10	N.	" " "
21	2	N.	" " "
22	10	N.W.	" " "
23	2	N.W.	" " "
24	0	N.	Storming.
25	18	N.W.	Very mild.
26	22	N.	Strong wind.
27	22	N.	Snowing.
28	24	......	
29		......	
30	14	......	Bright and clear.
31	1	......	
*	*	*	* * * *
Nov.18	2	N.	Snowing and drifting all day.
19	4	N.	drifting, cloudy.
20	12	N.	Light snowfall.
21	14	N.	Cloudy; clear towards evening.
22	4	N.	Cloudy.
23	14	N.	"
24	12	N.	Cloudy; north wind in evening.
25	3	N.	Mild; lake partially frozen over.
26	12	S.	Light snow; lake frozen over.
27	14	......	Cloudy; light snow.
28	−12	N.	Bright and clear.
29	−20	N.	" " "
30	−24	N.	" " "
Dec. 1	−30	N.	Cloudy; strong wind.
2	−22	N.	Storming.
3	−21	N.	"
4	−10	N.	Cloudy.
5	−10	N.	Bright and clear.
6	−10	N.	Cloudy.
7	−33	N.	Bright and clear.
8	−31	N.	Bright and clear; high wind.
9	−31	N.	Cloudy and storming; strong wind.
10	−30	N.	Cloudy and storming; strong wind.
11	−22	N.	Cloudy and storming; strong wind.
12	−14	N.	Cloudy and storming; strong wind.
13	−24	N.	Cloudy and storming; strong wind.
14	−12	N.	Cloudy and storming; strong wind.
15	−4	N.	Cloudy and storming; strong wind.
16	−20	N.	Bright and clear; strong wind.
17	−37	S.	Cloudy.
18	−28	N.	Bright and clear.
19	−34	N.	Cloudy.
20	−32	N.	Bright and clear.
21	−28	N.	" " "
22	−32	N.	" " "
23	−22	N.	" " "
24	10	N.	Cloudy; light snowstorm.
25	8	N.	Bright and clear.
26	−18	N.	" " "
27	−42	S.	" " "

Date.	Minimum Temperature.	Direction of Wind.	Remarks.
1879.	°		
Dec. 28	−38	N.	Bright and clear.
29	−11	N.	Cloudy.
30	−3	N.	
31	−5	N.	Snowing and drifting.
1880.			
Jan. 1	−18	N.	Bright and clear.
2	−27	N.	" "
3	−33	N.	Cloudy, drifting.
4	−22	N.	" "
5	−23	N.	Bright and clear; at noon −30°.
6	−45	N.	Bright and Clear.
7	−43	N.	Cloudy.
8	−43	N.	Bright and clear.
9	−45	N.	" " "
10	−44	N.	" " "
11	−45	N.	" " "
12	−44	N.	" " "
13	−40	N.	" " "
14	−30	N.	" " "
15	−28	N.	Storming and drifting.
16	−25	N.	" "
17	−41	N.	Bright and clear.
18	−26	N.	Cloudy.
19	−10	S.	Cloudy; light wind.
20	8	S.	Bright and clear.
21	4	S.	Cloudy; light snow in p.m.
22	0	S.	Bright and clear; heavy S. gale last night.
23	−12	S.	Bright and clear.
24	−10	N.	" " "
25	−30	N.	" " "
26	−40	N.	" " "
27	−43	N.	
28	−14	S.	Light snow; 8 a.m., 0°.
29	−4	S.	Cloudy.
30	12	S.	"
31	14	S.	"
Feb. 1	16	S.	Bright and clear: light snow last night.
2	10	S.	Cloudy.
3	24	S.	Very soft.
4	0	S.	Very soft; at noon, 12°.
5	4	S.	Very soft.
6	−14	N.	Bright and clear.
7	−22	......	" "
8	8	S.	Cloudy.
9	2	......	Bright and clear.
10	−18	......	" " "
11	−12	......	
12	0	N.	Cloudy; S. wind p.m.
13	−12	S.	Cloudy.
14	−14	N.	Bright and clear.
15	−14	N.	" "
16	−38	N.	
17	−12	N.	Cloudy; light snowfall.
18	−12	N.	Bright and clear.
19	......	......	Heavy snowstorm.
20	12	S.	Storming all day; heavy snows last night.
21	12	S.	Heavy snowstorm last night.
22	18	......	
23	−8	......	Bright and clear.
24	......	......	
25	......	......	Bright and clear; high wind.
26	−42	N.	Bright and clear.
27	−10	N.	Cloudy, mild.
28	4	S.	Light wind.
29	0	N.	Bright and clear.
Mar. 1	−34	N.	Bright and clear; 4 p.m., −7°.

Date.	Minimum Temperature.	Direction of Wind.	Remarks.
1880.	°		
Mar. 2	−39	N.	Bright and clear: 4 p.m., −2°.
3	−34	N.	Strong wind; bright and clear; 4 p.m., −8°.
4	−32	N.	Strong wind; bright and clear; 4 p.m., 12°.
5	−34	N.	Bright and clear; 4 p.m., −16°.
6	−14	N.	Bright and clear; 4 p.m., −12°.
7	−24	N.	Bright and clear: 4 p.m., 2°.
8	−12	N.	Storming all day; 30° above zero.
9	14	N.	Cloudy; strong wind last night.
10	8	N.	Bright and clear: strong wind.
11	−27	......	Bright and clear.
Nov. 1	......	......	Mild: light snowfall.
2	......	N.W.	" " "
3	......	N.W.	Mild.
4	......	N.	Very mild; raining.
5	......	N.	Very mild; heavy rain.
6	......	N.	Heavy fall of snow.
7	......	N.	Very mild.
8	12	N.	Mild, cloudy.
9	0	N.	" "
10	0	N.	" "
11	12	N.	Mild; raining in evening.
12	......	N.	Mild; rain.
13	......	S.	Mild.
14	......	N.	Mild: summer weather.
15	26	N.	Frosty, beautiful morning
16	14	N.	Cloudy; fine weather.
17	14	N.	Clear and bright.
18	14	N.	" " "
19	8	N.	Cloudy: light snowfall.
20	11	N.	" "
21	22	N.	Cloudy.
22	18	N.	Cloudy and mild.
23	13	N.	" " "
24	7	N.	Cloudy and mild; snowing in evening.
25	15	S.	
26	13	N.	Cloudy.
27	15	N.	Bright and clear.
28	10	S.	Cloudy; lake partially frozen.
29	18	S.	High winds: ice broken up.
30	21	N.	Strong wind.
Dec. 1	4	N.	Bright and clear; high wind.
2	−14	N.	Cloudy: lake partially frozen.
3	−15	N.	Cloudy; light snow; lake frozen over.
4	−6	N.	Cloudy; high wind.
5	−10	N.	Bright and clear; crossed lake on ice.
6	−20	N.	Bright and clear; strong wind.
7	−19	N.	Cloudy; strong wind.
8	−14	N.	Cloudy; drifting; light snow.
9	−18	N.	Storming and drifting.
10	−2	N.	
11	12	S.	
12	5	N.	Light snow.
13	4	S.	
14	15	S.	
15	−8	N.	
16	−14	N.	Cloudy: drifting.

Date.	Minimum Temperature.	Direction of Wind.	Remarks.
1880.	°		
Dec. 17	—15	N.	Bright and clear.
18	—12	N.	Bright and clear; south wind p.m.
19	—11	N.	Bright and clear; 8 p.m., —20°.
20	—23	N.	Bright and clear.
21	—18	N.	"
22	—21	N.	"
23	—21	N.	Cloudy.
24	—13	N.	Bright and clear.
25	—14	N.	"
26	—21	N.	Bright and clear; very heavy wind.
27	—21	N.	Bright and clear; very heavy wind.
28	—22	N.	Bright and clear; very heavy wind.
29	—16	N.	Cloudy.
30	—10	N.	Bright and clear.
31	6	S.	Light snowfall.
1881.			
Jan. 1	14	S.	
2	10	S.	
3	14	S.	Light snowfall.
4	4	S.	
5	5	N.	Light snowfall; cloudy.
6	6	N.	"
7	4	S.	
8	9	S.	Bright and clear.
9	4	S.	Cloudy; snowfall last night.
10	—2	N.	Windy; drifting.
11	—17	N.	Bright and clear.
12	—24	N.	Bright and clear; 5 p.m., —25°.
13	—29	N.	Cloudy.
14	—28	N.	Bright and clear.
15	—20	S.	Cloudy; noon, 0°.
16	2	S.	Cloudy.
17	2	N.	Bright and clear.
18	2	N.	
19	15	N.	Cloudy; light snow.
20	2	S.	Cloudy.
21	10	S.	Bright and clear.
22	20	N.	Cloudy.
23	10	N.	Bright and clear.
24	0	N.	"
25	—20	N.	
26	—17	N.	Cloudy.
27	—1	N.	Bright and clear.
28	—28	N.	"
29	—30	N.	
30	—34	S.	Cloudy.
31	—10	N.	Cloudy; light snow; drifting.
Feb. 1	—2	N.	Snowing and drifting.
2	—22	N.	Cloudy.
3	—14	N.	Snowing and drifting; heavy storm.
4	—19	N.	Bright and clear.
5	—14	N.	"
6	—10	N.	"
7	—14	N.	"
8	—16	N.	"
9	—12	N.	"
10	—12	N.	"
11	—11	N.	Cloudy.
12	—0	N.	Cloudy; clear p.m.
13	—8	N.	Bright and clear; windy.
14	—30	N.	Bright and clear.
15	—25	S.	Cloudy.
16	4	S.	Cloudy and light snow.
17	4	S.	Light snow.
18	6	N.	Light snow; drifting.

Date.	Minimum Temperature.	Direction of Wind.	Remarks.
1881.	°		
Feb. 19	—1	N.	Heavy snow-storm; drifting.
20	—29	N.	Bright and clear.
21	—37	N.	
22	—37	N.	Cloudy; drifting.
23	—4	N.	Heavy snowfall.
24	—16	N.	Bright and clear.
25	—37	N.	"
26	—38	N.	"
27	—5	N.	Cloudy.
28	—6	N.	Cloudy and drifting.
Mar. 1	—5	N.	Bright and clear.
2	0	S.	"
3	6	S.	Cloudy; light snow.
4	6	S.	Cloudy.
5	4	S.	Cloudy; snowfall p.m.
6	10	S.	Cloudy.
7	4	N.	"
8	2	S.	Cloudy; snow storm p.m.
9	2	N.	Cloudy; high wind.
10	0	S.	Bright and calm; light snow in evening.
11	8	S.	Light snow.
12	6	N.	"
13	—18	S.	Cloudy.
14	18	N.	Cloudy; light snow.
15	17	S.	Cloudy.
16	12	N.	"
17	7	N.	Snow-storm; drifting.
18	6	N.	Cloudy.
19	12	S.	Light snow; heavy thaw.
20	24	S.	Spring weather.
21	24	S.	
22	20	S.	
23	—2	S.	
24	8	S.	Bright and clear.
25	—6	S.	"
26	0	S.	"
27	above zero.	S.	Cloudy; light snow.
28	"	S.	Snow-storm; drifting; strong wind.
29	"	N.	Snowstorm; drifting; strong wind.
30	"	N.	Rain in evening.
31	"	N.	
May 25	......	......	Creek commenced to rise.
30	......	......	Highest water.
June 4	......	......	First trip of steamer to Thibert Creek.
			Very cold, wet summer.
Sep. 27	......	......	Snowfall in evening.
Oct. 6	......	......	Light snowfall.
21	......	......	
22	......	......	Rain.
23	......	......	
26	......	......	Very mild.
Nov. 1	26	S.	Light snow.
2	28	S.	Heavy rain last night.
3	31	S.	Snow all gone.
4	25	N.	Very light snow.
5	25	N.	"
6	23	S.	"
7	23	S.	"
8	19	S.	"
9	20	S.	Strong wind.
10	29	S.	
11	18	S.	Heavy snow; storming all day.
12	8	N.	Heavy winds.
13	3	N.	Heavy winds; drifting.
14	—5	N.	Bright and clear.
15	—15	N.	"
16	—20	N.	Cloudy; at noon, —4°.

Date.	Minimum Temperature.	Direction of Wind.	Remarks.
1881.	°		
Nov. 17	—4	N.	Lake partially frozen over.
18	20	S.	Heavy snowfall.
19	12	N.	Light snow.
20	21	S.	Bright and clear.
21	6	N.	Lake frozen opp. town.
22	3	N.	
23	10	S.	At noon, 34°.
24	23	S.	At noon, 38°; rain.
25	26	S.	Raining.
26	31	S.	Raining.
27	13	S.	Bright and clear; Indian crossed ice.
28	18	S.	Snowstorm.
29	18	N.	Bright and clear.
30	2	N.	Cloudy; lake nearly all frozen.
Dec. 1	16	S.	Ice broken up between town and Thibert Cr.
2	13	S.	Strong wind.
3	3	S.	Cloudy.
4	3	S.	Bright and clear.
5	0	S.	Light snowfall.
6	1	S.	Bright and clear.
7	5	S.	Heavy fog in morn.; p.m. clear.
8	—9	S.	Heavy fog in morn.; p.m. clear.
9	—0	S.	Light snow, drifting.
10	—14	S.	Bright and clear.
11	—21	S.	" " "
12	—11	S.	" " "
13	—25	N.	" " "
14	—20	N.	Cloudy.
15	—20	N.	Light snowfall.
16	—15	S.	Light snowfall; drifting.
17	7	S.	Bright and clear.
18	5	S.	" " "
19	22	S.	Heavy wind; drifting; heavy snow-storm.
20	8	S.	Bright and clear.
21	—7	N.	Cloudy.
22	—6	N.	Bright and clear.
23	—3	N.	Cloudy.
24	10	N.	
25	25	S.	
26	23	S.	
27	—5	N.	Bright and clear.
28	—10	N.	" " "
29	—5	N.	" " "
30	—10	N.	Cloudy.
31	—10	N.	Heavy snow-storm; drifting.
1882.			
Jan. 1	—15	N.	Cloudy.
2	—23	N.	Bright and clear.
3	—14	N.	" " "
4	—17	N.	" " "
5	—20	N.	Cloudy.
6	—11	S.	Cloudy; light snow.
7	—4	S.	Cloudy.
8	0	S.	" "
9	6	N.	Light snowfall.
10	—11	N.	Bright and clear.
11	—8	N.	Cloudy; light snowfall.
12	5	S.	Beautiful morning, like spring.
13	25	S.	Bright and clear; heavy rain last night.
14	—17	N.	Bright and clear.
15	—20	N.	Cloudy; light snow.
16	29	S.	Heavy rain, turning to snow.
17	25	S.	Heavy rain; light snow.
1882.	°		
Jan. 18	7	S.	Cloudy; snowfall.
19	20	S.	Cloudy, snowfall; rain in evening.
20	—1	N.	Cloudy; snowfall.
21	—13	N.	Cloudy.
22	—1	N.	Bright and clear.
23	—2	S.	" " "
24	—13	N.	Drifting.
25	—16	N.	Bright and clear.
26	—17	N.	" " "
27	—17	S.	Cloudy.
28	—20	S.	" "
29	15	S.	Strong wind.
30	10	S.	
31	5	S.	Strong wind; drifting.
Feb. 1	3	S.	Bright and clear.
2	—1	N.	" " "
3	6	S.	Cloudy.
4	6	S.	Bright and clear.
5	—4	S.	Drifting.
6	—3	S.	" "
7	—12	N.W	Very heavy drifting and snowing.
8	—11	N.	Drifting.
9	—25	N.	Bright and clear.
10	—20	N.	Cloudy; drifting.
11	—42	N.	Cloudy.
12	—20	N.	Light snow.
13	—10	N.	Heavy snow, drifting.
14	—14	N.	Storm.
15	—41	N.	Bright and clear.
16	—52	N.	" " "
17	—24	S.	" " "
18	—21	S.	Cloudy; weather changed.
19	—11	S.	Strong wind.
20	1	S.	Cloudy.
21	28	S.	Cloudy; strong wind.
22	12	S.	Cloudy.
23	—26	N.	Bright and clear.
24	—14	N.	Cloudy.
25	—3	N.	" "
26	—11	N.	Very strong wind; drifting.
27	—15	N.	Heavy wind; drifting.
28	—6	N.	Cloudy.
Mar. 1	—1	N.	Storming.
2	—26	N.	Bright and clear.
3	—31	N.	" " "
4	—3	N.	" " "
5	—25	S.	Cloudy.
6	4	S.	Bright and clear.
7	9	S.	Very fine.
8	13	S.	" "
9	—18	S.	Bright and clear.
10	—14	S.	Very fine.
11	0	S.	Rain in evening.
12	15	N.	Cold wind.
13	2	N.	
14	—3	N.	Bright and clear.
15	—26	N.	" " "
16	—4	N.	High wind.
17	—22	N.	Very cold wind.
18	—29	N.	bright and clear; strong wind.
19	—33	N.	Bright and clear.
20	—34	N.	Drifting; cold wind.
21	—16	N.	
22	—40	N.	Bright and clear.
23	—8	N.	Heavy storm; snowing and drifting.
24	5	N.	Heavy fall of snow.
25	14	N.	Storming; snow.
26	8	N.	Cloudy.
27	10	N.	Heavy snowfall all day.

Date.	Minimum Temperature.	Direction of Wind.	Remarks.	Date.	Minimum Temperature.	Direction of Wind.	Remarks.
1882.	°			1882.	°		
Mar. 28	—17	N.	Bright and clear.	Apr. 12	—2	S	Cloudy; cold wind.
29	—39	N.	" " "	13	—5	....	" " "
30	—39	N.	" " "	14	14	S.	" " "
31	—20	N.	High wind; drifting.	15	23	S.S.	" " "
April 1	2	N.	Cloudy; drifting.	16	27	S.S.	" " "
2	2	N.	Cloudy.	17	20	S.	Snowing and storming.
3	5	N.	High wind; drifting.	18	20	S.S.	Snowing in evening.
4	11	N.	Cloudy.	19	23	N.	Cloudy; cold wind.
5	11	N.	"	20	7	S.	Cloudy; storming in eve.
6	14	N.	Light snowfall all day.	21	22	W.	Storming; cold wind.
7	12	N.	Fine day.	22	24	S.	Bright and clear.
8	15	N.	Raw, cold wind.	23	2	S.S.N.	Cloudy; light snow drifting.
9	12	N.	Cloudy.	24	7	S.	Bright and clear.
10	20	S.	Bright and clear.				
11	—1	S.	Cloudy; cold wind.				

(4.) RECORD OF TEMPERATURE AT LAKETON, DEASE LAKE, B. C., DURING PORTIONS OF THE YEARS 1886 AND 1887, BY MR. ROBERT REED.

Date.	Minimum Temperature.
1886.	°
Nov. 20	—11
21	—21
22	—11
23	—14
24	—2
25	—1
26	—3
27	19 { Stormy.
28	16
29	14
30	7
Dec. 1	6
2	—4
3	—7
4	7
5	13
6	12
7	12
8	3
9	—2
10	3
11	—1
12	—5
13	1
14	—2
15	—7
16	—9
17	—18 { Lake frozen.
18	—16
19	—10
20	—8
21	—6

Date.	Minimum Temperature.
1886.	°
Dec. 22	—30
23	—44
24	—34
25	—30
26	—41
27	—40
28	—34
29	—43
30	—38
31	—35
1887.	
Jan. 1	—32
2	—25
3	—13
4	—13
5	—10
6	—23
7	8
8	10
9	11
10	—5
11	—6
12	8
13	—7
14	—28
15	—35
16	—51
17	—32
18	—27
19	—23
20	—20
21	—46
22	—39

Date.	Minimum Temperature.
1887.	°
Jan. 23	—30
24	—28
25	—34
26	—9
27	—40
28	—61
29	—61
30	—52
31	—52
Feb. 1	—12
2	—47
3	—56
4	—48
5	—37
6	—38
7	—5
8	—31
9	—40
10	—27
11	—23
12	—3
13	—31
14	—32
15	—1
16	—14
17	—33
18	—2
19	—21
20	—32
21	—35
22	—5
23	—23
24	—43
25	—45

Date.	Minimum Temperature.
1887.	°
Feb. 26	—40
27	—30
28	—31
Mar. 1	—55
2	—49
3	—13
4	—9
5	—15
6	—45
7	—32
8	—28
9	—15
10	—41
11	—31
12	—22
13	—12
14	—13
15	—7
16	—10
17	—5
18	—12
19	2
20	4
21	18
22	25
23	—20
24	—9
25	—2
26	—8
27	8
28	11

SUMMARY OF ASTRONOMICAL OBSERVATIONS BY DR. G. M. DAWSON, EMPLOYED IN THE CONSTRUCTION OF THE MAP ACCOMPANYING THIS REPORT.

NOTE.—The angular instrument employed was a sextant of seven inch radius, Cary, No. 938. The longitudes of places on the map depend on two small chronometers, Frodsham, No. 06859, and Arnold, No. 9699, running mean and sidereal time respectively. The first-mentioned was employed in taking time in all the observations, and has been given double weight in longitude determinations beyond Telegraph Creek, as it was an instrument of higher class than No. 9699, and proved to be extremely trustworthy. The chronometers were rated wherever possible, as shown in the annexed note. No. 9699 changed its rate suddenly on one occasion, in consequence apparently of a slight jar received on Finlayson Lake, but subsequently recovered a satisfactory rate. The longitude of the site of Fort Selkirk on the map depends entirely on that brought round by our route from Wrangell, as we are still in possession of the preliminary plotting only, of Mr. Ogilvie's Lewes River traverse. (See foot note on p. 276 B.)

The chronometers, in their cases, were packed together in a padded leather-covered box, which was invariably handled and transported with the greatest care. Comparisons were made throughout the journey on every second day at 8 P.M., approximate local mean time.

General Note on Rates of Chronometers, determined at Esquimalt, Dease Lake, Frances Lake and Camp near site of Fort Selkirk.

Frodsham, No. 06859, running mean time.
 Rate determined on board H. M. S. *Triumph*,
  at Esquimalt, May 4-9 . . . . ·2   seconds daily, losing.
 Dease Lake, June 5-7 by obsn . . . . ·37   "   "   "
 Frances Lake, July 11-16 by obsn . . . . ·48   "   "   "
 Camp near site of Fort Selkirk, Aug. 13-17,
  by obsn . . . . ·625 "   "   "

Arnold, No. 9699, running sidereal time. Rate given on mean time, and including the daily difference between sideral and mean time (=3 m. 56.555 s.)
Rate determined on board H.M.S. *Tri-*

 umph, at Esquimalt, May 4-9.... 3′ 53″·45 seconds daily, losing.
Dease Lake, June 5-7, by obsn........ 3′ 54″·078 " " "
Frances Lake, July 11-16, by obsn.... 3′ 54″·82 " " "
Camp near site of Fort Selkirk, Aug.
 13-17, by obsn................... 3′ 52″·6 " " "

(Chronometer received a slight shock since last determination of rate, which
accounts for its sudden change.)

Wrangell, Alaska, May 19, 1887.

	h.	m.	s.				
Frodsham, 06859.....	1	12	51·5	Obs. alt. ☉.....	88°	5′	20″
	1	15	03·5		88	34	30
	1	17	24.5		89	5	10
	1	18	12·5		89	15	30
	1	20	0		89	38	30
	1	21	42·5		90	1	30
	1	23	20·5		90	21	55

Index error and eccentricity............................. —2 9
Taking latitude of observation spot as 56° 28′ 18″, from
 U. S. Pacific Coast Pilot, Alaska, Part I, 1883.
Chron. 06859 fast .... 3h. 49m. 03s.

River-bank near site of H. B. Co.'s old post, Stikine R., May 21, 1887.

	h.	m.	s.				
Frodsham, 06859.....	1	5	17	Obs. alt. ☉.....	86°	57′	35″
	1	7	16		87	24	10
	1	8	26		87	38	50
	1	9	44		87	56	20
	1	10	41		88	8	30

Index error and eccentricity........................ —2 31
Chron. 06859 fast .... 3h. 46m. 33·4s.

	h.	m.	s.			
Frodsham, 06859.....	3	48	28·5	106°	48′	0″
	3	50	10·5	106	46	40
	3	51	15	106	45	10

Index error and eccentricity .... —1 52·5
Resulting latitude from above two series of observations.. 57 8 1
Longitude by Frodsham, 06859...................... 131 46 45

Glenora, Stikine River, May 23, 1887.

Jupiter, obs. merid. alt........................... 46° 4′ 5″
Index error and eccentricity....................... —3 49
∴ Latitude 57 50 10

Telegraph Creek, Stikine River, May 27, 1887.

Jupiter, obs. merid. alt........................... 46° 7′ 25″
Index error and eccentricity....................... —3 44
∴ Latitude...................................... 57 55 0

Telegraph Creek, May 28, 1887.

```
                         h.  m.   s.
Frodsham, 06859.....    12  27  16·5      Obs. alt. ☉.....   79°  55'   0"
                        12  28  21·5                         80   10  40
                        12  29  49                           80   31  40
                        12  31  29                           80   55  30
Index error and eccentricity............................      —2  48
∴ Frodsham, 06859, fast................................ 3h. 44m. 06·1s.
```

Telegraph Creek, May 29, 1887.

```
                         h.  m.   s.
Frodsham, 06859.....     2   0  22        Obs. alt. ☉.....   99°  25'   0"
                         2   2  28·5                         99   45  10
                         2   4   3                          100    0   0
                         2   6  12                          100   20   0
                         2   8  23                          100   40  10
Index error and eccentricity............................      —2  39
∴ Frodsham, 06859, fast................................ 3h. 44m. 04·5.s.
```

Telegraph Creek, May 29, 1887.

```
Obs. meridian alt. ☉........................................ 108°   5'  50"
Index error and eccentricity................................      —2  23
∴ Latitude ...............................................    57   54  56
```

Telegraph Creek, May 29, 1887.

```
                         h.  m.   s.
Frodsham, 06859.....     5  25  39        Obs. alt. ☉.....   99°   0'  50"
                         5  26  37                           98   41  10
                         5  27  51                           98   28  50
                         5  29  32·5                         98   11  55
                         5  30  44·5                         97   59  20
Index error and eccentricity............................      —2  42
∴ Frodsham, 06859, fast................................ 3h. 44m. 07·2s.
```

Telegraph Creek, May 30, 1887.

```
                         h.  m.   s.
Frodsham, 06859.....     6  37  51·5      Obs. alt. ☉.....   84°  34'  50"
                         6  39  51·5                         84    6  30
                         6  41  26                           83   44  55
                         6  43   3·5                         83°  22'  10"
                         6  45   2·5                         82   54   0
Index and eccentricity..................................      —2  42
∴ Frodsham, 06859, fast................................ 3.h. 43m. 56·4s.
```

Telegraph Creek, Stikine River (summary).

Diff. in long. between Fort Wrangell and Telegraph Creek,
by comparing two a.m. sets of observations :

Frodsham, 06859.. 1° 13′ 40″
∴ Chron. long. of Telegraph Creek 131 10 20
Latitude adopted 57 55 58

NOTE.—By Hunter's surveyed line, continued by that of McConnell to Telegraph Creek, the longitude, depending on observation point at Wrangell, (long. 132° 24′ 00″) is 131° 10′ 05″. As the chronometers were subjected to exceptional conditions while ascending the Stikine by steamer, this longitude is adopted for Telegraph Creek in preference to that resulting from observations.

Head of Dease Lake, June 5, 1887.

	h.	m.	s.				
Frodsham, 06859.....	6	32	22	Obs. alt. ⊙.....	85°	45′	40″
	6	33	44		85	27	0
	6	34	55·5		85	11	0
	6	36	2·5		84	55	20
	6	37	23		84	37	5
	6	38	30		84	21	50

Index error and eccentricity................................   −2 53
∴ Frodsham, 06859, fast .... 3h. 39m. 18.5s.

Head of Dease Lake, June 5, 1887.

	h.	m.	s.				
Frodsham, 06859....	3	29	34	Obs. alt. ⊙.....	108°	57′	15″
	3	30	38		108	58	10
	3	31	59		108	58	40
	3	33	45·5		109	0	20
	3	34	56		109	0	55
	3	36	8		109	1	5
	3	37	27		109	1	25
	3	38	21·5		109	1	30
	3	39	25·5		109	1	15
	3	41	11		109	0	35
	3	42	53		108	59	10
	3	44	14		108	58	30
	3	45	52		108	57	35
	3	47	14		108	56	40

Index error and eccentricity............................   −2 2
∴ Latitude .... 58 28 17·3

Head of Dease Lake, June 7, 1887.

Obs. merid. alt. ⊙ .... 109° 13′ 15″
Index error and eccentricity.................................   −2 1·5
∴ Latitude 58 28 6

	h.	m.	s.				
Frodsham, 06859.....	6	56	34	Obs. alt. ⊙.....	80°	33′	30″
	6	57	47		80	15	20
	6	58	38·5		80	2	50
	6	59	40		79	48	10
	7	0	40		79	33	25

Index error and eccentricity................................   −2 50
∴ Frodsham, 06859, fast .... 3h. 39m. 17·8s.

Head of Dease Lake (summary).

Diff. in long. between Telegraph Creek and head of Dease Lake:

Frodsham, 06859...................................... 1° 10′ 34″·5
Arnold, 9699.. 1   9 54·5
Adopted diff.. 1 10 20

NOTE.—Here, and subsequently throughout, double value is assigned to Frodsham, 06859.

∴ Chron. long. of head of Dease Lake...............=130° 0′ 00″

NOTE.—This longitude depends directly on Wrangell by chronometers. Taking into consideration the corrected longitude for Telegraph Creek, and assuming a mean value as between chronometer longitude and longitude by paced traverse from Telegraph Creek to head of Dease Lake, the longitude of head of lake is found to be 130° 2′ 0″, which is adopted.   Subsequent longitudes along the line of traverse are made to depend fundamently on this position.

Adopted latitude, from series of circum-meridian altitudes, June 5, 1887, 58° 28′ 17″·3.

Laketon, Dease Lake, June 17, 1887.

		h.	m.	s.					
Frodsham, 06859...∴		1	18	2	Obs. alt. ☉.....	93°	55′	5″
		1	21	33		94	37	0
		1	23	35		95	1	30
		1	25	44		95	26	30
		1	29	5·5		96	5	20
		1	30	2		96	16	0
		1	31	56		96	37	45

Index error and eccentricity....................................   −2 19
∴ Frodsham, 06859, fast ....   3h. 39m. 26s.

		h.	m.	s.					
Frodsham, 06859.....		3	42	31·5	Obs. alt. ☉.....	109°	57′	30″
		3	43	51		109	57	0
		3	45	16·5		109	56	20
		3	46	47		109	55	35

Index error and eccentricity..............................   −1 50

		h.	m.	s.					
Frodsham, 06859.....		8	14	20·75	Obs. alt. ☉.....	62°	24′	50″
		8	16	10·5		61	56	40
		8	17	16·5		61	39	5
		8	19	2·75		61	12	0
		8	20	1·5		60	56	50
		8	21	1·3		60	36	0

Index error and eccentricity...............................   −3 9
Resulting adopted lat. from second and third series of observations 58 42 20

By last observation :

Frodsham, 06859, fast ....   3h. 39m. 16s.
Diff. in long. between Laketon and head of lake by long bearings ....   3′ 32″
∴ Resulting adopted long. of Laketon.................   130° 5′ 32″

Sta. I, Dease River, June 19, 1887.

    Obs. merid. alt. ☉.................................... 109° 34′ 15″
    Index error and eccentricity.......................... —2   3
    ∴ Latitude... 58 56 38·9

Sta. U, Dease River, June 20, 1887.

    Obs. merid. alt. ☉.................................... 109° 13′ 50″
    Index error and eccentricity.......................... —2 03
    ∴ Latitude... 50   7 25·6

Sta. E, Dease River, June 21, 1887.

    Obs. merid. alt. ☉.................................... 108° 49′ 45″
    Index error and eccentricity.......................... —2   0
    ∴ Latitude... 59 19 35·2

Sta. M, June 22, 1887.

	h.	m.	s.		°	′	″
Frodsham, 06859.....	10	17	13	Obs. alt. ☉.....	50°	38′	40″
	10	19	17		51	0	50
	10	20	18		51	26	0
	10	21	2·25		51	37	0

    Index error and eccentricity......................... —3   1
    ∴ Frodsham, 06859, fast.............................. 3h. 36m. 16s.
    Lat. for above observation from traverse............. 59° 34′   0″
    Diff. in long. between place and head of Dease Lake, Frod-
        sham, 06859...................................... 44   0
    ∴ Chron. long. of place.............................. 129 18   0

Sta. U 2, Dease River, June 22, 1887.

    Obs. merid. alt. ☉.................................... 108° 4′ 15″
    Index error and eccentricity.......................... 1 57·3
    ∴ Latitude... 59 42   5·8

Lower Post, mouth of Dease River, June 25, 1887.

	h.	m.	s.		°	′	″
Frodsham, 06859.....	1	21	35	Obs. alt. ☉.....	93°	55′	25″
	1	22	46		94	8	0
	1	23	25·5		94	15	35
	1	24	8		94	23	50
	1	25	37		94	40	5
	1	26	41·5		94	51	30
	1	27	22		94	58	30
	1	28	6		95	6	20
	1	29	2		95	16	20

    Index error and eccentricity......................... —2 16·5
    ∴ Frodsham, 06859, fast.............................. 3h. 32m. 0·8s.

NOTE.—This series of observations was not employed in determining long.,
the sun being too near meridian.

	h.	m.	s.				
Frodsham, 06859......	3	19	34	Obs. alt. ⊙.....	107°	17′	20″
	3	20	24		107	18	50
	3	21	24		107	20	40
	3	22	44·5		107	22	5

Index error and eccentricity ....   —1 51
By a.m. obsn. and last, with interval of time.
Latitude .... 59 55 56·7

	h.	m.	s.				
Frodsham, 06859......	3	37	31	Obs. alt. ⊙.....	107°	30′	10″
	3	38	30		107	29	20

Index error and eccentricity ....   —1 51
By a.m. obsn., and this, with interval of time.
Latitude 59 55 55

Difference in long. between place and head of Dease Lake:
Frodsham, 06859...... ....   1° 32′ 24″
Arnold,   9699........... ....   1 30 40·5
Mean, (giving double value to Frodsham) 1 31 50
∴ Chron. long. of place 128 30 10
Long. ascertained by bearings carried through
   by Dease River........................... .   128 35 10 adopted

Sta. I, Cañon on Upper Liard River, June 26, 1887.

Obs. merid. alt. ⊙ .... 107° 16′ 20″
Index error and eccentricity......... ....   —1 58
∴ Latitude............ 60   1   6·2

Sta. P, Upper Liard River, June 27, 1887.

Obs. merid. alt. ⊙...... .... 107° 6′ 30″
Index error and eccentricity........ ....   —1 58·5
∴ Latitude..... 60   3 43·7

Sta. Y, Upper Liard River (confluence of Frances R.), June 29, 1887.
Obs. merid. alt. ⊙........................... .... 106° 29′ 10″
Index error and eccentricity............... ....   —2 19·5
∴ Latitude .... 60 16 35·3

Sta. F, Frances River, June 30, 1887.

	h.	m.	s.				
Frodsham, 06859......	9	10	54	Obs. alt. ⊙.....	47°	30′	25″
	9	11	49·5		47	17	10
	9	12	38·5		47	5	15
	9	13	25·5		46	53	45
	9	14	12·5		46	41	50
	9	15	1·5		46	30	0
	9	16	21		46	10	50

Index error and eccentricity.... ....   — 3 19
∴ Frodsham, 06859, fast .... 3h. 35m. 38·8s.
Lat. for above obsn. by traverse.... .... 60° 26′   0″
∴ Long. by Frodsham, 06859...... .... 129 11 46

Sta. H, Frances River, July 1, 1887.

	h.	m.	s.				
Frodsham, 06859.....	3	42	45·5	Obs. alt. ☉.....	105°	53′	0″
	3	44	9·5		105	52	30
	3	45	23·5		105	52	10
	3	46	12·5		105	51	20

Index error and eccentricity...... ....   —2   0
With time by last observation and long. of traverse,
Latitude...... 60   27   28

Sta. W, Frances River, July 3, 1887.

Obs. merid. alt. ☉......... ... . 105° 10′ 45″
Index error and eccentricity....... .. ..   —2   0
∴ Latitude..... 60   39   15·1
Note.—Observation fair only.

Sta. E, Frances River, July 4, 1887.

Obs. merid. alt. ☉..... .... 104° 41′ 50″
Index error and eccentricity..... ....   —2   15·5
∴ Latitude............... 60   47   53·4

Sta. P, Frances River, July 7, 1887.

Obs. merid. alt. ☉........... .... 103° 24′ 35″
Index error eccentricity.................. ....   —2   18
∴ Latitude...... 61   9   25

Cȧche Camp, Frances Lake, near mouth of Finlayson River, July 11, 1887.

	h.	m.	s.				
Frodsham, 06859.....	12	45	32	Obs. alt. ☉.....	81°	15′	30″
	12	46	41		81	28	50
	12	48	23		81	49	20
	12	49	15		82	0	0
	12	50	55		82	20	0
	12	52	36		82	40	0
	12	54	18		83	0	0
	12	56	1		83	20	0

Index error and eccentricity..........................   —3   17
∴ Frodsham, 06859, fast...................... .... 3h. 37m. 23s·9.

Cȧche Camp, Frances Lake, July 7, 1887.

	h.	m.	s.				
Frodsham, 06859.....	3	35	33·5	Obs. alt. ☉.....	101°	43′	40″
	3	36	32		101	44	25
	3	37	19		101	44	50
	3	38	16·5		101	45	0
	3	39	26		101	45	20
	3	40	24·5		101	45	40
Approx. app. noon					101	45	50
	3	43	20		101	45	30
	3	45	26		101	45	10

```
                          h.  m.   s.
                          3   46   36·5                      101  45   5
                          3   47   58                        101  44   30
                          3   49   1·5                       101  44   0
                          3   50   53                        101  42   40
```

Index error and eccentricity ....   −2   38
∴ Latitude 61   29   22

Câche Camp, Frances Lake, July 11, 1887.

```
                          h.   m.   s.
Frodsham, 06859 .....     6    29   1·5    Obs. alt. .....☉  83°  20′  0″
                          6    30   44                      83   0    0
                          6    22   23                      82   40   0
                          6    34   7·5                     82   20   0
                          6    35   45                      82   0    0
                          6    38   20                      81   28   50
```

Index error and eccentricity ....   − 3   16
∴ Frodsham, 06859, fast ....   3h. 37m. 29s.

Câche Camp, Frances Lake, July 16, 1887.

```
                          h.   m.   s.
Frodsham, 06859 .....     10   55   18    Obs. alt ☉.....   55°  5′   50″
                          10   56   18·5                    55   20   45
                          10   57   35                      55   38   30
                          10   58   31·5                    55   52   10
                          10   59   11                      56   2    35
                          11   0    6                       56   14   45
                          11   1    31                      56   34   30
```

Index error and eccentricity.................... ....   −3   40
∴ Frodsham, 06859, fast ....   3h. 37m. 22s.

Diff. in long. between place and head of Dease L. by mean of two first obsns.
Frodsham, 06859 ....   0° 23′ 36″
Arnold, 9699   0   21   22·5
Mean. (giving double value to Frodsham)....   0   22   51·5
∴ Chron. long. of place....   129   39   8·5 adopted.

Sta. P, Frances Lake, July 12, 1887.

Obs. merid. alt. ☉................... ....   101° 46′ 30″
Index error and eccentricity ....   −2   34
∴ Latitude   61   21   7·9

Sta. T, Finlayson Lake, July 24, 1887.

Obs. merid. alt. ☉..... ....   96° 53′ 30″
Index error and eccentricity.... ....   −2   37·6
∴ Latitude   61   40   12·9
                    Correction for temp. and pressure,—6.″

St. U, Finlayson Lake, 14″ south of last, July 24, 1887.

```
Frodsham, 06859 .....     9    43   48    Obs. alt. ☉.....   36°  0′   35″
                          9    44   47                       35   46   25
                          9    45   40                       35   34   0
```

	h.	m.	s.			
	9	46	37	35	20	50
	9	47	37·5	35	8	20
	9	48	20	34	56	30
	9	49	0	34	47	10

Index error and eccentricity............ .... —3   34
∴ Frodsham, 06859, fast .... 3h. 40m. 29s.

St. V, Finlayson Lake, July 25, 1887.

	h.	m.	s.				
Frodsham, 06859.....	12	51	45	Obs. alt. ☉....	77°	0′	0″
	12	52	47·5		77	12	5
	12	53	36·5		77	21	50
	12	54	25·5		77	31	0
	12	55	25		77	42	40
	12	56	13		77	52	10
	12	57	6·5		78	2	30
	12	57	47		78	10	25
	12	58	45		78	21	10

Index error and eccentricity......................... .... —3   23
∴ Frodsham, 06859, fast .... 3h. 40m. 46s.

Obs. merid. alt. ☉....... .... 96° 28′ 10″
Index error and eccentricity........................ .... —2   38
     Correction for temp. and pressure, —6.
∴ Latitude..... 61   40   0·6

Sta. V, Finlayson Lake (summary).

Mean of last obsn. and that of July 24. reduced to this point, gives,
  Latitude...... .... 61° 40′ 0″   adopted.
Diff. in long. between place and Câche Camp, Frances Lake:
  Frodsham, 03859.... .... 50′ 12″
  Arnold, 9699..... 46   51
  Mean, (giving double value to Frodsham).. 49   5
  ∴ Chron. long. of place .... 130° 28′ 13″.5
  Long. of place by traverse between Frances
     Lake and Pelly Banks.... 130   28   52
  Mean of this and chron. long............... 130   28   32·7   adopted.

Pelly River, First Camp, near site of Fort Pelly Banks, July 29, 1887.

	h.	m.	s.				
Frodsham, 06859.....	7	4	59	Obs. alt. ☉.....	70°	54′	30″
	7	6	46		70	32	35
	7	7	41·5		70	20	50
	7	8	33.5		70	10	0
	7	9	23		69	59	10
	7	10	14·5		69	48	30
	7	12	17		69	23	10
	7	13	15		69	11	10
	7	13	58		69	2	10

Index error and eccentricity............ .... —3   22
∴ Frodsham, 06859, fast .... 3h. 42m. 45s.

Pelly River, First Camp, July 29, 1887.

	h.	m.	s.					
Frodsham, 06859.....	7	57	32·5	Obs. alt. ☉.....	59°	1'	40''
	7	58	58·5		58	42	0
	7	59	46·5		58	31	10
	8	1	11		58	12	0
	8	2	19		57	55	50
	8	3	17		57	43	10
	8	3	58		57	33	30

Index error and eccentricity............................   −3 30
∴ Frodsham, 06359, fast .... 3h. 42m. 46s.

Pelly River, First Camp, July 31, 1887.

	h.	m.	s.					
Frodsham, 06859.....	12	36	49	Obs. alt. ☉.....	70°	54'	0''
	12	37	53		71	7	0
	12	38	56·5		71	19	30
	12	39	46		71	30	0
	12	40	31·5		71	38	40
	12	41	28		71	50	40
	12	42	31		72	2	55
	12	43	25·5		72	14	0
	12	44	23		72	25	20

Index error and eccentricity............................   −3 21
∴ Frodsham, 06859, fast .... 3h. 43m. 42s·9
Obs. approx. merid. alt. ☉...........................   93° 23' 10''
Index error and eccentricity............................   −2 42
∴ Latitude................... ....   61 48 59

	h.	m.	s.					
Frodsham. 06859.....	3	54	7·5	Obs. alt. ☉.....	93°	21'	50''
	3	55	12		93	21	20
	3	56	34		93	20	40
	3	57	50		93	19	15

Index error and eccentricity............................   −2 42''·5

	h.	m.	s.					
Frodsham, 06859.....	7	45	57.5	Obs. alt. ☉.....	61°	11'	40''
	7	47	1		60	57	5
	7	48	19·5		60	39	10
	7	49	10·5		60	27	55
	7	50	8·5		60	15	10
	7	50	45·5		60	6	45
	7	51	25·5		59	57	50
	7	52	7·5		59	48	5
	7	53	5·5		59	35	30

Index error and eccentricity..................... ....   −3 29
∴ Frodsham, 06859, fast .... 3h. 42m. 45s·8

Pelly River, First Camp (summary).
By last two obsns., with interval of time:
Latitude................................. ...   61° 48' 52'' adopted.

Diff. in long. between Cache Camp, Frances L.
    and place by mean of sets of obsns.

Frodsham, 06859....	1	22	7·5
Arnold, 9699......	1	21	39
Mean, (giving double value to Frodsham)..	⌐1	21	·58
∴ Chron. long. of place....	131	1	6·5 adopted.

Sta. X, Pelly River, Aug. 2, 1887.

Obs. merid. alt. ☉ (fair only)...............	92° 30′ 20″
Index error and eccentricity..	—2 44
∴ Latitude......	61 44 52·5

Sta. G, Pelly River (Head of Hoole Cañon), Aug. 3, 1887.

Obs. merid. alt. ☉..........................	91° 48′ 0″
Index error and eccentricity...........	—2 41·5
∴ Latitude......	61 50 28

Sta. H, Pelly River (lower end Hoole Cañon), Aug. 4, 1887.

	h.	m.	s.				
Frodsham, 06859.....	9	49	41·5	Obs. alt. ☉.....	30°	17′	50″
	9	50	31		30	30	0
	9	51	26·5		30	42	30
	9	53	8		31	5	40
	9	54	41·5		31	27	25
	9	55	35		31	40	10
	9	56	26		31	52	10

Index error and eccentricity..........................	—3 25
∴ Frodsham, 06859, fast	3h. 46m. 47s·5

Note.—For above obsn., lat. employed determined by paced
    line from Sta. G...... .... 61° 50′ 48″·8
Long. by chronometers (giving double value to Frodsham) 132° 1′ 51″

Sta. B, Pelly River, Aug. 5, 1887.

Obs. merid. alt. ☉....................	90° 4′ 5″
Index error and eccentricity.........	—2 45
∴ Latitude......	62 10 20

Sta. L, Pelly River, Aug. 6, 1887.

Obs. merid. alt. ☉ (passing clouds, approx.)..............	89° 2′ 15″
Index error and eccentricity	—2 54
∴ Latitude....	62 24 53

Sta. C, Pelly River, Aug. 7, 1887.

Obs. merid. alt. ☉.........	87° 57′ 10″
Index error and eccentricity..........................	—2 54
∴ Latitude.............	62 40 41

Sta. N, Pelly River, Aug. 8, 1887.

Obs. merid. alt. ☉	87° 12′ 10″
Index error and eccentricity..........................	—2 41
∴ Latitude....	62 46 4

Sta. T, Pelly River (6 m. above Macmillan River), Aug. 8, 1887.

Frodsham, 06859.....	9	31	23·5	Obs. alt. ☉.....	37°	8′	10″
	9	32	21·5		36	55	10
	9	33	25		36	40	50
	9	34	18·5		36	28	20
	9	35	7·5		36	17	10
	9	35	59		36	5	30
	9	36	39		35	56	0
	9	37	34·5		35	44	0
	9	38	9		35	36	0

Index error and eccentricity............................   —3 19
∴ Frodsham, 06859, fast .... 4h. 1m. 29s.
NOTE—For above obsn. lat. employed determined by traverse 62° 48′ 10″
Long. by chronometers (giving double value to Frodsham) 135 44 25·5

Sta. O, Pelly River, Aug. 10, 1887.

Obs. merid. alt. ☉ (approx.)..................................... 85° 52′ 25″
Index error and eccentricity.....................................   —2 58
∴ Latitude...... .... 62 51 10

Observations near site of Fort Selkirk.

Three-quarters of a mile below Fort Selkirk, Aug. 11, 1887.

	h.	m.	s.				
Frodsham, 06859.....	4	1	8·5	Obs. alt. ☉.....	85°	19′	0″
	4	2	0		85	19	40
	4	2	52		85	20	20
	4	3	58		85	21	10
	4	5	28		85	22	5
	4	7	3		85	22	55
	4	8	15·5		85	23	30
	4	13	17		85	24	25
	4	14	43		85	23	50
	4	16	47·5		85	23	35
	4	17	45·5		85	23	0
	4	18	38·5		85	22	40
	4	19	43		85	22	20
	4	20	50		85	21	35
	4	21	45		85	20	55

Index error and eccentricity.............................   —3 4
Correction for temp. and pressure, —6.″
∴ Latitude 62 47 32

Camp opposite Fort Selkirk, Aug. 11, 1887.

	h.	m.	s.				
Frodsham, 06859.....	8	12	7·5	Obs. alt. ☉.....	54°	37′	30″
	8	13	16·75		54	22	30
	8	14	2·5		54	12	40
	8	14	53·5		54	1	50
	8	15	30		53	54	5
	8	16	36		53	39	10

18

```
                    h.  m.   s.
                    8  17  35·5                        53  27   0
                    8  18  16                          53  18   0
                    8  18  58·5                        53   9  10
Index error and eccentricity.............................     −2  39
∴ Frodsham, 06859, fast ...... ........... .............  4h. 7m. 42s·3
```

Camp opposite Fort Selkirk, Aug. 12, 1887.

```
                    h.  m.   s.
Frodsham, 06859....  7  35  59·5    Obs. alt. ⊙.....  61° 30′ 50″
                     7  38  18                        61   2  30
                     7  39  22·5                      60  50  20
                     7  40  10·5                      60  40  10
                     7  40  58·5                      60  30  55
                     7  42   5                        60  17  30
                     7  43  20·5                      60   2  10
Index error and eccentricity...........................     −2  35
∴ Frodsham, 06859, fast ...... ........... ..........  4h. 7m. 46·5s
```

Camp opposite Fort Selkirk, Aug. 13, 1887.

```
                    h.  m.   s.
Frodsham, 06859.....  0  58  46·5    Obs. alt. ⊙... .  63°  0′  0″
                      1   1  22                        63  30   0
                      1   3   8·5                      63  50   0
                      1   4  52·5                      64  10   0
                      1   7  33·5                      64  40   0

                    h.  m.   s.
Frodsham, 06859.....  4   4  10·5    Obs. alt. ⊙.....  84°  6′ 55″
                      4   5  33                        84   7  35
                      4   7  57                        84   8  15
                      4   9   7                        84   8  25
                      4  10   4·5                      84   8  40
                      4  10  59·5                      84   9  10
                      4  12  44                        84   9   0
                      4  13  32·5                      84   8  50
                      4  14  39                        84   8  40
                      4  16  35                        84   8  10
                      4  17  46                        84   7  40
                      4  18  44                        84   7  25
Index error and eccentricity.............................     −3   7
          Correction for temp. and pressure, −6·7
∴ Latitude......................................... ... .........  62  47  32·4

                    h.  m.   s.
Frodsham, 06859....  7  16  30·5    Obs. alt. ⊙.....  64° 40′  0″
                     7  19   9·5                      64  10   0
                     7  20  54                        63  50   0
                     7  22  40                        63  30   0
                     7  25  16·5                      63   0   0
```

By the above series of observations, paired with a.m. series
by equal altitudes, Frodsham, 06859, fast............ ...... 4h. 7m. 47·5s

Camp opposite Fort Selkirk, Aug. 15, 1887.

	h.	m.	s.				
Frodsham, 06859.....	1	17	56·5	Obs. alt. ☉.....	65°	30′	0″
	1	19	48·5		65	50	0
	1	21	41·5		66	10	0
	1	23	32·5		66	30	0
	1	25	25·5		66	50	0
	1	27	20·5		67	10	0

	h.	m.	s.				
Frodsham, 06859.....	6	55	55	Obs. alt. ☉.....	67°	10′	0″
	6	57	48·5		66	50	0
	6	59	42·5		66	30	0
	7	1	37		66	10	0
	7	3	29·5		65	50	0
	7	5	19		65	30	0

By the above sets of equal alt. obsns. Frodsham, 06859, fast 4h. 7m. 40·5s

Camp opposite Fort Selkirk, Aug. 17, 1887.

	h.	m.	s.				
Frodsham, 06859.....	0	39	16·5	Obs. alt. ☉.....	57°	0′	0″
	0	40	55·5		57	20	0
	0	42	35		57	40	0
	0	44	16		58	0	0
	0	45	56·75		58	20	0

	h.	m.	s.				
Frodsham, 06859.....	4	7	38	Obs. alt. ☉.....	81°	36′	40″
	4	9	10		81	37	10
	4	11	5		81	37	20
	4	12	0·5		81	37	5
	4	13	29		81	36	30
	4	16	30		81	35	55
	4	17	32·5		81	35	20
Index error and eccentricity.....................................						—2	0
Correction for temp. and pressure, —5·3							
∴ Latitude					62	47	29

	h.	m.	s.				
Frodsham, 06859.....	7	36	25	Obs. alt. ☉.....	58°	20′	0″
	7	38	5		58	0	0
	7	39	46		57	40	0
	7	41	26		57	20	0
	7	43	7		57	0	0

By the above series of observations, paired with a.m. series by equal altitudes, Frodsham, 06859, fast .... 4h. 7m. 45s.

Camp opposite Fort Selkirk, Aug. 17, 1887.

Obs. merid. alt. Altair..	71°	35′	30″
Index error and eccentricity*..................................		+1	8
Correction for temp. and pressure, —4·1			
Latitude	62	47	28·3

* The adjustments of the sextant were changed here.

Site of Fort Selkirk (summary).

Reducing the foregoing latitude observations (taken at two different points) to the ruins of Fort Selkirk, we find:—

From obs. of 11th........................	62° 47′ 12″ adopted.
" " " 13th......................................	62 47 12·4
" " " 17th.....................................	62 47 9
" " " 17th (on Altair)................	62 47 8·3

Diff. in long. between Câche Camp, Frances L. and Camp opp. Fort Selkirk, by directly comparing two equal alt. obsns.:—

Frodsham, 06859...........................	7° 40′ 9″
Arnold, 9699..............................	7 42 34·5
Mean, (giving double value to Frodsham)....	7 40 57·5 adopted.
∴ Long. of Camp opposite Fort Selkirk......	137 20 6
Or reduced to site of Fort Selkirk..........	137 20 22 *

Lower end Lake Labarge, Sept. 4, 1887.

	h.	m.	s.				
Frodsham, 06859...	12	20	54	Obs. alt. Arcturus...	48°	58′	30″
	12	23	29		48	21	30
	12	25	35		47	51	40
	12	27	18		47	26	20
	12	28	38·5		47	7	30
	12	30	14·25		46	44	30

Index error and eccentricity..........................	+1 2
∴ Frodsham, 06859, fast..........................	3h. 58m. 46s.
∴ Long. of place...................................	135° 5′ 45″

	h.	m.	s.				
Frodsham, 06859...	12	36	22	Obs. alt. Polaris....	122°	46′	10″
	12	39	7		122	47	55
	12	41	11		122	49	20
	12	43	35		122	50	55
	12	45	44		122	52	30
	12	47	38		122	53	35
	12	49	57		122	55	25

Index error and eccentricity............................	+2 56
∴ Latitude..	61 25 13

Employing local time obtained from observations on Arcturus.

	h.	m.	s.				
Frodsham, 06859...	1	2	1	Obs. alt. Altair...	74°	20′	10″
	1	4	28		74	18	25

---

* The longitude thus determined for Fort Selkirk, depends directly upon Wrangell, and my line of traverse by the Stikine, Dease, Liard, Frances and Upper Pelly rivers. It is that used on the accompanying map. Since the map has been engraved, and after this Appendix was in type, a first computation (still subject to possible small corrections) has been made of Mr. Ogilvie's winter observations near the 141st meridian and of his instrumental traverse from Fort Selkirk to that point. His resulting longitude for Fort Selkirk is 137° 22′ 45″, the difference between the two independently determined positions being 2210 yards only. It is therefore probable that all intermediate places on my line of traverse are correct in longitude within small limits of error.

1	5	52·5	74	17	40
1	7	21·5	74	16	20
1	8	59	74	15	10
1	10	59	74	13	10

Index error and eccentricity............ ....   +1 20
∴ Latitude......... .... 61 25   0

Employing local time obtained from observations on Arcturus.

OBSERVATIONS FOR MAGNETIC VARIATION.

Mag. variation observed at head of Dease Lake.
Lat. 58° 28′ 17″·3.   Long. 130° 2′ 0″

June 5, 1887, 3.40 p.m., obs. var. E.................... ....   30° 26′ 0″

Mag. variation observed at Frances Lake.
Lat. 61° 29′ 22″.   Long. 129° 39′ 8″·5.

Date and time.	True bearing of object.	Mag. bearing.	Obs. variation.
July 12, '87, 6 a.m....	127° 37′	93° 45′ compass 1	33° 52′ ⎫ mean 33° 45′·5
" " " " " ..	127° 37′	93° 0′ compass 2	33° 47′ ⎭

Mag. variation observed at First Camp on Pelly River.
Lat. 61° 48′ 52″.   Long. 131° 1′ 6″·5.

Date and time.	True bearing of object.	Mag. bearing.	Obs. variation.
July 30, '87, 5.40 p.m.	202° 59′	167° 45′ compass 2	34° 24′ ⎫ mean 34° 30′
" " " " "	202° 59′	168° 45′ compass 3	34° 36′ ⎭
" " " 6.40 p.m.	308° 18′	273° 30′ compass 2	34° 0′

Mag. variation observed opposite site of Fort Selkirk.
Lat. 62° 47′ 30″.   Long. 137° 20′ 6″.

Date and time.	True bearing of object.	Mag. bearing.	Obs. variation.
Aug. 12, '87, 4 p.m......	169° 27′	134° 15′ compass 2	35° 12′*
" " " " "	169° 27′	135° 30′ compass 3	34° 0′*

Determined by Mr. Ogilvie at same place (with transit)....   34° 21′·5
  "   "   "   "   "   "   "   at Fort Selkirk...   34° 5′

---

*The differences between these obsns. and Mr. Ogilvie's at same place, were assumed as index error of instruments and applied to the obsns. at other places.